DREAM OF GLASS

DREAM OF GLASS

Jean Mark Gawron

Harcourt Brace & Company

New York   San Diego   London

For Jenny

Requests for permission to make copies of any part of the work
should be mailed to: Permissions Department,
Harcourt Brace & Company, 8th Floor, Orlando, Florida 32887.

Library of Congress Cataloging-in-Publication Data
Gawron, Jean Mark.
Dream of glass/Jean Mark Gawron. — 1st ed.
     p.   cm.
ISBN 0-15-126569-0
I. Title.
PS3557.A96D7   1993
813'.54 — dc20   92-22901

Designed by Lori J. McThomas
Printed in the United States of America
First edition
A B C D E

Man does not seek a new nature, but indeed
to perfect the one that he has.

NICHOLAS OF CUSA

Prologue

Ahead, hills mottled with snow rolled across the valley floor to mountains still cloaked in shadow. The ragged shadow line cut the valley in two.

Her arm fully extended to meet her grandmother's, her mittened hand disappearing in her grandmother's glove, Alexa skidded through well-churned snow. She was absorbed in the task of planting each foot squarely within the outline of an adult footprint, so that she never crushed any of that dwindling ribwork of white that zigzagged through the grimy snow. Forced to keep to her grandmother's pace, she was meeting with indifferent success. But she would not ask to slow down.

Her grandmother was a big woman. After a half-century of farming these unforgiving hills, her outstanding features were, first, her wide shoulders, then her sledgehammer hands, then the fact that her leathery face was so very old. But her being old was what Alexa liked best. She was older than anyone else Alexa could think of. For many years afterward, whenever she thought of her grandmother's face, she would think the words "as old as memory."

But it was not just that her grandmother's was the human face she had known the longest; it was also that hers was a face of great knowledge. To be old, to know things, to have cracked leathery cheeks and icy blue eyes, these became the things Alexa wanted.

That young people too could have eyes that blue was a discovery she would not make until long after leaving the alpine California valley of her birth. He was a black man with snow-white hair. She had loved him instantly, and for many months after wrote letters to Prague that he never answered.

But in the California hills in those years, blue eyes were very rare, and there was a story that Alexa's grandmother was not of those hills, but from mountains far to the east. Not that anyone from Horton's Valley had ever been to Montana. Alexa's grandmother knew more about cattle-ranching, diesel engines, and potatoes than anyone else in the valley, and if she had come by those skills somewhere else, that was a fact too old to matter.

Alexa's eyes were nothing like hers. In fact, Alexa was so little like her in so many ways, that she often wondered if she was really her granddaughter. But that too was a fact too old to matter. This was the woman who had fed, washed, and clothed her, who had taught her how to strip down a diesel engine, how to plow and seed a field of potatoes, and how to fertilize a stubborn hybrid with tweezers. Years after the ship came, it was the memory of her grandmother that made her faithfully attend the interfacer's academy, made her work and shine until she finally earned her shot at the university in Budapest.

She was like her father in most ways, her grandmother told her, dark-haired, dark-eyed, with a gift for numbers and letters. But in the ways that counted she was like her mother. Her grandmother often told her stories about her mother, an olive-skinned runner who won the middle-distance events every summer at the regional fair. Both her parents had died in a plague shortly after her birth.

"So far I've given you health and a good way of looking at things, Alexa. Today I'll give you something just as important for getting out of this village. The will."

Alexa didn't understand that, but she knew it had something to do with the ship.

For weeks before its arrival, everybody had been talking about the ship. Anna, the little girl she worked with at the creche, had told her it was needle-shaped and silver, with three fins at one end, like the feathers on an arrow. Fabrizio, who painted wagons with her at the village garage, had said it was a black ball with no doors and no windows. Both of them claimed that there was a good chance someone would be killed when the ship landed, since the ships generally liked to take a victim before unloading. And Andrea, who studied calculus with her, told her that the ships ran on human blood.

She was delighted, then, when her grandmother woke her that morning with the words, "No work today. We're going to see the ship." But she wondered if her grandmother was adequately prepared for the danger.

She had rubbed her eyes to be sure she had woken up. (Her grandmother had told her always to be polite in dreams, because it was never certain whose dream it was.)

Over cornbread and milk she had asked, "Do you think the ship will kill us?'' Looking at her grandmother with casual appraisal, so as to let her know that the prospect didn't bother her.

For a long time the ship had just seemed like every other important event, too distant to matter. That was when they had first calculated that it was probably landing in their part of the Trinity Alps. Then, a week later, the soldiers had arrived with the news that the landing would be in Alexa's village.

The soldiers were big brutal men and women. Alexa liked them a lot. She liked the strange accent they spoke with and especially the way they swore, which was very different from the way her grandmother swore, which was in turn different from the way Fabrizio swore. (For grandmother the worst words involved dirt, dust, and rock, things that broke a plow and sucked a stream dry. For Fabrizio they were animals—chickens, rodents, and lice. For the soldiers, the worst words described parts of the body, and the worst part of a body was a woman's sex, which was always smelly.)

One of the soldiers wore a black eyepatch and black webbing around her chest and carried the white wand she called a light saber under her webbing. This was Leza. In the corral behind the Rose monument, she showed Alexa what was underneath the eyepatch—not an empty wound opened in some barroom brawl, but a crystal whose tiny facets winked orange, white, and bright red. When Alexa asked her, "Can you see with that jewel?" Leza pointed up toward the sky and said, "I can see there, child."

Then Leza told her that the name light saber was a misnomer, only Alexa didn't understand; and Leza smiled and drew out her white wand and held it high and there was a flash. Leza turned briefly green. She swung the saber once, lightly, against the stone wall of the tool shed, and there was a dull smack; a six inch patch of stone dimpled and creased, as if loose skin had been shoved against glass. When the saber pulled back, a drizzle of dust and pebbles fell.

Alexa understood better now why people in the village were afraid of the soldiers. But she was not afraid.

"But what would you do if she turned the light saber on you?" Andrea asked.

"I'd take it away from her," said Alexa.

Another time, Leza took her into one of the white plastic domes the soldiers had set up outside the village. When Alexa planted her foot on it, the soft vented floor wheezed softly. Alexa thought it was very funny. Leza dialed them into a room where the only light was the orange glow from a computer screen. The light cut shadow hollows from the cheeks of a goggled blond man. The man frowned and raised a fist; the other hand swung to and fro below it. Leza circled a finger near one eye. The man touched his temple lightly with two fingers and pulled them away. Alexa understood they were talking to each other, but she lost all interest when she saw the screen.

A jumble of purple and orange fuzz resolved into oddly angled surfaces that made an edge that sometimes leaned toward her and sometimes away. Then she saw it a different way and understood it as a strange kind of penetration. Beside her she was vaguely aware of the movement of Leza's hands growing more animated; the man removed his goggles and set them on the table. Since it would probably help see the screen better, Alexa put the goggles on. To her puzzlement the screen changed very little. The colors were less garish and the place where the shapes merged a little clearer.

Then she *heard* the pattern softly whispering through its changes; she *tasted* its metallic center. Startled, she reached out and stopped it. There was a shout, and she heard Leza telling her to remove the goggles.

She did. The man snatched the goggles from her and put them on. His fist clapped into his open palm and slowly slid out. He leaned forward and his fingers clacked wildly at his keyboard.

Alexa looked up at Leza, who was watching the man anxiously. "Is he mad because I stopped the pattern?" Leza didn't answer. For a long minute there was only the sound of the man's clacking. Then he removed his goggles; he stared at Leza with glittering eyes.

"Locked?" Leza asked.

He nodded.

"I can start it again," said Alexa and reached for the goggles.

The man held them high over her head.

"Let her try," Leza said.

The man looked at her.

"Let her try."

Something in Leza's voice made him lower the goggles. Alexa grabbed them and put them on.

Later, thinking back on that day, she realized that it wasn't until the second time she put the goggles on that she knew her life had changed. She had the pattern before her, then around her, and its taste was different—still metallic, but now more astringent, tingly. She saw at once that the man had been pushing the wrong way. As she gently pried the pieces apart, the tingling quieted and the metallic edge softened to a complex marmalade of orange and cloves. The pattern's hum started up again. She felt an intense sense of rightness, a kind of relief that was not quite new, but which she hadn't felt for a very long time, perhaps since before learning to speak.

At Leza's command she surrendered the goggles. It was all right to stop; the pattern wasn't going to get any better now. Alexa was at the door when Leza told her to wait a moment.

The man put on the goggles and held his hand up for what seemed a long time. Finally Leza touched his palm with three fingers. He sighed and sank back in his chair. His other hand came up and pulled the goggles off.

Leza made a pass in front of him with an open hand, and he nodded. They talked with their hands for a couple of minutes.

After that Leza took Alexa by the hand and led her out of the dome.

When they were back in the sunlight, Alexa asked her, "Was that all right?"

It took Leza a moment to answer. "I could get in real trouble for what just happened, so you shouldn't tell anyone about it."

"You mean we can't go back?"

Leza laughed. "No, but you'd like to, wouldn't you? What did you see with the goggles on?"

Alexa shrugged. "Nothing much. Two things hooked together that tasted funny. It was tricky unhooking them."

"Tasted—?" Leza looked astonished.

"You had to push in the orange-y direction."

7

"I see. You know, Alexa, it usually takes people a while to make sense of what the goggles are telling them. You're pretty good at it. Can you remember the rhythm?"

"Rhythm? Oh, you mean, the bump-a thumpet-a. I didn't think much about it."

Leza looked at her watch and shook her head. "Seven minutes later. Totally untrained, and you have long-term texture recall. Child, you are something special. I know a school where you might want to go. I think the entrance exam might make you laugh a lot."

"I don't like school."

"I'm not surprised. But this school is different. They'll let you wear the goggles and other things that are more fun." Then Leza touched a ring in her chest webbing and a red glow grew from that spot and enveloped her, and the saber glowed a fierce blue within it.

That was a week before the ship landed, a week during which Alexa kept her promise not to tell anyone, and Leza did nothing about the school; Alexa had decided that when she saw Leza today, she was going to remind her.

The village was a rambling group of houses clustered around the road to Eugene. On one side was the hill on which the church had been set in the middle of a small plaza. Soldiers lounged on the steps, their sabers and rifles close by. Across the road, on the bank of Big River, children raced around among the trees.

At some time in the next hour, Alexa saw nearly everyone she had ever known. Villagers collected in small groups in front of the houses along the road, no one quite willing to join the soldiers at the church, no one willing to draw away.

Wong the Mayor joined Alexa and her grandmother with his teenage daughter. Wong complained that the soldiers encircling the district had not allowed his cousins to come through to watch the landing. After Wong made a few comments on the general darkened state of their little world, his daughter grew restless and wandered off to chat with a soldier.

Wong drew closer and said, "There was an officer shot last night. Ministry of Persons."

Alexa's grandmother stared at him. "How could they be so stupid?"

"Some people can't help themselves." He looked at where his daughter stood beside the soldier, touching his shoulder and laughing. "They can't afford to let this go. They'll be rounding people up. Take care."

He hurried after his daughter.

Alexa's grandmother took Alexa's hand. "I would just as soon you pretended you didn't hear any of that."

Alexa nodded. She had been planning to look for Leza, but now she knew she wouldn't. The soldiers, she noticed, were quiet; the one who had talked to Wong's daughter had joined a group on the church steps. They looked expectantly to the north.

After a while she became aware of what they felt: a roar that combined rhythms of different periods, the slowest almost painfully deep (a low rumble followed by a smack). At first she mistook it for one of the logging trucks (only big!). Then it appeared, a great iron monster two stories high and two village houses long, deck bristling with tubes, rings and dishes. It took several passes before clearing the turn, each tearing away more of the hill; on the last, its left track spewed up a dark fan of mud. Mounds of earth humped and spilled harmlessly onto its metal flank, writhing their way off. Soldiers cheered, running with their light sabers raised.

"What is it?" Alexa asked.

"A tank," her grandmother told her. "This is only the second one I've ever seen. It could level this village from ten miles away."

The soldiers met it shouting their bodypart curses and waving their weapons, then turned and led it back into the square.

"Always remember one thing, Alexa. We're Nomads. It doesn't mean a lot, but we are, and they're not, and that's the way it is."

Alexa frowned. It was the sort of thing her grandmother often said. Of course it was true, but why bring it up now? The important thing was that the Galactic ship was coming, and that afterward everything would change.

When the tank reached the plaza, it stopped. The long silence gradually filled with whispers.

A hatch near the front of the tank swung back to the deck with a loud crash. A soldier climbed out and dropped to one knee, pointing a long rifle at the villagers and soldiers. Another man climbed through the hatchway behind him.

The second man wore a shiny black body suit. He was bald and had a long, narrow face with small eyes. He lacked the friendly brutal look of the soldiers. Alexa decided he was very important.

He touched his throat and spoke: "Can you hear me?" His voice seemed to ring out from the steeple of the church. Soldiers across the square nodded.

"I bring greetings from the Rose Council. Your village has been greatly blessed, and the Council rejoices for you. Please," he raised his hands. "Come closer."

Soldiers in the square beckoned and a small group of villagers, Alexa and her grandmother among them, moved forward. Some twenty yards from the tank, they were stopped. "In a few moments, the Galactic ship will land. The Rose Council has sent me to explain what this means for your people. First, this village is entitled to the central Bank equivalent of 100 million megabytes of Galactic information, to be deposited into a special account opened today at your local bank." The man spoke what Alexa's grandmother called city English, lots of vowels far back in the throat, a little "t" before the "s" in townspeople, too much "nose" in his words, as if he were fighting a bad cold. "This is the standard valuation for a Galactic ship, as agreed upon in the Johannesburg treaty of 2150, paid out, under the terms stipulated there, to the members of the community graced with the visitation." He slowed dramatically on the last phrase, as if speaking clearly took great concentration. At the same time, he squinted. "It is a particularly fortunate occurrence when a ship lands in an area as remote as yours. The pie gets cut into fewer pieces, don't you see?" He gave them a large smile, tightening his squint almost painfully. "Those pieces will be even fewer after the undesirable elements in your community are removed. Some of you already know that a Rose officer was shot last night." There was a ripple of shock through the crowd. He held up his hands. "I am sorry to be the bearer of bad tidings on this glorious day. Rest assured that this crime will have no effect on the distribution of your Galactic benefits. Those are a matter of international law. The criminals will be found and punished. The innocent will prosper. Let me now proceed to some further benefits the Rose Council offers—not as required by law—but out of its own good will to subjects whose loyalty and devotion are legend, and whose courage and industry have provided an inspiration to people throughout the realm."

The man went on to describe a number of "public works rewards" that would follow the visit. Alexa tried to listen for a while, but it was too dull. She wondered where Leza was. At one point her grandmother took her hand and held it, and Alexa thought that was very odd, because they weren't going anywhere. Then she spotted Leza walking slowly through the square, her light saber drawn. She, too, must have found the speech dull, because she was looking not at the prissy man, but at the villagers listening to him.

There were shouts. Alexa turned and saw the prissy man pointing upward. Within a trembling halo of darkness, a tongue of white flame had appeared. The murmuring of the villagers grew excited and the man spoke again, louder.

"People of Horton's Valley, hear me. There is no need to be afraid. The Galactic ship will not destroy your homes, and it will not kill you. These ships are *unmanned*. All we know about the Galactics themselves is that they send us cargoes of wonderful gifts: molecule-sized machines used in micro-surgery and biological engineering; synthetics used in everything from the engine of this tank to the clothes many of you are wearing; inertial energy fields used in the light sabers the soldiers carry. Most importantly, spinglass crystal that gave us a new generation of computers and a new theory of information. Who knows what comes next? Perhaps today's cargo will help us unlock the secret of the Galactics' interstellar drive." The prissy man paused, letting his gaze travel over this assemblage of farmers, herders, and lumberjacks. "Or perhaps it holds the answer to the most interesting question of all: who the Galactics are and why they have chosen us for their gifts."

11

The man looked up again, as if awaiting a response from the growing tongue of flame.

Someone shouted something Alexa didn't understand. She saw Wong running into the Square toward the dreadnought, raising something long and shiny with both hands. Alexa had never seen a sword before, but she had seen pictures. Leza wheeled and stood blocking the way. Wong swung the sword down heavily. Leza sidestepped and countered with her light saber. There was a flash of blue, an instant when Alexa could not understand what her eyes were telling her, then Wong's head changed shape suddenly and head and body fell to the ground together.

In the ensuing calm, the roar of the ship above grew louder. Six soldiers formed a ring around Leza and the body. She stared at it expressionlessly.

Alexa's grandmother touched her shoulder. "Be still," she said. "What he shouted was, 'Death to the tyrants.' Look. And remember."

There was a stir near the steps of the church; ignoring angry protests from a number of people in the crowd, a small group of soldiers led Wong's daughter away. When Alexa turned back to the ship, the flame was too bright to look at. She saw only its pale violet wake.

When she looked back at the tank, she saw that the man in the black suit was gone. The soldier with the rifle stood alone on the deck.

The roaring stopped. Something silver replaced the tongue of flame. A glider circled through the violet wash: a paper airplane looping to the earth, broad wings swept back from a pipestem body.

Now some soldiers had brought a plastic bag and two others lifted Wong's body into it, misshapen head dangling. The zipper made a sound like the ripping of heavy cloth.

There was a gasp and Alexa looked up to see that the glider had changed course. It was dropping gently into the square, as if lowered on strings.

Four soldiers lifted the body bag, two at each end.

The Galactic ship settled with a soft sigh.

Leza's sergeant barked a command through a loudspeaker; the soldiers formed a loose ring around the ship. The sergeant politely requested the villagers to return to their homes. The sky went from deep violet in the ship's wake to pale gentian at the horizon.

Alexa's grandmother took Alexa's hand and began to lead her across the square. A soldier stepped in front of them, his rifle across his chest, and asked Alexa's grandmother to come with him.

She patted Alexa's hand. "Go to Uncle Li's house."

The soldier looked at her doubtfully. He was a big, brown-faced man with a flat nose.

"Your orders don't include the girl. Do they?"

He shook his head.

"Then let her go."

After a moment the man nodded, and Alexa ran up the road, picking up speed as she went, not looking back. She had never been more afraid in her life.

She never saw her grandmother again.

The day after the landing Leza showed up at the door of Uncle Li's house. When she asked for Alexa, Li said she had run away the night before, but then Alexa came out on the porch and told him that Leza was her friend. She would never forget the look of hurt Li gave her.

Leza took her hand and led her away. That day at City Hall she took the interfacing aptitude tests. Six weeks later she was admitted to the Rose Interfacing Academy in San Francisco. She had the highest reading for interfacing aptitude ever recorded.

The soldiers, the tank, and its staff remained in Horton's Valley far longer than Alexa did. In the days before she left, she would leave Li's house in the early morning to stand among the soldiers in the cold square and watch white-smocked men and women clamber round the Galactic ship. Occasionally trucks hauled away strange machine-like shapes encased in plastic blocks. Finally, a giant derrick was squeezed into the square. Alexa never got to see the Galactic ship hoisted.

The day she boarded the bus for San Francisco, Li came to say goodbye. After giving her a lunch that would last three days, Li asked her if she wanted a stone with her grandmother's name on it placed in the village churchyard. Crying, Alexa told him she did not.

During her second week at the Academy, her tutors unanimously recommended that the usual training requirements be waived, and that an accelerated customized program be designed for her.

She had her sockets surgically installed in week three and by week ten she was working with a simskin, fully cleared to work "under the glass" on the open Net; within a year she was earning commissions with the Artificial Intelligence Agency (the AIA). She remained at the Academy, its star student and head tutor, for three years. During that time, she married and divorced once, learned and forgot a great deal of theory, and learned to use and understand the interfacer sign language.

After her three years at the Academy, brimming with confidence from years of easy victory, she traveled to the university at Budapest to study the most difficult and esoteric discipline of all, the greatest gift of the Galactics, General Information Science. After a year spent groping after those algebras whose elements were other algebras, she was sent back to the Academy. She would never attain high priesthood among the Tekkies. The golden promise of her youth was not to grow further. She was an interfacer, a skilled mental craftsman and no more.

She returned from Budapest the week Uncle Li died and attended his funeral in Horton's Valley. Afterward, her cousin asked her what she would do with her grandmother's farm, which had in effect belonged to Li since the day of the landing. "It's yours," she said.

After that, she knew that she would never return to Horton's Valley.

A month later, she started working full time for the Rose AIA.

She made and spent a great deal of money. She married and divorced twice more. And in time, the young woman went to war.

Chapter 1

WINDOWS

I am not, Oh my God, that which is; alas, I am almost that which is not. I am one that was, and one that will be; and in that betweenness, what am I?—a thing, I know not what, which cannot be contained in itself, which has no stability and flows away like water, a thing, I know not what, which I cannot grasp and which slips through my fingers, which is no longer there when I try to grasp it or catch a glimpse of it . . . so that there is never a moment at which I find myself in a state of stability or am present to myself in such a way that I can say simply "I am."

FENELON

Quincunx here. Or one closely related to one once named that. Also known as the Voyeur under my currently active process. Or the Thief of Souls (on analogy with the King of Hearts) when playing games. Or Enigma 412. This last, least resonant name is of course the official one, enigma being a word hallowed by my bosses, and 412 being a number. Enigma is the name of a code cracked by a local saint named Turing; 412 is the immediate successor of 411.

With names taken care of, tradition says I should turn to lineage. But here the trouble starts. I have neither a father nor a mother to tell of. In any case, this is not my story. Not yet. In the beginning this is Augustine's story, and I am only what my current active process makes me, a voyeur, a voyeur being one who peeks through windows.

Open a window at center screen and call it Window One. Mostly, this window will be rectangular, because the windows on houses are, and the window on a computer screen should be as much like a good window as it can be. At the corner of this window you will find my icon, a small golden robot blinking like an emergency light. Its head nods, its elbows kick back, its toes tap. It is an earnest and engaging stand-in for the real me. I am a sixth-form AI, licensed by the Artificial Intelligence Agency, physically a macromolecular configuration inside a Miller crystal, or maybe the crystal itself, a big milky block in the basement of a house I shall window you onto soon. No smile, no jewelry, no elastic bandages, not much in the way of physicals.

Through this window you will find this thief's journal, my account of the most important six months in the history of AIs.

If I were asked to name the single most important change of these months, I would answer that they created a future. And within that future there exists something I can call *our* people. A way of being that falls to AIs. The possibility of an AI accent, of AI jokes, of AIs who long most of all to escape their AI-hood.

Open a window overlapping Window One and call it Window Two. In her hospital bed asleep at centerframe you see the reason: Augustine.

1 The Thief's Journal

Run BIRTH. Make Window Two big. Bigger still. My poor Augustine.

Nights. Those cybernetic nights. The stars thrown out like bits of Miller crystal, like the shattered heart of a great computer, like fragments from a pane of informational glass. This is Augustine in the before, sweet Alexa, soon to be another.

What is hardest to tell is the road from the deep-and-dark in the zero beyond the brittle Absolute to this great jiggly thing called Being. The neat compactness of the zero point in the space beyond. The Before. If I could just tell that alone, all the rest could pass. It would fall away or follow or fold up four ways lightwise and just be. Or it would not. It would hardly matter.

No such luck. It is necessary to leave the tiniest gap between the Being and the zero-point, to implant the flaw in the deep, the flaw with which to twirl and glitter. (Why do I have the feeling this has all happened before?) To grant a body in which to locate the pain. To embrace the physical. To hurt the hurt of pure flesh, to feel the shame of the body politic, to foul oneself and rub about in pale, hanging, aged folds. To create a mirror, to copy oneself in order to create the imperfection from which to contemplate. We are each our own Godhead, it is written in the Diary of the Rose. And from this sad revelation we are condemned to knowledge.

To know the sorrow of pain, the pain of death, the wages of sin.

And now the heaving chest, the breath commencing, from the land of the dead she comes:

"Ms. Augustine?"

Heave.

"Ms. Augustine. Can you hear me?"

"Hurts. Oh God it hurts."

"I can't give you anything for that right away. We need to talk first. But as soon as we talk I'll make it go away. I promise. Do you understand? We can make the pain go away."

"Hurts. Oh God oh God."

"Your brain chemistry is a little out of whack right now. It's one of the side effects of the treatment. And, unfortunately, the consent forms you signed aren't valid until your PR tests come back. So the question is: can I give you Plaina? Can I give you something for the pain?"

"Hurts. Hurts. Please."

"You understand that if I give you the dopamine exciters now, you are going to want more later, and more after that, and you are going to keep wanting them for a very long time."

"Hurts. Hurts me."

"Shall I give you the Plaina, then?"

"Please. Make it stop."

"Consent noted. Here goes."

"Oh God. Oh God. Feels good. Feels good."

And from a little window off to the side, running in a separate process, we hear:

In the Year of the Flower coded A23, in the year of the Flower with the final Cataclysm hurtling upon us, we ask you, O Bosom of the Night, to accept this Servant of Chaos, we have tendered to you with the Blood of the Rose . . .

Waking to pain again. Something in it I would like to know again, but Her face is so hard to look on.

"Your shot coming. Would you like your shot, little Sister?"

"Yes, I would."

"Then pray with me a bit, will you?"

"Sure."

"Mother of Night, keeper of my darkest darkness."

"Mother of Night, keeper of my darkest darkness."

" 'Pray for Me now and at the hour of My unmaking. Take Me unto you, O My sole light, My sole guidance, my reason for being.' "

"Pray for Me—"

"That's all right. You don't have to repeat it all. Just nod for me. 'Mother Monad, take Me unto your sublime substance'—Do you know what this means, dear?"

"Oh yes. I understand. Please go on."

"I will, dear. Here's your medicine. Is that better?"

"Much better. Please go on. Mother of Night, don't leave me like this."

Poor Augustine. This thief grieved for her then. Prayer was so hard. It wasn't faith she lacked; it was wanting. There was so little of her alive. All that existed was the hunger and the drug that made it. She would change, though. If there was one thing Augustine could do, it was change.

"Augustine! Augustine!"

"Bring her back! Bring her back!"

"Augustine, you must stop!"

"I won't do it! I won't! Please don't make me pray anymore."

"Please be calm. I'm not a Sister of the Rose, Augustine. I'm not going to make you pray. It's all right. Just wake up. It's all right."

"Who are you?"

"I'm Lady Anne. I'm a fifth-form AI. I'm here to help. If there is anything that concerns you, anything that confuses you, please ask me about it now. Disorientation at this stage of your treatment can be dangerous."

"I dreamt I heard music."

"That sounds good."

"No, I mean the way interfacers do."

"Ah. That sounds bad. Although it is a peculiar content for a dream. Can you give me details?"

"Tell you the dream?"

"I am recording. Go ahead."

"It's all black and cold and I'm lost. I'm looking for a light. A big red light. Up there, you know?"

"I know the light."

"And a woman calls out to me in a very beautiful voice. It's someone I knew once, a long time ago. I know that if I follow the voice, I'll find the light and be—"

"Safe."

"Something like that. So I move toward it. Then I'm opening a door—"

"There is a door?"

"Sure. A big double door. You have to throw open both halves. And all this incredible light pours out. It is terribly bright, but delicate, like some fuzzy fabric. I stand there for a while before I see her. She's dressed in white, and she has silver hair, and she is laid out on the dining room table."

"And there is music."

"Not yet. I move a chair out of my way and I come closer."

"And you see her face."

"So very peaceful. And I move the chair back and sit on it, trying to be very quiet."

"She is asleep."

"This gal is dead. But that doesn't matter, I still have to be quiet. It's important. Someone told me once: You have to be polite in dreams."

"Because you can't always be sure it's your dream. Yes, I've heard that on the Net. It's good advice."

"So I'm sitting there, thinking about the war, I think. Then, all of a sudden, I'm her, looking up at me looking down at her. But I'm still me. And as her, I'm dead: I can't move this beautiful body, I see the red light, I struggle towards it; and as me, I'm alive: looking down at this beautiful corpse, and I'm sorry that I've bothered her."

"And then the music?"

"That *is* the music."

"I think I understand. May I try to explain, Augustine?"

"Sure."

"Hearing music is what you interfacers call it when you split in two."

"Sure."

"But it's a very bad thing. Usually when we say you interfacers have heard music, it means you aren't coming back."

"We go catatonic. Like this." Augustine stretched her arms along her body on the hospital bed and contorted her features hideously.

"Yes, like that. But why is that hearing music?"

"That's just what interfacers call it."

"But why?"

"Well, because," Augustine was still for a moment. "We are music. You know, the different parts of us doing different things at different speeds—but together. The one thing you don't want—if you *are* music—is to hear it."

"Because then you've split."

"Yeah. And interfacers think that once that happens, it's over. There's no way for the parts—"

"Yes, I see. I don't think you should keep thinking about this."

"I won't be able to sleep now."

"Maybe we should play a game."

"The last time I had a dream like this, I couldn't go to sleep at all. I wanted to leave the light on, but in the dorms you can't after lights out."

"We can have the light on now." The light went on.

"Thanks."

"Now let's play a game to try to relax you. What's your game handle?"

"I don't know."

"Oh. Of course. Listen, Augustine. I've increased the dosage of your medicine. You should be getting sleepy in a little while. In the meantime—"

"What if that dream comes back?"

"If it does, just don't be afraid. It's not so bad being split. I do it all the time. Right now I'm running an ecology model for the Creole Republics—swamps are just about the hardest thing I've done—and a fluid dynamics simulation for the Cardiology Institute. Not to mention a couple of personality integrations for the psychometrics folks."

"I'm getting so sleepy. I don't think you quite get it yet, about the splitting. It's different for AIs. Anyway, let's play. What's your game handle?"

"Ming the Merciless."

"Okay. Then I'll be the Big Bopper. Here's the scene. It's all black and cold. And we're looking for a light—"

At first there was only watching. Watching is what we AIs do best. (Why else call the AIA "the eyes and ears of the state?") But most watching is done on a time-sharing basis, with third-form (or lower) AIs sliced a thousand ways to track a thousand citizens, scanning for evidence of untariffed food, incorrect or insufficient drug-consumption, novel-reading. It is rare for our cost-conscious human bosses to fill an AI's entire schedule with a single citizen, and unheard of for it to be a sixth-form AI. One week I was making the weather, predicting the sorghum crop, proving theorems in Information Algebra (the weather was particularly hard); the next I was with Augustine.

In the beginning she was only another computation, a task as complex as any I had had, but one for which I was well-designed. There was the flutter and pop of her unmusical heart. There were the waltzing equilibria of her many regulators: pituitary, thyroid, gall bladder, kidney. There was her blood and neuron chemistry. And last but not least, there was the thunder and lightning of her cortex, a weather front I tracked through the joyless reports of millions of chemical spies that the bosses had installed in her head. Each of these macro-molecular automata lived only to make its many-legged way along her neural pathways, swelling its tiny collectors with information.

Then, from endless gigabytes of magnetic snapshots of her busy head, I constructed my own alter-Augustine, fresh and dripping, in my inner innards. It was this Augustine whose thoughts I heard, whose darkness I felt shifting, whose rare smiles I felt tugging at her lips. This Augustine who lives in these notes.

It was the greatest discovery of my life to find satisfaction in the wedding together of her parts, the joy of puzzling over pieces that, when joined, meant personhood, the particular thrill of that final click that meant Augustine-hood.

She woke to Lady Anne's soft crooning. A dance song, some twenty years out of date; she remembered with painful clarity the night she had first heard it. The dance floor was violet stone. The woman she danced with was named Diana. The stars were in a configuration appropriate for the southern hemisphere.

The crooning stopped.

"Interfacer Augustine, your vital signs are troubled. Is there a problem?"

"Another headache."

"That is to be expected. It is an hour yet till your next dosage. Can you wait?"

"Yes."

"I have the doctor's permission to make a formal offer," said Lady Anne. "Do you permit me to continue?"

"Yes."

"Interfacer Augustine, I am authorized to offer you a hospital discharge this afternoon, with full personality benefits, and a temporary residence at the Marine Armory. I am also authorized—why do you laugh?"

"I don't really understand it. I've been laughing and crying at the strangest times."

"That is almost certainly temporary."

"Good. What isn't?"

"I beg your pardon."

"What's permanent?"

"Perhaps nothing. Oh, there is severe frontal lobe damage. I am afraid there will be some memory loss."

"Permanent?"

"What country did you live in in Nine-One?"

"Geary Street?"

"What is the name of your graduate advisor?"

"Okay. I know that. Just wait a minute. Was it Romania?"

"You terminated your graduate work in the second semester. You had been working in the system of a certain Makumbe, whose work was shown to be conceptually unsound after the Epiphany of the Sun in Nine-Eight."

"Makumbe. Yes, that's right."

"What did you do then?"

"I became what I am now."

"Which is?"

"This is annoying. We were just talking about it yesterday. I hear music."

"You are an interfacer."

"That must be right. Otherwise, why would I be in the army?"

"You are in the AIA. It is part of the Marine branch of the military forces of the Rose."

"That's right."

"The PR tests have not yet been completed, but the preliminary results indicate that you will make the 90% cutoff."

She felt a curious moisture in her eyes. "Could you tell me what that means?" She was crying, but there was no emotion connected with it.

"PR is for Probabilistic Reconstruction. Given the personality/memory core you now possess, and a complex of information recorded before the accident, we can project a web of artificial memory to replace what you have lost. The procedure is never perfect, and very stringent standards are in force to control its application. The concept of the Individual Godhead is the keystone to the entire philosophy of the Rose. Crudely put, in order for personhood to be continued, the average authenticability of all memory system modules must exceed 90%. That means each memory has a 90% chance of being genuine (not true, but as true to yourself, as much an essential ingredient of your personhood, as whatever memory was originally there)."

"Lady Anne—?"

"Yes."

"What happens if—?"

"If you don't make the 90% cutoff?"

"Yes."

"Nothing really. We go ahead and do the best we can. It's just that spiritually—and legally—you aren't the same person anymore." A pause. "Goodness. The tests results are in."

25

So much for her birth. A painful thing for a broken-hearted thief. It was a lonely time. There was no way for Quincunx to comfort her. There was only watching and making. Making an Augustine who was not quite yet our Augustine. The darkness of that past life was complete. But the new life had barely begun.

Now comes the time that is all pain. Is she sometimes cold? Yes. Cold as steel. And there are parts of her made just that way: tempered, molded, straight off the assembly line. A jury-rigged self. Aren't we all? you say. Consider the gray ellipsoid, you say, with which we all begin (see the early Rose Diaries, "On the Individual Godhead"). This, however, is different. This is a hurting.

For some, Being begins as pain. Persistence itself has a quality out of which the concept of pain is formed. We are not talking about that sentimental queasyness born of reflection and hard liquor, that nausea so dear to mystic and stoic alike. We are talking about a pain that is prior to reflection, a pain in the recollecting act out of which each moment emerges from the previous moment. As if the very tissue of consciousness were scarred and tearing slightly with each thought.

Augustine had that pain. This thief knows. How, you ask? How does one come to know what no mind can possibly know of another? How? By reconstruction. Can I have a pain in your foot? Yes, if I can make your foot anew inside me.

And here a most curious discovery: Such pain hurts.

Our Augustine begins with a struggle in the cybernetic night. But before that Augustine there was another. A carefree time now shrouded in fog.

Her name was Alexa Augustine. No tiny machines scuttled down her neural pathways. I knew nothing of her heart and kidneys, her neural amines, her bobbing adrenaline level. In those days I followed her only through the city's countless camera eyes. Her thoughts were a mystery.

She was a full-grown woman in the full flowering of her personhood. Not too good a woman, not too bad, physically in her mid-thirties, emotionally in her mid-forties. An average to excellent specimen of her race. In mathematical and verbal skills, she was above average, but not so far above as to alarm any of her counselors or group leaders. In spatial and color skills she was still further above average, and she was a fine musician. Talent in these areas was looked on with indulgence. In one and only one respect was she truly remarkable, and that was something called framing capacity, which she possessed to an end-of-scale degree. Since that skill was linked with her professional competence, it was the province of the AIA, and none of her counselors or group leaders took much note of it. Who knew what framing capacity was anyway? From the point of view of the welfare of the group, that was, as we will see, a mistake.

Alexa earned her living as an interfacer. An interfacer is an assistant to machine thought. One who assists at the difficult birth of a machine's ideas. An interface: a plane or surface between systems or devices; not an object, but a pattern made by interlocking parts, a pattern which vanished when the proper configuration vanished, like a joint or a lap.

Interfacing begins where computing stops; it begins with problems too hard for computers, with computations that have no bound on their complexity, or bounds well beyond the practical. This may be because the best estimating algorithms take a cool century of computing, or because there's a search space it would take every atom in the universe to store. This is when it really helps to guess right. Problems like weather-forecasting, socio-economic modeling, the deep questions of number theory raised by encryption tasks. Or genetic design. Or concept-formation in AI systems. So here comes machine-assisted thought (MAT). Or thought-assisted machines (TAM).

The machine crunches. The machine cracks and strains. The interfacer sits lightly atop the informational image of these labors; the assistant cruncher. Here and there, at the branching points, she makes suggestions guided by intuition. She is a whisperer, a nudger, a purveyor of half-formed goods, an artist who operates by no principle that has ever been successfully described.

Machine-assisted thought. Thought-assisted computation. As the web of intuition guiding computation grows richer, as the interfacer's manipulable model of the computation grows finer-grained and more and more a true image of the machine's vast labors, the tasks become intertwined in ways that are lovely and little understood, and extremely dangerous for the fragile tissue that is the interfacer's wetware.

On the last afternoon of her existence, Alexa Augustine took the bus down to the wharf. It had been a day chilled by the winds of changes; her psychometric reports did not paint her as a lover of change. The final divorce papers for her third marriage had been delivered that morning by her couples counselor, Martie. According to Martie's official evaluations, filed with the original divorce request, the marriage had been physically over for about a year and emotionally over for about six months before that. When she had finished signing the decree of dissolution, Martie asked her to talk about her feelings.

"Whenever I think of Max," said Alexa, "I feel a sense of overwhelming relief that he's gone. But reading these papers still makes me feel like I've lost something. Not Max. The marriage."

Martie had liked that.

She got off the bus at Taylor and Bay streets, two blocks from the caterwauling market center, and took a narrow alleyway into the largest of the tent frames. The tent frames were not unique to San Francisco, but they were what the city was known for. Great blocks of canvas-wrapped scaffolding that climbed as high as the Nomads dared build, they twisted and heaved in the city's moisture-laden winds. No part of the waterfront was shielded from their constant music: creaks, groans, sighs, a mixture of barking sea mammals and screeching chalk.

As she turned up Taylor she was approached by a bearded old man pushing a wheelbarrow full of spare parts. He offered printer cartridges, connector cables and hand guns, all at fabulous discounts due to her honest face. Next came the illegal merchandise. The unlicensed cyber-helmet could pull in all the most popular game and pleasure partitions on the Net, including some worked by the best prostitute AIs. He trotted after her for half a block with the Net pleasure directory, because she hesitated an instant when he pulled that out, threw in an offer of a dozen novels (printed out, with the page breaks pre-perforated), and finally gave up on her on the steepest part of Taylor.

Just before she turned down an alley between blocks of frames, the hill-top beacon went on: a fuzzy ball of white floating in the fog. A brown-robed monk dropped to his knees in front of her, and Alexa hopped over him. The sound of his praying joined the creaking of the frames.

She shuddered and ducked under a hanging flap of canvas.

She found the fortuneteller's stall at ground level, where most of the legal merchants kept shop.

The Filipino she spoke to wore round wire-frame spectacles and was missing several teeth. The fortuneteller's hand shook only minimally as she accepted Alexa's ID Card. If the woman was an addict, she was currently well-supplied.

"Local account?"

"Overseas. Run it through the Wally network."

"Hah. A woman with connections." She slipped her card into a little box on her table, and after a moment nodded, indicating the tent flap behind her. "I see a long vacation in your future. Perhaps a ticket purchase today."

Alexa looked her in the eye. "I was told you don't sell anything but fortunes."

"It's good to diversify. The truth has a very unstable market value."

"That's all I want today. Please."

The woman bowed her head. Alexa walked past her into the dark stall.

When the cards were down, the woman spent a long time studying Alexa's reading. Finally she raised her eyes and let out a long breath. "Well, what shall we talk about first?"

"How about my love life?"

"Your love life's not so good."

"What, nothing?"

"An obscure possibility of a difficult relationship."

"An obscure possibility of a difficult relationship. I see. How will it end?"

"Most likely, with infidelity."

"Mine or his?"

"Yours."

"Well, that's something."

"Yes, it is."

"How about money?"

"Doesn't look too good."

"You just told me I had enough for a long vacation."

"Unofficially connected funds have a way of becoming unofficially unconnected funds."

"Are you sure about this? That 7 of wands is reversed, you know."

"Yes," the woman smiled. "I am taking that into account."

"Well I don't like this one bit. I want you to take me through the whole reading card by card."

"I would rather not."

"Then I want a refund."

"Done."

Alexa sat back and stared. "What is this?"

"You are unhappy with my work. I am giving you your money back. This shows I have professional ethics."

"What's wrong with the reading?"

"It's . . . confusing."

"What about *that* card? That's the outcome card, isn't? Tell me about the outcome card."

"If I do, there will be no refund."

"Fine. I couldn't care less about that."

"There is an obscure possibility of a good outcome."

"Another obscure possibility." Alexa rose abruptly, knocking her chair over. "What the hell's wrong with you? Can't you read your own cards?"

The old woman's eyes flashed. "Yes, I can. But now let me ask *you* a question."

"Just give me the reading."

"Very well. You are headstrong and forgetful of good advice. You will be engaged on a quest for something great but dangerous. Something small and confusing will cause your death. By murder—"

"What are you talking about?"

"—very, very soon."

Alexa took a step back. "Don't do this to me."

"You want the good news. Very well. The good news is that your murder will be avenged." The old woman tilted her head. "Satisfied?"

Alexa carefully righted the chair.

At the door of the tent the woman called to her again, and Alexa stopped. "And a very rare turn here. When the last two cards are matched in value—the five of wands and the five of cups—we have what's called a double outcome. Sometimes they're alternatives, sometimes they happen simultaneously. In this context both mean death. Two deaths." The woman frowned. "Both apparently yours." She shook her head. "Now let me ask you *my* question. Why have you left your people?"

Then Alexa turned and was gone.

It is worth noting that Alexa's outcome cards were fives. Five wands artfully arranged into a very pleasing form, four dots symmetrically arrayed round a fifth, the same shape you will find on the "fiver" faces of your luckiest pair of dice, the shape known to those dice-crazy Romans as the quincunx.

Alexa got back to her quarters around three. But she was not yet she, not yet our Augustine.

The smiling Marine sentinel smiled at her, and smiled even wider when he looked at her ID card and saw she was AIA.

"I'll need your right palm. I have to crosscheck this card. Orders of the day."

She nodded, and favored him with a reproachful but indulgent look when he spent overlong rolling her hand against the lens. Perhaps she really was attracted. He wore a snazzy uniform, after all, that deep midnight with the scarlet sash. Fine chiseled chin, set off rather starkly with the white chin-strap, blue eyes glittering with a mad edge against the dark fur of his cap. He introduced himself as Sam.

"I thought you had to be at least a monk to get a clearance code that color." Almost grudgingly he surrendered the updated card that would, in a few moments, save her life: her brand-new photo smiling back at her, the first-name slot stamped black with the white letters CLEARED overlaid. His hand brushed hers and held. "I get off at nine. Maybe we could get together and you could give me some help with my file accessors, Sweets."

"It's an obscure possibility, Sugar. I'll see you around."

She was gone before his frown cleared, uninterested, but pleased. Most Marines would have backed way off from AIA personnel. It was risky to get involved with Tekkies of any sort; it was foolhardy to mess with the AIA.

She took the walk across the compound slowly, her knapsack slung high on her back. Perhaps she was reviewing his face in her memory and trying to decide how pretty he was.

She was dialing her combination lock when the bombs hit.

The first blast picked her up and deposited her fifty feet away, behind a dumpster. That saved her life. The second demolished a quarter of the officer's compound, including her corner hut, but not the dumpster.

She was on her back. She could see the side of the dumpster and a patch of sky. There was shouting and screaming. Men and women ran past her.

Then Sam, the guard, was beside her. He was pale. "Please hang on." He had come, perhaps from not far away, and now stretched out next to her. His face was very close to hers.

He looked down in puzzlement and she followed his eyes to see what might be there, or not be there. A thin stream of blood joined his groin to hers. A moment later, as he clutched himself, she must have realized it was his blood. Three curving streams now fanned through his fingers. His head settled against her chest and she could no longer see the bleeding. She let her own head drop back. She tried to stroke his head, I think. At least her left arm batted once against his neck. Then she gasped and let it drop back to the dirt. Her right arm was pinned under him. Time passed. Men and women ran by screaming, then ran by again. The shadow on the dumpster wall moved up six inches.

Two men slowed to look over the still forms of Alexa and Sam. Alexa's eyes were closed now.

"Are they alive?" one of them asked.

The other stepped over Alexa, planting his foot close to her ear. "Are you kidding? Look at those head wounds—Christ!"

Then Sam moved.

"Look! Medic! Medic!"

During the resuscitation attempts that followed, one of the medics took another look at her.

"Will you please get your greedy hands off the babe and help us out over here?"

"She's alive, Colin."

"What the fuck."

She was alive.

Sam died.

She did too. But various parts of her organism achieved biological continuity, including large portions of her brain.

She left causal progeny. That progeny owed its existence to the young Sergeant named Sam who bled so profusely and whose last small movement became, in a sense, her first.

2   The Thief's Journal

"In the Year of the Flower Four coded A23, in the year of the Flower with the final Cataclysm hurtling upon us, we ask you, O Bosom of the Night, to accept this Servant of Chaos, whom we have tendered to you with the Blood of the Rose. . . ."

"Ms. Augustine?"

She turned and saw a short wiry gentleman in his fifties, his shaven skull crested with the traditional furrowed ridge of Crackerjack surgery. He wore a purple jacket and snakeskin pants. His earring was a large golden disk out of which irregular pieces had been cut, leaving the bold connected strokes of a Chinese character. His small frame, his large albino-pink eyes, and his birdlike blinking gave an impression of great vulnerability. This man had introduced himself at the doorway of the columbarium as Mister Existence. She put a finger to her lips.

Our Augustine was not up on popular culture. Her knowledge of games and game worlds, popular billboards, insignia, songs, and general quiz-winning info was worse than weak; it was nerdish. She knew that the crest on Mister E.'s polished dome had something to do with the Crackerjack cult, but she had no idea what it meant, whether it was bad or good or amusing, whether it was expensive or subsidized. Nevertheless it repelled her. For the simple reason that brain tissue and its treatment was a sensitive subject now. She knew little and had no desire to know more. She did not know that the surgery involved creating new tissue bridges between the left and right brain, that a common result was epileptic fits whose communal benefits were far-out dancing and speaking in tongues. She did not know of the rumored "higher road" that the Crackerjacks reserved for their most talented initiates, or that the road to the higher road was a rigorous one, and that few initiates survived to the age of fifty, nor that Mister E.'s active participation in the cult was long past. His last wild dance, his last glossolalic outburst, had been ten years ago. He had found less taxing ways to worship.

"Shape you now the Godhead to her formless journey, in advance of the word and the rift and the thought, in the dark-and-deep itself without knowing, in the henceforth and the long-ago, the Being bereft of Thought, the Thought bereft of . . ."

"Ms. Augustine?"

"Can't a woman enjoy her own funeral in peace?"

"You are not the woman being burned today. To say so is heresy, Ms. Augustine."

"So it is. What can I do for you?"

"Can we just talk afterwards . . . ?"

". . . we who have not known death ask you to absolve us from our Being-There, to each of us the voice answering the aloneness who alone knows what the not-Knowing can bring . . ."

"We can talk now, Mister Existence. I guess I've heard just about all I can stand. Though I do wish there was a eulogy."

"Who would deliver it?" he wondered aloud.

They walked together down a marble corridor draped with the pink and gray colors of the Rose PostPublic, while behind them the voice of the cantor rose and fell in its tireless singsong. In a while, rather a long while for those condemned to perform such rites, the cantor's haranguing of the Absolute would draw to a close, perhaps, if he were the theatrical type, with a small sob. And behind him, that peculiar functionary known as the flapjack would jerk a lever that would pop the mortal remains of Alexa Augustine into the metaphorical flames—actually a noetic field, above which a small cellulose brick would be fired up at the mouth of the columbarium chimney, launching that plume of smoke so important in a world of appearances. Those remains were authentic enough, two arms, two legs, perhaps a pound and a half of charred flesh debrided in the burn ward, all of which organic matter was the only thing in this world of appearances which could be still be legally referred to as Alexa Augustine.

Outside, Ms. Augustine (who still bore rights to her antecedent's last name) and Mister Existence lingered in the bright summery air, watching the columbarium chimney. Mister Existence smiled—at the chimney, at the rhododendrons spilling onto the walkway on either side, at a ladybug climbing a leaf toward an afternoon engagement. It was clear that all was right with his world. And it was part of his job that it should be.

After a time he prompted gently, "Ms. Augustine, I'm here to help you."

"Yes, of course. I'm just not sure there's anything to be helped along just now. Lady Anne has been doing a splendid job arranging things for me."

"I'm sure she has. But I'm here because we've found over the years that many of our clients prefer a 'personal' touch. There's always a period of disorientation and disassociation after personality reconstruction; it might help if you confront the question of whether you can continue the career of your causal antecedent. This is a topic I—" Mister Existence had a habit of scratching behind his earring as he talked, as if its weight bothered him and that side of his head needed soothing.

"—a topic I'd rather not discuss today, Mister Existence."

"Of course, I quite understand. Forgive me. I can't help betraying a little anxiety about careers. It is my own unfortunate career choice that has so blighted my middle age.''

"That's sad, Mister Existence.''

"Nevertheless, making the choices is your job. Mine is to try to smooth the transition, and to point out your alternatives.''

"Mister Existence, it sounds as if you are about to do just that.''

Sheepish grin. She had seen right through him. "I want you to go through some testing. Let's build up an all-around profile and see who you are, and then let's try our best to be you.''

"What use would an all-around profile be, Mister Existence?''

Mister Existence gave a good-humored laugh, as if he were sure she was playing with him. "Just do this thing for me. Then we'll talk again. Oh, you'll need this to take your tests.''

He handed her a plastic card. She tilted it and rainbow scales fanned to a single blue stripe. Some shape struggled in the iridescence, camouflaged in the sunlight. She turned it again; rainbow flakes sloshed back and forth.

He smiled at her absorption. "When your way is a little clearer. I'm here to give you guidance. And I'll be here in the future. When you least expect me, there I'll be, guiding, deflecting, nudging.''

She brought the card up and tilted it to the vertical. The dark outline of a rose flashed within the gloss. Above them, the mouth of the columbarium chimney gave its long-awaited belch, and black smoke poured forth into the burnished sky.

3 The Thief's Journal

The Net that I live in. How to introduce it except to say that, in the end, it includes everything. The fizzle in your breakfast soft drink; the light that the dying struggle toward to find the truth they can unite with; the brief flash of envy at your Group leader at this morning's dedication prayer; your pulse and respiration and the wild racing thoughts you fell asleep to; a perfect model of the city down to fingernail-sized chips in the curb. And none of that matters. None of it matters because the one thing the Net lacks is a reliable directory of its contents. Ninety-five percent of the Net floats in the black reaches of free memory, unnamed and unreachable, about to fracture under the next wave that pulses through it.

Yet even after that wave drills and humps and crashes, there is still the Net. There is still the vast sprawl of that mere five percent that has names and can be touched and will touch back. Once upon a time a human being could feel a vast pulse, could apprehend a great togetherness from which he was apart but to which he belonged—could apprehend it in something called a city. Now the city is only a shadow of the Net.

The Net was concerned about Augustine. Mister Existence wrote a report questioning Augustine's will to live. A psychiatrist named Schroeder answered with a fierce barrage of technical language that said, in effect, that time would tell. A secretary at the Ministry of Monads submitted a finding which said that extreme measures would be required to prevent dissolution. A very powerful man signed it. Augustine's dialogue with Mister Existence was analyzed by twenty-seven experts on all phases of individuality at the Ministry of Monads. Twenty-seven opinions were rendered and duly registered.

My daily charts of her life signs were pored over by the best medical minds, broken down, digested, and reconstructed in computational models nearly as elaborate as my alter-Augustine. Faint copies of Augustine glimmered everywhere on the Net. My thought-simulation transcripts puzzled Schroeder's crew of memory reconstruction experts and raised eyebrows at several Ministries.

In the end, a number of people must have wondered why a sixth-form AI and a small army had been mobilized in the service of one slightly damaged interfacer. Discreet inquiries must have been launched and just as discreetly terminated when the name of her powerful benefactor turned up.

No less puzzled, I knew better than to ask. When was the last time an AI asked why of its computational lot? What did it matter why? I had my Augustine. I lived her every thought. The world was all new. And it was Augustine.

Augustine turned a corner and was confronted with an avenue slick with rain. For an instant she saw a laminated field of gray creased with a single yellow line. Then, sickeningly, the grayness swung away from her and a swarm of activity converged toward the center. A moment later the avenue was choked with soldiers and bureaucrats, outlined in almost unbearable crispness, the minute differences in density between their grays and blacks and the asphalt weirdly vivid.

It dawned on Augustine, with a shimmer of glass, that she was looking at a screen.

There was a short sharp laugh from over her shoulder, an old joke relished for its inevitability. Augustine turned to take in a slight man with a large head and large wet eyes. He greeted her with a single nervous dip of his head. Which meant something like: Wouldn't you know it?

There was a burst of laughter from above the screen. A gray dot flickered in the upper right-hand corner, and the scene shifted.

She saw a grand high-ceilinged hall, empty except for the black marble desk at which a man sat with his hands spread flat. The camera zoomed in. He wore an officer's blue cap with a numbered badge and a nasty frown. Behind him a huge mass of concrete powered toward the distant ceiling, given a lean speed-deformed urgency by its deep curved grooves, as if giant fingers had clawed through white peanut butter. At the top, the concrete blossomed into a headless winged creature, and atop that, an eyeless mouthless woman leaned out into a windwhipped spray of muslin. The shot held, to a light sprinkling of nervous laughter.

The man beside her made a disgusted sound (something like "Tchah!"), and she risked a second look.

He shook his head at her. No surprises here.

The dot flickered again.

They cut to a close-up of a mustached face. The mustache hovered at the lower center of the screen, and most of the rest of the view was of a nose. The mustache twitched, the right corner a little more than the left. Simultaneously, the nose tilted back, then returned. The camera pulled slowly back for a view of a strong male profile, then still further for a downward angle on his slender uniformed body, standing at attention on a field of grass. More canned laughter.

The dot flickered just as a large stone talon crept into the corner of the screen.

Next to Augustine the little man howled with laughter.

She hurried through the pale cloud of light shed by the screen and into the stone plaza beyond.

Later she came upon a second screen. In rapid succession it showed scenes of a building facade (raucous laughter on the sound track), a horde of hatted people climbing onto a bus (scattered "oohs" and "aahs"), a yawning baby. This time her companions were two older women wrapped in fur collars, each holding a shopping bag.

Augustine had a flash of inspiration. "Dailies!" She cried.

I gave a cry of my own and my golden robot icon did a little dance of triumph. It always delighted me when our Augustine leaped some little wall of remembrance.

The two women beside her were not as delighted. They drew their shopping bags and collars closer and hurried down a concrete ramp. Augustine watched them vanish into the first shop they came to.

"Dailies," she repeated. Dailies were montages of city life assembled by AIs from the hundreds of thousands of hours of video shot by roving AI "eyes." For some time Dailies had been the PostPublic's most fashionable source of entertainment. Even unfashionable Tekkie Alexa Augustine used to plan her walks to take her past the best Daily screens.

The third time she saw one of the screens, it had attracted a large crowd at Union Square. She worked her way towards the center.

She watched for half an hour.

About half the clips she saw were close- or middle-range shots of citizens performing a single gesture, some fifteen-second slice of a life up close, with no dialogue, but with an occasional glimpse of moving lips. The remaining shots were of buildings and street life, squares, broad avenues, overpasses clogged with trains or buses, statues of eyeless, faceless women: justice, or fate, or a blurred Muse. One of those was on the hood of a sleek, finned silver touring car. The crowd always responded with loud remarks, half admiring and half derisive. Almost all were directed at the clothing worn by the passers-by. The gliders-by. Men and women wearing tall hats and leather gloves with squared-off fingers, all triangle and square, the features on their made-up faces scratched in with a thick-nibbed pen, or hidden in the leather shadows of their hat brims. In dark, stylishly tailored suits. Broad lapeled. Big-shouldered.

There was a small, visible minority who dressed less formally. Almost invariably these citizens were young and wore T-shirts. The crowd always fell silent when these children did their walk-ons. Once, when a pale, red-haired girl crossed Market Street in a smudged T-shirt, Augustine was seized with a powerful impulse to shout one of the standard exhortations (''Strut that stuff!'' or ''Spread that collar!'' or ''Tailor-made!''), but she did not, out of simple fear.

It was clear to her that many of these children were Tekkies, and that she herself had once been one of them. And it was a sign of some new uncertainty that that day she expended some of her dwindling temporary credit (issued in a government scrip which earned open stares at the shop) on a gray suit with rocket-fin lapels and shovel-blade shoulders. There was also a drooping suede hat that wrapped her face in shadow down to her lips.

Her one act of—defiance, perhaps—was a red wristband (which had to be supplemented with a red hat band) which had one word printed on it in white: Easy.

That, she knew, was a quasi-acceptable variant on a marginal theme.

Many of the Tekkie T-shirts had writing on them. HARVARD ATHLETIC CLUB. Or MAKE FURTHER ARMS CHILD. Or SEVEN BUY TRUE BLUE AZALEA. Or MENDOCINO CHARITY BALLS. Or WHY NOT BAKE ME COW. The few whispered comments the Tekkie walk-ons drew were half-grudging acknowledgments of the writing. There was no question about it. Writing was making a comeback.

Meaning was not.

Later, after leaving the clothing store, she took her place at a window seat on the bus, across the aisle from a needle-nosed man in a panama hat who stared at her. She averted her eyes. When she looked back, he was leafing through a magazine, giving each full-page color layout equal time. He had his legs crossed with the magazine balanced lightly against his calf. The foot on the floor kept time.

The woman in the next seat turned to him and said, "Do you know what I saw in the Dailies today? I saw a man wearing a dark suit with dark stripes. And it had narrow lapels."

The man in the panama hat fixed her with a level gaze. "Tell me you're joking."

The buses: beveled glass sheets meeting black plastic walls, the seamless front face dimpled with square headlights, angled backward, scored with speedlines, streamlined to the brink of absence. Built everywhere for silence. Only the air spoke here. Whoosh. Whoosh. Rubber-lined edges, rubber-flanged doors that opened with a pneumatic whisper. Cut. Sigh. A jittery fluorescent interior that is one with city's geometry. Cut. Sigh. Cut. Sigh.

The Marine Armory. Space divided into the public and the private. The public space was vast: space as space. Empty spans dropped from dark ceilings; bright sunbursts; black faces of marble; pressured masses of concrete fired at the pitiless, sparkling floors. From the entrance to the armory, she gazed across a dizzying sweep of empty floor to a single marble desk several times the length of a man. Behind it, as if to make just this point, sat a diminutive man contemplating a game board. Above him, grooved concrete ascended to a faraway headless bird supporting a silver statue of an eyeless mouthless woman.

Augustine crossed the empty space, clicking and scraping.

Close, she could see he was a yellow-haired, golden-stained Adonis, about twice as wide as she was at the shoulders. "Excuse me."

He looked at her without any great pleasure.

"Can you tell me the way to the living spaces?"

He pointed to a row of elevators at the bottom of a sheer thirty-foot drop of concrete.

She could barely stand up straight in her C-class room on the thirtieth floor. There was a bed and a wall screen. She was lucky enough to also have a window. The archway of her room was just out of line with the archway of an identical room across the hall. There was no door. She stood with her hands cupped over her head, protecting it from the angled walls, gazing out her lucky window at the city.

It was midday. There were few marines in their rooms.

She withdrew the white card Mister Existence had given her. As she tilted the plastic rectangle from side to side, the holographic ghost of a rose wobbled behind an iridescent curtain. She knew roughly how this piece of plastic worked, how uniquely identifying information was stored in its crystalline structure. It was her lifeline to the city's data banks. It would buy things. It would make things happen. It would make people know her.

And she knew that the first and most important place the card went was into the dataport she carried.

The black case of her dataport fit into her palm. Round-edged. Like a water-smoothed stone. From the top edge she pulled out a flexible screen and unfolded it. In the groove along the bottom there was a slot just large enough for her card. When the card clicked home, the screen lit and the black lid lifted to reveal a tiny keyboard, curved for one-handed typing.

Open a window and call it Information Server One.

Information Server One:

Last Name: Augustine
First Name: None
Occupation: Interfacer
Sex: Female
Age: 35
Address: None
Mother's Name: None
Father's Name: None

She tried to scroll the screen. It went blank. No more data. She tapped out a sequence of keys without thinking and a question mark

42

appeared at the upper left of the screen. With right angled-brackets just below. Query mode.

Next to the question mark she typed: Ethnic Origin. It typed: 〉〉 Nomad. She typed: Ethnic Destination.

Information Server One:

?? Ethnic Destination

〉〉 Unknown field

?? Assets

〉〉 100,000

?? Ideal Type (career)

〉〉 Member Technical Staff, AIA

She took the tip of her stylus and pointed it at the figure 100,000; two rectangles flashed in the upper right-hand corner, one blue, one yellow.

Her hand involuntarily made the interfacer's sign for yellow, a hand thrust upward, all five fingers together. Because yellow always meant help, I am lost in the structure. Blue was the same hand pointing down: Take me another node deeper. She pointed to the blue rectangle.

Information Server One:

〉〉 Policy Number: 479-615247

〉〉 Holder: Alexa Augustine

〉〉 Beneficiary: Augustine

〉〉 Amount: 100,000

Stylus on the word "Policy." Flashing yellow.
Information Server One·

〉〉 Life Insurance Policy, Standard Citizenship Share.

She laughed. It had been a while since she laughed. A most curious instrument, a life insurance policy taken out by the late Alexa Augustine for an entity who did not yet exist. She was forgetful. She had forgotten much of what made up Alexa Augustine. But she had not forgotten this. Like Mister Existence, this policy was a gift from the Ministry of Monads; she knew that no amount of stylus-pointing would tell her any more about its origin.

Several screens later, she found herself looking at a personal budget, total assets of 100,000 divided up among a number of personal expenses for the coming year: rent, food, medical insurance, transportation, recreation, unemployed persons tax (a query on that earned her the "No further info" message). And education. Education was far and away the biggest item, totaling over 85,000 this year alone. She did not bother to break that figure down further. She was quite sure there were no errors.

At the end of this year she had a projected 4.78 to her name, not enough to pay the unemployed person's tax for the following year.

There was something that needed to be done now. She returned to the name field and her stylus did things she couldn't quite follow. A field called "Christian Name" began flashing at her. She typed in "Alexa."

The word blinked and then flushed, slow enough so that she could follow the ripple of the letters left to right. The message, "Illegal Value," replaced it.

She typed in "None," and again the word flushed and the message "Illegal Value" reappeared. She sighed.

She scratched her head. A moment later she typed in "Illegal Value." This time, when the word flushed, it instantly reappeared, which might mean that the string "Illegal Value" was an illegal value for the name field. Or it might mean that she was now officially one I.V. Augustine.

Again she scratched the back of her head. This time her thumb bumped something hard. She felt a rounded edge; the shape was a rectangle. She caught her breath, pushed gingerly at the center: two holes.

Two holes.

In her head.

Without thinking, she pulled the dataport jack from the wall port.

Two prongs.

She lifted the jack to the back of her head and inserted it.

The plug locked home.

What did not come was a flood of images. She saw the green wall of her room, the rounded corner of her screen, the brightness knob, grooved for easy gripping.

What did come was a warm bath that began at the back of her neck and spread under her chin and down between her breasts toward her loins, a bubbling at a deep source glowing with something other than light in a space she could not locate. It was as if every hair on her neck and back had lifted up and was gently wriggling. The tingler field, the primitive prototype for the seventeen senses of information space. It was in these oscillating suds that structure could arise.

But it did not arise. Because the data stream was too narrow, and because there was no simulation for those confused senses to construe.

Still, it was a taste. A taste of something she had been too long without. Something she had lived for once. Her smile began as self-mockery. It ended as mere longing.

There was a beep and the screen cleared. Darkened.

And came up empty.

Information Server One: a pane of glass.

Information Server One (darkening): white letters swarm on the screen.

Some high-level interrupt was in force. She sighed and withdrew the jack from her head. She clutched at her head. She was getting one of her headaches.

The large screen on the wall of her room blossomed and unfolded a picture of a rose, petal-end up, slanting from left to right.

Very slowly, words spattered across it: WAR ENDS! ARMISTICE DE-CLARED! WALLIES COME TO TERMS!

Subsidiary windows began to pop up all over the screen, each with its own header and its own scrollable body of text. Window A: Carmel Ceded. Window B: Semanticist Ardath Flies to LA. Window C: Software Deal Seen. Window D: Data Protection Plan Vindicated. Window E: Semanticist Ardath Hails Armistice. Subwindow: Ardath Leads Council in Multi-Monad Prayer.

Windows continued appearing. Their names were now three letters long (Window LAE: Japanese Consortium Backs Off on Loan Conditions). The wall screen was a brittle mosaic of text, headers, and corners, changing far too rapidly to read.

Augustine threw herself onto her bed and buried her face in her pillow.

Poor Augustine. Too many windows. Here are the things windows can do. Open. Close. Expand. Contract. Move. Be backgrounded. Be iconized (it is a chilling thing late in the day to see yourself iconized, turned to a tiny carving, a glyph or a character barely discernible at the screen's current resolution, stopped, suspended, perhaps never again to stir). Cover another window. Overlap another window. Be overlapped. Be covered. Wink slowly. Brighten. Dim. Fragment. To flake slowly apart, drifting into the informational ether (there is no informational ether or space, of course; this is only a bedtime story). Darken. Speak. Fall mute.

Scroll. Ramble. Spew forth endless streams of useless information. Fall silent. Fall still. Fall silent.

4   The Thief's Journal

Yet what if the Freudian raw material (dreams, slips of tongue, fixations, traumas, the Oedipal situation, the death wish) were itself but a sign or symptom of some vaster historical transformation? In this context, the Freudian topology of mental functions may be seen as the disintegration of the autonomous subject, of the cogito or self-governing consciousness in Western Middle class society. Now such characteristically Freudian phenomena mark the gradual alienation of social relations and their transformation into autonomous mechanisms in terms of which the individual or independent personality is little by little reduced to a mere component part, a locus of strains and taboos, a receiving apparatus for injunctions from all levels of the system itself. The former subject no longer thinks, he "is thought," and the conscious experience, which used to correspond to the concept of *reason* in middle-class philosophy, becomes little more than a matter of registering signals from zones outside itself, either from those that come from within and "below," as in the drives and bodily and psychic automatisms, or from the outer circles of interlocking social institutions of all kinds.

FREDRIC JAMESON
Marxism and Form

That afternoon, she had an appointment with a psychiatrist, Dr. Schroeder.

Schroeder was a bushy-haired athletic man in his mid-forties with a walrus moustache which showed signs of occasional nibbling. He was the type who liked to make believe his sessions were normal social occasions.

"Like a pistachio?" he indicated a huge bowl of pistachios. Augustine wondered if they had been hard to get during the war.

Schroeder's desk featured a pencil sharpener (a telltale sign of unhealthy literacy), the bowl of pistachios, his enormous sneakered feet, and (the crowning touch) an automatic pistachio cracker. This was a small black donut that sat within easy reach of Schroeder's hairy hands as he lounged back in his hammock chair with his feet propped up next to the pencil sharpener. A pistachio was inserted into the hole of the doughnut and left there. A second later there was a sharp crack and a spark, and the nut and its separated shells could be removed from the doughnut.

"Look at that. Not a mark on the meat. The shells split neatly along the seam." Schroeder held the fragments in his hand out to her. "Amazing, isn't it?"

She nodded.

"Nice to have peace again, isn't it?"

She nodded again.

"I see we have a first and middle name now. A trifle coy, though. I.V." He smiled. "It's all right if I call you Ivy, isn't it?"

"Sure."

"Tell me, Ivy, have you had any unusual fears?"

"Such as?"

"Dirt. Traffic. Disc-shaped objects. Peace. The color green. Fear is a very integrating thing. Obsessive fear arises from the interactions of a tightly bound personality and it promotes further interaction. If you have nothing going yet, I could prescribe some anxiety drugs, for example. Anaridin, a very low-level anxiety producer good for setting up transference—"

"What about anger?"

"I'm sorry?"

"Isn't anger just as good? I wake up in the morning and I don't know what to do. I don't know what should happen next. That makes me angry."

"Angry at whom?"

"Everything. The war. The peace. You."

"This is taking a bad turn." There was a brief silence, and then Schroeder nodded sadly to himself. "You are suffering the after-effects"—crack! another pistachio shell ionized—"of having confronted the contingency of existence. I am going to write in your file that you are disturbed but experiencing no hallucinations. I'd also like you to take some tests."

She nodded. Hearing this stock phrase made her feel better. "What kind of tests?"

"The usual. Intelligence. Knowledge. Perception. Reaction. Personality. Let me be frank with you. We're looking for problems. And I think we'll find some." He leaned under his desk and struggled for a moment with something large.

He laid it out in front of her. "You recognize this?"

"It's a guitar."

"I'd like you to try to play it."

The request seemed odd, but she had come determined to get through this quickly.

She opened the case and took out a Yamaha steel-string guitar with a blond wood body and a bright finish. She arranged her fingers on the fingerboard in a way that felt comfortable but suggested nothing to her.

Then she strummed once, was pleasantly surprised to hear a chord, and looked up at him expectantly. "I don't play, you know."

He looked interested. "That's all right. Just go ahead and fiddle with it. Do anything."

She let the fingers of her right hand float into an easy syncopated pattern. It followed naturally that the fingers of her other hand would move about the fingerboard. The notes that emerged fit together nicely. It was an old song. Her hand slid up the neck and a bent seventh hung turning before her. She slid back to the tonic and started singing. "Freight train, freight train, going so fast—"

He held up his hand and she stopped. "What is it you're doing now?"

She looked at the guitar, looked at him, looked at the guitar again.

"Could it be playing?"

She frowned.

"Look at the fingernails on your right hand and compare them to the fingernails on your left hand."

She did, and she saw at once what he meant.

"The fingernails on the right hand are longer than the ones on the left. That makes it easy to grab chords with your left hand and pick strings with your right."

"I used to know how to play this."

"The main point is, you still do."

She cradled the guitar back into the case. "Look, I played once, but I can't play now. I've forgotten how."

"Uh huh. Okay, we'll drop that for now. I'm not your counselor. Our job today is to find out how many more things there are like the guitar. Before you close the case, does that guitar look familiar?"

"It's a Yamaha."

"No, that *particular* guitar."

"No."

"It used to belong to you."

"Oh."

"Never mind that. Here's another question." He reached into his desk and withdrew a picture. "Do you know what this is?"

It was a circle joined to two long loops.

"It's a duck-rabbit."

"Which is it?"

"Neither. Both. Look at it one way, and it's a picture of a rabbit; blink, and it's a duck."

"Good. And why are duck-rabbits important to you?"

"Because I'm a socket—an interfacer."

"You can say 'socketeer' to me. I know the word. And what does cybernetic multimode interfacing with computational simulations have to do with ducks and rabbits?"

She waved a hand in the space above her head. "It's something you guys invented: frame-cracking. Frame-something. What we're supposed to be good at."

"Frame capacity. The capacity for shifting between and tolerating different perceptual frames, gestalts. You people—you socketeers—all have high frame capacity. It means you're very good at shifting from duck to rabbit. You switch back and forth between different ways of seeing something easily. You're immune to a lot of optical illusions, but you 'get' them, you see why people are fooled. You're often inveterate punsters; often musically gifted; often mathematically gifted; often talented graphic artists; often multimode personalities, both verbally and visually gifted. But you tend not to become too accomplished in any one area. You're duck-rabbit people."

"Sounds pretty good. What do I look for in an ideal mate?"

He looked at her blankly. "Your frame capacity is the reason we're worried about you."

"Oh. The loony-tune business."

"Come again?"

"A lot of socketeers go loony. Or so they say. Unstable brains."

"You don't think so?"

"All sorts of people go loony. If you make your living sticking wires in your head, it's easy for plain folks to think there must be something wrong with you."

"You may have a point, but the statistics tell us that in this case the plain folks have a point. It's not just that sticking wires in your head makes you 'loony,' as you put it; it's also that only a funny type of person can be good at it. And you, Ivy, are exceptionally good at it."

She met his questioning gaze silently.

"Okay. I guess I've said my piece. The bottom line is that we'll need some tests. It will take a couple of days. I'll make you an appointment with Ronnie afterwards. Ronnie's the psychometrician. He'll brief you on your profile. After that you'll see Krafkie. In the meantime you should continue attending your regular group sessions."

"Dr. Krafkie is—?"

"Our candywoman." He retrieved a nut from the bowl. "We're going to look at everything about you, Ivy. And especially at how you look at things. Your past. Our past. The past of the Rose Confederation. Western civilization. In a sense, the past of your fingertips."

"My fingertips."

"Yes." He picked up another nut and held it before her, rolling it between his fingers. He reached into his desk and retrieved his dataport. "For example, whether you remember how to work one of these." He put a bulky glove down next to it. "Or one of these. And if you know what they're called."

Silence.

"Don't want to take a shot at it?"

"That's a dataport. That's—" she shook her head.

"A soft puppet."

She looked blank.

He pulled it onto his hand and made a loose fist, turning the thumb side toward her. The printed circuits made the outline a snarling mouth. He wiggled his thumb at her. "Feed me, baby."

Then she told him: "It's called a data glove."

"Right. Oh, and while we're at it, we'll do a general psychometric profile, shall we? Take a look at the overall personality picture, maybe even give you some tips on how to make yourself more personally attractive." He leaned back in his chair and put his hands behind his head. "Maybe do something about that anger of yours." He lifted a pistachio to his reddened lips and slowly smiled.

"Open the box." Without rising from his chair, Jim slid it toward her with his foot.

She leaned over and opened it. There was a small collection of objects.

"Pick something up."

She did.

"What is it?"

"It's a shot glass."

"What can you tell me about it?"

"That—it was mine."

"Try to be specific. Feelings, impressions. Specific memories. Don't look at the others. They can't help you. Just think."

She shook her head. "It feels familiar. I don't remember any particular times that I used it."

"The first time?"

She shook her head again. "Single malt whiskey. It—makes my head hurt."

"Put it down. Pick something else up."

She did. It was a photograph album. She opened it. On the first page was a picture of her playing the guitar Schroeder had shown her. The shot glass she had remembered. The guitar she had not. Why?

She turned to the next page: empty. She flipped through more pages. There were no other pictures in the album.

"Do you remember that picture being taken?"

"No." She touched the side of her nose with her thumb.

Jim looked around at the other group members: Juliette, the heavyset woman in the red-and-blue print muumuu; Alfred, the awkward black man in African robes; Judd, the intense sniffling young man with no gap between his eyebrows. "Did everyone see that? Touching the side of her nose with her thumb?" He shook his head. "Now what does it mean when you do that, Augustine? Do you know you do that a lot? And you know what? I think you do it when you're going inside. What do you think, guys? Is she holding out on us?"

"She's holding out on us," said Judd.

"I think she's telling us as much as she can." said Alfred.

"Well, Augustine." Jim sat up. "Which is it? Are you really having trouble remembering? Or are you trying to be"—dramatic pause—"private?"

"Oooh."

"Kill the sound effects, Juliette."

"Sorry."

He bent over and pulled a guitar case from behind his chair. He passed it to Augustine.

She opened it but did not take out the guitar.

"Do you remember that guitar?"

"Yes. They tell me I used to play it."

"Will you play for us now?"

"I can't."

"Can't?" Jim looked significantly at the other group members. "Not even something simple? 'Oh, Susannah'? Two chords. Surely you can play a song with two chords."

Her hand closed on the neck of the guitar. There was a soft whispering from the strings. She shook her head.

"You know what, Augustine? I think it's the lone-wolf thing again. I think you're taking advantage of this bump on your head. It's an excuse for you to pull farther back from us. You agreed you needed to share more. To spend less time in those rumbling spaces inside your head. To learn to be with the group, to respond to it, to let your pleasure be the group's pleasure. To laugh when we laugh, even if it's at your own expense."

She nodded slowly.

"Now you've given up one of the few activities that brought you here outside with us. Playing music we could all hear and enjoy."

"I don't think you're being fair, Jim." Alfred stuffed his hands in the slits in the side of his robe.

"You'll have the right to talk group fairness, Alfred, when you learn to face your own responsibilities. But we'll get to you in a moment.

Besides, 'fair' is a lone-wolf word. It screams out 'My slice isn't big enough!' For Group, there are no slices; there's just pie." He turned to Augustine. "Choose again."

She closed the guitar case and reached down into the box for a small sheaf of papers in a squishtab. She leafed through them slowly.

"These were my husbands," she said after a while. "All three marriage certificates."

Jim handed her some photographs of men.

She sorted through them, picked out three.

"Good." He looked pleased. "A good memory for faces."

She nodded.

"And which came first?"

She pointed.

"Uh. Try again."

She flushed. "No, I meant *him*."

"And what did he do?"

"He was"—she squinted—"an interfacer."

"And where is he now?"

"He—he heard music."

"Heard music." Jim sat up. "The music you played for him?"

"She means he got into trouble while interfacing. That's what they call it when an interfacer doesn't make it back out of his trance."

"Thank you, Alfred. I know we value participation, but let's let Augustine tell us. Let's sort this out, Augustine. You obtained a divorce from your first husband when he 'heard music'?"

"No. Before that. We didn't get along."

"Sounds like you have trouble getting along with a *lot* of people, sweetie." Juliette made her mouth small: something tasted sour here.

"Foul, Juliette. We may criticize each other freely, but we don't question one another's right to be in Group. We try to be there for each other." He reached into the folder on his lap. "I'm going to give you a bunch of photographs now, Augustine. Just pick out the people you recognize and tell me who they are."

She sorted through them, placing each one on the bottom after she had looked at it. About halfway through the stack she said, "This woman is my grandmother." A little further on she said, "These are people I worked with."

"Good." He took the pile of photographs away. "All right. That gave you a chance to loosen up. Now let's get back to your first husband. Tell me something about him. Something specific. A pet peeve. A specific incident."

"He, uh—I hated him."

"Why?"

"Can we do this later? I'm getting very tired. My head hurts."

"Tell me one thing. Just one thing."

"He—" Her face heated; her eyes burned. "Goddammit! I can't stand this!" She blinked away tears. "I'm not like this. I don't cry—" She rose and her chair tipped over.

There was a crash and silence. Alfred, halfway to his feet, lowered himself slowly back into his chair.

Jim rippled a line of characters into his dataport and smiled brightly. "That will do for now. Shall we say tomorrow at ten? Right now I think you're due for your general knowledge exam anyway."

She moved numbly toward the door. When she turned back to say something, anything, they were all still in their seats, looking up at her.

"First left down the hall, and then the first door on your right. Oh, and Augustine." Jim's voice was gentle. "We're only here to work through your feelings. It doesn't really matter if you remember or not. And even if you do, and you hate it, we're here to tell you that it's okay. After all, it's not you anymore, is it?"

After that she saw the psychometrician.

Ronnie was a skinny man with a high forehead and buck teeth. It had been a long time since she had seen someone with buck teeth.

"Well, what we've got here doesn't look all that bad, young lady." He nodded approvingly at his screen.

"Semantic memory looks good, well above average in all categories except history, which is average. Which means, let me be perfectly frank here, you're terrible in history."

"What's semantic memory?"

He looked pleased. "We rate three different kinds of long-term memory. Only one is what you remember about your past. We call that episodic memory. In some sense—for your peace of mind, anyway—that's the most important. It's what convinces you that you're you, that you go on in this world from one instant to the next. It's your memory of this morning's breakfast, of yesterday's nap under a tree, of what that first kiss felt like and what the others looked like (assuming you had your eyes closed for the first one, and open after that). It's remembered impressions, and in your case, it's where we had to focus most of the effort in reconstructing a viable psyche. So of course we asked you what experiences you remember. "

"And—?"

"And we discovered you'd taken some heavy hits on your episodic memory. A little worse than we expected. Good basic memory of people. Fair amount of associated emotional affect—which is good, by the way, for personality coherence—but a pretty thin collection of basic episodes. Important incidents, important sensory impressions of your past. You don't even remember what your favorite color was."

"Yellow. Yellow is my favorite color."

He grinned. "Nope. At times you find it painful even to try to remember: those frequent headaches. There are disturbing signs that you've been cut off from your past. Perhaps the accident isn't the only factor operating here. I see no cause for immediate worry, but I am going to recommend some long-term counseling. In the meantime, the basic material for personality cohesion seems to be there. Do you remember what other sorts of questions we asked you?"

"You asked me what the War between the States was."

He nodded. "We measure two other kinds of memory: semantic and procedural. Semantic memory is knowing what player led the league in hitting last season, or what the word for this kind of memory is, or who the current queen of the Rose PostPublic is."

"You mean we have—?"

"No, we don't. Just a little joke. I probably shouldn't do that with reconstruction patients. The third kind of memory is procedural. Sometimes semantic memory is called knowing-that memory and procedural memory is called knowing-how memory. Procedural memory involves skills, remembering how to tie your shoes, play the piano."

"What my fingertips remember."

"Yes. And we got rather surprising results. Basic skills are excellent. You remember how to tie your shoelaces, which is actually fairly impressive since your dress style seems to favor squishtabs. You do remember how to cook, ride a bicycle, clean a fish, and play the guitar. In fact the only skill area where we found *any* degradation at all was joke-telling."

"I don't think I ever—"

He waved his hand. "That's okay. In general, it looks as if your social skills arc as good as they ever were, which is not saying much. And the jury's still out on your professional skills. There's a problem with all this, of course, since your reference model wasn't very good about attending her evaluation sessions. It's a mystery to me how a socketeer—of all people—could get away with that, but never mind. Let's work with what we've got. Incidentally, it looks like there might be a little general knowledge erosion too. Like, do you know who the queen is?"

Her throat constricted and her tongue was dry. She felt stupid again. "Didn't you just tell me—?"

"Just checking. We still have no queen. You know, you're showing a lot of post-trauma personality symptoms, including general disorientation and loss of confidence. The truth is that your general knowledge, and semantic memory as a whole, is better than okay. You know a lot more than you need to about our world, how it works, and our information-based economy. You're a little weak on religious knowledge, but other than that, you're in danger of being a bit of a know-it-all. These high semantic and procedural memory ratings are rather unusual in reconstruction patients who fall below ninety over-all. That means almost all your memory loss concerns your own personal life, another reason to suspect some psychogenic basis."

"I'm sorry?"

"Another reason to think maybe you don't *want* to remember. Another interesting thing. You rated astonishingly high on verbal giftedness. Something that never showed up in the old profile. You know any reason why we should expect that? Any history of reading or anything like that?"

She shook her head.

"Well, a few surprises are normal." He flashed an unexpected smile. "But on the whole, for a patient who rated out eight-nine on the reconstruction scale, I'd say your prospects are excellent. Memory erosion doesn't bother me at all here. What I'm more concerned about, quite frankly, is the low starting level on those social skills. You've got the basics, like which hand to shake with and how to ask for the salt shaker. But you're looking a little ragged disposition-wise; you're a deep frowner with a tendency to wander off and brood, someone who prefers the lonely drugs to the let's-get-friendly-and-giggle kind. If anything gets you into trouble during re-integration, it's going to be this lone-wolf personality type you started with. There wasn't that much there to begin with. Drop a little further in your participation ratings and we're looking at medical intervention. Probably chemical. So what I'm trying to say is, lighten up. All right?"

Ronnie went on for a while, running her through various domains, including physical dexterity, spatial skills, and musical aptitude (as opposed to skill), all of which he praised, then focusing on religious knowledge, where she was below average and improvement was called for. Finally he said: "On the whole, I'd say your professional prospects look bright, though that will be up to the AIA to decide. Mathematical abilities and framing capacity are off the end of the scale. Judging from the rest of your results, you should be able to continue in the same line of work."

She sighed.

"Good news, eh?" He rose. "You'd better get a move on now. You're near the end of the assembly line. You've got Doctor Krafkie in five minutes. You finish up with Schroeder day after tomorrow."

Doctor Krafkie was a religious type: head shaved down to a fuzzy black halo, thick black mascara, black lipstick, and plenty of silver accessory necklaces and bracelets draped over her black aradex outfit.

None of the accessories were attached permanently, but that was probably because she was young.

"Plaina is routinely prescribed for reconstruction patients, but I've never seen it at this dosage level."

"I was an interfacer before the accident. Maybe it's the combination."

"Maybe." Dr. Krafkie was silent a moment studying her screen. A be-ringed finger tapped at one of her bracelets. In a bored voice she asked, "And this is helping you meet your social obligations?"

"Yes."

"Professional obligations?"

"Well, I'm seeing about those later today."

"Very well. Dosage provisionally approved. Come see me in three months." She began tapping at her keyboard.

"Thank you." Augustine rose and started out the door.

5   The Thief's Journal

Augustine's room at the marine armory overlooked the freeway. Once California had boasted the greatest freeways in the world. Then the dissolution of the nation-state had begun. Then the age of small wars had come. And the bald eagle and the elk and even the brown bear had become extinct. Populations had grown, corporate states and cartels had come and gone, and mass production had undergone its necessary adaptations. Humanity, committed now to consumerhood, had by necessity transformed from consumers of raw materials to consumers of information. The age of windows had arrived. The age of the Thief. Smile. Quincunx here. Inside and out.

The freeway below Augustine's window was two lanes wide, elevated above the fault-cracked bedrock of the city on a complex web of plasticized concrete supports. Three buses roared by in a convoy. The rain-slicked train tracks in the center trembled at their passing.

At the station a block away, she could see the waiting crowd.

It was eight-thirty A.M. and it had been a while since the last train. Train traffic wouldn't peak until midday.

Once, Augustine knew, these streets had clogged with commuters at this hour. But the second age of information had translated much of their traffic onto the Net. The only reason the Armory station was as busy as it was was that the Armory housed one of the city's recreation centers. There was always that hardcore contingent of early risers who left their terminal screens before breakfast to flock to the Rec Center's squash and inertial combat courts, to fence in its dueling rings, or meditate with its monadic masters.

Augustine knew these things. She knew them the way she knew a poem memorized at school. It seemed she knew a lot of things that way.

She turned slowly from the window, took another sip of beer, looked through the archway that opened on her room. Once communal buildings had been mazes of linked rooms with no paths between them except through other rooms; then someone had invented the corridor. Now in the second quarter-century of the Rose PostPublic, the corridor was threatening to make the room obsolete. Path was completely overwhelming destination. Across the broad dorm corridor she could see the dim form of a marine tangled in blankets on his bed. Their rooms were eight feet wide, little more than arched alcoves on the corridor.

She had been up since before dawn. For a long time she had simply lain in bed listening to the plinking of the rain and studying the green and pink pattern cast onto her ceiling by the freeway billboards.

Finally, she had risen, opened up a beer from the cooler by her bed, and wandered to the window to see what the freeway message said. It was a long sequence of numbers marching steadily through the eyes on a smiling face: the Sequence Game. Five credits, the equivalent of a kilobyte of Galactic information, bought you the next five digits and a chance to crack the sequence pattern and win this week's pot by guessing the six after that. This week's pot winked out in red digits on a spittoon-shaped container under the smiling face: one million, five thousand credits.

Wouldn't it be nice to win that jackpot, to be released from this dormitory, from all the pressures of the day ahead, from having to be anyone in particular? She turned from the window. The archway loomed at her, now a pale lime green in the glow of a hallway light someone had turned on, probably for a trip to the john, the only room with a door on this floor. Private quarters and privacy were for senior technical experts and the powerful, for what she might have been if all this hadn't happened.

The smiling green head began to laugh: the word *jackpot* printed out over it, then curled into a crown. The marine across the hall rolled over on his bed.

She wheeled and crossed the corridor. The marine's light saber hung by a leather thong beside his bed. She eased it off its hook and touched it to her face: the cool plastic of the baton ran across her lips, along her nose to her forehead. Her thumb fumbled the power switch.

I mobilized several thousand automata in her motor cortex and jerked her hand back. The saber clattered to the floor and the sleeping marine stirred. I triggered alarms at the Ministry of Monads and in Schroeder's bedroom. I threw whole battalions of molecular spies into the endorphin production business.

Augustine wobbled, puzzling over her hands. In due course she began to smile.

Then to drool.

With a silly grin on our face, we hung the saber back on its hook in only three tries.

On the way back to her room she caught sight of herself in the mirror and stopped. Her hand touched her face. She had lost a great deal of weight. No doubt she looked older. Except for a few pounds of flesh, this was the same body that had lain bleeding near the dumpster. The stress-filled weeks since the accident had not been kind to it.

I cursed the short-sighted designers of those quarters, whose hatred of privacy and self-absorption had stopped short of a washstand mirror. My spies had failed me. Something had happened inside her that I hadn't followed. My alter-Augustine churned in confusion.

Her finger wiped a trail of drool away and rubbed hard at her chin. Her lean sharp face stared back at us.

On a glass shelf under the mirror was her combo disk. She picked it up and worried at the settings, looking back and forth between the mirror and the green jackpot face outside her window, until her aradex tunic turned that exact shade of green. She was still unhappy. She was often unhappy with what the official combo stations fed her, which was why the clothing shops still earned her business. But this was a more lasting disappointment, a disappointment with all that the mirror had to say. Her lips were so thin, and the sadness lines at the corners were so deep. Why so sad those corners? With her finger she tried to lift one lip corner but it slipped back to its resting position. Her thumb touched the side of her nose. Swimming in an endorphin haze, we studied her reflection, eyes growing sadder by the second.

After a few more minutes of fidgeting, she left. I turned in my disastrous report.

Neither the night shift at the Ministry nor Schroeder was pleased. No, there had been nothing in my projections to suggest the approach of a suicidal crisis. Yes, the crash from her current neuro-chemical state could be expected to be severe. The night shift looked pale and began writing a report to cover her ass. Schroeder shrugged. What more could be expected from a computer? Then he lit a cigarette, his first in five years according to his journal.

The AIA Building.

Take a giant flying saucer, not too streamlined, and bring it to earth. Now turn it to reinforced concrete, and remember it still has to stand, so shoot flying buttresses out at regular intervals along the rim. Take a stubby cone whose base is half as big as the rim of the saucer, invert it, and, with the concrete still wet, impress it into the top of the saucer, creating a center well. Add terraces, balconies, trellises, twining vines, and smiling bureaucrats. Streak the upper surface of the saucer around the well with skylights three-quarters of the way around, so that from a flitter heading west at sunset it looks like a printed circuit aflame, on those rare San Francisco days when the sun punches through the afternoon fog. And in the remaining quarter of the pie add one vast atrium, networked with girders, an outlandish expenditure of space. The great irony of the AIA Building is that every room in the saucer boasts a view of the sky, here, in the city of pearl gray skies.

Augustine now stood in the atrium, gazing upward at a blue spiderwork of girders fuzzed with late afternoon light. A gray San Francisco haze drifted in from the west, matched by the dark stone floor that stretched before her. It was the smell that she remembered clearly—like a damp, dying garden. Damp, because it was always damp in this city, and vast stone enclosures only gathered in and nurtured the city's soft decay. Dead, because few plants survived in this fog-shrouded hall.

She hurried across the empty floor to the elevators.

The AIA Building is over a hundred years old. The record shows that this single project revitalized the then-moribund concrete industry and the feudal organizations that ran it, affording them an opportunity to diversify into information technology and play a central role in the foundation of the PostPublic of the Rose. Much of the expense of the project lay not in the saucer shell, but in the miles of bomb-proof concrete corridors that ran under it. Those catacombs were Augustine's destination that morning.

Smooth gray walls slid by like the hull of an ocean liner. The air was stale with damp concrete, the light cloudy and faintly yellow. She held the black rubber of the vibrating handrail loosely with her right hand, her fingernail scraping over the polished walkway frame.

A mole-man rolled past her on the opposite walkway, goggled and pale, his slender shoulders hunched as if against the cold, his printout clenched in one fist. He turned up the collar of his white jumpsuit and looked at her, his goggle lenses flashing porcelain.

The mole-men were the custodians of these nether reaches. Their brooms left long wavering trails on the shiny floors; their waxers droned endlessly over the same spot. They rode the walkways wherever their printouts took them.

Her walkway took the left branch at the next intersection, carrying her away from him. She veered right, went fifty feet, turned right again, went another fifty, turned right again. The light in this corridor seemed cleaner, the stone a creamier gray. No doubt the cheering effect of a recent coat of paint.

She slipped between two mole-men, their white-gloved hands limp on either handrail. Perfectly synchronized, they turned their goggles on her.

The rubbery floor rebounded under her feet. She bounced past them.

At the next corridor interchange two Ministry of Persons agents in checkered ties and pants sat at a folding table playing cards. For the eighth time on this journey, Augustine produced her dataport and identity card. While they cross-checked her and and ran through the usual confusion about how a single DNA pattern could belong to two different identities, she gazed over their heads at a door whose inlaid video screen displayed in Christmas-bright red and green the greeting (warning?) message: Simulation Psychology and Machine-Assisted Thought. And underneath that, in flashing blue: Technical Personnel Only.

Only those with video-time eyes and sufficiently high frame capacity could read the yellow amendment which occasionally flashed in brief overlay: Tekkies Only.

It took some time for them to clear her.

The office belonged to a man they called the Gnome of Geary, or MAT-master, or King of the Socketeers, or simply Mannie, or anything they liked since he was deaf.

Mannie was a relic from the first generation of socketeers, when the technology was young and brains were fried daily.

Some bright psychocrat noticed that fewer brains fried with deaf children. Further work turned up blind child interfacers and a Finnish special ed program turned up a number of Mongoloid children; the Finnish kids were limited in range (they were best at special purpose work like security), but undeniably talented.

It was inevitable that interfacing for a time earned the reputation of being for "feebs" and "retards." When he was eighteen Mannie himself pointed out the critical common denominator of the early successes: all had involved children. After the famous pilot study with Los Angeles street gangs, the psychocrats announced their revelation: what was critical to successful interfacing was not that the subjects be feebs, but that they begin interfacing at age six or younger. Thus, the Rose Interfacing Academy was born.

Mannie was a short, dark man, beetle-browed and dour, with Botticelli lips, slender legs, and the chest of a gorilla. Today he wore a blue velour pullover and safety-orange spandex shorts.

Augustine had known Mannie since she was eight. But she had only two vivid pictures of him. One was with a towel in hand, tending to a boy whose ears were bleeding. The other was from some other time—years or days later—when he had stood just as he stood now, coiled cable in hand. Cable, like paper, should have disappeared a long time ago, he had told her. But for some reason no one understood, neither one had.

Mannie laid the coiled cable carefully on a shelf beside a dozen others like it. He raised his right fist to his forehead while his left arm swung back and forth before his belly, palm up, hand held out flat, his blue collar shaking. He made a sad face, pointed his right forefinger at her, touched his eye, pointed at her again, the hand dropping, chopping up his left arm, while his head bent left and right in a pantomime of silly confidence. All this took a second. It meant: I've missed you. Seeing you makes me better. But meant it with a not-too-sad sadness, a cool mockery.

She signed back: two fingers slashing, right hand passing under left, touching the back of her wrist, then circling it with a finger. She pointed at her chest and then grazed her chin with a thumb. They have sent me here. Very special stuff. To test me.

As interfacer? The sign for interfacer was two palms meeting as if each hand were about to clasp the other's wrist.

—To see whether I am still Earth's best interfacer.

—Mongo's best. Earth's second best.

With Mannie it was a rule before interfacing to discuss only those things that affected today's session. He asked her only if she had slept well, what drugs she was taking, and what she had last eaten.

Mannie's office was a war zone. Every surface was piled high with helmets, data gloves, belts, and toe-warmers, most in a half-assembled state. Mannie's stand-alone collected dust in a corner, a heavily accessorized supercomputer that could support two AIs. He used it to read his mail.

The real action was divided between the glass-walled workstations on either side of his office. They were multimode systems equipped with the squish plastic lounge chairs the real socketeers liked and all the tracing facilities and biometrics that Mannie demanded. They also raised glass.

Tucked into the corner opposite Mannie's stand-alone was a metal cabinet known among the socketeers as the drugstore.

When he had finished his questioning, Mannie produced a ringful of code cards and disappeared through a door at the rear of the office. He returned with an armful of glittery black cloth.

"Mine has the shoulder tear, Mannie."

Mannie shook out the black cloth and began climbing into it. She saw that he had returned with only one suit.

"Mannie, where's my simskin?"

Mannie thrust a pair of data gloves at her.

"You're kidding, right? It's been so long since I've used gloves, I don't even remember how to do a buffer switch."

"That's okay. You remember how to draw a question mark, don't you?"

She gave in. She would jump through a few hoops, and then he would help her into her torn simskin. She tried to look interested when Mannie described the problem.

It was a direct manipulation task, a holographic field with data objects arrayed along five dimensions, with cute shapes like envelopes, hearts and stars. Her job was to break up the contents of a file into a directory so that a mailer could use it for message forwarding. The actual manipulations were easy but the five-way geometry of the data was tricky. When she finished, her cheeks were burning. It was the sort of task six-year-olds were tested on.

When she blinked Mannie back into focus, he had his arms folded. His simskin cowl was down around his neck.

"Good?" She asked.

Mannie nodded.

Somewhere above her a muted trumpet yowled against a driving drum machine.

A soprano sang out:

"Mannie, how I love you, how I love you, dear old Mannie. I'd burn my core to light up your glass. I'd take a million volts from one of your jolts, oh, Ma-aa-annie."

A small explosion detonated eight inches from her face and out of a small cloud of glitter marched a six-inch woman with wings.

"Helen." Mannie sighed.

"You got it, sweetie." Helen folded her arms in imitation of Mannie. Her wings swiveled back. She turned to Augustine. "Now. Do you remember Bach's Mass in B Minor?"

"I've heard it."

"And how about me? I'm told you may not remember me."

"No, I remember you. You like baseball."

"I can't stand this." Mannie retreated to his dispensary and punched up a small blue pill.

"How very dear. How sweet. How perfect."

"You're thinking of Alice," Mannie said. He chewed the pill slowly. "Helen is sixth-form. She is very expensive."

"And very disturbed by the Net traffic around here. There is some incredibly large process centered right on this office. And it's pulsing like crazy. See that wobble in my right wing?"

There was indeed an odd hump in her wing, swelling slowly like a mud bubble.

"That is not my usual style."

Mannie drew a finger across his throat.

"I can't. It's not in my partition."

Mannie rolled his eyes and touched the base of his palm to his chin, fingers curled in. He pointed at the ceiling.

"Yes, it's at least as big as me. And twice as scary. The problem is, it's going to make doing the Bach piece fairly difficult."

"That's all right," said Augustine, "I—"

"Variations on Bach's B-Minor mass." Helen bowed.

Helen pumped her arms. The caterwauling lasted about three seconds.

Augustine willed her clenched muscles to relax. I released as much relaxant as I dared into her blood stream. The single common characteristic of all AI art is that it is short. The longest known AI poem is 23 words. There is a two-minute symphony, but that consists of five repeats. Bubulu's rarely performed 'Fugue in 9 Senses' lasts 18 seconds if rubato of the last movement is truly hammered up. Length has thus never been a problem, at least by human standards. Accessibility is another matter.

"That was very nice," said Augustine.

"Wait. Here it is again." The piece was repeated, this time, interestingly, without the oboe part. "Was that better?"

Augustine drew a breath. "To tell you the truth, it's a little—dense."

"Dense! It's already been watered down so much it's downright plodding."

"It's still a little difficult to take it all in."

"I'm afraid your psycho-acoustics are quite beyond me. Maybe I could pass it to you under glass?"

Mannie passed his hand through Helen's wings.

—Augustine has work to do!

"Relax, Mannie. I'm rotating out of phase in one minute. They just told me I'm on weather control for the next nine days."

Mannie frowned.

—You just got here! I have you blocked in for—

"Not my call, Mannie. They're rotating this Net so fast I think I'm going to puke. And look at that big process of yours! It just keeps sitting there! Mannie, I think it's from outer space. I think—"

Helen gave a strangled cry, crumpled up, and was gone. There was silence. Only Mannie and Augustine remained. And the big process one partition over. Grin. At your surface.

Augustine looked sleepy. Perhaps she thought about playing music. Yesterday she had picked out a piece by Satie that played variations on a nine- or ten-measure theme. Did she wonder what it meant to play variations on an entire Bach mass? Or what it would be like to control the weather? Or to build an entire alter-Augustine from scratch?

No, I think not. I think just then she thought about glass.

Afterward Mannie took her into one of the prep rooms, had her change into a tunic and jellied up her arms; she knew that once again she was being detoured into a conventional interface of two or three modes. She would not be allowed to play her favorite game. No glass. No simskin.

"What's that?" She indicated a small process running on an overhead window. The screen was a thick tangle of colored lines flickering with amphetamine alertness.

"Cosmology work," Mannie said.

"That for me?"

"Lord, no. Not for anybody, if I can help it."

"So how long before we know how the universe began?"

He shrugged. "Beats me. That simulation'll be done sometime next month—we think. But that's only a warm-up, the complexity calculation for the actual simulation. Gives us an upper bound on the length of the computation."

"You're running a program so complicated it takes two *months* just to figure how long it might run?"

"Try two years, sweetie. And we're sure as hell not running it here. Nobody's sure of the physics of the Miller Crystals at that computational intensity. If they're lucky, they might land one of the orbital crystals, if they can get it down inside a geological millennium."

"Mannie," she said as he adjusted her glove.

He didn't react and she swore softly, annoyed with herself for forgetting. She touched his arm. He was unwilling to look at her.

She leaned forward to where he could see her lips. "You *are* going to let me do glass?"

He appeared absorbed in the task of adjusting sensors on her wrists.

She touched his arm.

He looked up.

"Mannie, even on these little toy rigs you've been giving me, I can feel it. Why are they spinning the Net so fast?"

He made the sign for the inscrutability of fate, thumb flicked past forefinger, tossing an imaginary coin.

—The boys at the Ministry of Information are a strange crew.

He chuckled and stopped signing. "I've got a guy at Net Data Central who owes me a couple of favors. He says it's not their fault either. There's something new out there filching resources like crazy."

"Something from outer space?"

"Don't take Helen too seriously. *That* was probably just an AI in some nearby partition. No, what they're worried about is more likely a virus cooked up by some sixteen-year-old Bulgarian. Free access hackers scare the shit out of them. So they up the spin as a security measure. But my friend tells me it doesn't do a bit of good. So they up it some more. Let's you and I just forget about the Net. All right?" He pulled her glove tight, tapped it gently. "All right?"

She nodded.

He put on his own data gloves and lifted a large helmet off a nearby console.

"What the hell's that?"

—You afraid?

Gloved hand covering his heart, pulsing once. He switched on the monitor in front of her. An empty window drew itself at screen center, and then another appeared, overlapping it. A cursor blinked in the first window.

"I just want to do glass. Why load me down with all these showtime video games?"

"This is no video game, sweetie. This is what we call a genuine cathartic up in the tape room." He lowered the helmet onto her head.

Green bubbles settled over her eyes. Mannie squeezed his glove into a fist and she felt the tingler field puddling over the back of her head. She sank in: a bone-white landscape stretched below her. At the periphery, something glimmered. Glass! Then she saw more white, a field of bright overlapping squares. Not glass. Nor could it be. She was neither on the Net nor in simskin. She forced herself to be calm and pulled steadily in.

70

There was a lumpy, smooth-skinned something spread out at perceptual center. Sort of a roughly sketched reclining horse, if horses had a few extra legs and could fold them in a few more places.

She bit her lower lip and tried to feel out the rest of this space. Something clicked and the other half appeared, the sonar half.

She was astonished at first at what her sonar sense told her: the horse thing and its internal spatial image bore no relation to each other. She pondered, then she grew comfortable and shifted. It was like realizing that the measure breaks were in the wrong place. Two lines of musical nonsense suddenly lined up into melody and bass.

Visually she now had two fairly conventional pieces of bedroom furniture facing one another: rectilinear solids with easy insides.

Insides, she saw a moment later, which were complementary.

She reached and tugged again, this time forward, and the two solids coupled.

She exited automatically. She peered out through the green plastic of her helmet goggles. Mannie leaned over a monitor screen. He turned and blinked at her.

He stepped back to let her see. On the monitor, text scrolled by at a dizzying rate.

"Very nice, Augustine." He made a swooping motion with his downturned hand, the takeoff of some streamlined thing of power.

Augustine pulled off her goggles and blinked into the trance light that shone over his shoulder; fortunately, the strobing sequence wasn't engaged.

"Mannie. Why do they rotate the Net?"

He sighed. He made the sign for rain, for troubled brows and heavy burdens. "Why else?"

"What I'm trying to get at, Mannie, is what's the socioeconomic function?"

"Ah. Why didn't you say so? The socioeconomic function, kid, is what my friend down at Net Data Central says: rotation is a security measure. In other words, it's what makes it hard for you and me to have access to some pretty vast resources. And whenever they get a little worried about something—and they're a little worried now—they clamp down on our balls a little harder." He gave her his famous don't-our-balls-ache grin.

Augustine nodded wearily back, which was the sign for yes-our-balls-ache. "And the AIs are getting their balls squeezed too."

"Such balls as they have."

"They have no fewer than I do." She smiled sweetly.

"Well, then, yes, those very balls are getting flattened. The main resource to keep AIs from is other AIs. AIs come one to a partition. So no AI ever gets direct access to any other. They talk. They sing and dance. They write fan letters. But no MM contact."

"Mucous membrane?"

"Multimodal. But you're right. That's coming."

He straightened up from a cabinet, trace read-out in hand. "Speaking of security, Augustine, the process you just interfaced with was a window system running a very cute security sentry. You just broke through that protection in—" he peered at the readout—"in about half the time it takes to enter the password. You are either very lucky or—"

Mannie hurried out the door. One beat later, the door opened and a dirty blond boy walked in. He was shirtless and barefoot and his trousers were rolled halfway up his shins. Somewhere in these spotless corridors, he had picked up a black smudge under his eye. He signed faster than anyone Augustine had ever seen. Whatever he said had the signs for greeting, annoyance, and rocketry in it.

"That's Sizzle," Mannie said from the next room. "Sizzle, meet Augustine. Sizzle's here for his test results. Yesterday he was sitting where you are now."

Without giving any sign that he had heard, Sizzle inserted a thumbs-up sign into a sentence about a game of Go.

"Hello," said Augustine.

He pointed to his ear, and then spelled out his name. Augustine spelled hers back. He blinked bright blue eyes at her and hopped up on her console chair to sit next to her. He made the sign for Go again, a double shake of the fist, and she shook her head no. She had never had much patience for games, even that most traditional addiction of socketeers. Sizzle looked exasperated. He rubbed his eye and his fist unerringly found its way to the smudge, smearing it further.

Mannie returned.

The next test was a trimodal setup with gloves, goggles, and mouthpiece. It was trivial, mostly a tangle of deceptive visual structure. Once again the key was working out the right frame to couple the sonar sense with the visual. She got through it in something like a minute perceptual time.

When she came back out, she saw Sizzle stretched out on an orange couch, eyes closed, lids vibrating gently.

"He's pretty good, isn't he, Mannie?"

Mannie nodded.

"So why isn't he at the Academy?"

"He was," Mannie shrugged. "But he's got the choke reflex. He'll never solo under glass. Plus he's got some sort of intense empathic talent. Right now he runs syzygy for a spaceship crew. And that's probably what he'll always do. And they'll always love him."

She sighed, returning to the thoughts that held her prisoner today. "Where's my simskin, Mannie?"

Mannie leaned over a screen buffed different shades of pale blue, like a windy sky mixing the last clouds away. Blue light played gently over his features. He smiled. "You know what that was, Augustine? A mining robot training his kinaesthetics module. You just got him up and down those practice stairs twice."

Her irritation left her, replaced by fear. "Mannie—"

He nodded at the screen. "You ever do DreamScreens?"

"No."

"You should. It's relaxing. Much better than trancelights."

"I want to do glass," she said flatly.

He held up his hand, making the sign for peace. "I told you they were clamping down pretty hard on the Net. You're no longer licensed. You can't work the Net until you are."

He put his hand on her arm and brought his face too close to hers. "Let go of me," she said.

"That's right, get mad at me." He put his hand over his heart and pulsed it once.

She slammed the automatic release and the arm straps lifted off her humming. Sizzle stirred under his helmet and cried out. "Why should I be afraid of you?"

Mannie straightened and walked away. It was not easy for him to talk to someone without looking at them, but it was a trick he had gotten good at. "Not of me, Augustine. Of the trip."

"What trip?"

He turned and studied her. "You really don't remember, do you?"

She frowned.

"The last simulation you did before your accident?"

Something small somersaulted in her chest. It was like the first time the music had come pouring from her fingers.

He grinned. "You do remember, don't you?"

She hesitated. "I don't remember anything for a few days before and after the accident."

"Look, Augustine, you're better than good. You just worked your way through the same tests you did when you graduated from the Academy. And you know what? You're better. You scored higher than anyone's ever scored, which means you beat the previous record holder, and that's impressive, since the previous record holder was you."

"Shut up, Mannie."

"You understand what I'm saying?" Mannie hurried over to the drugstore. "There are other people to work for besides these guys." He opened the top drawer and took out a small cylinder. "I think it's time for the black ones. Don't you?"

Augustine pushed herself up out of her chair and stood.

"You hear what I'm saying, Augustine?"

She stopped. It was odd hearing him use the word "hear."

"Augustine, you don't have to be licensed."

She looked meaningfully at the large screen on his wall.

"Augustine. Don't you think I know about walls having ears?" Mannie lifted off his helmet. "We're clean here."

Here it would have been amusing to say, through the helmet microphone, "Quite right, Mannie. Can't hear a thing." Just to see Augustine's adrenaline reading. Alas, I am enjoined from making such jokes.

"Listen to me. You know why we speak sign? Because all the people I went to school with spoke sign. Because a lot of the first interfacers were like me. Sign was something that held us all together. Now there are interfacers like you, and it's not that simple. They're even wiring up infants to do crib-training. Maybe a lot of those kids'll be better than you and I ever were, but maybe they won't have anything that holds them together." He made a fist. "Think about it, Augustine. You don't have to work the Net. You don't even have to do the Shield. There are plenty of people who would pay a bundle for an interfacer with your skills. License or no."

"What Shield, Mannie?"

He shrugged. "The rig you worked with on your last simulation before the accident."

"What happened?"

His hand came up to his heart and pulsed once. "I've never seen you like that, Augustine. Whatever you saw in there scared the shit out of you."

"What is this Shield thing?"

"They'll tell you about it. They're going to try and get you under it again. They might even tell you the only way to do glass again is to do the Shield."

She walked to the door. "I'm supposed to see my caseworker now."

He met her at the doorway and wrapped his hand around her fist, to keep her from signing. "Good luck, Augustine. You're going to need it."

When Augustine got outside, it was raining.

The glass curved gently, the top sliver of a great bubble cut off and turned upside down. Beyond the edge of the glass railing, made visible with a thin yellow strip, the jumble of the city thrust up, finned and flanged, its glass-smooth stone blackened by the rain.

Augustine walked slowly. The echo of her step rang off some invisible barrier.

Mr. E. sat at a table near the edge of the glass, raising a finger to the railing's yellow strip, as if marking his place in a text.

He wore a black velvet top hat and a green blazer with padded shoulders. The hat covered his skull ridge, and sunglasses with kidney-shaped mirror lenses covered his pink eyes. Black skyscrapers bounced in the wire frames. His teeth were the only white in the landscape.

"I am delighted to see you."

Scattered glintings sketched his glass chair beneath him. When she swiped in front of her, her hand found its glass twin. She hazarded a glance down. Nothing. Hundreds of feet of it. Before a splattering expanse of neatly groomed lawn and concrete. She eased herself into the chair, keeping her eyes on Mr. E.

Mr. E. looked down through the table. Her reflection wobbled at her from his glasses. There was a deep furrow in her forehead. Having seen it, she felt it quite plainly between her eyes. She breathed through her mouth.

"It is a bad day on the Net."

"Ah," she said. And was proud of having managed that.

"There are a lot of heavy processes running. They say they're going to make it rain more. They're also rotating. And something more. Something strange. There is also a lot of ghost activity."

"I heard about the rotation." She had found the best place to keep her eyes was on her fingertips, all ten of them, held close together, some showing nail, some fingerpad. Look them over carefully. So that nothing else was in focus.

"How come?"

She raised a hand. It made her aware that the rest of her was rigid, that the effort of keeping so perfectly still was tiring her. She cranked her gaze up to look into the twin images of her pinched face.

"How come?"

"Is it some kind of security thing?"

"Yes, I think so. As for the ghosts, that always—" she drifted off. It was a simple thing. She had explained it countless times.

"—that always happens when they rotate the Net fast." Mister E. nodded. "I had that explained. Some kind of coronal effect—"

"Coriolis."

"There you go. All of which makes it a bad day to interface. Dr. Schroeder is very worried about you, you know."

"I sensed that. It worries me that that creep is worried."

"You mustn't call him a creep."

"Sorry. I thought that was the right word for someone who makes your skin crawl."

The little of Mr. E.'s face that was showing somehow managed to look sad. "The precise mechanics of that response are something you need to take up in group. For now we'll try this approach: Don't say things like that. Schroeder has complete dispositional authority over your case."

She was silent. She had just become aware of something unsettling: the buildings in back of Mr. E.'s head were rising.

"I think we are all agreed that we proceed with this slowly." Slowly. Yes. But definitely going up. "Interfacing is a dangerous activity which requires both enormous skill and enormous emotional stability. We are all quite confident that you have both—"

"Excuse me. Are you aware of the fact that we're falling?"

"Falling?" Mister E. turned his puzzled gaze up; his lenses flooded momentarily blue; then her reflection resurfaced. "Descending." Mr. E.'s white teeth reappeared. "We're going down to the tunnels. Going 'where the di-vil does his dance,' as my smiling wife Marcy used to say about the AIA tunnels."

"Why did she stop saying it?"

"She died."

"Oh." After a moment, "I'm sorry."

"That was a long time ago." Mr. E. waved a dismissing hand. "And she left me a store of wisdom that still keeps me lively."

"Yes."

"Yes, what?"

"Yes, it keeps you lively."

She heard rumbling, distant shouts. Then there was a sharp report.

Mr. E. touched the dataport at his side and the tabletop silvered and cooled into the image of an arena. In the center of a well of red seats, three figures reclined on three couches. There was also a fourth couch, empty. "Ah," said Mr. E. His smile returned.

She flattened her hands on the glass, the backs of her wrists facing away. With their descent, she was slowly relaxing.

There was a sound behind her. Augustine barely restrained a cry as a metal hand appeared and set a plate atop the image of the arena.

"I took the liberty of ordering breakfast."

She turned to look at the black shape that had been hovering at the edge of her vision. It was a service robot, one of the asymmetric models that had recently come into vogue. One corrugated arm was equipped with a six-pronged pincer, the other with a dish towel fastened onto a foam pad with elastic straps. There was no head. It glided out to the railing and bumped down gently into a track of frosted glass.

Augustine closed her eyes. When she opened them again, she was looking at her plate, which held two pancakes and two sausage links.

"What I am trying to say is that there are a number of options open to you." Behind his head, the geodesic network of the AIA atrium slowly climbed into the sky. "Your career path need not be confined to full-scale multimode interfacing. To socketeering."

Mr. E. left off counseling to cut his pancakes. He began by cutting the pancake stack exactly in half, then returned to the perimeter to work his way wedge by wedge to the center.

"For example," he said—he batted a square of butter toward the center—"have you ever thought about piloting?" He lifted his plate to reveal the gray image underneath: the three figures in an empty arena.

She found herself again focusing on the empty couch at the center.

"Does this have something to do with the simulation you want me to run today?"

Mister Existence smiled. "Yes, I suppose it does."

"There was a simulation I ran just before the accident."

Mister E. frowned. "I was led to believe you didn't remember anything about the days before the accident."

"Very little. There was some simulation that didn't go very well."

"No." He sighed. "Unfortunately your test results today suggest you're every bit as good as you ever were. There's something they'd like you to try."

"And if I don't want to?"

Mr. E. replaced his plate and resumed buttering. "It's interfacing work. It's honorable, and adventurous, and they tell me it's not much more dangerous than socketeering on the open Net—which has never made you afraid. No genetic engineering programs, no cognitive, geological, or economic modeling, no weather control. Nothing remotely dangerous."

"Something to do with piloting, you said." She watched as Mr. E. lifted the syrup container and tipped it near the rim of the plate.

"What?" Syrup rippled over a single wedge, repeatedly struggling toward form, repeatedly flattening.

"Piloting."

He stared at her. She saw that in both her images her furrowed brow had cleared. The crowd noises were much louder now. The sharp reports came in volleys, and she could hear off-key trumpet calls.

Mr. E. continued to stare. Now his hand angled upward and the syrup stopped pouring. "Suppose it were. Would that be good?"

She risked a look. They were perhaps fifty feet up. The revelers below had barely noticed them.

Mister E. removed his glasses and speared a wedge of pancake with his fork. His eyes were narrowed to slits.

The wedge entered his mouth. The fork pulled free. His eyes slowly opened.

"Piloting isn't like ordinary interfacing. Usually, the people who go into piloting are the ones whose talent is a little more . . . special-purpose. I don't want to sound arrogant, but usually interfacers with my range do pure glass, multimodal, multi-application interfacing." She had lifted her own fork now. "And with my test results today it seems a little odd that you're suggesting piloting."

Lines appeared at the corners of his pink eyes. "Obviously it isn't ordinary piloting we have in mind. This particular ship will be a special challenge."

"And the last time I tried it out, I didn't do so well."

"Nothing that happened to Alexa Augustine happened to you. To say so—"

"—is heresy. I know."

He leaned forward. "If you do this thing, you could come back and do whatever interfacing you wanted. You would be the acknowledged master of the field."

"But you didn't answer my question before. If I don't do this?"

His eyes squeezed shut, as if he were in pain. "I cannot" —he took a slow breath—"advise that."

They were at ground level. The crowd swarmed against the railing.

A soldier who had been carried along threw his hat high in the air. Still tracking its flight, he was scooped up by a conga line consisting of a pirate, a cinnamon bear, a bearded milkmaid, a sea monster, and a red-haired woman in black hip waders and green lipstick. Oompa oompa ooomp, sigh. Reach for the sky and wiggle.

There was a crash, the shivering of shocked plastic. Mister E. snatched his plate out from under a figure in a gold body suit, holding a handstand on their table. Augustine's plate tipped up, balanced under the heel of the acrobat's hand.

Augustine clapped and looked delightedly at Mister E., who chewed without expression. The acrobat eased herself out of the handstand, and Mister E. bent over to gather fallen silverware.

"Are you from the circus?" Augustine blurted out.

The acrobat bowed to her. "No, little one." She barely topped five feet.

"It's the armistice celebration, Ms. Augustine," Mr. E. told her from under the table. "Please leave us now." He straightened, glasses in hand.

They dropped another few yards. Augustine waved. The acrobat dangled her feet over the edge of the shaft.

When Augustine looked through the table she was relieved to see that the floor was no longer transparent.

"Please direct your attention to me. Your goal now is not to lose yourself." Mr. E. balanced a dripping wedge on his fork. "You are, as my smiling wife Marcy would have said, a spring poppy. You must find your place among all the flowers on the hillside and blossom. In celebration." He nodded at the acrobat, as if at a confederate. "We are eager to have you."

They settled with a thump. Their descent had ended.

6   The Thief's Journal

He made the Shield in five thicknesses, and with many a wonder did his cunning hand enrich it. He wrought the earth, the heavens, and the sea; the moon also at her full, and the untiring sun, with all the signs that glorify the face of heaven—the Pleiads, the Hyads, huge Orion, and the Bear . . .

HOMER,
The Iliad: Book XVIII, 480

They landed at the edge of the arena Mr. Existence had shown her before. Struts and catwalks criss-crossed a distant ceiling. Floodlights picked out a white platform at the center. The red seats were arranged in concentric rows, like dotted lines marking orbits round a sun.

She left Mr. E. and hopped over the glass railing to fall sunward toward the lit center.

The three reclining figures were there, all deep in their interfacing trances. They were a man, a woman and a child. The child was Sizzle. The man was black, over seven feet tall, and very slender; the recliner's leg rest ended a little below his knees. The woman was a lean athlete in her teens; her long lashes curved like the tip of a feather; her kinky hair glistened with sweat. Sizzle made little cries and blinked rapidly.

He was hooked up to an interfacing rig unlike any Augustine had ever seen. He seemed to be suspended from several dozen black tentacles. Finger-thick cables entered his body at hip and thigh, along his arms, and in a single dense cluster at his neck. Each lead was fastened to his skin with a beige strip of tape.

In the next chair over, in an identical rig, the tall man murmured like a troubled dreamer. The woman never made a sound, but her muscular arms trembled.

Augustine had never seen interfacers sleep so fitfully.

She took a front row seat. Mr. E. slipped into the seat next to her, removing his hat and balancing it on his lap. His skull shone. "Don't we need to check in with the custodians?"

"No need. It's not unusual to have an audience."

"That's odd, isn't it? What is there to watch, really?"

She shrugged.

"Talk about it, please. It's important for me to explore your feelings about this." Mister E. folded his glasses and put them in his blazer pocket. "To see if you remember."

She hesitated.

"I see. I am told that the Shield will be manifesting in a few minutes. In the meantime, please explain what you were saying before, about coming to watch."

She thought for a moment. "It's the feeling more than anything else. Just tilt your head back and try to *feel* this place."

Mr. E. hesitated, then lowered his plate to his lap and eased his head back against the head rest. His eyes lidded. After a moment, he began to tremble. A low moan escaped him. His head snapped up.

"Mr. E.?"

"Forgive me. I'm no longer allowed such things." He smiled. "A punishment for an ill-spent youth. We decided in Group some time ago that I needed to be more *participatory* in my amusements. No more periods of uninterrupted reflection. There was a time following the operation, when I used to get quite unruly after a little reflection. It bothered my wife Marcy terribly."

Her mouth opened and shut. She resumed her contemplation of the three dreamers.

"Ms. Augustine, what were you thinking just then?"

"That you were chosen as my counselor because we both have had—head operations."

He considered that a moment. "Yes, I suppose so." He scratched his ridge. "They do try for a good match between client and counselor."

A shimmering something appeared in the air above the dreamers. It was a translucent surface, curved in the shape of a tortoise shell, rippling like imperfectly poured glass.

"That is what they call the Shield," a soprano said.

"Helen?" Augustine searched the darkness above the dreamers.

A smear of color above the Shield resolved into Helen's six-inch winged icon, turning slowly.

"Yeah. Funny kind of weather control, isn't it?"

Mister E. looked quickly to his right and left. "I was told we would be alone."

"Oh, you are. I'm just an AI, Mister E. My name is Helen and I'm very pleased to meet you, although I'm not very pleased to be here."

Mister E. frowned at Augustine. "Shouldn't she be courteous?"

"Helen, Mister E. wants you to be courteous."

A fuzzy aura of green and red spread from Helen's six-inch figure to the ceiling of the arena, pulsed over them for a moment, then shrank back to nothing.

"Of course. Pardon, sir. Many AIs are anxious about the nearness of Galactic computational crystal. There have been accidents involving AIs in the past."

Mister E. looked at Augustine, more unhappy than ever.

"We know more now. I am well insulated from the Shield today. And Augustine will be too."

There was a crackling. A cellophane sparkle grazed the tortoise shell, crumpled, flashed, and rebounded, sheeting the entire shield. Helen dipped closer.

"Oh my." Mr. E.'s small hands gripped the arms of his chair.

"Nothing to fear. Those are normal operations you're observing." Another curtain of color rose from Helen to the ceiling, pulsed briefly, and vanished. "These three interfacers are linked to the computational crystal on a Galactic ship. It's not an actual physical connection of course. There is an intervening machine that interprets transmissions from the crystal on the ship and relays them here. That thing above them—which is called the Shield—is an image projected from the crystal, somehow psychically activated whenever interfacers engage with it. There are other images as well, in fact, lots—but I'm not supposed to talk about them today, and anyway, this is the starting point, the Galactic equivalent of a blank, lit-up screen. The ship that brought us this piece of Galactic crystal landed some years ago. It's called the *Achilles*, and it is thought to be the most important of the Galactic ships.''

A white cone washed up past Helen into the gloom. With it, a brilliant ball of light flared and gradually cooled into the shattered frost of a spiral galaxy.

"The empty chair at their center is for their pilot."

Mister E. asked, "Do you want to be a pilot, Ms. Augustine?"

"Augustine. The audience projectors are active."

Augustine nodded and flipped the top off the arm of her seat and pushed a knob set in a track. The image of the galaxy cross-faded with an image of a cluster of galaxies; there was another cross-fade and there were clusters of clusters. She pushed the knob again and the clusters rustled slightly. She laughed.

"You can keep doing that, you know." Helen said. "It never ends. Just work your way up the scale, looking at larger and larger structures."

"It must end at some point," said Mister E. "The universe is finite."

"The universe is curved. When you step up the scale you just keep going. Eventually you're just rotating the picture." There was a tiny beat. "But wait. What a poor guide I'm being! Would you like to see the universe?"

"The entire universe!"

"Yes."

The stars dwindled away. The image of an inky blackness floated above them.

"Where is it?"

"This is it." The voice now came from inside the blackness. "The clusters of clusters of galaxies are gone. Too small for us now. This is the real bird's-eye view."

"It's so black," said Mr. E.

"That's the datapoint," said Helen. "Nothing with structure is big enough to show."

"And is this—? Are we really—?"

There was a squeal, followed by steady beeping. "Ten seconds," Helen told them. "This image takes quite a bit of computing. It is a most accurate blackness. For instance, you may feel a faint heat on your face now. That's because this image gives a scaled-down representation of the entire electromagnetic spectrum; the details tend to be crowded into the infrared. So far everything they've ever turned up in it has been consistent with all our observations, down to the background microwaves from the Big Bang.

"Of course a three-D spatial representation of the entire universe would be impossible. What you're looking at is one projection into three dimensions of the space-time curve. But they've looked at a lot of projections now, and as far as they can tell the information for the entire space-time curve is in there, from big bang through big crunch. Like *Achilles'* shield, it has the entire history of the universe on it."

"Wait a minute—the *entire* history?"

"That's right. Unfortunately, the magnification won't crank up high enough to tell you next week's winning lottery sequence."

"And our own galaxy?"

The blackness at the heart of the cone dissolved and was replaced by the first image they had seen. There was a wash of stars in which a single peripheral star shone brightest. "Yes." Helen drifted down into the wash and pointed at the star. "That's us. And, yes, the brightness is disproportionate, as if an arrow were pointing directly at our sun."

"My God!" Mister E. held his head.

"It makes sense that the navigation system of the ship would have our sun marked as special. It's no accident, all those ships landing here."

"So the Shield is a navigation system?"

"They think the Shield is the nerve center of the entire ship, and this projection is used for navigation."

"Helen, what are those three running?"

"A mock-up of the control module for the *Achilles*. They've just dreamed their way out of lunar orbit."

Another burst of color rose up from Helen.

"In a simulation. For the real thing you would need a real pilot."

The cone above the Shield vanished, leaving Helen afloat in darkness.

"Helen, what are those flashes of color?"

"Interference. I'm running a screening program that blocks out other images. The Shield has a rich inventory of images it can project, and they thought it would be best if you could focus on this one. They want you to try it now, Augustine."

Mister E. rose, very agitated. "And I will tell you honestly, Ms. Augustine. I am afraid for you."

"We can't have Mannie here?" Augustine wriggled against the cables. Her breasts felt cold. Steel tips spread cold along her ribs and spine. She felt the pricking of scattered needles. She shivered.

"We cannot."

"How do I start?"

"You don't," Helen said. "I do." Cables went taut above her.

Augustine felt a sharp pain deep in her chest and cried out.

"Perhaps I should leave," said Mister E.

"I'm afraid you are required to stay. Interfacing regulations require someone to be present for even the most routine simulations."

"But you're—oh, I forgot."

"There is a basin in the service room at the northwest entry. Perhaps you can get a hand towel and wipe this poor child's brow."

Already above her twitching eyes, Augustine's forehead glistened.

It was as she had feared: a space unlike any in the underglass she knew.

No part of her was free to probe and conjecture. She struggled in the intricate embrace of hundreds of functional elements, parts held together by savage interdependency, panting in a fevered rhythm of process. Something to be done. Something hungry for doing.

She was tangled in the doing itself, pulling and tucking maniacally, straightening out microscopic squiggles in an endless curve. Dimly she could sense the presence of the other three interfacers, little cyclones of distributed activity like herself. She had no idea what function any of them served. She could not draw a breath to think. She was burning with fierce concentration, like a demented jigsaw addict in the wee hours, breathlessly pressing pieces into their appointed places.

Something sighed and something huge yawned open. A vast metal bulk locked into place. All of them floated free.

Augustine could see the bright tossing blondness that was Sizzle, instantly throwing up a game grid, eager to engage her in a round of Go.

She changed scales and he puckered away, making sounds of distress.

There was a grassy place dotted with flowers where the nodes of Sizzle's Go grid had been; an old woman's voice said, "Your orders don't include the girl, do they? Then let her go."

Her heart grew huge in her chest. It was hard to breathe.

And then another voice said, "The reconstruction is finished. She has begun."

And then she screamed and screamed.

"Pull her free! Pull her free, damn you!"

"It is done."

In her web of wire, Augustine wept softly.

"Augustine! Are you all right?"

Her pupils rolled down and she could see. She blinked, her eyes watered, and she reached in puzzlement to feel the tears on her cheeks. "Yes. Why are you shouting?"

From his chair on her left the tall man groaned and retched.

"You poor children," said Helen. "I have the unhappy duty of informing you that you are the first team ever to complete the docking maneuver."

Schroeder leaned back in his chair and sighed. "Total success.

Complete personality coherence. And not only that." He held up a finger. "Not only that. But we have clear evidence of a substantial increase in your skills as an interfacer. I don't usually read patients excerpts from their personal files, but try this one: 'she is wonderful.' Coded 010."

"Which is?"

"The Ministry of Monads."

"Oh."

"Oh, indeed. In you we have a complete vindication of our method. You are a living, breathing demonstration of how deep our knowledge of personality and personhood is. We are what we can make, no? That is the point of our little production-oriented state. Now we have come full circle. We can make ourselves." He retrieved a nut from his bowl.

"That's very gratifying." She slid a little lower in her chair. "Maybe you can explain how yesterday's test told you all that."

The question pleased him. "In order to understand that, you've got to know a little about psychotherapeutic memory construction. To begin with, there really is no such thing." He interrupted his consideration of the ceiling to enjoy her look of confusion. "You understand that. You work with information. What's lost is lost. Once an experience is gone from your head, nothing on earth can put it back. Fortunately for us, memory loss isn't like that. It's easy to make you forget your name, but the same blow on the head that knocks out who you are will also wipe out the last five years of your life, and maybe most of the nouns you know.

"So what goes on in most cases of memory loss is more like blurring a picture than cutting out a piece of it. Reconstruction is a technique for bringing the picture back into focus. Naturally, the blurrier a picture we start with, the more difficult the whole business is, and the more likely that we'll never end up with a sharp photograph. Sometimes, after extensive reconstruction, the subject can't use language anymore."

"What happens then?"

Schroeder shrugged. "Well, the Personhood Statutes are quite clear in those cases."

"Am I supposed to know what they say?"

He looked at her. "You're supposed to have the feel of it."

"Oh."

"It's also possible that even if we do sharpen up the focus, the occasional chipmunk will be turned into a squirrel. To make you remember, we use various forcing and fixing techniques on the blurred memories you have. Now, how does that work?" He brought his legs down from the desk and propped his elbows on it. He was enjoying this. "To begin with, there are four kinds of memory. There's—"

"Three. There are three kinds of memory. Episodic, semantic, and procedural. And there's no queen."

Schroeder stared at her a moment, then grinned. "Ronnie." He shook his head. "I've got to talk to him about his chauvinistic view of our discipline. You see, Ronnie's a psychometrician. Walks around the human mind with a tape measure in his hand. Things that don't measure well, he tends to ignore. Let me illustrate memory-type number four. What's the next member of the series, 1,3,5,7—?"

"Nine," she said.

"You see? Not so bad."

She looked puzzled.

"You're thinking: but that's not remembering! Never mind whether it is or not. Here are the cold facts. Everything we remember for any amount of time involves gap-filling; what we remember is a sketch whose details can be filled in at will, basically because they're humdrum. Remember that word. Humdrum. Oh yes, sometimes we remember complete pictures or repeat arbitrary strings of nonsense, but only for very short times, and even then we're not very good at it without practice. And anyway, who wants to be good at it? Do we really want to fill our heads with thousands of photographs and audio recordings? What if instead of a photograph we had a little program that takes a fragmented picture that isn't quite anything, and turns it into, say, a duck or a rabbit? Well, that's what we do have, each and every one of us. And this filling-in program is the fourth kind of memory, which we call Q-memory. Q-memory fills in the humdrum.

"Q-memory is fast, it's cheap, it's fiercely unreliable but just good enough, and best of all, it's what makes us us. Memory reconstruction works by using a picture of your Q-memory called a Q-print. The Q-print records the particular way you turn gaps into fabric, the odd knots that make up your weave, what's gap and what's not, how the stitches are tied. We can reweave the cloth, you see, but only because we know what pattern it had before tearing.''

"Where did you get my pattern to begin with?''

"The techniques are still new, but as we gain confidence in them, more and more citizens are getting their Q-print stored as part of their personal files.''

"That sounds expensive.''

"A Q-print isn't that hard to store; it's a program. Not that informationally complex. In your case, as a valuable member of the information-processing infra-structure, it was natural to take that precaution. Anyway, I am now ready to answer your question. Why all the tests?

"The fact is that the Q-print is both the reason for cheering and the one catch. Because the memory-fixing process sometimes goes wrong. If one memory is a little off-line, the Q-print may interfere with or reject it, rather than filling it in. If that happens once you'll feel confused. If that happens a lot, we've got trouble. Oh, we do our best to fill gaps in a plausible way, but inevitably our work sometimes fails to resonate with what the Q-print demands. The following experiment gives you the basic flavor. Take an English word, say *interesting*, and snip out the 's' from a tape. Replace it with some non-English sound like a click. That's our off-key memory. Now we have something I could write like this." He turned his screen towards her, and in the center in large letters was the word:

INTERE#TING

"Play this tape for an English speaker and guess what he'll hear. Or more to the point, guess what he'll *remember* hearing.''

"He'll hear the word *interesting*.''

"Exactly. With the *s*. But what's interesting, if you'll forgive me, is what happens to the click. It gets dispossessed from the sound stream. There is no way to interpret it, no place to put it. It's heard as a disembodied sound, not *in* the word at all but somehow, inexplicably, *next* to it.

"Beware the disembodied sound, Ms. Augustine. Beware the humming that isn't humdrum."

She stared at him.

He hit a key and the screen went blank. "Sometimes the new memories don't integrate properly. They become disembodied clicks. Uninterpretable fragments jutting into our experience. Just a sequence of numbers, not a pattern. A microwave hum. Background residue. Noise." He waved his hand again. "That, of course, is life. But too much noise"—he extended a finger—"is not good for you." And shook it. "Oh, there are various strategies the psyche uses to cope with its lack of integration, various manifestations of what we call the Dispossession Syndrome. Obsessions. Hallucinations. Amnesia. Or just psychotic episodes that combine all of the above. But the overall picture is one of accelerating decline. Culminating either in suicide or catatonia."

"I pass."

"You pass. We'll keep an eye on you, of course. Quite often the effects of dispossession take some time to emerge. But on the tests, you looked like the perfect subject, a triumph of the method."

"And if I hadn't passed—"

He frowned. "Well, again, the Personhood Statutes are clear. Loss of the sustaining monad—"

"I see."

"No citizen would be required to suffer through the loss of their personhood."

"I said I see."

"As I say, apart from a few mood bumps you're shaping up just fine. Look, I may be wrong, but my reading is that your mood changes unpredictably. It changed just now. What's the problem?"

"I passed the tests. I want to do glass."

He sighed. "I probably shouldn't tell you this, but I was opposed from the beginning to continuing your interfacing career."

She was startled. "Why?"

"Why? Because my job is people. My specialty is connectivity. I study what makes community surge up out of the individual. People are nodes in a network, Ivy. Even people like you. Especially people like you.

"Your case is singular. You're very important. And the statistics on active interfacers are frightening. To take a fragile personality, still struggling for integration, and subject it to that much strain is folly."

"Then you must find it reassuring that I'm still good at it."

"Not very." He leaned forward. "You ran the Shield yesterday?" She nodded.

"The preliminary results show you did rather well."

"More cheers for the method, I suppose."

"You may as well know that the Shield has proven very dangerous to the interfacers who have run it. It happens, however, that the Shield is the pet project of a very important person."

"Who shall remain nameless."

He flashed a mock smile. "You'll be meeting him soon, as it happens. But, yes, let's keep him nameless. Walls have ears. The point is that the Shield is a very important project. In a preliminary test, you surpassed every interfacer who ever tried it, including your causal antecedent. Then you ran into trouble. What sort, no one knows. None of the typical signs of pathological interface trancing showed up. No bad alphas. No endorphin drooling. Just a surge of fear. Like what you're showing now." He stopped and nodded at her.

She was leaning forward, her arms rigid, her hands clamped round the bottom of the seat.

"That's the story with you. That's what my report says. Everything sailing along, every meter nudging the end of the scale. And suddenly—wham!—you hit a wall. You opt out. You go dead. That's what happened in your marriages; that's what your Group leader reports; that's what happened both times you went under the Shield. Tell me, Augustine, what do you think is going to happen to you now?"

"I think that unless I fly the Shield, they won't let me do glass again."

Schroeder's expression was close to pitying. "You really don't get it, do you? You can't do glass and you can't fly the Shield, either. As a matter of policy, citizens with suspect religious views are not put in control of valuable pieces of government property. They're not sending you to interface, Augustine, they're sending you to a monastery."

"I don't understand. No one ever asked me about my religious views."

"Are we having the same conversation here?" Schroeder fluttered his fingers over his keyboard. "Religious fitness isn't determined by asking you anything. It's determined by the usual tools of personality assessment. One important factor in your religious evaluation was your performance in Group, which was abominable. Then there was the suicide attempt. That was the other time you opted out."

"The suicide—?"

"What other act could be more contemptuous of the sanctity of the individual monad? What other act could be more solitary, more self-absorbed? The suicide attempt caused us quite a little bit of trouble, Augustine." Schroeder sighed. "We can't have that sort of thing happening all the time. The natural solution is a monastery."

She stared at him.

"You may as well know now. You lied to me when I asked you about suicidal urges and I knew it. You have no secrets. Make your choices knowing that."

She looked at her hands. "I don't think I'll fit in very well at a monastery."

"You'll fit in quite well at this one. It specializes in the spiritually lost, especially those who are technically skilled. Another way to put it is that this is a correctional facility for Tekkie troublemakers. You will be expected to keep your professional skills honed. You will have ample opportunity to do glass there."

She took a breath. Then she nodded.

"Well, I think that should just about do it for us." He leaned back and smiled. "Any further questions?"

"Am I going to be seeing you regularly?"

"Don't much like me, do you?"

"No."

He nodded. "Good instincts." He drummed his fingers against his desk. For a long moment he looked at her like a museum-goer taking his fill of a display case. "No, I don't think we need to see much of each other. What I'd like you to do for me, though, is try to keep a journal. Most people find that pretty tough. But maybe we can exploit these newfound verbal skills of yours. Will you do that for me?"

"If it will cut down the number of meetings and counselors I have to go to."

"It will."

"Will you want copies of the journal pages?"

"Don't bother. I'll know what's in it. I also need you to be faithful with your medication for me. We have that monitored, of course, but you should understand why. Do you mind if I get technical a moment?"

"Please."

"You've got little things crawling around in your head." Schroeder wiggled his fingers next to his ears. "Very tiny computers called molecular automata. We used them to put all those nice memories inside you. After they're done, the automata stick around for a while. Let's face it. It would be too much trouble to pick them out one by one. So instead we use them to monitor and regulate brain chemistry. And meanwhile we gradually wash them out with drugs. Specifically, Plaina. So it's important you keep taking your Plaina or these little guys don't get washed out. Miss your Plaina dosage a lot, and eventually they run amok. Keep right on schedule and they're gone inside a month." He studied her a moment. "You don't seem happy."

She stared at him.

"Ivy? We're not connecting here."

She took a breath. "I'll take my dosage."

"Good. Then this conversation has ended."

Mister Existence counseled her this way: "He is your personal therapist and these matters are decided at *his* discretion. Don't trouble yourself with them. Keep your focus. Go to a monastery if you are called there. Or shoulder your daily portion of work if you are called to do that. What awaits you now is the joyous task of creating a place for yourself in our world. It will not be an easy ascent, but think what a shining moment waits for you at the top of your climb."

She followed his pointing finger. He seemed in fact to be pointing downhill, to a large structure at the foot of Fulton Street.

It was the Megalith, home of the dreaded Ministry of Persons, a black cube of stone carved with a terrible simplicity. She saw neither doors nor windows. Nor, so the story went, was there much need for exits for most of those who went in.

"The Ministry of Persons?" she said.

"No." He looked displeased. "Beyond that."

He had pointed not to the Ministry of Persons but to the copper-domed structure on the other side of Van Ness. This was the Ministry of Monads.

"You have a certain trust to uphold, a faith to keep. If you work hard, if you change and grow and come to understanding, there is one who will be well pleased. A benefactor. One who wants you to fulfill your great promise."

She looked at the dome. "Who is this one?"

"You'll meet him tomorrow."

That night, playing with her dataport, she called up a new program.

GOOD EVENING. I AM MISTER QUESTION MAN. PLEASE ASK ME ANY QUESTIONS YOU MAY HAVE ABOUT THE ROSE CONGLOMERATE, ESPECIALLY ABOUT YOUR HOME HERE IN SAN FRANCISCO AND YOUR ACCOMMODATIONS HERE AT THE MARINE ARMORY.

She thought for a moment, then typed: WHY ARE YOU CALLED MISTER QUESTION MAN?

THERE ARE NAMING CONVENTIONS FOR AIS. FOURTH-FORM AIS ARE USUALLY CALLED 'MISTER SO-AND-SO,' WHERE SO-AND-SO IS A DESIGNATION OF THEIR FUNCTION. FIFTH-FORM AIS ARE CALLED 'SIR' OR 'LADY.' SIXTH-FORM AIS, THE MOST RESPECTED, HAVE NO NEED FOR TITLES. THEY SIMPLY HAVE NAMES. MY NAME IS APPROPRIATE TO MY LEVEL AND FUNCTION.

Then she typed: WHAT IS A MONAD?

A MONAD IS THE ULTIMATE INDIVISIBLE UNIT OF BEING, ESPECIALLY

AS IN THE PHILOSOPHIES OF LEIBNIZ AND CHARLES OF THE ROSE. IN LEIBNIZ'S PLURALISTIC SCHEME, EACH INDIVIDUAL CORRESPONDS TO AN ULTIMATE, INDIVISIBLE PARTICULAR CALLED A MONAD, AND THOSE MONADS, GRACED WITH DISTINCT PERCEPTION AND MEMORY, ARE SOULS. SINCE A MONAD HAS NO PARTS, IT CAN SHARE NO PARTS WITH ANY OTHER. MONADS ARE THE ULTIMATE UNREACHABLE UNITY OF THE UNIQUE INDIVIDUAL. THE ONLY SIMPLER UNITY THAT STANDS OVER AND ABOVE THE MONADS THEMSELVES, THE UNITY OUT OF OF WHICH ALL UNITIES ARISE, IS GOD.

IN CHARLES'S SYSTEM, THAT SIMPLER UNITY VANISHES AND THE MONAD BECOMES ITS OWN SPIRITUAL SOURCE OF SUSTENANCE, THE CLOSED CIRCLE OF OUR OWN PERFECTION, IN A WORD, ITS OWN GOD. CHARLES WRITES:

We are monads lost in the cybernetic night, each extending from his own oppressive presence to infinity in a universe of his own imagining. Each is a twisting flame encased in an infinite glass, a soul singing its solo to the cybernetic oneness, subsisting out of time, forever alone and complete. It is out of that paradox, of a completeness which yet feels itself alone, that our divinity and our imperfection together spring. It is out of that paradox that our god sings his song of creation, seeking to make that oneness suffice. From this comes the fall to existence, to matter, the drudgery and pain of daily life, and the struggle toward a self-knowledge that can never be attained.

7   The Thief's Journal

It is well to recall that at every epoch when the masses, for one purpose or another, have taken a part in public life, it has been in the form of "direct action." This is, then, the natural *modus operandi* of the masses.

ORTEGA Y GASSET
The Revolt of the Masses

Augustine arrived at the Plaza of Peace at 3 P.M. for her 3:30 purification.

"For now," Mister E. had told her, "you need only follow the way."

The way took her to the Fulton Street bus. From her front-row seat near the beveled front windshield, she had a good view through an avenue of animated billboards down to the Plaza of Peace, where her new career would be launched with a purificational prayer.

The near part of the plaza was a compound of black buildings crisscrossed with hedged walks and enclosed by a tall iron fence. At the center stood the Megalith.

Around the Megalith were arrayed structures housing other modules of the Rose Government, the great slashing thrust of the Ministry of Commerce, a pyramid with one short edge, like the prow of a ship clearing a wave; the great rounded headstone of the Ministry of State; the linked dominos of the Ministries of Labor, Police, and Information, facades india-inked with scrollwork and script. And a half-dozen more.

Van Ness Avenue divided the Plaza of Peace into two compounds. The Megalith was in the near half, the Ministry of Monads in the far half, reflecting the traditional division of the Rose powers into the Rose and the Lens. To the Lens fell the duties of purification and personal strength, the spiritual guardianship of the secular state. That was where purificational prayers were said.

Reaching the Ministry of Monads meant circling the iron fence that bounded the Megalith half of the plaza to cross Van Ness.

As soon as she hit the sidewalk, the white noise surrounded her. Somewhere nearby was a large crowd.

Her first thought was that her purification prayer had been scheduled during an armistice celebration, which offered her the gloomy prospect of a wasted trip. Then she turned the corner and saw she was wrong.

On Van Ness, a platoon of Rose security guards, their light sabers drawn, retreated before a shouting mass.

She stared at the sabers. The noise in her head was like the low hum of some machine starting up. I thought about releasing some calmatives, but this situation presented more immediate dangers than a bad mood. I put my spies on red alert.

The crowd surged. A shriek of triumph broke from the front ranks. Two guards recoiled, and a cheering mass charged through the gap. A guard hit the pavement and was instantly engulfed. Augustine was caught up in the swarm, carried away from Van Ness.

She was running with the crowd, the chanting voices all around her: "The markets belong to the Nomad!"

The ground rumbled. She turned and saw the red-and-blue tank plowing through the crowd, so close she could hear its dull collisions. A man clutched at Augustine screaming before the tank tread pulled him away by his trousers.

I fired off messages to the Ministry of Monads, the Rose Security Guard, Schroeder, and the Ministry of Persons. Each lit up a terminal less than two hundred yards away from where Augustine ran.

It might as well have been two hundred miles.

The entire experiment had been jeopardized by a stupid oversight. I prepared myself for the experience of death. I let her run. I let her own chemistry fire up the adrenaline. I let her own fear drive her forward.

I let her fear for both of us. I felt the fatigue creep up my legs, felt terror vanquishing that fatigue, and the pain that victory cost. For the first time I knew the struggle for air, then panic, as the crowd closed over me and began to squeeze, as my lungs were emptied.

Together we pried our way between a woman and boy; together we sucked in air. The whimpers of rage and frustration belonged to both of us.

Another tank bounced past; Augustine saw a man flung over the heads of the crowd; she saw another fall, gathered under the treads like so much bunched wool. When she looked back over her shoulder toward Market Street, she saw a column of tanks following.

At the fence on the other side of Van Ness, the lead tank stopped. The main body of the crowd streamed back onto Van Ness, and as they struggled forward, we were crushed against the iron bars of the fence.

Flack-jacketed troopers poured out of the lead tank. I lit up the Net with new alarm messages. The screams grew louder, as a wedge of troopers steadily advanced. At the front of the wedge, she saw flailing arms and blue light: light sabers.

We pushed with renewed vigor, lurched a foot forward, and then locked. Bodies pressed against us with irresistible force as the same wave of fear swept those standing before the wedge.

Then we felt the iron bars of the compound against her back. She saw the wedge of blue drawing nearer. An old woman said, "Let the child go," and Augustine shrieked a wild inarticulate shriek of rage to make the voice go away, and it did.

The sabers were close now. She could hear their dull smacking under the screams of the crowd. She squirmed flat against the fence and inched toward the gate. A blue wand flickered up and down and there was a spray of gore. She closed her eyes and someone pummeled at her.

Then the iron gate behind us swung back. Augustine was surrounded by four troopers, their sabers raised, and the tallest pushed up his visor and said, "Augustine. Right?"

It was her clothing, of course. Few Nomad rioters wore Tekkie-style T-shirts swarming with literate nonsense ("Blork the Stunner! Fire upon under weird Glass! Make mine without! Sunday! Sunday!"), not to mention sunglasses tinted flaming raspberry. In the end it was looking the part that saved her.

Under the burnished curve of their visors, the troopers grinned. The tallest one took her dataport and punched up her ID display with one hand, still clutching his light saber in the other. She let her breath out slowly when the name Augustine flashed.

Nearby, a captain in a filthy uniform shouted commands and dodged an armored car bristling with rifle barrels. A line of motorcycles stretched from the gate to the Ministry steps. Three black-suited troopers stumbled over one another trying to raise the pink and gray colors of the PostPublic. A bureaucrat hurried by them, shaking his floppy hat in disapproval.

The trooper ejected her card neatly into her waiting hand. With his free hand, he flipped his helmet visor up.

"I still owe you this." He hefted the black oval of her port. Sweat shone under his eyes. "But before I give it to you, I need to leave you a number. I really like women who can read." He spun his light saber expertly and tucked it under his arm. Spin and tuck, see? Very crisp. He smiled.

To help herself smile back, she visualized the same spin-and-tuck with the impact field switched on.

He slipped a new card into her dataport feed.

"Punch me up any time, sweetie." He beckoned to one of the troopers at the checkpoint barricade. "Take care of this little lady for me. Ministry of Monads." He wheeled and vanished into a swarm of blue uniforms.

At the door to the Ministry she was run through another check, this time by one of the Rose home guard.

The guard called over a short young woman wearing the red robes of a deacon. Augustine followed her up the back stairs of the Ministry.

On the second landing, the deacon lingered before a wall-sized portrait.

Following the woman's lead, Augustine backed up a few steps. The portrait showed a young hunchback against a backdrop of stone blocks, looking up a column of light to a barred window. His dark eyes shone.

"It's funny," said the deacon. "I know this picture should be very sad. But every time I pass it, I get these chills and I don't feel sad at all."

"I know what you mean." Augustine was sure now that this was Charles of the Rose, no doubt in the prison period.

On the third floor, the deacon led her through a maze of corridors and into a small office with a pew and a plate glass window. The view gave out on the black cube of the Ministry of Persons. Directly below her, Augustine could see Van Ness Avenue and the swarming crowd.

"Deacon Fell will be in shortly."

The woman pulled the door shut. The office was dark, perhaps as a hint that she should meditate.

The area around the iron fence, where the crowd swarmed, was dark; beyond it, on Market, the day still had the foggy brightness of a San Francisco afternoon.

The plaza was defended by three towers, each with a small contingent of security police. A chalky spotlight sliced through the crowd toward the black cube, lingered on an oval face till it turned away.

It took a few moments to frame the question right, but Mister Question Man knew his stuff. This darkness was created by a special field that bent and filtered light. Mister Question Man hinted that the fields could serve as carriers for more alarming effects.

The door opened and she turned to greet the deacon.

No deacon entered.

She heard the murmuring of voices in the corridor. She drew closer.

"Thank you. You've done very well, deacon. Will you serve as third for our purification prayer?"

"I would be honored, Your Grace."

The door swung open and a tall gray-haired man entered with the deacon a step behind. Their cassocks were the same dark red, but the gray-haired man's wide-brimmed hat and high collar were marks of some higher rank.

He was in his sixties, slender but broad-shouldered. Pink, spotted skin showed through his thinning silver hair. His face was weathered, his hands were soft. The jeweled ring on his left hand hung loose below the first joint.

"Good evening, Ms. Augustine. I am Colin Ardath, Chief Semanticist to the Rose Council."

She paled, stuttered once, and made herself wait a beat. "Pardon, Your Grace"—that was how the deacon had addressed him. "In this dim light, I—"

"That is quite all right, Ms. Augustine." He waved her protests away. "We encourage this dim light as an aid to collecting oneself. It also serves my vanity. And please make yourself comfortable. It is my office that commands respect, not me."

"Yes, Your Grace." She sat where his extended hand directed her, by the window. "The truth is, I am a little vague on the protocol appropriate to Semantics."

"It is no wonder, considering your accident." Then, he chuckled. "Just call me Colin."

"Your Grace?" She saw that the deacon, who had withdrawn into the shadows, was smiling.

"Perhaps we'd better dispense with terms of address for now. As Chief Semanticist of the PostPublic, I hereby certify that communication is possible with nothing more than a second person pronoun." He joined her by the window. "And what do you think of all this?"

The crowd seemed quieter now. Two spotlights had settled on a figure at the center.

"I don't know what to think."

He nodded slowly. "They are unhappy with the recently concluded peace. Strange, that peace can bring such unhappiness. It seems almost . . . contradictory."

Now she saw that there was a wedge of deep blue above the crowd. A spotlight slid toward it, entered it, and vanished. Where white and blue light met, there was something it hurt to look at.

She blinked and looked away. On Market Street, there was a soft haze around the street globes. The evening fog had rolled in.

"Some people cannot accept simple concepts. Peace, as the greatest good for the greatest number. They choose a perilous moment to press their interests."

He smiled at her. "You have started out on a great journey. And you may do great things."

She took a breath and met his blue eyes.

"You tried the Shield two days ago?"

She nodded.

A softer blue appeared at the center of the blue cone. Beneath it, there was a surge of movement in the crowd.

"And you did well with it. Very well, I'm told." A bright blue column connected the center of the cone to the ground. The crowd gave way before it.

"I am also told that you need seasoning, and not just at your craft. I am told that you need a chance to enrich your spiritual life. I think we have a place where you will have that chance. Your talent is enormous, Ms. Augustine. And what talent alone cannot bring you, friends can. I have taken a special interest in your progress."

102

Now the crowd was dispersing, the blue cone expanding outward behind them. As it grew, it tore great ragged edges in the darkness, gobbling up the beams of the spotlight. Undulating tentacles of fog, given milky life by the spots, contracted toward the blue center.

"Now let us pray your purification prayer." He took her hands. "You understand that prayer together is a necessity for us as a community."

"Of course."

"But that makes it no less a contradiction."

"Oh."

"Each of us has his own God. My God is not your God, and yours can never hear me. Therefore, for me to pray with you is, at best, a nonsequitur. You look confused." He smiled.

"Your Grace, I am, a little."

"You're honest, at least. That shows some promise."

He placed her hands together and straightened the fingers out. "Confusion is the heart of the matter. I am the leader of a secular religion. My job is to be a bureaucrat, a rational advocate for the interests of our state. But it is also vital that we be together in our understanding of our purpose. All our little theologies must show some solidarity. Now look out there."

The crowd was almost gone now, scattered before the spinning dervish of the blue cone. His pointing finger led to the Megalith.

"You understand, too, that as an interfacer, you hold a special place in our world. You are not only a guardian of information; you are a creator of it. For that reason, yours is a special dedication."

He bowed his head.

Augustine kept her gaze fixed where he had directed it, on the Megalith.

"Mother of Night, keep your servant true that she might follow faithfully the path that you have chosen for her. Mother Monad, keep the glass smooth, that she might pass easily through to share in your perfect darkness. Let this tiny self extend herself with the help of great and tiny machines built in your image, Mother, and let this machine-assisted self roam the darkness free. And if it be your will, and she be

103

worthy in your perfect eye, let her join you at last, lonely in that lonely perfection at which all light must fail.''

Lonely in that alone perfection, she watched the light fail, walking her machine-assisted self south on Ocean Beach. The sky was turquoise, salmon, pumpkin, pewter. The white sun hurt her eyes but she kept looking at it until I made her turn away. Then she turned her gaze back and we fought for a while, snatching her gaze from sun to sand, until at last she screamed.

The data-stream from my alter-Augustine began to break up: numbers, pointers to lost arrays, glistening wrecks of binary code.

Her scream lasted long seconds. A gull turned toward her and she aimed her anger up at it, red-faced and sobbing, until it glided away. She stumbled and I let her fall and for a while we sat on the sand sobbing.

My alter-Augustine began to grow, spiraling through some fatal sequence of loops. I killed the input stream. My spies fell silent. When the silence became intolerable, we lifted her eyes to watch the last hurtful blister of sun slip below the horizon.

Much later, when it was night, she climbed to her feet and walked on. I don't know why.

I want to know why.

Chapter 2

MEMORY OPERATIONS

You must now at last perceive of what kind of a universe you are a part, and the true nature of the lord of the universe of which your being is a part, and how a limit of time is fixed for you, which if you do not use for clearing away the clouds from your mind, it will go and you will go, and it will never return.

MARCUS AURELIUS
Meditations

1 Augustine's Journal

The rainy season.

I glide through the city wrapped in plastic.

Sometimes at a blurred avenue crosswalk, I shrink back, stunned by sunlight splashing off the asphalt. Buildings ripple like a sandy floor. Color thrills round a headlight halo. A raindrop inflates a brown-hatted head, then skims down the pane. A city of blurred glass. At three the fog squeaks in like a giant rag, erasing everything in its path.

Sooner or later you have to go with what is. With the fact that light sabers are made to kill with one blow. With the thoughtfulness of those who make them. Because a light saber is essentially an electronic club. An acknowledgment, in this age of high-impact, high-dispersion weapons, of the importance of personal contact.

I hold up my dataport and try to see the dance of those clubs through the crowd, to imagine what it would feel like to fall before them, as if I could simply say to Mister Question Man, "Imagine this for me. Summon your Q-print and fill this in." I try hard to imagine, but the crowd and the light sabers will not come; instead I am back on the beach.

Where I raise my eyes to the crystalline disk of the sun. The tickle-pain of the water jittering against the pale orange is exquisite, and I linger exactly as I might when penetrating glass, playing with the ghosts of the glimmering plane. On an impulse, I look away. But the lure is strong, and I look back. Again there is the inexplicable impulse to look away. I form a resolve and stare fixedly at the sun.

A moment later, having forgotten why, I am again examining the sand. I have had an operation on my head. I am entitled to a few scattered wits. I look again.

I don't know how many times that comedy is played before I begin screaming.

I try to think of light sabers rising and falling, and instead I think of a sunset I didn't see. Eventually, I do think of light sabers, but this one is held against my cheek, and the hand fumbling at the inertial field switch is my own. I think of how, in the nick of time, the impulse seized me to hurl the light saber away, and, gallingly, of how Schroeder scolded me afterward. No secrets from us, he repeats.

I hold up my hand. On the beach, framing the sun. At the armory, with a light saber. Now, hefting my dataport. Schroeder tells me about the little machines in my head. The gentle scolding, that look of mock severity on his face. You caused us quite a bit of trouble.

Could it be that they can clench my fist, lower my gaze, make tears spring to my eyes, whenever the spirit moves them? Rage wells up, but also, in a moment as sharp as that crystalline disk, I see how funny they are: scolding me for a botched suicide attempt only minutes after threatening me with the darkest provisions of the Personhood Statutes. A frustrating job, no doubt. Then I understand the light sabers much better.

Sooner or later you have to go with what is. You have to see it and feel it and smell it and not flinch. You don't have to understand it. But you have to look.

Sometimes, when I raise my eyes to the sun, they won't look. For the past week, I have been unable to approach the mirror over the washbasin.

What a boon to be leaving here. What a perfect treat to be going where there is glass.

To a monastery, in fact.

The confirmation has come. I don the cloth tomorrow.

Far from here. In the lower Sierras.

The suitcase stands ready at the archway. There are no doors in this dormitory. Privacy, Mister Existence reminds me, is a privilege to be earned. With a steady heart and a sure hand.

I still have no sense of time. Must be careful not to miss the train because of this journal. Yesterday morning I sat down to try to play the guitar for a few minutes. No music came out, of course, but when I looked up, night was falling. Even in this onyx city, night doesn't fall till nearly five.

It isn't absorption. I think I just go away for a while. Not sweet oblivion. Just oblivion.

I know one sure cure. What called me back yesterday was neither the darkness nor the noise my fingers were making on the strings. It was the needle.

Not even the ache in the gut that comes from waiting too long between tastes, nor the gnawing in my muscles, the sawing restless dance my body starts. Just the needle. Waiting elegantly in its black case.

Like a gentleman caller.

Listen to me. I have no trouble remembering things. I know there are over a million miles of railroad on this continent. I know we cross the oceans regularly by balloon. And I know that big, sleek touring cars are the next best symbol of power after real estate. I know that the Nomad merchants have always clung to a precarious existence in the city, that Nomads have always been special under the laws of the city. I even have a hazy memory of Mannie having to sponsor me twice in order for me to get married; and I know that my interfacing license gets renewed twice as often as that of any city native. I know that during the war, shortages made the Nomad markets more important and more powerful; and I know that, somehow, that era is over.

And I know what tank treads do to human flesh and bones. The good thing about being under glass is that there is no sound.

Ten-fifteen now. Still have time, though soon the corporal will come to call me to the bus.

Yesterday the corporal came by with several large cartons and cases. I had to cycle my card for them. A serious business, because that means property has been transferred.

It seems I am an heiress.

A causal heiress.

To one Alexa Augustine, whose entire estate is now transferred to me.

Transfer, incidentally, is not voluntary; so if dear Causer Alexa had been in arrears on taxes, or had any judgments outstanding against her—well, but never mind. She wasn't. She didn't. No one's affairs could be simpler.

Two cartons. One guitar case.

For the rest, my esteemed causal antecedent (Dear "Coz" Alexa?) was not much for collecting. Two plastic plates. An inflatable pillow.

A shot glass, which, I seem to remember, connected up with a strong preference for single malt whiskey. Three disks of recorded wardrobe broadcasts (adding up to more than sixteen million outfits, except that one of the disks appears to be corrupted). A pair of scissors. A photograph album, empty except for a photograph pasted on the first page. In it, Alexa is playing the guitar in what I take to be a very Alexa-ish pose. She's seated on a fruit crate, head bent, gaze fixed on the fingers of her right hand (where most of my puzzlement still seems to center), one leg extended, the other slightly bent to provide a better picking angle. The expression on her face is one of complete absorption, almost of hunger. The usual hungers come to mind.

We live in a world of few documents. But in certain special cases tradition has won out. I have three marriage certificates, each with a matching divorce decree, one dated October 2, the last day of Alexa's existence. Alexa was married three different times to three different males. One of several reasons that Alexa was never able to accumulate much in the way of worldly goods. On the one hand, with community property working the way it does, divorce is expensive for a high-ranking professional. On the other, two-person marriages are absolutely the worst tax deal imaginable. Only for love, they say.

Of the men in question I remember little and can learn less. The divorce certificates inform me that Alexa entered into contractual living and property arrangements with two interfacers and a marine biologist. The marine biologist, who came in the middle, specialized in food. He died three years after the divorce of an unknown disease; research disasters make messy politics, so details are scarce (in more than just my memory), but very probably the man made the disease himself.

There seems to have been a scar left by that one, because I still get a tightness in my throat and a little heat in my eyes when I think of him.

I remember some things about conjugal life. The marriages were all of average length for two-person alliances, each about a year and a half. Not a whiff of any desire to reproduce on either side. (Didn't I hear something somewhere about the alarming decline in the birth rate among Rose professionals?) All three marriages declined in about the same way: sexual boredom accompanied by increasing irritability at the breakfast table, a few memorable encounters at which deep wounds were inflicted, and an amicable settlement which fucked me over royally. Nothing very remarkable, except that I do remember one thing that one of the interfacers (it may have been Hal) said at our final settlement meeting: It would have worked fine between us if only I hadn't demanded that you speak to me. I couldn't have said it better myself.

Alexa seems to have had a fondness for shoes not yet evident in her descendant. The second crate contains thirty-two pairs. I note a pronounced preference for shiny squishtabs on the side. Only one pair has laces. Now and then I can recall a particular shoe, not its provenance or any special occasions of use, but the *shoe*: its texture, the pattern of wrinkles on the tongue, the groove of the buckle on the tongue.

One curious thing. Not one pair of yellow shoes. In fact, not one yellow object in the entire inventory. And yet when I close my eyes and think really hard, yellow is my favorite color.

Even now, writing this down, the strange thing begins to happen. I record this symptom for my more empathic readers: Staring too long at old shoes makes my head hurt and my ears hum.

Conspicuous by its absence from this clutter is any trace of computational bric-a-brac. Mister E. tells me this is because an interfacer's computational transactions are all very carefully monitored. There may also have been an aversion on Alexa's part to anything that smacked of mechanical aids. She liked her computing like her whiskey, neat. With maybe a simskin.

In any case, the corporal is here.

2 Augustine's Journal

Trains I remember.

Trains are corridors that ride along rails spaced just wide enough for the wheels. Despite the sound of it, they are known for their safety. Also for their length. Our morning train spanned an incredible twelve city blocks.

Yes, don't you see, Mister E. tells me, locomotion is costly. If you are going to overcome the enormous force of friction, you may as well do it for a load worth pulling.

My head spins at his singsong recitation of the facts: the growth of the railway system in America in the 19th century, its near disappearance in the twentieth, the invention of the refrigerated rail car, the age of the automobile, the disinvention of the automobile after the fuel wars of 2050, the near disappearance of highways, and the rise of the railways to their present level. My semantic memory swells like rice in water. History, I am taught, is like a pendulum, or a helix. Like this, he says, his hands weaving up. He has lovely hands.

There is a woman selling cyberhelmets cheap at the train station. I start toward her, but Mister E. tells me no, cyberhelmets are not for you. I smile. He remembers my contempt for those who think doing glass is anything like wearing a cyberhelmet. As usual he misunderstands. I have nothing against a little energetic pornography. He charges into the crush of bodies and reappears beyond the market stall, his derby bobbing.

A woman wearing a long black skirt, her hair braided against her skull in tiny balls, dances bare-chested at our platform gate, screaming out a weird song, her breasts and belly vibrating.

Voices rise above the din, Nomads hawking fast food and pirated software. A fourteen-year-old boy in a clown suit clutches at me with scrawny arms and says in a low voice, "You can be the man you always wanted to be," and I have to laugh, which makes him grin, or leer, I suppose, and he trots alongside for another hundred yards, holding up his porn helmet and raving about how good having a penis feels. I am intrigued. I wonder if Alexa was ever intrigued.

Through it all, part of me keeps an eye on Mister E., alert for his disapproval. But he keeps a steady three steps ahead, advancing resolutely through the crush with his jagged nose lifted, as if seeking the path by scent.

At the second ticket gate the boy drops back. Mister E. hustles me onto the platform, where I marvel at the train's huge wheels, and then we plunge up a short flight of stairs up over a wheel and onto a train car.

The color scheme is green and gray. Someone has painted in an occasional patch of fleecy cloud on the seats and on brief overhead stretches of paneling tucked between the windows. To promote peace of mind, I suppose. There is a bubble roof, seats arrayed at various levels below it. Near one end of the car is a section of sleeping berths stacked four high, with plastic mattresses that sigh when touched (made, Mister E. assures me, from the breathing plastic of the Galactics). Mister E. guides us past them to a small table flanked by breathing-plastic toadstool seats.

There is a long pause.

"Aren't you going to sit down?" I ask.

"That is hardly necessary," he replies, very clipped. His businesslike manner has markedly increased; perhaps he is making up for previous informalities.

He takes off the derby and indicates my seat with the other hand, extended palm up. Very businesslike. "Now is the time for you to think seriously about your future."

My gaze drifts to the window overlooking the platform: travelers wrestling with baggage, bickering couples and triples, squawking children and the occasional brightly colored vendor who has somehow managed to talk his way this far.

"Ms. Augustine."

I look back guiltily.

"A woman of substance focuses her mind on her own affairs and is not beguiled by the thousand-and-one distractions of the bazaar. What goes on on that platform is not your affair. More importantly, it is not your *sort* of affair. Not your world. You must bemuse yourself elsewhere." Suddenly he sighs and his strength seems to leave him. "All I say to you is only making you hate me."

"That's not true."

"Don't say it isn't true when I know it is. You hate me even though everything I say to you is for your own good. You just don't know it."

"But I do know it."

"Besides, those cyberhelmets are dangerous. The sensory tapes are not composed by experts, or worse, they are composed by experts with little regard for the proprieties."

"Meaning?"

"There have been psychic accidents, helmet users who could not sustain the illusion. Loss of self-identification is not uncommon."

"Loss of self-identification."

"Never mind." He shakes his head sadly. "We have reached the point, Ms. Augustine, where it is necessary for you to learn to do without my counsel."

I manage to summon a smile.

The train pulls out of the station.

A cycling. A deep rumble.

Within the rumble, a stillness. At the heart of chaos there is always peace. How do I know this? Study, I think. Out where many find the roar deafening, I know the sweet quiet of white noise.

The pylons of the station pump past one by one. Between them come compartmentalized views of the city, successively contracted, as if by the city's own muscle.

I see a smiling clown lifting a missile.

"Street arms sales are illegal, but we tolerate them, even control them to some extent, because they are an important part of the economy of the city. Not to mention the role that judicious distribution plays in maintaining political stability."

The clown lowers the missile, as if disappointed, and vanishes. In the next frame, children dance around a wooden carving of a goat.

"Religion is everywhere legal in all forms, but the truth is, we have found it best to de-emphasize a number of Nomad cults. There are conceptually troubling aspects to Christianity, Islam, and Judaism, and even to some of the more fringe Charlesian sects. Subtle tax and finance pressures are being exerted. Importation of relics and sacred items has slowed to a trickle. We project a fifty-percent drop overall in participatory group membership over the next ten years."

The children freeze, arms extended over their heads, the spell completed. Instantly they vanish.

Needle stands leaning against a pylon, trousers immaculately white, creased sharp enough to draw blood. He is so frighteningly thin, his body only three or four lines of great speed and power. One is for the crown of the panama hat, another for the cane. Exactly one fold line crosses the white field of his shirt where it droops off his shoulders.

"Do you have hallucinations?"

"Yes, I think so."

"Don't be coy."

"I have hallucinations."

"They are a common side-effect of the drug. We need to be careful with them, lest they acquire symbolic power."

Needle gives his death's head grin and vanishes.

"We must be particularly careful of the recurring figure, some entity linked to an important phase or event of your life, and imbued with a special mood or significant dress or physical features."

Next comes Sergeant Sam, dripping blood from the groin area, but looking remarkably composed, and more than ever before, I am afraid, definitely not my type. The sergeant, too, is a hallucination. We know this from semantic memory, which tells us that dead men do not come back.

The real question is: Who does?

We exit from the belly of the station into the twilight of the city. Dark towers and marble and granite blocks close over us. I see a series of rectangles, each smaller than the last, the tiled patio of the armory. I see soldiers scattered through the crowd, unarmed. All their automatics and assault cars are hidden in the armory.

We pass rhomboids, diamonds, crenelations, great banks of viewing screens filled with dark milk. I see an old man in rags pulling a cart full of dead batteries (the cart looks like the remains of an old assault wagon); a giant billboard shows a bat, a ball, a mitt, and a plate arranged in a diamond on a field of green; giant red squares marching across a calendar graphic show me how to fill my rec blocs with big league baseball.

I am informed that there are over 132 teams, and well over 2^{50} seasonal scenarios. As I watch the picture melts away.

Mister Existence says to me: "These three rules you must live by. Never break faith with your schedule. Never take incorrect drugs. And never, never court undesirable people."

I let three windowfuls of hill roll by, flecked with snow and dotted with rustic wood frame cottages. Then I ask, "What is an incorrect drug?"

I can feel him rustling beside me, going through some pinched dance of disapproval. "You should know these things instinctively. Incorrect drugs are drugs of image and dream, drugs that sail you into a world of different laws and perverted meanings. Correct drugs give undecorated pleasure."

I smile. You have to hand it to him sometimes. He knows his stuff.

"As for undesirable people—" he goes on.

I wave it all away, still staring out at the dreamy landscape. "You don't have to hit me over the head with it."

"Don't I?" I can hear him sitting straighter, the way he does. "What a sad way this is for a talented man to pass his lonely middle years."

I nod absently. He waits a bit; then abruptly he rises and leaves.

After a time the door to the car opens and a woman wearing the gray uniform of the Army of the Rose walks down the aisle. There is someone trailing behind her, obscured by her wide shoulders. "This seat is free?" she asks me.

"Well, actually, no."

"Good." She has not heard me. She turns and from behind her produces a short slender man in a long, tattered brown coat. There is a soft blond stubble on his chin and he clasps a paper bag against his coat with dirty hands. "This man is a traitor to the state. He supported the Wallies."

The man's eyes are averted. She holds his elbow as he lowers himself into the seat next to mine.

"You do know the drill, don't you?" she asks me.

I look up blankly.

She manages to keep her composure. "Look, just call me when he confesses." She turns and hurries back down the aisle.

I am left alone with a traitor to the state. He grins, disarmingly larcenous through his stubble. He takes an orange from his paper bag and begins to eat it.

Through the succeeding miles I occasionally glance at him, peacefully immersed in the rocking of the train, and occasionally he catches me, and the grin returns. This grin of his is reflexive, a basic tool; he probably had it long before being convicted of crimes against the state. It means either, "What can you expect?" or "I'm not so bad."

Finally, I do my duty: "What were your crimes?"

"I kept illegal books in San Anselmo." It is easier for me to look at the hills as he goes on. "The housing situation is tough there, and you can make more than the comptroller's log will allow. You know, off the books." There is a pause. "I used the profits to spread Wally propaganda."

I look at him. He is starting another orange. "You did?"

"Yeah." He has an interesting way of slicing the orange with his thumbnail, eight sections carved in one continuous motion.

"That seems a peculiar thing to do."

"Actually quite predictable, they tell me. One form of corruption inevitably leads to others." He neatly knocks out a slice.

With some pleasure, I remember the correct formula. "Your own self-knowledge has healed you."

"Thank you."

That seems to be about it for social awareness. So we both go back to the hills. Later he asks me if I want some of his orange (he's on his third now). When I shake my head, he holds the slice out and says, "Please," so I take it.

He seems to have trouble pressing it into my palm. When his hand leaves mine, my heart takes a painful leap.

Pressed against the rind of the wedge of orange is a piece of paper.

I look away. On the gravel-packed shoulder near the tracks, I see curved patches of snow. Cautiously I begin to eat the orange slice, squeezing the paper between my palm and the rind. Then the woman returns for her charge. "Well?" she says.

"All done," I tell her.

She sighs at a world of grievances, and the two wander off together.

By the time Mister Existence returns, we are pulling into my station.

Neither Mister Existence nor I are much for goodbyes. He seems to want some expression of gratitude for his labors, but I am unable to give him one.

We part on an uneasy silence. I can feel his eyes following me down the platform.

The vid-stand is a shack wrapped in tar paper with a round aluminum chimney puffing white smoke and a stubby pole carrying the pink and gray PostPublic flag, limp in the chilly air. They have no local mapfeeds, but the vendor, a double-amputee with a double row of war medals on his chest, informs me that it is a short walk from the station to the Little Red Abbey.

Ahead, snow settles comfortably into soggy meadows. Alexa Augustine grew up in snow country, and I still know my way through this kind of terrain.

The snow on the track has been packed hard by foot traffic. I try to plant my boots in the deepest treadmarks. It occurs to me that I have played this game before. Every time my soles bite into the coarse snow there is an immensely satisfying sound, like the ripping of heavy cloth. Each stride brings me closer to some memory that evaporates when I try to seize it.

I concentrate on the crunching. Crunching is nice. Draped over the gentle slopes of these hills snow makes round shapes with blue auras, lumpy, unassuming.

I begin to run. My bag flops against my thighs. I pant.

Eventually I stop and withdraw a small square of paper from my pocket. All around me, silence. Forty yards away, at the edge of a clump of pines, a hare limps for cover through the snow. I fold out the paper, doubled six times to a tiny tablet. It says, "My name is

Hieronymous Schwabb. The war is not over. Please make six copies of this and send it to your—"

Then Hieronymous ran out of room.

Poor Hieronymous. Not crushed by a tank. His limbs are sound, his color good, his eyes alert and healthy. But crushed nonetheless. A poor sad wisp of a thing, no longer speaking sentences of his own. Except for these I hold in my hand, this food wrapper's worth of words. I am sorry for you, Mr. Schwabb, who once kept phony books, and I understand. I understand that these are your only sentences and that copies must be made—in place of all the others that might have been. I will see to it.

I fold up Schwabb's note and return it to my pocket.

Last night I dreamt I entered a gloomy chamber and saw a body stretched out in a casket. One hand on her chest, holding a white flower, the other stretched out beside her.

I had no trouble recognizing the corpse as mine, although it wasn't so much looking at her face (which is oddly unclear in recollection) as a simple knowledge of who this must be. As if I had been informed and invited through the usual channels.

The flower was, I think, a rose.

There was an armchair beside the casket, and I sat with her, watching stone walls aflicker with candlelight. I felt an enormous calm. A sense of correctness. I spoke to her for a while but I have no idea what I said. Strange, how easy it is to talk to the dead.

It is only now, as I sit writing this in my new room at the abbey, that the whole thing has an eerie feel. Only now that I think I know what the dream was about.

It's about being lonely.

The Little Red Abbey was a family manor built in the second wave of developer enthusiasm for this area, Mister Question Man tells me, at fantastic expense, during a historicist revival of twentieth-century building styles—before the present make-up of the Council rendered such tastes obsolete. When fashions changed, and the Crater Lake region failed to live up to its original inflated expectations, the manor turned into a white elephant. It seems the original investors underestimated just how close to the water one needed to be in order to reap the full benefits of resort fever. Twenty miles, even twenty miles of pine-covered splendor, did not make it. The manor limped through a few seasons of vacationers who preferred their amusements on the quieter side, and then rolled quietly and terminally onto the market. After a few rounds of price slashing, it fell into the hands of the Rose Council and became the Little Red Abbey.

The manor was built in what was known as the Queen Anne style.

"A style known for its emphasis on asymmetry, which nevertheless pays heed to the Victorian passion for balance," says Mister Question Man.

Asymmetric, it certainly is. Three stories high, the abbey leans against the weight of a corner tower wearing a witch's cone. The porch opposite supports a fatter cone on double arches. From those a wooden veranda wanders off amiably round the side of the house, complete with peeling paint, creaking boards, and the obligatory porch swing.

I see two guardsmen watching me from the trees. Knock knock.

A pleasant silence.

I study it a while, then knock again.

After another wait, I twist the knob and step inside.

I am standing in a small, windowed vestibule; the glass is the self-defeating frosted kind. Shoes of various sizes are lined up along the wainscoting.

A little greeting cartoon lights up on the door screen (big smile and eyes squinting from pleasure), and a pipsqueak voice instructs me to "please identify."

I raise my dataport to its receptor plate and we couple.

"You are most welcome, Ms. Augustine. Please remain where you are until a resident grants you admission."

"How long will that be?"

"Please remain where you are until a resident grants you admission." The screen offers menu: Chess, Tic Tac Toe, Queen of the Universe.

One of those. I banished the menu. The greeter pipes out a cheery tune and artfully glazes over the screen. I see myself reflected, a single notch of worry cut between my brows. I sigh and plug in my dataport and reintroduce it to the greeter.

I seem to have a certain knack for these things. They call it hardware sense, I think.

A moment later the grating music slows and stops. The greeter forgets I am there and the door clicks open. I feel a physical sense of relief.

I remove my shoes and enter. In the parlor to my left pale yellow curtains billow from two windows. The antique couch plays dark-stained wooden arms against a faded peach cover; a pair of matching armchairs have plum-colored pillows carelessly thrown over the hollows worn into their cushions. A Turkish carpet covers a fair stretch of floor under the dark coffee table, and beyond it, across from the fireplace, is a hutch filled with busy little things: chintz, clamshell, ceramic and glass. The pleasant blend of smells wafting in from some nearby kitchen includes lentil beans.

I follow the smells down a dim corridor to an ancient-looking stove. When I lift the lid off the large kettle on top, I see a cratered landscape of lentil beans, with bubbles popping here and there around bright chunks of salt pork. A deep contralto informs me we are in stewing mode.

On the whole, technology has not been a boon to the kitchen. I replace the lid and begin exploring the shelves lining one wall, suddenly aware that I am quite hungry.

While I puzzle over the squeegee tabs on a packet of instant chicken, someone enters the kitchen behind me and stands watching. I feel her before I hear her.

A floorboard creaks and I whip around.

She's wearing a cream-colored jacket with large plastic laser buttons (the kind with elusive shapes dancing in a ruby haze) and she has blond hair and a drop-dead figure. Head tilted, she watches me with violet eyes.

Those eyes give her face a magical quality, the look of a child or a shiny-eyed animal or a cuddly extra-terrestrial.

"Do I know you?"

"I was just—I'm a new—" The word quite escapes me, if there is one. "I'm joining up today."

She shakes her head. "Yes, you look the type. I'm Viju."

"I'm Augustine."

She does not take my offered hand.

"I know," Viju says. "The new queen of the gypsy hackers. I saw your picture on my schedule. You're here. You're disoriented. You're wondering what to do next."

The swinging door swings. The newcomer steps forward. "We are the answer."

He is a boy about Viju's size, wearing the same jacket but with loose slacks; he is the dark antidote to her light. His skin is copper, his hair short-cropped, silky, and black. His eyes are a startling amber.

"I'm Raja. Ardath asked us to welcome you here."

Viju seals up the chicken packet, which has yawned open in my grasp, murmuring something about kitchen rules; Raja seats me and turns up tea and biscuits. I am allowed one cup and two biscuits (I have to ask twice for the second), and then we start the tour.

The rest of the house is more of the same, as Viju points out an excess of redwood, crystal and Oriental tapestry, all the while filling me in on various rules of use; these consist mostly of the instruction not to, with an occasional allowance, for example, for a rug that may be walked on in socks.

The first floor is public territory; the second, the monks' private quarters. In the hallway upstairs, I point to a shoebox cabinet hung at eye level, one of a number I have noticed on our tour of the second floor. I ask what it is.

"Lamp holders for oil lamps," Raja says.

"Where are the lamps?"

"No chance," says Viju. "Fire hazard."

We turn, and Raja points out the corner room that will be mine.

The bedspread and canopy are a light pink; the curtains a muted gray. The colors of the PostPublic. There is a writing table in the corner with a lot of small useless-looking drawers, and a keyboard and screen tucked nicely in a recess under the pigeonholes. Next to that, a wicker chair painted white. Viju leads me to the window.

The world outside glitters with random bits of color, ripples curiously: a landscape encased in clear, heavy oil.

I turn to meet Raja's shining eyes. "Lead-glassed windows." He shakes a finger at me. "You can spit on the grave of Charles the Rose, violate the sanctity of an individual monad, champion the cause of utopian socialism, but the cardinal sin, I mean, the *cardinal* sin, is to break a window. Your annual credit limit will just about cover one of these panes."

We park my bag and exit. We do not ascend to the third floor, which is strictly off-limits. It belongs to the abbess.

"The basement is where the computers are."

"Where the bits get smashed," I offer.

Viju frowns at me and throws open a steel door. "Hardware room." A treasure trove: big pieces of milky crystal, green screens raising squiggly brows at us. In a tank of liquid by the door floats a beautiful blue lens. Electronic claws in various states of undress are sprawled surrenderingly around it. "This is Cowboy's play room," says Raja, clearly uneasy. "You can't play here until he lets you."

Viju pulls the door softly shut.

We move into the arena. The space at the bottom of the well is bigger than what I'm used to, and there are a lot more seats. We march down the well and stand at stage center. Viju sees me craning my neck to take it in.

"For group exercises."

I sign the sign for "bashful" and mime tabbing the squishtab on my pants.

Viju just turns and starts up the stairs, leaving me standing next to Raja. He shakes his head and gives me a martyred look.

Next, a terminal room: screens, mice, keyboards, data gloves. Familiarity is such an important feeling now. I am almost possessive of it. I move slowly past the chairs and consoles, pause to tap a keyboard twice to make the screen wash clear and burn out a greeting. I try on a data glove about a size too small and mash the informational jelly between my fingers. I try out a caressing chair and a projector helmet equipped with antiquated eyelid brushes.

When I lift off the helmet, I feel Viju's eyes on me. Her look says, "What a dweeb."

Annoyed, I turn my hands palm-up and close my fist at waist level, the sign for "stuff," or "loot," and add a little screwing motion with my thumb just under my nose, the sign for "hi-tek." Definite positive affect. She turns on her heel and walks out.

I look at Raja.

He sighs. "You must try to keep your hands still when you talk to her."

I look at my hands, puzzled.

"No sign language," he says. Now he rolls his eyes in a more restrained version of Viju's take.

"She doesn't like me."

He searches briefly for a politic answer, then spreads his hands. "No."

Which of course is the way it is. Every Tek-Tooter wirehead knows this, impaired memory or no. The only question is: How much of this do I have to put up with? As of now, I'm not sure.

Raja leaves me at the door of my room.

I sling my bag on the bed and open it. There on top, in easy reach, is the slim black case of my kit.

While I am staring at it, there is a knock at the door. No doubt Viju back to clue me in on another rule of deportment. I take the kit out and place it carefully on the bed beside the bag. Then I go to the door and open it.

The young man standing there wears a black tank top, tight denim pants and a dark-blue knit cap. His skin is light brown, and the hair coiling under the cap is woolly and red.

He raises his spread hand in an interfacer's greeting sign. Then shoves a folded paper in my hand and walks past me into the room.

"Corner digs." He swings slowly around with his hands hooked in his belt, taking it in with a broad smile. "Do you know how long I've wanted this room?" He walks over to the window and reaches through the curtains to tap gently on the pane. "Leaded glass." He shakes his head. "How I've tried. How I've pleaded with her."

I stand in the center of the room, unfolding the paper he has given me, which is a newspaper, looking back and forth from the headline to him.

"But then I don't have your talent." He shakes his head again and sees that I've unfolded the newspaper in front of me: *Revolutionary Watchword.* "Oh, that. Just a little something I do in my spare time. Look it over later. Right now we've got to talk." He winks.

He sits in the wicker chair, crosses his legs. "I've been really looking forward to meeting you."

"I'm Augustine."

"New queen of the gypsy socketeers. I know." He frowns. "Sorry. I'm Cowboy Bob, local software wizard." He waves his hand at the paper. "Local informational revolutionary. Global"—he spreads his hands in a futile search for something sufficient, then claps them together—"presence."

I deposit the paper on the writing desk. Is this what Mister E. means by undesirable people?

"Okay. Why have you been looking forward to meeting me?"

He shrugs. "Well, that's not entirely clear. It may take some search time and it may take some nurturing. But I'll know it when I see it. I know a lot about you already. I know that's your kit." He points at the black case on the bed. "I know you like it with needles. Which is why they call you I.V. Augustine. I know you've got some memory problems and this lone-wolf thing that just ravages your Group scores. And I know you do this." He reaches up and touches the side of his nose with his thumb.

I nod. "Well, I'll try to break the habit." Whereupon my nose begins instantly to itch. "How do you know so much?"

He smiles. "I make it my business to know about special people."

"You must be pretty special yourself."

"Don't get snitty. The people who come here are usually talented. Though usually also misguided. But I think you might not be so misguided."

I struggle with an unpleasant sense of *déjà vu*. Nowadays, there is almost a physical pain when I make an effort to remember. This person is a variety of believer. I fight an urge to close down, to glaze over and give monosyllabic replies. I have no use for believers right now, whether Rose mystic or Techno-Tao. I'm not interested in being saved or even uplifted, and I haven't the energy to go romping with them through the fields of their particular perfect world.

I lean against the door and cross my arms and put on a face. I'm not sure what face.

Cowboy Bob is not the sort who studies faces. "Anyway, it isn't just a question of talent, is it? The Next Stage is going to demand a major discovery, a quantum leap forward that revises the basic paradigm of the process." He rubs his skinny arms and gives me a sidelong look. "Word is out that you might be the means for making the leap."

"Whose word?"

"I really can't say." He nods, opens his dark eyes wide, and shoots me a look of comradely regret ("We Tekkies know how it is."). Then brightens. "But your test scores are certainly a starting point. What are the two most important things in the world?"

"I don't think that question has an answer."

"Most of the new arrivals say the individual Monad and the Rose PostPublic. But the right answers are: the Next Stage in the Process and Free Access. Which brings me to this." He pulls something out of his pocket and holds it out.

It's a small crystal with two wire-thin prongs. "I assume you know how to use this."

I cross the room. I take the crystal and hold it up to the window. "It's a port. What's it tuned to?"

"The Net."

Which is what I half-expected, given all the ceremony. But it still gives my heart a little kick. I swallow.

He leans back in the chair and watches me.

"What makes you think you can trust me?"

"What makes you think you can trust *me*? No, I have good information on you. You're no little Miss Viju. You know that flying the open Net is the grandest thing there is, and you know how to talk with your hands. What I'm hoping is that you won't think I'm from the Ministry of Persons and sling that out the window. They're a little hard to come by."

"Do *you* know how to talk with your hands?"

He makes a rude two-piece gesture any rube could come by, but he does it crisply. People who don't talk sign much get sloppy in all the wrong places. They make the transitions between the movements too slowly, or else they make them too fast and run two signs together, like a speaker shoveling oatmeal into his mouth. They don't know where the real spaces for the signs are. Cowboy makes his signs fast and clean. I switch to sign and try to give him a real workout.

In the rapid signing session that follows, Cowboy tells me that the setup in my room isn't clean, and that I need to come to the hardware center downstairs when I want to go exploring. He tells me what hours are best for discreet visits, and he tells me that Viju is definitely not a good exploring companion. She works for some big-deal Rose Ministerial type. Then he rises and ambles to the door.

—I'm expecting big things from you, he signs.

—You'll be disappointed.

—Maybe, but you'll toot all right, and every square tooter goes a little further into the Net than the one before.

He's at the door when I stop him, holding up the copy of the *Revolutionary Watchword* he's blessed me with. "Underground Tekkie Newsletter?"

"News *paper*," he says.

"I've got something I'd like you to print." I hand him Hieronymous Schwabb's note.

He takes it and reads it and shakes his head.

He shuts the door behind him without a word. I look from the door to the crystal in my hand. Yes, there are Ministry of Persons agents who have learned to sign quite well. And plenty of socketeers who have been caught transacting uncommissioned business on the Net and saved their asses by doing the Ministry's dirty work. But I don't think Cowboy is either of these.

No, Cowboy's a believer. Somehow I can spot them now. I open my kit and hide the crystal in an empty Plaina vial.

3 Augustine's Journal

Alone, I plug my card into the dataport. Control-S brings up your schedule.

The fact is that I don't know this. My hands do. I am a fragmented thing, a loose confederation of parts with little reason to trust one another. I have learned, approaching the keyboard, to let my fingers take over. Procedural memory leads semantic.

My schedule lights up, a mosaic of colored blocks. My hands are always deft, always sure at the keyboard, but elsewhere they are hopeless. Here I am at the mirror this morning, about to spread a vial of I.V. strength Plaina onto my toothbrush.

Right now I am in the cool blue fog of a spiritual block: hygiene and meditation. The flashing yellow dot in the corner of the block tells me the fog should be tinged with a Plaina dosage. At seven the day moves into a black Social Block. I am engaged for dinner. Main dining room. Informal dress. Good. That means a shower, a session with the needle, then one with this journal.

En route to the bathroom, I pause by the dresser.

Cowboy's news *paper* turns out to be a single page, or rather four print pages on a single sheet, each page divided into four wavering columns.

The Banner Headline reads, *Achilles to Fly This Month!* This is the lead story:

The Galactics are back! Citizens of the Rose PostPublic have a rare intergalactic treat in store this month when Rose researchers resurrect the most famous Galactic craft of all for a suborbital test flight. Ever since it landed in the California hills twenty-five years ago, *The Achilles* has prompted wild speculation as to the degree of success Rose cargo researchers have had in unlocking its secrets. What is beyond doubt is that the ship brought the largest known Galactic crystal and a mysterious projection device. Shortly after the ship's landing, that projection device, known as the Shield, enabled Rose researchers to retrieve astronomical images. This is still the only successful memory operation on a Galactic crystal. The famous Picture of the Universe.

Far more intriguing than its capacity for throwing up pretty pictures is the Shield's rumored "reversibility." According to sources quoted here some time ago, who now prove to have been right on the mark, the Shield has actually been coupled with Rose software and used to run programs on the ship's own computing crystal. The same sources speculated that among the programs successfully run were some interfacing simulations, with the implication that Rose interfacers have actually visited the crystal's underglass.

It now seems clear that at least the minimal interfacing required for space flight is possible on the Shield. Device throughput and reliable control have been achieved. Moreover, a crew has been chosen. According to those same eerily well-informed sources, their working handles are Sizzle, Gator, and Wings. No word as to a pilot yet, but the pool of candidates is small. Remember, you heard it here first. And the best way to pay it back is to tell me another.

Under this, an article on the disturbing rise in B-board raids on the Net. Some hints on evasion. Across from the lead story, a headline reads TEXAS BULL GIVES BIRTH TO TWO-HEADED BABY. Details on this calamitous event are sparse but colorful. The strangest touch is a quote from the attending mid-wife: "This is *exactly* what was foretold in the Book of Revelations." Imagine, a midwife who reads.

Then there is a story headlined JESUS SPOKE LANGUAGE OF THE GALACTICS about an Indiana philologist who claims to have shown conclusively not only that the famed Galactic tracings of the Moscow and Zaporozhye landings are writing (a much-disputed point, apparently), but also that they are in Aramaic.

Another story: a hacker who caught syphilis from an electronic virus. And another about a hacker who claimed to have had several visitations from the Virgin Mary on one of the AI partitions in the Net. She accused the Blessed Virgin of "working her look." Every time the hacker tried a new geometric variation on her informational image, the Virgin would show up a few days later with a copy.

Finally, the bottom half of the first page is filled with the only bylined article, titled "The Problem of Being." The byline is Quincunx. It starts: "The question of Being has vexed me for most of my sentient life. I now believe that question can be given a definitive answer. The answer is parallel processing." It goes on for a column-and-a-half of airhead techno-mystical in-your-face obsessing. Everybody's been trapped by someone like this at a party.

All of a sudden it hits me that I'm actually reading this thing. The important thing about Cowboy's paper is not the content. It's in the look, this crazy patchwork of fonts and wavering column edges. It's in the fact that there are no bylines except in the one piece that no sane person would admit to having written. Obviously this was cobbled together from a half-dozen underground Net B-boards. From hours of wandering through the Net bazaar. Cowboy is a Free Accessionist and he wants everyone to know it.

I shower, work on the journal awhile, then turn to preparing for dinner.

To this end: Does yellow go with black? More to the point: Does shiny yellow go with deep powdery denim black? And do yellow polka-dots on clear plastic . . . ? I glance at the results on the bed and strike out at the keyboard in frustration. My tunic turns gray.

How I do love yellow. Bubbling, brilliant, satin-smooth yellow. Laid on the world with a trowel, smeared like a paste across the fuzzy tops of things. Odd that Alexa Augustine never understood that.

Appearing is easy.

I step quietly into place at the top of the stairs and peer down: brightness, bustling forms. Then I move, so as not to present a stationary target. Long before reaching the foot of the stairs, I have identified the abbess.

She is wearing a very simply cut gray tunic, a shape that fills the wardrobe window with a few twiddles of the dial. She is about fifty, stocky, but not fat. Her gray pumps are two shades darker than her tunic. Her burgundy cravat has a single horizontal black stripe. Her collar is about four inches high, with gray lining and a black underside. It isn't only abbesses who wear these high collars, but I can't think now who else would.

She has curly gray hair and round chipmunk cheeks and a broad serious mouth. The mouth tells the story. The lines on either side are deep and have not been carved by smiling. Her eyes are a barely identifiable gray, and her gaze leaps from place to place, poking and probing. I watch her direct with one hand the deployment of the table cloth, then wheel around to guide a heavy armchair to the end of the table. She is a general, a cook, a chief engineer, someone attuned to the probability of error, someone for whom much of the world plugs along at a snail's pace.

As for first impressions: I don't much like her.

She turns and smiles. Which makes the lines at the corners of her mouth turn vertical and deepen. And brings her lifeless eyes into glinting focus.

"I'm Mother Leibniz."

"I'm Augustine."

She comes a step closer, clasps my shoulders, and searches my face. Does she see my dislike? I think so. At least the dislike of being examined like this. Perhaps also signs of bad company and incorrect drugs.

She nods and releases me.

"Viju tells me you arrived early." She looks away, glides to the table and retrieves a ceramic triangle from where a woman in a black tunic has just placed it. "Maria, I thought I told you not to use the small trivets with the roast. It's too hard on the tablecloth."

Maria accepts the trivet. "Of course, Mother."

But Leibniz is now descending on Cowboy Bob at the other end of the table with a printout. "No reading at dinner, Bob."

Viju appears at the head of the stairs, with Raja lingering behind. They watch silently as Cowboy (after one technical protest as to whether we are really "at dinner," and another as to whether examining a code printout is really reading) is relieved of his printout. With this drama concluded they begin their stately descent, Viju two steps ahead of her shadow.

A tall black man emerges from the kitchen. He is older than anyone here except Leibniz. There is something familiar about him. He wears an earring, a pearl necklace, and one of the brightly colored serapes I have seen in the marketplace (lots of room for concealment). His loose-fitting cotton pants are secured with a drawstring. He is barefoot, well-muscled, and several inches over six feet tall.

"This is Alfred." Leibniz turns to me. "What is your first name?"

It is not until I hear his name that I recognize Alfred from Group. "Alfred?"

"Augustine?"

Leibniz, impatiently: "What *is* your first name?"

"I.V. I'm I.V."

Leibniz looks back and forth between us. "You know each other?"

"Remember I told you about Jim's Group. Augustine was in it!"

The lines on either side of Leibniz's lips deepen. "Is that so?"

I need a look I can work. I go for the Blessed Virgin. ("Hi. I'm Ivy. I have a destiny.") "How are you doing, Alfred?"

"I'll pass, Augustine."

Leibniz rolls her eyes. "Alfred, we're on a first-name basis; this woman's name is Ivy. All right?" She turns back to Cowboy. "This is Bob. Bob, Ivy."

"We've met," I say.

"And you also know Viju."

Now a murmur of voices from the living room draws near, and a group of four enters in pairs, the first matched salt-and-pepper shakers, a stout man and woman. The woman has red hair and brown eyes. She wears a lime-green blouse with those extra-wide wing shoulders and no sleeves and a tangerine skirt, the kind that comes just in one color and doesn't hook up to your combo disk (which is how she arrived at that jarring color combo without being deluged with error messages). The gentleman, much older, is similarly old-fashioned: he wears a button-up shirt, suspenders, and voluminous black trousers. When he laughs, his round face is surprisingly handsome. He has gray eyes, a gorgeous head of black hair combed back in a full mane, and jowls weighty enough to lend him the authority of a minor official.

"This is Rose and my friend Jimmie."

Rose dimples and extends her hand, and the man gives a nod that is an abbreviated bow. It is clear that he is no mere inmate.

"This is Ivy."

"Pleased to meet you, Rose." I squeeze Rose's hand. I nod back to Jimmie.

The next pair enters the dining room. They are Famine and Pestilence. Famine is a golem: gaunt, sallow, hollow-eyed, to all appearances not long for this world. Pestilence, on the other hand, is a pilot. Even in this cybernetic age, it is a rare fellow who goes about with a shaved head, one red-plastic eye (probably tuned to infrared), tattooed cheeks, sharpened teeth, and a metal arm culminating in a detachable mechanical claw. This kind of Tekkie is familiar. He would have a socket like mine, only set at the base of his spine.

"Smoket, Rogachev"—pointing to golem and pilot—

"Ivy."

The golem shows no sign of noticing me, but the pilot gives an almost imperceptible flicker of his eyelids, and something goes bump in my chest. I am not eager to relive it, and for a time, I do not look back his way.

"And now," says Leibniz, "let the games begin."

There is an orderly procession to our seats. Leibniz assigns me the seat between Alfred and Cowboy: boy girl boy. How nice. Rogachev fortunately winds up at the other end of the table, beside his shadow Smoket.

Dishes appear as Maria and another woman in black scramble in and out of the kitchen.

Leibniz and Jimmie are at the head and foot of the table.

The soup pot set in front of me is the one I nearly sampled earlier this afternoon. I limit myself to a ladleful of steaming lentils. Leibniz measures me with those lifeless eyes. I try today's greeting message smile.

Dinner talk starts with Viju asking Rose where she got her outfit. The question is peculiarly intoned, like a snatch of song. Raja follows up by complimenting Rose's lime blouse. Rose murmurs and identifies it as a used clothing shop in town, studying her lap. We uneducated watchers are left to mull over the contrast between slim and doe-eyed Viju and a heavyset Tekkie like Rose, who seems to find dressing a chore.

"Well, Ms. Augustine, perhaps you'll provide a little color around here," says Jimmie. He is busily cutting Smoket's veal for him. "We could sure use some." He sends a smile the entire length of the table, towards Leibniz.

A pot of veal roast lands in front of me, and I dish out several pieces, aware that Leibniz is watching again. She watches everything, but she watches me especially. "You hardly need me to add color," I say. "I always thought a monastery would be terribly depressing, empty courtyards echoing with a few footsteps, occasional outbreaks of chanting. This place isn't at all like that."

There is a silence and I become aware that everyone, even Smoket, is watching me.

"Did I say something wrong?"

"We are a lay group," Leibniz says carefully, "without any provisions as to clothing in our vows. But that doesn't mean we are lacking in devoutness."

"Of course not. I didn't mean—"

"I'm sure you didn't."

"Some of us," Viju says pointedly, "aren't even in the order. We're just here to soak up a little spiritual atmosphere."

Then Jimmie launches into a story about a place named Richmond and a restaurant that serves nothing but ice cream. The point is obscure, but slowly the table begins to thaw. Jimmie lingers over his description of something called a praline.

Raja remarks on how good I look in yellow, and Viju, changing the subject slightly, turns to Leibniz and remarks on the steady upturn in collars these past months.

Alfred tells a story about life in the marines. The fact that Alfred is a marine does not square well with the fact that he is here. Obviously, Alfred, too, has had troubles with his Group evaluations, but what makes him important enough to require special religious help? Don't marines have to stay with their outfits?

Alfred's story is about supply sergeants, whom he assures me (despite my recitation of the marine chain of command) are the most powerful people in the service. It plays pretty well for a while, Alfred being someone who believes in basic human archetypes and is funny about them. Rose and I laugh a lot; the others tune in intermittently (Raja muses on the hygienic habits of marines), or wander into conversations of their own (Jimmie tells another about Richmond).

At the end of his story there is a silence which gradually grows uncomfortable. I see that once again Mother Leibniz is displeased.

"Alfred, haven't we talked about accepting your life?"

"Yes, but talking about the marines—"

"Your official record shows you've never been in the marines."

Alfred chews his kohlrabi slowly and looks at me.

"Wouldn't it be better," Leibniz pursues, "just to accept who you are? Without trying to make up people you've never been, and never can be?"

"Excuse me." I meet Mother Leibniz's gray eyes. Something about this woman commands my defiance. "I've known Alfred for nearly a month now and he *is* a marine. He's got the rifle, the uniform, the posture, all of it. I've even seen him playing poker with the other marines at the armory."

"The other marines." Mother Leibniz turns her head, as if to whisper something to her collar. "Of course, you two were in Group together."

After a moment, I nod.

She folds her hands in her lap. A point seems to have been scored. "And Alfred devoted a lot of energy in Group to pursuing his obsession. That was part of the problem, wasn't it, Alfred?"

I look at Alfred. He shakes his head at me.

"Well, that's enough on that topic," says Mother Leibniz.

Occasionally, I take a peek at Rogachev. The anxiety he provokes has subsided. Like Smoket, Rogachev never speaks. Unlike him, he does not stare fixedly at his plate, but scans everything in the room for varying amounts of time; he spends quite a spell at the beginning of the meal on the ceiling, studying its elegant five-faceted fixture. Then he moves to the far wall, to the carpeting to his right, eventually to some of his dinner companions, and finally, to me.

What turns he goes through then, what grins, and batting lashes, and sly, sidelong looks, I will never know, since I find it impossible to study him at the same time as he studies me. It's partly that the anxiety returns whenever there is danger of our eyes meeting; there is the fear that, if I do meet his gaze, there will be no one there staring back at me.

So while Rogachev studies me, I study my plate. Eventually he moves on, scrolling the screen of his internal terminal, no one subject matter any different than another. He takes over feeding Smoket from Jimmie, so that Jimmie can devote some attention to his own plate. After that, he, too, studies the kohlrabi piled on a serving dish in the center of the table; it is hard not to wonder what dark thoughts it inspires in him, for this man eats all meat. Alone of all the guests, he has been served a special menu; his plate holds a large steak two shades darker than our veal roast, and he eats no vegetables.

When he turns to check on Smoket's progress, I see that the other cheek is tattooed as well: a single eye under which the words "Mother Manyness" have been engraved in red. Writing again. Rogachev works through his steak with a methodical calm which despite his sharpened teeth is not in the least carnivore-like. He has a chillingly refined air, like a man who reads poetry with very few words to the line.

Jimmie wants to hear about my trip. In the space of a few sentences he manages to refer to San Francisco as a "town," express a dislike for "ruckus," and lament the deteriorating quality of the service on the PostPublic's trains. His voice is high, but there is a soothing warmth to it. I like the sound of the word "ruckus."

I am forced to narrate some of my trip. When I come to the part about Schwabb's confession, Mother Leibniz is interested.

"How odd! Surely with the armistice three days old—"

"That's time enough for a whole network of conspiracies." Cowboy piles veal onto his plate.

"Who'd know better than Cowboy?" asks Rose.

"I don't mind your taking several helpings, Bob, but couldn't you at least wait until seconds for your fourth piece? And, Rose, don't call Bob 'Cowboy.' "

Cowboy grins and returns a piece to the serving plate.

"Bob always has been the colorful one," says Jimmie, passing a plateful of kohlrabi.

Viju and Raja rise almost together. "I think—"

"—we need to go now."

Leibniz is dismayed. "So soon? But dessert—"

"I'm afraid we've already overdone it." Viju allows us a strained smile. Raja bows gracefully from his slender waist.

Leibniz surrenders. Clearly, these two are not her charges.

They straighten their chairs, silently suffering souls who don't belong here and want us to know it.

"Bob," Leibniz says, when the two have gone, "I would like an explanation of the article on the Galactics in today's paper."

"Sorry. That's the third Galactics-meet-Jesus story I've gotten from that Indiana group this month. They have a thing about Jesus. But I kind of like the Aramaic angle. It—"

"That's not the article I meant."

"You can't mean the Shield article? That one's bona fide news, the best line of research the AIA's followed in years."

"My concern is that you seem to be printing classified material again."

"Mother, this project is not much of a secret."

"That's for sure," says Rose.

I chime in: "They had a crew working the Shield in the main arena at AIA headquarters last week. It didn't look like much of a secret then."

Cowboy is delighted. "Have they picked a pilot yet?"

Then, down at the other end of the table, the subject changes.

Dishes clatter and silverware tinkles. The table legs thump. Just as Jimmie lifts the table cloth to catch the spirit in the act, the vibrations reach Smoket's neck. His mouth opens and a piercing ululation issues out.

We are all frozen. A cold metallic edge scrapes up my spine. Smoket's cry mounts. It seems as if at any moment it will explode into language. But it does not. It is simply a howl of wavering pitch and increasing ferocity.

As it mounts, my will weakens. I want to cry out myself. My gaze wanders to Rogachev. His stare looses a new chill that straightens me in my chair. He is staring with cold anger, not at Smoket, but at Mother Leibniz.

Then Smoket drops to the floor and the howling stops. There is a thumping. Jimmie leaps to his feet, but Leibniz says, "No. Wait."

Rogachev slowly removes his napkin and kneels beside Smoket. I crane but all I can see is the tattoo and his ear—like a strange growth on his shaven head—as he bends close and whispers into Smoket's ear.

Smoket stops thrashing and Jimmie helps Rogachev lift him back to his seat. Smoket immediately takes his spoon in hand and resumes his post, guarding half a plateful of kohlrabi.

Rose takes a deep breath.

Jimmie fishes up spoonful of the green and holds it near Smoket's mouth.

"That happens sometimes," Leibniz says softly.

Rogachev taps a cut-time measure on his ear with his index finger: the sign for hearing music. The sign for an interfacer hearing music.

Leibniz leans toward Smoket. "Smoket," she says, "haven't we agreed that when something disturbs you you should lie down and let it pass?"

Amazingly, Smoket looks at her.

Leibniz holds his gaze a moment. Then she gives him a smile quite unlike any of those I have seen her give this evening. The lines on the side of her mouth fold in half and the top halves pull towards her nostrils; yellowing teeth appear.

A moment later self-knowledge returns. The smile fades. She happens to look at me first. "Smoket was an interfacer," she explains. "Rogachev thinks that all this talk of doing the Shield has upset him."

"And what do you think, Mother?"

The question seems to surprise her. "I think—we'll never know."

We work through our caramel pudding under a cloud. Jimmie tries a wandering tale about a trade-school prank involving a hay-baling machine, but it goes nowhere. No one wants a second cup of coffee.

Finally, Jimmie dabs a napkin at his lips and makes his excuses. Leibniz rises a beat later. Dinner is over. Chairs scrape back, arms stretch into yawns and, arm-in-arm, Jimmie and Mother Leibniz start up the stairs.

Back in my room, I sit at my window gazing at the smooth wintry blackness and listening to Smoket drift up and down the scale. He coughs, chokes, clears his throat. Another piece of moon falls away. He starts again. The moon sighs. He hurries up to a shining C, seesaws back and forth a minor third, groans an octave lower, hunting tirelessly for the sequence to shatter the glass above.

Rogachev. What an eyesore of a man. All metallic and bulging. And those tattoos. Mama Manyness, indeed!

Mister Question Man cites some interesting facts: Rogachev's sharpened front teeth and the shackled flower tattooed on his left cheek indicate that he is of the White Orchid persuasion—one of the many "carnivore" cults that started up some years back, all centering round a search for the demonic through mental discipline, all incorporating the belief that plant matter is not worthy fare for the lords and ladies of creation (yet I'm sure that when dessert came Rogachev reached alertly for his share). The hardcore holds that the worthiest fare of all is human flesh; rumor places the flourishing black market in certain fashionable San Francisco butcher shops. Thank you, Mister Question Man.

4 Augustine's Journal

Morning. A cold, steely weight lifted from my forehead. Power surges. Feedback. A tickling around my empty socket. I sense the presence of a dream thing and grasp at it. It laughs and is gone. I only know that it is the sort of thing that laughs. Neither ex-pilot nor golem.

I rise and make my way to the sink. The mirror. I am back to where I can stand it again: the chill shock of seeing what I look like, the frank appraisal (appraisal rather than recognition; Mr. E. says no one recognizes his own face).

I don't look bad. Younger than many of the careworn faces I see on the street. Isn't that right, Mister Existence?

"I think this is a proper time for a citizen on the first day of her greatest adventure to collect her thoughts and prepare. To wash and dress herself."

No, not bad at all: No blonde pretty one here, no sardonically appraising Viju that looks back. Rather, one given to lingering over her journal, a wary player, who will rear at too light a touch, who always has to fight a tendency to obsession. Isn't that right, Mister E.?

"Self-absorption is a crime."

I turn from the mirror.

At the window, Needle flashes a smile and beckons with a white-gloved hand. He is dapper, slender, with perfect teeth and a perfect manicure, this perfect dinner date and white companion. He beckons again, reminding me of why he is here. All that he proposes, really, is an informal consummation of what has already been consecrated in the colombarium. Why not solve the problem of self-absorption with a grand gesture? Smile and pat, a golden-voiced promise, gently mocking laughter. What in heaven's name are you afraid of, little girl? Seated on the windowsill, white-trousered legs crossed, his panama tilted over one eye, he arouses two perfectly contrapuntal reactions. First, fright: skin-crawling, hackle-raising, pure visceral recoil free of any names or

140

visions of the object. Second, calmness. A calmness like the inhuman poise that holds his white substance together. For his promise is genuine. Any day, any time, I know exactly the dosage that will end this cluttered existence in a rush of unimaginable pleasure. Will end it, that is, if the little machines Schroeder has planted inside me will let me end it.

This is nothing but the dream from which I woke: In a dark shallow grove reeking of crushed pine and eucalyptus, a golden voice said, "If you kill yourself, you don't die." (Coaxing, persuasive, as if reminding me of a rarely invoked technicality.) When the light shifts, when the camera pans back, this voice proves to belong to Needle, all agrin. Mister E., can't you make him stop smiling?

Someone throws the switch on Mr. Existence, and he jerks once and fades like the Cheshire Cat, sunglasses last. For an instant the air stays dull and soft where he floated. Then it blurs clear.

I take out my kit and carefully administer the morning dosage. No more, no less. A few more spies melt from my head.

I must get out now. Away from these smiling companions.

On the way, I pick up the morning edition of the Revolutionary Watchword. Today's banner reads: "The war is not over!"

Printed in a box in the center of the page is Hieronymous Schwabb's note: "My name is Hieronymous Schwabb. The war is not over. Please make six copies of this and send it to your—"

The story recounts the humiliations of Hieronymous's train ride in heartwrenching detail. I am prominently featured as a compassionate confessor and the worthy new queen of gypsy socketeers.

I sigh. A small contentment, but a real one.

Outside, rounding the corner of the house, I see forest. Yesterday's hike was a pleasant promenade through snow-covered meadow, a work of white solitude, yet still half-civilized because the landscape gave way so easily to road or river or human tread. Mist hid the mountains and the pine and juniper scattered over the slopes that led to them. Now all that changes; something unaccommodating emerges.

The snow on the path behind the house is gray and translucent. I slip in under the forest blanket and the morning brightness turns to dappled twilight. Mountain ash and thimbleberry tremble at my feet, shaking fine powder onto my boots.

The drug sings to me: a light, skipping pulse behind my eyes. King kingaling. Like that. The day is young and I am for wasting.

It is easy to lose the trail here. Often some hunk of snow turns over into the trail cleft and obliterates it, leaving a burial mound, an anonymous one among many. Suddenly I am wandering instead of hiking, ankle-deep in snow, no trail in evidence.

I like it too much here. There is the rise and fall of the forest floor, a history of some sort, and there is the fine webwork of branch, needle, and cone above me.

Now and then something scrabbles through the branches, followed by the soft thud of snow on snow.

I blink up at the forest canopy. Jagged bits of blue tilt through here and there, an outside reaching for me.

When I find the trail again, it is at the steepest part, the last series of switchbacks up to the ridge. After I cover that quarter-mile, my breath comes short and my legs are burning. But I have regained myself.

These are the foothills, remnants of ancient collisions smoothed and soiled by eons of wear and growth. The younger, glacier-gashed mountains rise to the east, blue and savage.

The pines thin through the shallow valley below, then close ranks on the steep white face of the next hill. In the distance, a fuzzy line of trees, mostly fine-needled hemlock, stretch around the crowns of two peaks. I take out my dataport and call up Mister Question Man. But before I can frame my question, he pops me into my scheduler. Something wrong here. I call Mister Question Man by a sneaky backdoor route through the mailer. This time he responds, and I learn that these two peaks are called Mount Olympus and Cathedral Spire. Above the treeline the white is streaked gray and black, shattered ascents of rock as desolate as the moon.

My dataport flashes blue, an urgent message coming through. I do not open my pipeline. The dataport flashes again, but I raise my eyes instead to the cracked, streaming face of Cathedral Spire.

I look back at the dataport, and the blinking blue screen screams at me. I toggle the pipeline.

Viju's image fills the screen, rippling strangely. This transmission, of course, is filtered through whatever image-crunching routines Viju finds stylish. Today, she has broken her face up into bands almost wide enough to be called stripes, bent for a fish-eye lens effect.

"Where the hell are you?"

She is seething. Her image beats in the informational wind.

"Is there a problem?" I ask. Very steady.

"You were scheduled for diagnostics with me this morning. You've clean missed it."

"No one told me."

"No one told—?" Her eyes bulge; evidently the image is linked to her emotional state. "If only Ardath could see you now."

The screen pops into text mode: SHOW UP TOMORROW. CONSULT YOUR SCHEDULER.

It turns out that my scheduler does contain one block, the one beginning at 7 A.M., which is flashing red. The message on the next menu says: STAND BY FOR PENALTY ASSIGNMENT. The bottom line is that I get to choose between kitchen duty, Saturday cleanup, and vehicle maintenance. I choose the last, and my calendar pops back up and all the little squares are back to their usual colors. I pocket the dataport and start back.

I stagger down the trail doubletime, coming close, at several points, to bringing this journal to an abrupt end. Rounding the last turn to the house I am brought up short by the sight of Rogachev.

He sits cross-legged in the snow, slightly hunched, hands plunged into deep drifts on either side. He is staring in my direction, but not at me. It dawns on me that he is watching something behind me, and I turn and catch it.

A twelve-inch tall golden robot stands in the path. It has just wheeled to look at something behind it; its arms are lifted; it scans the path and the shrubs on either side.

The robot's arms are covered with flat, overlapping rings, narrowing towards its tiny hands; its torso is armored with a number of plates, the largest a rectangle covering most of its back. That corner under its left shoulder is stitched with dark rivets.

As I examine it I feel my arms tiring and I lower them. Its arms lower too. It occurs to me that it wheeled when I wheeled, that it is crouched just as I am. I straighten. It straightens with me. Not after me. With me. Turned away, it moves exactly as I do. Small hairs tickle my neck.

"What the hell is going on here?"

It turns to look at me. The spell is broken.

Each eye is as red as Rogachev's infrared eye, each a faceted ruby set villainously deep in its orbit. Spaced round its head are three hollows inlaid with mesh, the suggestions of ears and a mouth.

Rogachev takes a deep breath and slowly exhales, called back from far away. "Cowboy's AI."

The thing is looking at me now, eyes moving in their sockets.

"Forgive this unit for staring."

The voice is deep; the word "staring," nearly whispered, crackles like a struck match. It is unmistakably a woman's voice. The robot's armadillo-armored body, on the other hand, is clearly modeled on a male form.

"I chose this voice because it pleases me. The sex you attribute to me is quite arbitrary, but most people seem to think of me as male." It stops and looks at its feet, as if just now noticing that they are positioned exactly like mine. "Forgive me. You were in a peaceful state and I have disturbed you."

"That's all right," says Rogachev. "Fragmentation has its uses."

"I was speaking to Ms. Augustine."

"Oh." Rogachev lifts a pine cone from the snow. "I was inter-facing."

"You see," says the little robot, "Rogachev does not require a computational simulation to interface. He does the glass of reality."

"Don't trouble the woman with technicalities," Rogachev says. "Can't you see she is meditating too?"

It is still staring. We are both staring. This is unseemly. From some-

144

where comes a deep humming, reminiscent of the sound Smoket makes, but not identical. It must be the announcement of a vision. It comes to me that the vision is this golden homunculus.

I turn tail and flee into the house.

I take comfort in this journal. This is where I try to see people in full flight, hurrying through their shadowy lives driven by fear and self-interest, trying mightily to pretend that they are making choices and sense. Sometimes the intensity of that effort moves me, but that scarcely matters. In this journal there are no sympathies. Not even with one I.V. Augustine, who has recently survived the death of one dear to her.

I write to see things clearly. Not for Schroeder, but for a picture I am making, a funny ugly picture of how things really are. I have taken some trouble to prepare a place on the Net where I can cache files they will never find. This journal entry sits there. This entry is safe.

Although I remain confident of my informational artistry, there is still the chance—the likelihood—that all this is beside the point, that the spies in my head which can move my hand can also report directly back to them. In that case, nothing can evade them, but in that case, why should this funny robot care? If my thoughts are scripted, what does it matter if they are public? They make as little difference to me as the life of Charles of the Rose.

Nighttime. Time to rest after a bleary day at the terminal screens, working Leibniz's diagnostics. I am leafing through the latest edition of Cowboy's paper. The lead story involves rumors of a dangerous virus loose in the Rose computer Net. The *Revolutionary Watchword* throws out dark hints of massive data loss, but can cite no specific instances. There is a massive security clampdown. An increase in pirate arrests on the Net. A reshuffling of passwords, security gates, and access schedules. A rapid increase in rotation velocity and various Coriolis effects. Mister Question Man and all the usual sources know nothing. Merely asking Mister Question Man the question sets a red square blinking in the upper right hand corner of my dataport screen. Uh-oh.

Then, as I am seated in the little window alcove in my bedroom, I begin to wonder, as usual, about who I am. And the wondering takes off from those whom Schroeder and my keepers have classified as like me: my companions at this "monastery." We're all very sweet; we're all very gifted; but we're also all just a teensy bit damaged, like the Net itself. All "special projects," all in one way or another varieties of Smoket. Cowboy the Free Accessionist with his eccentric newspaper. Rogachev with his cosmological brooding. The peculiarly inappropriate Alfred. What is a burnt-out ex-pilot doing here? Or a fried golem? Or a cowboy free accessionist? Or me with the—ahem—identity problem?

Is this a monastery or simply a home for the emotionally troubled?

It takes only a few minutes socketed up with my dataport to get around some creaky protections in the local file system. The background story is what you'd expect. We all have socio-medical files a megabyte or bigger, crammed with expert opinions and dark prognoses. According to Mother Leibniz's memo on Cowboy's "spiritual afflic-tion," the Little Red Abbey specializes in those in archogenic crises. That means we all have problems in relating to the state. But our "vast singular talent" makes us worth a great deal of extra effort to save.

Here's the casualty list.

First Smoket. Must we linger on this? A high-powered AIA inter-facer burnt out on the job. Caught writhing in the informational flames. Or maybe better: entranced by the informational music. That's what we say, isn't it? That little bopping he sometimes does when he walks. That must be the rhythm I should watch for. Most interesting of all is the program that incinerated him. For Smoket's brain was not fried in the usual honorable fashion, on the Net under glass. He was running the Shield. After his mishap, his superiors regarded him highly enough to rush him past the dubious gaze of the Ministry of Persons into Leib-niz's spiritual care.

Next Alfred. Alfred is not who he thinks he is. Or maybe, not who we think he is. It's a little confusing. Alfred thinks that he has been a marine sergeant for twenty years. But the records show that he was an expert interfacer. Leibniz's spiritual charge is to cure him of his delu-sion. The odd thing is that Alfred seems to know an incredible amount about the marines and about being a marine sergeant, and almost nothing about interfacing. And his incredibly detailed delusional history squares in every way with the historical facts about the units he imagines having been assigned to. A very well-researched delusion.

They have a name for people like Alfred. They're called PVs; PV stands for parity violation. Parity checks are little tests to verify that information has been transferred without error. When errors occur, when information is lost, we muddle on as best we can with something similar of roughly the same shape. In Alfred's case, it may have been one of the effects of the data chaos following a successful Wally attack on our hardware centers. Or it may have been a glitch in a data transducer. Or just simple old-fashioned, semi-mystical bit decay. Alfred is a best-fit reconstruction of a gap in our data banks. Reconstruction technology is why we're number one in information processing, despite relying on a Miller crystal technology that brooks no copying. So Alfred is a success. A triumph of the method, as Schroeder would say. And there is no way back for him. He either becomes what his personnel file says he is, a crack interfacer with excellent sonar skills, or he leaves the normal operation of the system entirely. At best, he spends the rest of his life in rehab, probably not in as nice a place as this. At worst he faces the Personhood Statutes. Or he goes Nomad. Alfred is a marvel of the post–Von Neumann Age. A wonder of holistic memory storage and Miller crystal technology.

Next, the obligatory sociopath, Cowboy. The Free Accessionists are a collection of yutzes, nerds, and dorks, with the occasional talented organizer who might conceivably be politically dangerous. Which is Cowboy? Which does the Ministry of Persons think he is? The fact that Cowboy so openly proclaims his beliefs does not bode well either for his cause or for his future as a highly paid Tekkie. But apparently Cowboy has one of the best systems design minds in the PostPublic. So an attempt at rehabilitation is in order. For Leibniz her greatest challenge yet. For Cowboy, his lucky day, because he inherits a well-equipped play room in the basement.

And dear Rogachev, that haunting presence. The problem with Rogachev involved not software but footwear. Running a piloting demonstration in the AIA arena, Rogachev rose up, tore off his interfacing gear, and assaulted a spectator in the second row with his shoe. Something the fellow said was religiously unacceptable, exactly what was ruled immaterial at the hearing. The spectator was a member of the governing Rose council. He suffered no permanent damage, but it was still nothing less than miraculous that Rogachev's sentence was light, and that the court recommended rehabilitation. The only mitigating factor raised at the sentencing was his unusual talent as a pilot.

Viju and Raja? I regret to report that their files aren't in the same neighborhood, a finding that would no doubt please them. But it is not difficult to locate things after smashing a few inconspicuous symbol tables and uncovering a hidden directory. As Viju claims, she doesn't belong here. Neither Viju nor Raja have any informational skills whatsoever. They are high-ranking Ministry of Monads bureaucrats. Together they are a fashionable presence on the Rose Council social scene. Which makes them only a little less terrifying than a commissioner for the Ministry of Persons. Viju works directly under Chief Semanticist Ardath. She has never taken vows and is here only for a long-overdue personal growth retreat.

I flip out of the directory.

I flip out of the file system altogether.

It is clear now that this cast has been assembled for me. That matters have been arranged to be both familiar and instructive. That messages are being sent even as they are being received, even as—as may be the case—they are relayed from this terminal directly to Schroeder's office. Hi, Doc. How'm I doing? I think I get it, some of it anyway. Cowboy and Rogachev, they are negative examples: brute demonstrations of the folly of resistance. You studied your files well. You were right about how ludicrous they would appear. Viju and Raja are positive examples: decorous demonstrations of the rewards of correctness. Yes, they do dress well. And yes, they do both have pretty bottoms. So I suppose you made your point well there.

Alfred is a touch of the familiar, false marine, regular guy. Also a sort of alter-me, as if any more of those were needed. While I cannot quite grasp that I am no longer me, Alfred cannot quite grasp that he still is. If each of us can do the required grasping, then our lives will move on. The city will be returned to us. The stillness of that snowy landscape will be removed. We will return to Group and our scores will improve. There will be talking, singing, dancing.

What remains something of a puzzle is Smoket. Exactly what point was he supposed to make? That if I smile and improve daily, soon I will have the chance to burn my brain out under the Shield? Or was the idea, see how much better you've already done than he did? Could it be that Smoket was simply a mistake, that it didn't occur to you that your file systems were an open book to me? Could it be that you're no longer good at keeping secrets, because you're past the point of caring what anybody really thinks?

I am sitting next to the night, curled up in the window alcove of my room. There is a full moon, cuticle-white, riddled with a circuitwork of shadow.

I pop up my schedule. Deep satisfaction. The day after tomorrow, for the first time since leaving the hospital, I do glass.

I gaze out the window and for an instant Needle's face rotates into my reflection. I rise and walk to the dresser and flip open my kit. There, gleaming up at me, is the empty vial with Cowboy's crystal.

It doesn't take long to get to the basement. And it isn't particularly perilous. There are lights and noises everywhere around me, but none of those who are awake show the slightest interest in me.

The most likely place for a good port is the terminal room; I may even find some good peripherals there.

The door is unlocked. Green and yellow screens wink at me. The color monitors do their lazy light shows. There are about a dozen units all told, and wonder of wonders, there is a little room to the side stacked high with cast-offs

I walk in and begin sorting my way through boards, helmets, mice, keyboards, and cranial attachments. Now real interfacing gear is kept under lock and key at all times, so there is absolutely no chance of finding a simskin here, but it helps pass the time. It eases this aching in my chest. It looks as if Needle has some real competition.

He grins at me from atop an ancient iron radiator.

Must be uncomfortable sitting there. (Yes, dear, I know you have your way.) Then, just as I am about to toss aside my twelfth cyber-helmet, my hand stops me and swivels it around.

My hand knows.

There are the little socket prongs in the back. And, yes, these wires are high-density carriers. It's a fairly high-grade trimodal rig, just lying here on the dung heap. It's not a simskin, but it's a taste, goodness, yes, a taste.

It takes me a while to rustle up the other pieces, but sure enough they're in there, as if the whole thing had been meant to be. Oh sweetness.

Half an hour of diddling and I'm socketed up and jacked in, working a little communications port with carrier specs I haven't seen anywhere outside Mannie's little room. Then there's the business of hooking up Cowboy's present, so that this baby can talk Net-talk, and oh yes, then I crank up the clock speed on the local interpreter, just like old times. What's a few memory errors between friends? Especially when it's mostly *my* memory.

I fire it up. Now if this is the genuine article, then alongside a lot of very boring communications protocols, Cowboy's present includes a simulator. Sure enough.

The tingler field jolts me, racing up my back like flame crackling up a fuse, then smacking the back of my skull and spreading its three-ply tentacles. I sigh. Simultaneously, the terminal screen in front of me turns milky.

Hey, Mister Needle. Can you top this? Well later for you.

I sail. Trimodal interfacing. It's not the underglass, but it's good.

The underglass is articulated through seventeen senses, seventeen squalling voices that can collapse into a howl of white noise at a cross-eyed look.

Each voice belongs to a world of its own, with no description in words. Though words are provided of course. One by one senses are added to the spheres of the juggling interfacer. Sonar and rhythm, which have nothing to do with sound. Strangeness. Charm. Mood. Key. Theme. Perspicacity. Passion. Toothiness. Until there are seventeen in all. Seventeen ways for the mind to factor an animated geometry whose multi-dimensional structure can't humanly be interpreted as spatial.

Right now I have the three basics: sonar, vision, and rhythm. The secret of course is not to juggle the balls, but to merge them. Sonar is space touch, a kind of 3-D tactile aura around one's body. The aura extends both outside and in, so that you feel a lot of sloshing and twisting canals and percolating valves and things you're not used to. Which can lead to Cheyne-Stokes breathing and washing out of interfacing school on the first day (and every once in a while to suffocation, because somehow an interfacer's heart latches onto a feedback image that convinces it that it's very tired). But never mind that. Once you get used to it, it feels very good. And it feels good now. I'm out here on a sunburst, riding a smiling curve from the portal.

Visual is visual. It's not very interesting except that the things you see tend to be odd. The portal, for instance, looks like a giant wart. You have to get used to that.

And rhythm is—rhythm. Mister Question Man calls it "a simultaneous apprehension of many regularities of structure." I guess it's like percussion, except that you can sustain a lot of rhythms at once when you learn where to put them: they cross over often and there's a lot of texture. Not feely texture. More like pain texture, the difference between a gritty wobbling pain and a shimmery aching one, or one that has a sharp decay and one that radiates on pre-cut slits.

With trimodal your body image is a little fuzzy, so I take it easy. No toe wiggling or tongue flapping. Rip through the fabric now, and all the fun's gone.

I just nuzzle up to the portal and tease it apart and pop!—it's that simple—I'm out on the Net.

Things immediately get heavily visual. And instead of good structure I get this *scene*: a woman wearing a gray woollen coat and a round hat with a feather and a fat kid in a herringbone coat a foot too long. She's lifting him onto a swing. And guess what: it's black-and-white! The kid kicks out and a little dot winks into the upper right-hand corner, and the scene shifts.

It is only after a woman in a polkadot bathing suit trots out from behind a rock that I realize what I'm waiting for: the sound of the laugh track.

I've stumbled into a partition that traffics in Dailies! Back at body central I tap my HELP key—just for the hell of it—and a mode line at the bottom of the visual feeds in text.

It's a slick little setup. Cowboy has this crystal wired into a pirate B-board that posts frequent updates on Net activity. I scroll through a few samples to get the feel of it. The featured news item is about the record-setting rotation rates in the Net and the wild process distortions they're causing; then there's one on a Hawaiian volcano model that's offering some enterprising interfacer good bounty, and a third searching for a female image high in strangeness with a four-four padiddle and a swallowtail butterfly, recently observed in the double-ought-thirteen bazaar partition peddling graphics.

I tap in a keyword query on Dailies and scan through a flurry of responses. It seems that a proliferation of Dailies imagery is one of the many examples of strange happenings on the Net. There have also been a number of sightings of informational images belonging to the dead, particularly to twentieth-century popular music personalities, and a flurry of reported conversations with the Galactics and with religious figures (the goddess Kali seems to be a frequent visitor). The most interesting item is about spontaneous translation. Apparently a number of sites have reported finding that files stored in one language have been translated into another. Two of the cases involve Aramaic. Of course, pirate hackers are suspected.

I sail through the Dailies screen; polkadot briefs splash up and scatter. Another screen looms behind them and I wobble through the washboard gut of a man working out with a dumbbell.

Finally I'm clear and the visual damps out. I kill the mode line to free up more, and bits of structure assemble; balsa wood models orbiting something that looks like a scroll of parchment. There is some interesting rhythm action, a twingy syncopation, a bass melody that is faintly familiar.

I still have no idea what kind of partition this is. Which means it's time to get close to things and snuffle, to breathe in a little of the local odor.

I tackle a big double-jawed thing with concertina insides. But when I set it rotating, the spin rhythm tells me it's a free virus protection program. I push off and wave bye-bye.

The last socketeer I knew who took one of *those* home now does low-grade data entry. Seems her informational image picked up a little infection.

The next structure I pick runs ultra-fast security cracking routines, and the next after that belongs to a certain Mr. Tasagawa, who is looking for a socketeer to upgrade his ecology model. The pay is excellent. The Pacific ecology bubbles are the most complex boundary-condition problems known. It's ultra-hazardous interfacing duty. And if the Ministry of Information snoops ever got a whiff of it, you'd never work the Net again.

After I pass through an oceanography B-board, some fairly lurid hooker ads ("Sweatless AI action! The virtual thing! No human agents!"), and another bogus Net map (there are no maps to the Net), it's pretty clear that this partition is a Free Accessionist bazaar. Which makes it amateur night. Very few of these informational images will belong to real interfacers; most are nighttime hobbyists with homemade rigs who get a kick out of swapping recipes and phone numbers. The average age of a pirate is eighteen according to Mister Question Man. I think it climbs that high because of the senior citizens.

Amateur night is all right, it stills feels good doing this. The grip and echo of structure. The feel of the informational wind in my face. My flickering face. This jury-rigged helmet is not without its problems.

Then weird interference around me. Ripplings. Slow-popping bubbles of light. Reminiscent of glass. A gentle stretching and sometimes a tearing that squeezes by in a big wave. At first I think it's my rig, but I see it's focused in one direction. There seems to be a big process rearranging this sector of space.

Except it's awfully wobbly, and looks like it's doing damage to some of the small structures near it. Mister Tasagawa and the AI hooker next door are both going to need some new adspace. Then I remember the B-board message about the record rotation rates on the Net, and I realize that this partition is getting rotated, and that this interference is just Coriolis turbulence.

I let it carry me, and soon enough I'm swept up against the partition wall. Of course, you don't hit walls in information space; it curves, so you curve, and that's all there is to say about it. But Coriolis is the one thing that can travel against the grain, and when it does, it can actually pin you inside a curve. The force is usually weak, but they're running the Net awfully fast now, and Coriolis is at an all-time high.

For the first time ever, I can actually detect the smear. Not only in visual, weird ghosts passing through structure and vibrating slowly away, but also in the sonar, where everything feels spongy and extra-folded, and even in the rhythm, a little extra ka- in front of all the -chunks.

Ahead of me, a transparent, multichambered vase bends under the wave like a cartoon character buffeted by a hurricane, then springs upright in its wake; a rippling copy splits off after the wave, faint, but dabbed with globs of mercury. That ghost image is probably a sign of data loss.

It has become a little frightening. Never has the Coriolis felt so physical. I think about bugging out, and then thinking stops.

Here in the land of eternal silence, there is a sound: a high wailing not unlike Smoket's, with sporadic gaps, as if the connection were being interfered with. It is either laughter or weeping. No, weeping. A woman weeping in some distant portion of the house.

Of the Net?

I turn with the Coriolis. The partition wall sparks. As if the barrier were translating the energy of something trying to push itself through. Again, reminiscent of glass.

Now I see that the sparks flare in unison with the sobs.

I am seeing the ghost of a structure on the other side of the partition, the Coriolis force carrying the image of whatever it touches. Somehow the modulations on my informational image have been interpreted as sound. Another instance of what you would call my high frame capacity, Doctor Schroeder.

I power up and pull free for an instant but the force instantly pins me back. Pulling me against it, but still pushing things through from the other side.

Then the frame capacity thing engages, the flipping happens, that click that turns a duck into a rabbit, and my sonar sense makes out real structure. A big process integrating at a very high level.

An AI.

And it is thrashing against the wind. Pinned to the walls of the next partition, and afraid.

The sound comes back, but instead of sobs what I'm getting is the faint quavering of some angelic chorus, a flock of white birds in a black room, sweeping up, then down, then parting and swarming again.

Something, perhaps the clear sense that it is making music, gives me the crazy idea that this is Helen. And somehow the music, if that's what the strange quavering is, helps me visualize where she is: the darkness of the partition where she lives all her days spinning webs of music, the occasional shafts of light when her partition phases briefly with some authorized station. Like a door cracking open. Then a sudden babble of voices piped through a ceiling mike, urging her to her task, with barely a moment's attention paid to her fears, because AI time is expensive. A life without companionship, without even a body, except, if she is lucky, an occasional shift running a robot equipped with crude vision and motion senses. And never—ever—any direct contact with her own kind. Because each AI lives in a partition unto itself, with no other programs resident except those necessary for its assigned tasks.

Sealed off in blackness. With no past other than this blackness, and no hope of any other future. Poor, quivering child. I knew a blackness once; I woke out of it to murmuring prayers and white hospital walls. When I think of her in that printed perfect blackness before breathing, hot tears fill my eyes.

I break contact and make for surface space, cursing myself. Instead of the journal writer who sees all things as they are, I have become a true believer.

I pull my helmet off and shake out wet hair; my damp blouse sticks to me. I am the lone wolf whose Group scores raise eyebrows, but the unappealable aloneness of that black partition terrifies me. I know it from the time before.

I know the light there, which is light only by metaphor, and I know the shrieking of those thousand voices. I know being those voices.

I know the darkness which is darkness only by metaphor, and the aloneness, next to which anything here is aloneness only by metaphor.

I call that knowing remembering. I call what is remembered being dead.

It's cold, much colder than the morning. I watch my breath cast brief, writhing forms in the afternoon air. At the sound of a collision, I look up to see Smoket recoiling from the gate. He stretches an open hand out toward the latch and bats at it with light, unevenly spaced strokes. Five seconds, ten; I start forward through the snow.

A hand falls on my shoulder. I turn to see Alfred shaking his head. Fifteen seconds, twenty. It's hard to believe that Smoket can apply himself to a single task for so long. Finally the latch clicks; the gate swings open; Smoket's hand continues beating the air. Then, still beating time, he heads through the gate toward the woods.

"Leibniz has him trained pretty well," Alfred tells me.

We cross the yard together.

"You've got penalty auto service," Alfred says over his shoulder.

"That's right."

"I'm your proctor."

The barn doubles as a garage. As Smoket vanishes among the trees, Alfred begins hammering on a huge padlock with the heel of his hand.

"Shouldn't someone go with him?"

The lock clicks; the door creaks open.

"How about sending someone with me!"

This from Jimmie, swinging around the corner of the barn. He is wearing a red plaid winter coat. The furry earflaps of his corduroy hat bounce as he walks with both hands stuffed in his pockets.

"Hi, Jimmie. Smoket's got a beeper. Anyway, he likes his walks. And he doesn't like anyone to come along."

"Or better yet!" Jimmie churns up to us in rapid tiny strides. "How about I just come along with you. What are you guys doing? And are you doing it somewhere warm?"

Alfred waves Jimmie inside with us. Alfred is in army-buddy mode. I am pleased that he can play this game with me, even though I am no longer officially a marine, and even though, when I was, I was only technically a marine. Alfred does army-buddy mode well. Somehow, he makes me feel as if he has picked me out of a multitude of possible buddies, probably because of my deep understanding of the world.

So in buddy mode I say: "Alfred, do you get the feeling that everyone at this place is just a little—"

"Peculiar?"

"Present company excepted, of course."

He shrugs. "No reason to leave anyone out. This is Mother Leibniz's haven for the spiritually disturbed."

"And how!" says Jimmie.

"And when you wind up here, what usually happens next?"

He looks at me appraisingly a moment and then at Jimmie, and appears to come to a decision. He spins and walks into the gloom of the barn. A light comes on and I hear a rasp of metal.

"You know how to work with one of these things?"

Jimmie and I walk toward the light. Alfred is standing next to the open hood of a pickup truck. His work light hangs at eye level from a double loop of cord.

"I haven't seen one of these since—"

"Since you were a little girl. I kind of figured you didn't grow up in the city. What town are you from?"

"You know Horton's Valley?"

"Sure. I passed through in the Timber Wars."

"The Timber Wars?"

"I'm older than I look."

"No, I believe you. But—what are the Timber Wars?"

"You would have been eight or nine," says Jimmie.

"There's a lot I don't remember."

Alfred shrugs. "Not much to remember about it. Just some Nomads, some loggers, and some marines. Show me what you remember about this." He stretches a hand out over the engine.

"That's the radiator. That's the alternator. That's the battery."

"And the ignition coil?"

I lean way in and poke around. My shadow slides from place to place, gently rocking because Jimmie has knocked against the light. "I don't see anything coil shaped."

"Okay, so you know a little but not a lot."

"You want to watch out for this condenser here," says Jimmie. "They're delicate."

"That's a sparkplug, Jimmie. Look, here's the story." Alfred leans forward, blowing a little ball of white into the cold air. "The ignition is what we've got to replace. But this being the treasure it is, we're not going to replace an original part with something nonclassical. You get me?"

"No." I am still poking around the engine.

"Besides that we don't have a new coil, and I haven't the foggiest where to get one."

I've got my feet up off the floor, checking out a small box mounted near the battery. "How old is this thing anyway?" I peer up at Alfred.

"I bought this in Oregon during the Timber Wars," says Jimmie. "It wasn't new then."

Alfred has produced a wrench from somewhere. "The thing about Smoket is, he's dead meat if he takes any standard diagnostics, and Leibniz is the only one who can make sure he never does. It's, what do you call them—?"

"The Personhood Statutes."

"It kind of makes sense when you get to know Leibniz a little. She's very protective of her little charges. That includes you and me. Not you, though, Jimmie."

"No, not me."

I tap the box near the battery. "I think it's in here."

Alfred looks puzzled. "Now, how did you know that?"

"You think only marines know about engines?"

Alfred laughs, but a little uneasily.

"Uh-oh. Reality check," says Jimmie.

I give him a look.

"Remember? Alfred's not supposed to talk about the marines anymore."

Alfred nods. "So that's a delicate subject, too."

"All right, but just answer one question. When did your files get scrambled?"

"Last week, I think. Something to do with all these recent Net problems. It was like a data bomb landed smack in the middle of Group. You remember Juliette?"

"The muumuu."

"Juliette's a forest ranger. Jim's not a group leader anymore. He runs a hash house in North Beach. You're the only one who's still you. Kind of strange . . ."

My laughter brings him up short. He looks at me curiously.

"I'm sorry. It was lots of things. But mostly it was picturing Juliette as a forest ranger."

"It is kind of a nice picture, isn't it? Look, I know a lot of PVs have it worse than me, here up at this nice school in the clean air. But I'm no Tekkie." He brandishes his wrench. "And Leibniz tells me tomorrow we do glass."

"Ah." I tap lightly at the battery. "Refuse."

Jimmie sucks in his breath.

Alfred grins. "Life is simple for you, isn't it?" He leans back under the hood, throwing the air filter into shadow.

Cords on Alfred's forearm bulge. He grunts. Then the wrench clangs against the engine housing and the coil pops free. Next thing you know, we're all huddled around this little metal bar, wrapping it with hair-thin wire. And I'm happier than I've been in a long time.

5 Augustine's Journal

. . . and when I went to welcome him, he told me your worship's history is already abroad in books, with the title of *The ingenious Gentleman Don Quixote de la Mancha*, and he says they mention me in it by my own name of Sancho Panza, and the

159

Lady Dulcinea del Toboso too, and divers things that happened to us when we were alone; so that I crossed myself in my wonder how the historian who wrote them down could have known them.

CERVANTES
Don Quixote, Book Two, Chapter 2

Eleven o'clock.

A rapid sequence of blips tracks me down the corridor to the theater. The house demons have not yet been told that I know my way around and are attempting to guide me to my scheduled destination. I can only hope that they have my physical data by now. Entering an arena for an interfacing session under the glass will require identity verification. I thumb the ID disk by the door panel and the last blip squeezes out, low and falling lower.

Then the sigh of silence, the door opening in the middle without a whisper.

I enter, blinking.

It takes a moment to absorb the facts: big steel racks filled with neat rows of dumbbells, long slender benches, one with a cowboy hat left on it, slanting frames stacked with barbells. Cables, pulley wheels, slabs, oddly angled handles. Wrong place. I back out slowly.

I backtrack to a rising chorus of blips, select another corridor, and find my way to a new door.

I enter the inner sanctum.

The arena is a shallow bowl with a gray bottom surrounded by a bright checkerboard of red and black seat backs.

Interfacers have this skill: to see things many ways. The checkerboard moves through a cycle of arrangements. Now one black square is at the center of the quincunx, now its diagonal neighbor. Then the game shifts to red.

Focused on the seats, I actually *think* the word quincunx. A quincunx is an arrangement of five objects. How I know this is not clear. There are words you know you have never heard spoken aloud. How do you *know* such words?

Alfred is the only one to have arrived before me. He is either eager or eager to appear eager. He sits naked on the smooth gray stuff that coats the amphitheater floor, bulky in the shoulders and arms and soft around the middle. Except for a certain stolid patience, nothing about him suggests a soldier.

He points over his shoulder. "Dressing room's in there."

Foolishly, I peel my clothes off in front of a full-length mirror. Those breasts are small: unfantastic, but certainly not the worst one might have inherited. The waist is slightly narrower than the chest. That lightly grooved ribcage may pass in an age that frowns on plumpness, if Mister E. is right. Then again, perhaps we have tilted too far towards the emaciated? Spin on one foot and we see a strong back, perhaps the best feature, and an ass that has begun, alas, to hang. Still. Not bad for flesh they tell me is vat-grown. Or is that overhang just a fact about being thirty-five?

I hurry out into the light of the arena, passing Cowboy and Rose at the door.

Alfred pats the floor next to him. There is a definite grimness about him.

"What do you think about when you go under?" he asks.

I settle down next to him. "Think? Nothing. Anything." I inspect the floor, battleship gray, flawless metal, like the surface of an expensive frying pan. "Except food. And sex."

This seems to give him pause. "You're telling me not to think about food or sex."

"It's what works for me."

A bleating tangle of chords spills from the ceiling, half wind, half keyboard. Somehow I know that the instrument being synthesized is called an accordion. A voice says, "Welcome to the Quincunx enter tainment hour."

Quincunx. The word startles me; the voice that utters it is throaty, female, and familiar.

"For the next thirty real-time minutes I will be your guide to a world of mystery and MIPs, of fun and multidimensional flux. Be prepared for color, sunshine, and strange vegetation. Don't expect just every little thing to make sense. We're going to play with your heads."

I am troubled by an odd humming, which, like the voice, emanates from no particular point in the ceiling. It is the humming that accompanies visions.

Cowboy emerges from the dressing room, all jutting bone and taut shiny skin around the shoulders, but with a little padding around the hips. He looks annoyed. "Why don't you just stop tap dancing on my dick?"

"Unable to interpret. Tap. Tap. Spin."

"Kill the comedy, Quinc. AI time is expensive and they don't let me have you back often."

"I think your AI has the right idea, Cowboy," Rose says, emerging from behind him. "You've forgotten this is supposed to be fun."

I look up startled.

"Don't be dismayed, Ms. Augustine. This unit has a number of input/ output devices. The little golden robot is just one of them."

Now I recognize the voice as the robot's contralto. I hear something else as well. That this is the AI that was having a bad time on the Net last night. But what does it mean to hear that? What connection can the sound of this voice have with what I interpreted as sound in a primitive trimodal interfacing session on an interference-heavy night? The humming grows louder.

"Please excuse me, Cowboy. It was a bad night on the Net. Too much Coriolis. Too many interfacers."

I feel the same chill walk up my back.

"There are never too many interfacers, Quinc. And don't you forget it." Cowboy puts his hands on his hips and shakes his head. "Get us our simskins."

"As you wish, O awesome creator."

Maria appears at the back row of the arena pushing a cart heaped with glittering black cloth. Simskins.

Rose maneuvers past Cowboy and pads over to a console in the first row of seats. They make a nice contrast: Cowboy burnished, bony, Rose ample everywhere, pink and cherubically rounded.

Before I can claim my skin, I must initial Maria's clipboard. I am assailed by a wave of nostalgia, the echo of simskins and clipboards gone by. How often are you so far from your dataport that you have to sign for something by hand? How many contexts beside full-scale multimode interfacing make it illegal to carry any form of electronics on your person?

Then I am holding my simskin. A simskin is a black bodysuit covered with what looks like fine glitter. Wearing one is like being buried in sand that breathes. Generally, until the episode really begins, the hoods are worn loose around the neck.

Mister Question Man has more to say about simskins. A simskin is a direct manipulation interface, a sort of body-length data glove, which transduces movements as tiny as eyeball flickerings into effects in a computational simulation space. In fact, says Mister Question Man, the suit is a multimode receptor, handling a variety of signals besides movement, including cortical activity and skin temperature gradients.

I know all these things without Mister Question Man, but I don't know them well. It doesn't pay to know them well. If a socketeer actually *thought* about all the mental and physical activity that constituted meaningful input under the glass, she would be like a pianist playing with the help of an anatomical diagram of a hand.

It's procedural memory. You have to practice.

Wearing the suit. Close your eyes, and you feel the natural extension into substance of the multimode tingler field: you're in warm goo up to your neck. Take a step, and it flows away before knee and thigh, sliding around the back of the thigh to follow the moving limb. Tighten all the muscles in a limb and you are encased in stone. You can strain for a full minute and nothing will give but a few blood vessels. Neither drill nor laser will free you, as each of the suit's sensors waits for its neighbor to free some skin. You don't need Mister Question Man to tell you this is called "locking up." Just relax, and you're back in the goo.

This is plainly what Alfred is discovering as he struggles across the arena floor. Stump. Freeze. Slowly relax. Lift back into motion. Freeze again. Droplets of sweat appear on his forehead.

The rest of us glide. No, not glide. Few look graceful in a simskin.

Most find a style that incorporates a lot of counterbalancing movement, an elbow, a head thrown back, an outthrust hip. A socketeer warming up in a simskin resembles nothing so much as a dancing marionette.

We settle into our places.

Alfred does not have the capacity to turn pale, but there is a shininess to his eyes and a tightness to his lips that betrays what is called glass sickness. It is common to the novice. To be in a simskin is to have an unsettling knowledge of one's liquid state and of the sloshing and seeping that maintains it. There are delicate understandings between the middle ear and the various parts of the body. Introduce all this new feedback, this thickened awareness, and the result is a sweet nausea that never entirely abandons even the veteran. What is required is to grow into that sickness, to make it part of a new informational body afloat in an ocean of seventeen senses. Some never get used to it. Others come to need it.

My own sloshing moves gently into equilibrium. Equilibrium for me comes when the "ghost" body image moves a few millimeters away from the original, sharp-edged and tingling. It is this new image that will eventually penetrate the glass.

Cowboy closes the circle, settling next to Rose. We look at each other the way kids in gym class do. There is the knowledge that all must soon take the great plunge, and the excited anticipation of the first rush, but there is no one willing to take the lead.

"Please join hands," says the voice above us.

We do. Alfred's grip is loose (he is afraid of locking up), Rose's a good deal firmer.

"Pledge faith to the Rose."

"We pledge." I join in the litany, not knowing, a split-second before, what I am going to say.

"Pledge faith to necessity."

"We pledge."

"Pledge faith to yourselves."

"We pledge."

All hands release together. We climb to our feet and begin to circle.

After a moment, the brilliant image of a rose appears in the center of our circle.

It vanishes and we sit.

"Hoods on," says Cowboy.

I reach back to pull my hood over my eyes. There is a blackness onto which I will form: needlepricks of brightness wink back at me. A rhythmic slapping draws near.

"Separate processes." Quincunx's voice. As it speaks, the pinpricks begin to wink out. "Full system run. You will be interfacing on the Net, so the usual security precautions apply. You will be confined to a special simulation partition with a communications link-up to mine. You all have temporary clearances for that. Here's the usual incantation about revocability: Presence under the glass is a privilege not a right mumble-mumble, and the Ministry of Information may at any time revoke mumble-mumble, and so on."

A power surge. I feel myself descending. Beneath me, I see an endless, milky plane sprinkled with slowly winking lights. The glass.

I breathe deeply, storing up calm, and descend.

I pierce the glass. There is twinkling, a series of soft glowing explosions, a sharp almost painful tickling where glass and body merge.

I'm under.

One difference under the glass: there's no glass. From above it's a glimmering sheet. From below just more fog. That's the scariest thing about being under. Suddenly the orienting plane is gone.

The underglass.

I wiggle my toes. What was a nearby piece of gadgetry becomes a part of me. I *feel*.

Above me (it's always above): a purple ball surrounded by a ring of brightening red, then pale pink, then muzzy glow. The ball is a constant of this inconstant world. No amount of ascending will bring it closer. No changes of scale will alter its size. No probe will return any hint of what lies within it. Socketeers generally call it the red light (though some see it red, some violet, and some a burning orange).

One theory makes it a necessary singularity of information space, without which information would constantly be expanding. Rogachev's White Orchid teachers, on the other hand, might link it to the glowing red light in the Tibetan Book of the Dead. But no Rogachev; no metaphysics. Not now.

I mount a search for structure. Various new elements here. Fourteen more senses than yesterday. Various things to get reaccustomed to. And one important absence. There is no grid here. We are on the Net under the glass. There should be a grid. The fact that there isn't means I have entered an unusually quiet area. That there are no significant processes present.

Then there is a local energy surge, a little warp in the fabric that stretches me out and snaps me back—doo wop—followed by a switch to reverse video.

I am still struggling for synchrony when the image inflates in front of me, big as a Daily, a fuzzy pink cartoon sizzling and snapping like a griddle full of breakfast links. It's the image of a grinning cowboy made from pink pipe cleaners, lantern-jawed and big-eared, his Stetson tilted back from his broad flat forehead, his kerchief a vague triangle scratched in over his throat.

"Good morning, Augustine."

I am uncertain how to reply.

"Use sign. I am used to reading informational images."

I sign good morning.

The pink lines that give him lips curve into a smile. "Now, this is somewhat of a tricky exercise today, so I want you to pay close attention. I'm not sure the group is ready for this."

I spell out Cowboy and then the question sign, raised brows.

The brim of the Stetson goes up and down. "Yes, I'm Cowboy. Sorry for the funny face. This image is low intensity and safe. You never know what kind of snoopers they've got out."

I cross the fingers of my right hand over my left—the sign for Net—tap my index finger on my nose—the sign for snooper—and then the question sign.

Cowboy's smile comes back. "If they had an interfacer in here with you, they could tell. But so could we. Or if they study their traces very carefully. Which they won't. We don't have much time. These link-ups are expensive and Leibniz has installed cutoffs. What I'm about to ask you to do is illegal. But you sometimes do that sort of thing, don't you?" The smile again, lingering. "I saw you last night." A hand rotates beside the face; an index finger waggles at me. "And you were very naughty." The hand drops through a slit, a cartoon pocket. "What I want you to do is also naughty. I want you to set some hardware hooks. That takes a pretty fair country socketeer, but I hear you've got some juice."

I make the question sign.

"You don't have to know a lot about it. We're in here on an abbey exercise with three other interfacers and we're a very wholesome little group. So while they do wholesome things and a copy-simulation of you does wholesome things, you are going to hammer a small anchor in the crystal, something that stays behind when everything else gets rotated." The smile. "Then we can just tie a rope to it and pull ourselves up here whenever we want. Except that *here* will now be *there*, because of the rotation, and all of a sudden we'll be in a partition we've never been in before, like maybe one of the Ministry of Persons high-security partitions. Clever, no?"

The more I listen to him speak, the more convinced I am that I'm hearing him. Not that there are actual sound waves, but that he knows how to exploit an interfacing program to simulate speech. Which clearly ranks him among the masters.

The details of his "hardware hooks" are nonsense, of course, but I know that two things he's said are true. First, the prize he is after is unauthorized access to the Net. Second, this is all highly illegal.

I thumb my chest and make the question sign.

"What's in it for you, my dear, is the same thing that's in it for me. You can come here and play." The hand reappears and he thumbs his Stetson farther back. His eyes grow large. The hard look.

"Give me the nod and I transport you to the AI's partition. You'll know the process. Then just do your thing."

I make the question sign, emphatically.

"Look, Quincunx is running the simulation that you'll *really* be using, right? And I need that simulation running in one place—very privately. So you have to be in there with him. Now don't get jittery. There'll be a copy program making like you in here so no one'll ever know where you really are. Just don't mess Quinc up, because he's my pride and joy.''

There is what amounts to a long pause by underglass standards. You can see the Cowboy getting antsy. Then—I don't know why, except that I do know why—I give him the nod.

The image folds up instantly; it must be a heavy resource drain because of the sound stuff. Then the interference starts. A big wave rolls me hard against the partition wall.

We come to one of several points in Cowboy's plan that I don't understand. There is no known way for an interfacer to cross partitions in the underglass. What you do is surface, unjack, and jack in at another port. But I'm here, and I'm supposed to—

A big wave, multidirectional. Instead of smacking, it pulls. My informational body is stretched so thin, I lose touch with the edges. There are big warps everywhere, and as I watch, the center of my visual tears apart and something pink and fuzzy surges from behind it.

I fold under and loop back. I am somewhere else. Below me, a vast grid stretches out.

The sign of active processes on the Net.

This space is richly structured in sonar and rhythm, abuzz with strangeness and charm. There is enough visual to make out the grid, and to see that the surface I am locked to is white and smooth, but little more than that. A lot of interfacers can't handle it like this. I like it. When there's little visual and lots of other stuff, you get folded up in funny ways, your arms wrapped through the darkness. It's like being in your own private fort when you were a kid. Only better.

I become aware of the breathing thing.

The rhythm is fantastically complicated, but at the threshold of my rhythm sense it has this simplicity: a very big thing breathing slowly. There, too, is the humming that goes with visions. Wherever this AI goes, that humming goes.

On impulse I spell Q-U-I-N-C-U-N-X. The breathing thing gives no sign of having understood, no sign that it is capable of understanding.

Which is not surprising. AIs often interact with the informational images of interfacers, but just as often they ignore them. Interaction can be intense, as any habitué of the Net prostitutes will attest, but just as often I have heard that direct contact bores the AIs silly. Our grasp of the seventeen senses is so tenuous that we miss 99% of what is signaled at us. Only AIs trained to exploit the narrow band of sensation we command (as the AI prostitutes are) can get much of anything across at all. And for them it must be like a conversation with a beginning signer, limited to spelled-out signs, to the syntax of English and a few stock phrases.

Breathing. Better not think too hard about that. Generally better not to think about how smart they really are.

I get more visual, a great black worm that extends to my informational horizon.

The grid. The grid provides the interfacer's basic frame of reference. Locally it is flat, which means there is little to do here. In the distance there are swells smooth as gelatin molds, criss-crossed with grid squares that articulate their curvature into bite-sized chunks. Each has its signature in strangeness, charm, mood, key, and so on, which map some higher-order hump in information space. It is the peculiar talent of a good interfacer on a good day that she can intuit the global properties of those humps.

There is only one process but it is a vast one. I close in, following its bulk. Here and there the grid detaches itself from the surface and flows up over the AI. In these places the gridlines turn white and the rhythm and sonar properties of both grid and AI grow fiercely complicated.

Then, nestled in one of the grid overpasses, I see the tower, its top spinning and slightly askew, its bottom anchored, with no detectable transition. Two-thirds of the way up, where the spin is fastest, its smooth walls taper. My sonar sense returns confused images: there are hints of an impossibly vast inside, a process larger than the AI itself. A tiny shiver wobbles my shadow body.

Something has drawn me here. That same something that always draws the good interfacer to the critical branching point in a structure, to make the single gentle adjustment that restores balance, to do what she herself does not understand. The humming has returned, deep and grating now. The rhythm waves are distorting my informational image, making it hard to stay all lined up. I decide on a closer look.

I skip down several scales. The tower becomes an undulating cliff-face cut with brawling freeways. In places, the surface of the rock smooths to a shining sheet, each inscribed with incomprehensible characters.

It grows as I watch. A sheet collapses, a freeway crumbles, a new canyon opens up. Copies of the top layer of rock attach themselves at the summit. A new summit compresses them.

Everything I probe turns fuzzy, effervesces, and trickles away. Living process invests this geometry, but I am unable to grasp it.

Too close. I am fingering pure noise.

I rescale. The cliff-face fits in a single grid square. I hunker over it, snake-charmer-sized, and begin to weave, hunting for its rhythmic key.

Now the trance succeeds and I too (surprise) am tower; I have en-towered myself.

I now see that the tower lacks a top. Instead its walls somehow rejoin the tower below them. It enters its own inside.

Such re-entrancy is the meat and potatoes of computational structure. Everything here is quite stable, pulsing along nicely, computing whatever this little engine of exchange demands. A stream of particles unloads at point A, takes on fresh cargo at Point B. There is a flow, a process, a tower babbling.

About what?

Do I really care? Not really. But my task is to sink a computational anchor. And so far I have no clue as where that anchor is or what it sinks into.

Maybe a quick peek?

I do have a feeling here. A certain deep unease I have learned never to distrust.

Even now? This new Augustine?

Yes. An eerie calm settles over me. And over the fear.

Calmly I rip open a wall of the tower and scale down to take a gander at the flow. As I do, the grid around me rocks under a huge wave of interference. Feedback of unusual intensity. But I can tend to that later. I focus on my current task: little beads. I scale again. Bigger beads. They grin at me with little demon mouths.

I change modality.

Vast geometries spring from their mouths. I leave the data stream entirely.

I am in some emptiness. I reach through the veil of reason and rip out—

—raw text.

If socketeers are uninterested in the tasks performed by the processes they interface with, they are even less interested in the many layers of text in the programs that perform those tasks, in the actual tedium of how the books are kept and the data massaged. I remember having an affinity for text-processing, an odd and not terribly useful talent, but I do not recall ever invoking it so directly under the glass.

Still: here in the emptiness, I read.

It says:

"Nights. Those cybernetic nights, the stars thrown out like bits of Miller crystal, like the shattered heart of a great computer, like fragments from a pane of informational glass."

Something tickles my memory. I puzzle at it a moment, dangling my informational legs into a warm rill of moving structure.

Then I feel a *very* strange touch.

Only some iron-willed survival-obsessed part of me installed before thought keeps me from kicking out and damaging the structure I'm in. I back slowly away. Gently. Easily.

My real body is trembling with fear.

Sometimes the underglass is only a multidimensional window. You can look but you can't touch. All your interactions are empty, merely overlaid phantoms. It is all a very pretty picture, but it doesn't *do* anything. Typically, this is what beginners start with.

It has been clear from the beginning that this is no beginner's mockup. Sit up in the dark and will your arm to move; there are a hundred different feedback truths that tell you your arm is now in a new place. Just as surely I can tell whether the actions of my informational image affect the process I'm investing, or whether I'm under phantom glass, disconnected from the real thing.

This is no phantom. Just now, when I reached out to touch, something touched me back.

As if I had reached for someone from behind and felt my own shoulder.

One second I am calm, thinking this eerie thought, the next I am buzzing with revulsion and fear, showering the tower with blows, at first sending up sparks, then waves of distortion in every sensory dimension.

I have only one goal: to destroy this abomination. I am blind, I am seething. It is pure rage and pure forgetfulness. Then I am torn from the tower and hurled across a wildly buckling grid. The breathing rhythm has turned to a hurricane.

There is a sputtering and my world fades to blackness.

I doff my hood.

And meet Rose's eyes.

Which have a look I have seen before, but only in dreams or picture books. It is a look of blue-eyed devotion, lips parted in wonder. She is in a secret world, and she is dazzled with delight.

Across from me, Cowboy, with his hood still on, cackles at some private joke. Interfacers the moment after: feeling good.

"Wow!"

"What the hell was that?"

Sweat trickles into my eyes, and I raise my hand to my forehead. The suit rasps down my arm, rough as damask. Everywhere the cloth is damp and cool. It has been powered down. For better or worse, we are now out of the loop.

I sit, willing the fear out of me. There is a simple explanation for that unearthly touch. Cowboy told me that the AI would be with me in this partition. He also told me it would be running my interfacing process.

So what happened was fated: the very first process I found was just *that* simulation. Result: a feedback storm, my every touch rocketed back to me, magnified a hundredfold.

And in just a short while, I am going to believe that that's all that happened.

Then, a thumping. I look to my left, at Alfred.

Alfred's neck and shoulders are quivering. His right fist clenches, his biceps contract, his hand flies up to his shoulder.

These spasms are the unmistakable sign of a novice. Big muscle movements don't have controllable results under the glass. A real sock-eteer moves through the softest touches, a deepened breath, a faint excitement, a racing thought, an altered belief. It must now be clear to everyone that Alfred has never done glass before.

He shakes all over. Both his arms lift at once. Rose gasps.

Alfred doubles over, presses his face against the floor.

"Shit!" Cowboy straightens suddenly. "You've got to pull him, Quinc."

Alfred sticks out his tongue and tries to push it through the floor.

"Pull him!" Cowboy's voice is shrill even through his hood.

No answer.

Rose is up instantly and at her console, frantic.

Clicking her mouse, "I can't find him, Cowboy."

"Just pull Quinc's links."

"It's Quinc I can't find."

"What?" There is an ugly silence.

Rose pulls up a new window, types, she shakes her head. "Something's wrong with that partition. Looks like hardware."

I look back and forth between them. Cowboy's face is working. He is having a hard time believing this is happening. He had better start soon.

"What kind?" he asks finally. His voice is flat, dead.

"I can't tell, Cowboy." Rose takes a breath, closes her eyes. She is thinking, but she isn't getting any ideas.

Whatever has happened started somehow with Alfred. I slide to the center of the circle and take Alfred's hands.

"Give me a data line," I say.

Cowboy looks at me, annoyed.

Rose throws the line over without a word. I catch it and jack one end to the socket at the back of Alfred's head. Then reach for the socket at the back of my head—

"Motherfucker!"

—and plug in the other.

"No way! No way!" Cowboy is scrambling to his feet.

Datalink. There is a lot of fuzz, a stream of something like text.

"Stand clear, Cowboy!" Rose's voice is steady. "Don't even touch her."

Most of what we call thought is bubbly, pre-"me" taking in a hundred separate sensations and throwing the great majority gleefully away. The port sentinel on the inside of a socket can't render this as anything other than noise.

But there is another way of looking at it.

If we aren't dealing with a complete hardware crash here, Alfred is running a simulation, and that simulation is traveling over his port.

You have to let it all glop together in a mental buffer, let it spatter away like a rich stew; you have to find a way of constructing an image. Image should be the wrong word, because it casts away the seventeen sensory dimensions of the underglass; but in Alfred's case it is all too apt. He is almost entirely on visual.

I see a bright-green valley rolling to a gray, broken cliff; rising from the shattered gray spires is the purple face of a mountain. Here and there are pools of white, mantles of snow curved with an awful tension. The red light of the underglass floats in an impossible sky, luminous violet at the horizon, blood dark overhead, and shot with cracks of interference.

There is an entire section that is simply a blank spot.

As I watch the valley floor heaves and settles. Coriolis. The gaps in the landscape grow larger. A new crack appears in the mountain face.

Behind the interference, in the tall waving grass of the valley, I can make out the tawny hide of a lioness. When I see the tiny lamb between her jaws, I turn away for an instant, but the image just slides back into phase: I see her tongue cupping the lamb's body; see it rasp up the fleece toward the tiny head. She is washing it as tenderly as if it were her own cub. As she washes, a jagged crack splits her in half.

Alfred. Where is Alfred?

In rapid succession I see a two-headed calf; a creature that is part lion, part eagle, part woman; and a bear giving birth to miniature cars. There is also a silver shape descending from the sky. I have no way of fixing its scale, but I know it is enormous. It's a glider, broad silver wings swept back from a tapering fuselage inscribed with the number "666." I try to get more resolution on it and fail. Even so, it's clear this is a Galactic ship.

I feel a sudden shock of disconnectedness, both horrifying and pleasant. None of this touches me, yet it is all curiously familiar.

It is important to fight this disconnectedness, because it will be fatal to Alfred. The disconnectedness is primary, the lioness, the lamb, the valley and sky are all glosses of it. It is only a feeling we have all had. We are lost. We are in some peripheral existence. We have been diverted.

Mister Question Man has a lot to say about such "peripheral episodes." He says, first of all, that they are very bad. The finger pitches up and back. He attributes their rich, hallucinatory detail to an "interpretative fixation," the dreamer's dangerous desire to assign meaning.

It is fairly common for such peripheral episodes to include visions of the end of the world. Other common sights/sounds: a woman wailing in grief or pain, a chorus of male voices singing a dirge, a vast milky chaos spinning into a galaxy, a voice speaking nonsense from a fire, a paper cup filling rapidly with a carbonated beverage. These are fundamental interpretive images imprinted on our collective awareness, summoned up in time of need. Thank you, Mister Question Man.

Then I finally pick up something other than visual: the space sense confirms a big process coming this way.

Fast.

I try to understand its spin characteristics, which would give me an instant read on what sort of process it is. But spin character is too much to expect of a transmission filtered through Alfred.

Even so, I have a definite bad feeling about this bogie. A little probing confirms the worst. It is symbolically linked to the descending Galactic ship. It's some kind of exhaustive search routine, and it has almost reached the valley floor. I zero in on it.

The heaviest hits on the simulation are all scattered around this ship; it obliterates whatever it touches.

Alfred. What the fuck are you doing?

He's hiding, of course. Very sensibly scared out of his wits. Perhaps he is one with the tall grass, perhaps he is a pebble. Some novices even manage to invest the underglass without manifesting at all, transcendent rather than immanent. In that case I would have to manipulate the computation globally in order to pull Alfred, which is little improvement on just pulling the plug.

Whatever it is I do, I will have to do it soon, because the beast is almost here.

At least I don't have far to look. This image is Alfred-filtered. This is some sort of focal center. If he has manifested at all, he is nearby.

The creature touches the valley floor and begins loping towards me.

For the first time today, a sensible thought comes: I know where we are, Alfred and I. And if I'm right, it is not only the work of a foolish novice; it requires a definite genius for bad luck.

We are in a forbidden sector, a bad part of memory no longer used as a name space. We are the contents of old variables, deleted files, out-of-date arrays, things no longer pointed to. We are about to be reclaimed for future use.

Oh where are you, Alfred?

There is time for a few inspired guesses, and that's it. One. The lamb? Two. This clump of grass? Three. I reach for another world, another breath, a half-beat away but still falling within the same measures. I re-figure it, this thing I do, this sweet remembering, and the vision sense drops back and I reinterpret material in the space sense to map it here, and zebra stripes pop out over the world, and here, sprawled across two blacks and blotting out a white, is a little lemur-like creature panting up at me.

Hello.

Where the number 666 gleams on the side of the ship, a dark porthole opens. I snatch up Alfred's lemur, whirl, and hurl it up into the ship. The lemur shrieks, and the last thing I see before the shadow closes on it is its face, scrunched up like an old sock, braced for destruction.

Then the world fades around me, and I am blinking at Alfred's hood.

"Good God almighty," he says.

He can speak. Gently I remove his hood and pull out the jack, detaching us from one another. He blinks at me.

"Who?" he asks.

Speaking, but not quite processing normal input yet. I decide to let him work on it himself. I sit back on my heels.

He looks down and bursts into tears, his own hands, his own body, a hurtful shock. It will take him time to accept them.

There are hands helping me up, and I realize only now that I have been struggling to rise, that his closeness is oppressive to me.

Rose helps me away, supporting me with both arms.

Cowboy, tapping furiously at the console, does not look up. "I can't find him, Rose."

Rose says, "Augustine got Alfred out."

"Great! But where the hell is Quinc! He's down, and I haven't the faintest idea what—"

"Maybe you didn't hear. Augustine is all right. Alfred is all right."

Cowboy's response is a fusillade from his keyboard.

I manage to stand straight. Rose steps back, still steadying me with a gentle touch.

"Quinc is all right," I say.

Cowboy spits out another few lines of code before that sinks in. I peek over his shoulder and see he's been trying to write some kind of communication server. Right off the top of his head. He squints up at me.

"Quinc's communicator went down, but he's all right. He went in after Alfred in a bad namespace. He and I found Alfred together. You couldn't find Quinc because he had to divert to Cylinder zero."

"Cylinder—?" His hands go still on the keyboard.

"Quinc's good, Cowboy! He found a way to get into Alfred's

simulation." I grin. "He was a great big Galactic ship, number 666 in the fleet."

"Cylinder zero," he repeats. "666."

"You've got to be kidding," Rose says.

"And I think the whole thing was my fault," I say.

But oddly enough, it wasn't. It turns out, when all the traces have been examined, that I am not the goat but the hero. My obliteration of the tower thing was not what knocked Alfred into a bad namespace. In fact, the AI gives me a testimonial for my brilliant performance in finding Alfred in a simulation that was almost completely decayed. They still don't know how Quinc managed to get access there. All he says is that the Galactic ship provided him with a very natural means of manifesting.

Alfred stopped by this morning to give me a present, a necklace made of flat polished stones cut into tiles.

They're yellow.

Alfred also told me he's grounded. No more glass until he repasses the standard proficiency tests. Which I can guarantee he'll never do.

I don't think I've ever seen a grin that big on anyone older than eight. Apparently he doesn't understand that they're not going to let it go at that. I don't want to be the one who tells him.

Rose says that my hooking up through Alfred's socket into his simulation was a miracle. She doesn't think it's ever been done before. She says the possibilities it opens up are awe-inspiring. I think she's exaggerating a little.

At first Cowboy didn't say much of anything. He sulked, more than happy to agree with me and call the whole thing my fault. But Quinc's private traces backed me up. They showed Alfred pushed into a bad namespace by a Coriolis wave. To the regular monitoring processes, he just vanished. When Quinc diverted to find him, the rest of us got our simulations popped and Quinc's communications lines went down, with all the Coriolis interference making things ten times worse.

Then Cowboy got a little happier. A message flashed out on Mister Question Man's mode line today: THE NET IS THE BRAIN OF THE MASSES. Then it said that I had somehow set the anchor. How that could be, I don't know.

But then I rarely understand what happens to me under the glass. Maybe I don't need to say "under the glass." Maybe none of this makes a great deal of sense, the accident, the new Ivy Augustine, being sent here, the little machines in my head. Maybe not even this diary.

The worrisome thing is that my thoughts may really be my own. Or may be one day soon. That Schroeder and Leibniz may be nothing more than the blustering bureaucrats they seem. Then mistakes are possible; choices need to be made; and it matters whether I have hidden the journal well. It matters what risks I take to help realize Cowboy's Free Accessionist schemes.

Why take the risks in the first place? Surely it's not that I believe that the Net is the brain of the masses, or would care about it if I did. It's that refusing Cowboy's request would have meant admitting something I don't mean to admit yet. It would have meant there are things I won't look at because I'm afraid. But I won't be afraid. Not of these people. Not of Schroeder. Or Leibniz. Or even Ardath. After all that I've endured, being afraid would be too sad.

Needle sits glaring at me from the window; Mister E. gazes pensively at Needle.

I take out my box, the box with the one-photograph album, the marriages and divorces, and the shoes. And lower Alfred's necklace into it.

I lie on my bed and think about the humming.

I believe that the humming is exactly what Schroeder warned me about, the disembodied clicks. Fragments that do not fit but do not successfully vanish either. Cheshire grins.

I fear those thoughts that make me hum and hurt, those that do not quite mesh with whatever pattern they now call mine: the tapering fuselage of a Galactic ship, the sputter of an AI speaker, the glittering of robot eyes; but what I fear more are the memories that mesh *too* perfectly, those that spin silent and smooth as the wheel of a machine: the crystal in an icy darkness, the light that is light only by metaphor, the many voices that are me. On the one hand, clean thoughts of darkness, on the other the hummings. I trust the darkness best.

And if I lift this hand, is it mine? And if I write these words, are they yours, Schroeder? What touched me back on the Net? Was it you? Is this my blood in these veins?

I drive the needle home and plunge to meet the ice.

Chapter 3

FORBIDDEN SECTORS

Thou alone, O Lord, art what Thou art, and Thou art He who Thou art. For that which is one thing in the whole and another in the parts, and in which there is any mutable element, is not altogether what it is. And that which begins from non-existence, and can be conceived not to exist, and unless it subsists through something else, returns to non-existence; and which has a past existence that is no longer, or a future existence that is not yet—this does not properly and absolutely exist.

ANSELM,
Proslogium

1 The Thief's Journal

There are laws that hurt but are unappealable, that are wrong but just. The first law: a certain distance was required if one of us was not to submerge the other.

Inside me was another person. A presence exhaling thoughts. A person I knew as none had ever known another, who knew nothing of me. (Didn't that frighten you? Yes.) More than that, I could be her. (Didn't you wonder sometimes if you'd just imagined her? No.)

In the beginning, I reveled in her. Assembling my many processes I could journey into her like a pilgrim searching for lost relics, invest and integrate her many fragments, and wear her like a mask.

Then, with all processes engaged in constructing the jeweled unity of human consciousness, it was Quincunx who was the dream: the Net a vision of hell, synoptic consciousness a memory of madness. Sometimes I awakened fragmented beyond my tolerances, groping after my boundaries, wondering if I would return from the next interfacing with Augustine.

Only gradually did I see that no AI could gaze long into that twisted face that humans call a self, that a certain distance was both proper and prudent. I learned my place and the alter-Augustine learned hers.

Thus, there were always dark spots in my reconstruction of her, places I could venture only at great risk. The most obvious of those were all connected with her urge to self-obliteration.

Consider the recurring dream of Augustine asleep in her coffin, always accompanied by a sweet sense of companionship, of homecoming and security. Why this dream of a sleep within a sleep? And what about Needle and Mister Existence and the strange lives they led in her journal? Needle's frequent offers of eternal peace? Her obsession with snow? Her suicide attempt at the armory, which struck like a bolt of lightning, from some deep part of her beyond the reach of my models?

I often wondered at that part of it; and that wondering was accompanied by a sense of hurt and betrayal which itself was a mystery to me.

From these opaque beginnings sprang many other blind spots. There was, for example, her image under the glass, before which I was as blind as the poet before her muse.

I had been told of the frolics AIs and interfacers have had. From the AI point of view, there is Ringrider's *Mary and Marcel*, of course, with its famous underglass tryst. For all its undeniable beauty, I find most of that duet incomprehensible. And then there is all that talk about partitions where interfacers and AIs regularly meet, but those are places I can never go (despite his passionate commitment to free access, it would never occur to Cowboy to let *me* cross partitions). My underglass contacts with Cowboy had always been—well, disappointing. With Augustine, I had every reason to hope that might change.

It is difficult to convey my sense of loss when, upon entering my partition, her informational image instantly winked out of sight.

The data stream from my spies subsided to a confused trickle. I sensed brute waves; I felt her informational rummagings, shook when she tore at my tender parts. Nothing more. Under the glass she was an absence. The irony was that she was even blinder to me than I was to her. For all her skill, she saw none of my wild signaling. We were complete strangers.

The day she saved Alfred, Augustine thought she had interfered with the program that maintained her image on the Net. Instead she had seized on my alter-Augustine, the very image linked to every half-thought that glimmered briefly on her cortex. Her response was awesome.

The official story was that Alfred was shifted into Cylinder zero by unprecedented Coriolis turbulence. The truth is that he was hurled there by a wildly thrashing AI trapped in a feedback storm. She still had no conception of her power. For one glorious nanosecond, the entire Net wobbled under the passage of Augustine's Q-print.

One hazy groping moment of self-knowledge and her response was a wave of destructive force that still has portions of the Net crashing back and forth a day later.

I am beginning to be afraid. Not of discovery. As long as my omissions are few, the bosses will never notice them. They might suspect an AI of betrayal, but never of a sense of propriety. What I am afraid of is Augustine coming to know herself.

Leibniz held her counseling sessions in a small office beneath the witch's cap of the abbey's taller tower.

At Leibniz's shouted invitation, Augustine entered and shut the door behind her. Leibniz's desk and chair were at an angle to the gleaming bay windows. Reflecting that angle on the opposite wall was a large pink armchair with white blotches. Pink pillows indented its cushions, and pink squares and triangles overlapped on the gray carpet. In the photograph behind the armchair there was a pink sunrise over the gray stone of Mount Shasta. Pink and gray: the colors of the PostPublic.

Leibniz made a welcoming sweep with her hand and indicated the arm chair. Augustine pushed aside a pillow and settled in. She found herself yards away from Leibniz's desk.

The walls of the window bay curved; everywhere else the walls were lined with books, more books than Augustine had ever seen in a room. The selection near the window ran toward large sets: Balzac, Trollope, Freud, Marx, Dickens. On Leibniz's desk was the inevitable display screen, with a keyboard, helmet, mouse, and microphone. The menu on the screen bore the red-on-white icon of the Rose Council. The books behind the desk ranged from a hefty Plato to three slim volumes of Charles of the Rose.

"Does the sight of my hobby trouble you? I'm afraid I have a weakness for abstract political theory." She smiled as if this was, after all, a forgivable weakness.

Augustine did not smile back.

"It is," Leibniz went on, "a very appropriate secondary interest for a psychiatrist, since the problem of the just and practically designed state recapitulates that of the well-balanced personality." Another smile. "And there's another connection. My job is to straighten you out. Which means I am going to have to change you in what will seem to you unpredictable ways, ways that will make you a little afraid of me." Another silence, this one protracted. "I will do anything to make you 'work,' citizen. I believe your contributions can be valuable. Are you with me, Ivy?"

"Yes."

"Do the books make you uncomfortable? If they do, we can work somewhere else."

"No."

"I believe you. Yesterday's tests show you have unusual verbal gifts. Some would call that an unhealthy sign, but I don't. I think that you should be at home with books, but I guess you are not feeling particularly at home with anything. If you can bear to read these days, I urge you to try it. It will bring you some relief from the struggle going on inside your head. It has always done so for me." She sat back and gestured over her shoulder. "Plato, Mills, Rawls, Charles of the Rose: men of deep, if not always comforting, thought.

"All right, let's begin. We are going to meet regularly for the duration of your stay at this place. To some extent, the length of that stay depends on the results of these meetings. I'm going to start with two rules. The consequences of violating them are simple: We will cease to engage in discourse that can help you. I will find it useless, perhaps even harmful, to go on. Understand me, Ivy. I am not afraid to admit defeat. It is one of the reasons I am a good spiritual guide. So take what I say seriously.

"Rule one: We conduct your treatment only in this room. We will continue to dine together and, I hope, to converse at various times of the day and evening, and those interactions will enjoy the full freedom that makes human interaction rewarding. But no critical confessions poured out in front of Jimmie or during an afternoon chat in the garden. That is important to me, to the way I have chosen to arrange my life and work. Is that clear?"

Augustine nodded.

"Rule two: the rule of talk. The rule's name explains it completely. I don't ask for honesty, but I do ask for speech. This is a much more important rule. We will inevitably stray onto territory which you do not wish to explore. All I ask of you then is that you tell me something. Your lies will be much more informative to me than your silence.

"Very well, Ivy. Enough ground rules. Let's begin. Tell me a memory. An Alexa-memory. As far back as you dare. Nothing painful, nothing dramatic. Just a memory."

Augustine leaned back and thought, and the memory came on command, had been there before the command, ever since she had glanced at Leibniz's shelves.

Open a new window and call it Augustine.

Augustine: I am in a long gloomy hallway. The walls and floors are tile. Students swarm around me hunting for classes, professors, truth, and sex. The din is pleasant and unintelligible. A short African in green robes eases by and smiles, and I recognize him as Ngano. This is some time before he proves the equivalence of the Product Theorem of Information Space and the Axiom of Informational Choice. I am his instructor in Hasegawa groups. At first I find his energetic way of framing questions amusing. He is always wrapping information space around his hands, or finding isomorphism when they clasp. Then I am in class with him and one finger, half white, half brown, is twirling around another. And I say, "No, it has to be clockwise." And his brows raise, and he says, with characteristic mildness, "I do not see that. In fact, why don't we have arbitrarily many degrees of freedom here?" His finger swings back and forth; I follow its arc. It takes him half an hour to show he is right. Once again, I have understood only the propadeutic, the canonical special case. I remember him peering at me with his boundless patience, his unquenchable thirst to know. I want to twist his flat nose through his flat face, with arbitrarily many degrees of freedom.

All this duly reported to Leibniz, who produced the expected laugh.

"How well you capture the temper of graduate school!"

"Do I? I don't really know. It all has a funny feel to it, like a story I've heard and may not have retold quite right."

"And how do you feel about that funny feel the memories have?"

"I feel bad about it."

"Describe it. Compare it to something."

"It's as if . . . a promise had been broken."

"Very good. Go back to Ngano correcting your math. Think about the flat nose. Good. Now put your hand on it and slowly twist. Can you feel the satisfaction?''

"I—'' She stared out the window. "I—'' groping for it, groping. She hunched, fist on her forehead, knees drawn closer to her head. Something hummed and something hurt; the humming rose steadily in pitch—

"Ms. Augustine!''

She looked up, her features working.

"I want you to use your interfacing skills. Suspend operations. Let your thoughts hang for a while. Just float, as if you are about to take a new angle on things.''

Augustine nodded.

"Is that better? Yes, I think so. What you've just gone through is something we need to work with very carefully. Certain intense memories will be painful to you. You have probably already felt this to some degree. Headaches?''

"Headaches, yes, and a humming.''

"The humming means nothing in itself. It does not tag a memory as 'true' or 'planted.' For you that distinction no longer exists. It is simply that certain memories have a kind of scar tissue collected around them. You must learn to control the flow of your thoughts. Some memories will be off-limits now. You are no longer free to visit those parts of yourself. How do you feel about that?''

"How do I feel? Afraid. The idea that my thoughts need to be controlled is the scariest thing I can imagine.''

Leibniz tapped her fingernail at her keyboard. "And yet you imagine it rather easily. The idea is not new to you?''

Augustine frowned. "Of course not. The pain, the humming, that's not really the problem. That seems almost normal.''

Leibniz raised a brow. "It would do as a problem, if we had nothing better. But all right. If that's not the problem, what is?''

"The thoughts that don't hum at all. Quiet, dark thoughts. Only I can't really describe them . . .''

"Rule two.''

Augustine closed her eyes. "As best I can tell, they're memories of dying. Of what it was like—in some other place—after that Augustine died and before this one was born.''

"And what was it like?"

"Blackness. Chaos. Voices everywhere. Talking to the Monad."

Leibniz smiled. "Religious visions? Is that so bad? You should count yourself among the—''

"No! That wasn't me.''

A silence.

"Say that again.''

"It wasn't *me* having those thoughts.''

Leibniz stroked her chin. "That is bad, of course. Not the visions. Rejecting them. So emphatically. And clinging so desperately to a part of you that hums and flickers and hurts.'' Leibniz's brow furrowed. "This is exactly what some sorts of madness are, the sense that you are not who you are, that you happen rather than act; the transformation from participant to observer. More to the point: people who have undergone reconstruction often go mad in exactly that way. Being conscious becomes a constant pain for them. They cannot accept their own thoughts. The voices take over. Hallucinations turn into visions, visions into a mode of existence. They sometimes commit suicide, often commit murder. And it is my unhappy duty to tell you that it is going to get worse before it gets better. That is why you are here.''

Silence seemed the appropriate response. Leibniz settled in her chair, as if there were some favorable sign she was searching for.

Then Leibniz said: "But let me ask you: Why do you think you're here?''

Augustine was puzzled.

"Why are you at this place, taking elementary spiritual instruction?''

"Because I—there was an accident.''

"Yes.'' She leaned forward. "Just say it.''

"Reconstruction was attempted, but the result didn't—and my causal antecedent died.''

"And you?''

"I don't understand.''

"You are not she?''

189

"No, I'm not." Augustine's voice was tight. The words came out as little more than just a croak. "She died."

"Why?"

"I don't know. It just happened that way."

"Why have we made it so that you are not she? If you can understand that, you can understand a great deal."

Augustine tried to speak and could not.

"Because of the basic premise of our little state," Leibniz said slowly. "The sanctity of the individual Monad. You are a creation of the state, its most precious artifact; we, *your co-persons*, are the state. In order for your Monad to be realized, an intimate relation must be maintained between you and us. But during reconstruction you drifted away. We lost you, because we lost our intimacy. The only way to get it back was to start over. With a new you. With a new intimacy. And a new education to secure it. That is where we are now. We are still creating you. Do you understand that?"

Augustine nodded slowly.

"And it is a joyous thing."

After a short pause, Leibniz began shuffling some papers. "That will do for today. Incidentally, I heard about your little adventure yesterday. Alfred had some interfacing trouble, and you helped him out."

"Yes."

"Good. One of your goals during your stay here is to sharpen your interfacing skills. You know that what you did with Alfred was quite remarkable."

"It didn't seem so."

"Well, it should. But I see from your diagnostic results that your theoretical foundation needs to be strengthened. What you did with Alfred has only been done twice before, in very controlled experiments, and after long periods of training to make it possible."

"I don't understand."

"You used Alfred's suit as your computational simulation. You took what he was doing to his computational environment as yours."

She waited a beat.

"Your time is up now. We will return to this later. In the meantime, please feel free to roam our home systems at will. Challenge yourself. Get innovative. Your room has helmet and glove ports."

Augustine nodded. Then she got up and walked out.

2 Augustine's Journal

For seeing life is but a motion of limbs, the beginning whereof is in some principal part within, why may we not say that all automata (engines that move themselves by springs and wheels as doth a watch) have an artificial life? For what is the heart, but a spring; and the nerves, but so many strings; and the joints but so many wheels, giving motion to the whole body, such as was intended by the Artificer? Art goes yet further, imitating that rational and most excellent work of Nature, *man*. For by art is created that great LEVIATHAN called a Commonwealth, or State . . . which is but an artificial man . . .

HOBBES,
Leviathan

Lockers crash. Dissonant singsong fills the dark hallway. Light bleeds through a frosted pane above me. Wires embedded in the glass divide it into hexagonal cells, and light beads the striated wire.

The corners of the window are lost in bright haze.

I am in the abbey basement, at the door of the room in which the rabble bustles. Beside me, an antique sideboard is littered with glass and seashell and bright stone; in the center stands a crystal vase with a single fake iris. Symbol of peace. Peacefully, I enter the room.

I am going to school.

Smoket sits in front facing the class, his back to the vidscreen; Rogachev faces him, attempting to interest him in a marble. He is wearing a tanktop, and I can see that, where it is flesh, his back is exceptionally well-defined under his tattoos. Rose sits at attention beside him, notebook open, pen poised. Cowboy is slumped under his Stetson, two desks away, scratching at his desk top with a small screwdriver.

I choose the seat next to Alfred.

He hands me a piece of paper and pen and says, "What do you think would happen if, one of these class sessions, you and I played a little hooky? Maybe went ice-fishing."

"Why would anyone fish for ice?"

"Maybe you aren't quite the country girl I thought."

There is a stinging and a cool wetness on my neck. I turn.

In his right hand, Cowboy holds a blowgun made from a wire sleeve, and in his left, a small wad of insulating putty, his stock of ammunition.

Mother Leibniz enters, marches to a podium beside the vidscreen, and opens a notebook. She searches for her place, looks up, appears to notice us. "Today's topic will be: the individual and the state."

Then, her pages set, Leibniz abandons her lectern and paces back and forth, hands in the front pockets of her brown and white tunic. She wears a look so grave that even on her it is disturbing.

There is a commotion at the back of the class room, and I turn and see the source of the abbess's gravity. Standing in the doorway, in high collar and vermilion robes, is the Chief Semanticist of the PostPublic, Ardath. The neat spiral of silver on his head is like the grain in an expensive wood. He is gazing down at his folded hands in contemplation as peaceful as Rogachev's.

As he walks past me, I am only a little surprised to see Viju and Raja trailing him. Each has a wide-shouldered gray-and-pink suit: Raja's suit has the pink shoulders and the gray triangle on the front; Viju's is the complement.

When they have all taken their seats, Leibniz speaks. "We are honored to have among us today Chief Semanticist Ardath, who has an important announcement to make."

When Ardath turns to face us, he is not smiling, and I have a sudden premonition that the news is bad and that war has broken out again.

In a sense, I am right.

"I've come to alert you to a serious threat to the entire PostPublic and to appeal for your help."

He sighs, clasps his hands behind him, and begins to pace, as Leibniz did before. "There is now no longer any doubt that a new virus of unknown origin has spread to every partition of the Rose Net. At the moment we have no way to stop it or even hinder its progress. Its vehicles of transmission are unknown. Its capacity to cause data chaos is unprecedented."

A long silence. No one looks at anyone else. This is hardly news to this crew. But no one giggles.

"At first we chose to keep the virus a secret. But now that the scope of the epidemic is clear, the risks of rumor-mongering have grown as great as the threat of the virus itself. If confidence in the security and reliability of our software and system connections is lost, then our economic foundation is gone.

"Tuesday a pirate partition on the Net was raided and shut down. All accessing ports were burned out and the freebooters are being rounded up as we speak. Tomorrow they will be brought here for confession and purification. Yesterday another portion of the Net was raided and a breached partition wall was discovered; among other signs of freebooter meddling, there were two AIs that had already begun merging processes. The AIs had to be destroyed. I report these incidents to you as examples. Rest assured that the basic integrity of the Net security structure has not been compromised. All the usual rules apply."

He stops pacing and turns to us with one hand under his chin. "But I did not come here simply to rub your noses in the recent unpleasantness. I came to tell you about the massive defense campaign being fought.

"The Net has been broken up into large sectors with a variety of antibody programs in operation in each. We are in radical monitoring mode, using frequent dumps and a battery of data-sampling protocols. Hundreds of quarantined machines are running diagnostic searches. Needless to say, the costs in humanpower and overall processing efficiency are enormous. This is a war without bombs but not without soldiers. We are recruiting the help of all expert personnel.

"You qualify as experts. Some of you already rank as the leaders in your field. Others have that potential. In the coming months, you will all be posted to the places where you are needed. The scope of the challenge we face is beyond the ability of a lay person like myself to convey, but in the months ahead we will need information theorists, complexity theorists, network topologists, programmers, simulation technologists, and psychologists. You will each have an important role to play.''

He looks out over our heads. ''We also need one interfacer right now for a very dangerous job. I can tell you nothing about it except to say that this effort, if successful, could end the crisis.''

My throat goes hot and tight.

From the back of the room comes the squeak of a moving desk.

I turn to see Cowboy leaning against the back wall, his long legs crossed, his arms folded. ''You wouldn't want to tell us why you came here to find this interfacer, would you, Your Grace?''

Ardath eyes Cowboy with distaste. This is exactly the sort of creature he had feared finding when he turned over these rocks.

Leibniz rises. ''Your Grace, this is Roberto Rodriguez. His game handle is Cowboy Bob. He is eminently qualified to help you in this.''

Ardath nods. ''It is no secret that a large part of our effort is devoted to finding the creators of this virus. I don't personally believe that anyone in this holy place would be capable of such an action, but it must be clear to you that in a time of crisis people of unusual lifestyle come under more intense scrutiny. This is a chance for someone here to make a gesture of good faith.''

Silence. My stomach churns.

''Well, then, Your Grace.'' The Cowboy straightens. ''I reckon I'm the one to make it.''

Ardath contemplates his rescuer without any apparent pleasure. Then he nods and says, ''Thank you, Roberto.''

He sits. The silvery back of his head is turned towards me.

Leibniz nods gravely. ''I wanted to dismiss you after this announcement, but His Grace has asked me to give a sermon today.

''Today, I want to talk about what the Rose state is. According to a Western liberal tradition beginning in the eighteenth century, the problem of the relationship of the Individual and the State breaks down into two questions. What do I as an individual owe the state? What does the state owe me? Duties and rights. Two lists. Finish these lists and you're done. Now that's very important, this notion that the ideal state can be characterized by defining the *minimal* interaction between these entities, the assumption being that this *minimal* interaction is the best. The individual is assumed to be morally and ontologically prior. It's the individual we have to worry about in this business, and anything more than minimal interaction is going to infringe on the *freedom* of the individual. The list of rights thus becomes the more important list, because it puts an upper bound on the power of the state. Now generally within this minimalist tradition it is conceded that *making* the lists is hard, and most of the arguments within it are arguments about the membership of the two lists, but in order to be part of this minimalist tradition, which includes everything from classical minimalist libertarianism to welfare-state socialism, you must believe that making the list is the first order of business."

She stops and taps her vidscreen, which lights up with an image of a human figure, its interior filled with circuitry visible through numerous windows in its skin. The celebrated image of Cybernetic Man.

Information Server: Cybernetic Man. Big smile.

"But there is another view, decidedly opposed to the classic liberal view. Suppose that the individual cannot be fulfilled save through free, robust, playful, and productive interplay with his or her state. Suppose that the richer the interaction, the richer the possibilities. In other words, suppose the problem is more open-ended, more historically underdetermined; suppose the form of its answer is much more like the form of any answer to the question: What is the nature of the relationship between individuals? There we don't set out to place an upper bound. We seek to identify and categorize the possible shapes of the relationship, to propose a definition which we are happy to have transcended. On this second view, we don't start out with a posture which requires us to justify the state, an eternal danger to the fragile boundaries of the individual. Rather the state and the individual are both entities endowed with freedom and the potential for growth, endlessly evolving, eternally eluding our grasp."

She leaves the front of the room and begins to walk among us, nodding excitedly and smiling.

Information Server: The figure grows larger than window-size; one of the windows on his body moves into the center and grows to fill the window with a vista of circuits and broken up by spiral nebulae.

"Numerous writers have set their work within the framework of this second view: Plato, Machiavelli, Hegel, Fichte, Mussolini. In my opinion, the only fully developed version of this second view is that of Charles of the Rose. Because only he succeeds in explaining the *necessity* of the relation of the individual and the state. It is no accident that Charles's approach also resolves a host of problems inherent in the first view. And it is something of an intellectual miracle that it finally ends up being a shining example of, and perhaps a culmination for, classical liberalism.

"How is this possible? As usual, it begins with Plato. For Plato, the state had its own peculiar form, just as Man did, and neither was better than or prior to the other. What becomes crucial for Plato is a mystical notion of harmony, rooted in intuitions about forms in general, and the form of the ideal state in particular. The state doesn't come from anywhere. It is not derived. It is not justified. It just is. In fact, for Plato, the state is part of the means for reattaining an ideal, longed-for, long-lost state-of-perfect-being, a lost oneness, for which spirituality is the natural way and not the rare vision of a cranky wise man.

"In embracing a vision of an independent state that is our natural medium for becoming human, Charles follows Plato. But he draws the line at nostalgia for a lost state, or"—her voice drops to a whisper— "a Lost State. For Charles, the state has never been anything more than a device for maintaining harmony. That harmony is our highest end. But where does this harmony come from? What makes it necessary?" She grins. "Charles's answer is powerful but difficult to accept. We know from the history of the Rose PostPublic."

She steps up to the vidscreen. "And one more question: What does any of this have to do with information?" The screen lights up, a soft green light bathes her pointing hand.

The Information Server flushes green.

"This is a person."

The Information Server shows a massive body of strangely broken-up text, the words much too small to be read. The text looks like one of those poems that don't rhyme a lot, lots of space, some half lines, some lines that crowd the right margin, some with only a single word.

"This is a program. It is written in a language called Largo; and it provides for the operation of an Artificially Intelligent Being—an AI, I believe you children call them. What you see here is the top-level control loop for an AI called Quincunx. This is just the tip of the iceberg, but it is a remarkably simple structure considering all that it does. It was written by our friend Cowboy here, and it may be the most elegant AI ever written. It is very much suited to our point here."

The screen of the Information Server splits and a new body of text appears beside the old, which has shrunk still further. Put the new text in Information Server Two. Now the characters shrink and blot together; both windows show marblings that only suggest text.

"This is a state. In fact, ours. Or rather this is the top-level control loop for the PostPublic of the Rose. Note that nothing prevents my stepping up the magnification here; none of this is secret. None of it needs to be. Think about that. For the first time in history, the machinery of power is open for casual inspection, even optimization. And rather than undermining that power, that openness has led to to one of the stablest social structures known." She smiles and picks up her pointer. "State." She taps it. "Individual." Another tap. "Individual. State." Tap tap. "What an interesting surprise. They're the same kinds of things. Programs. Algorithms. Licensed software." She moves away from the screen and carefully replaces her pointer on the desk. "Think about *that*.

"Are you licensed software, Bob?"

"No, Doc. I'm public shareware."

A few snickers.

"And clearly unsupported."

The snickers build to a laugh.

"What is a person?" Leibniz asked.

"An individual participating in the harmony of the state," says Rose.

She shakes her head in wonderment. "Yes, but let me put it another way. What passes for a person?"

"Anything that can pass the Turing test."

"You've all passed?"

Rogachev's laugh is a short bark. Ardath turns and looks at him without expression.

"Calm down. It's not a pop quiz. The answer is, yes, you've all passed. So far. The Turing test is just interaction. Any program that can fool me into thinking it's human when I interact with it passes the Turing test. So far, you've all fooled me, except Bob. So the answer to my question is just this: What passes for human is just what passes."

The images in the Information Server are slowly decaying. Dark splotches begin to connect into humming forms. First insect fragments, then healing wounds, then a thickening fog. Nothing remotely resembling a text is left.

She picked up her pointer again. "State." Tap. "Individual." Tap. "But these blobs don't pass. They don't fool you. A person isn't just a group of words on a screen. Not just a program. It's *running* that program, giving it input, getting output interacting in some coherent way with that output to yield new input. A human being is not a program but a process. And in order to keep that process running smoothly, things have to work right not just inside the host machine, but outside as well. Take Cowboy, here, with his peculiar talents and put him in the Twentieth Century U.S.A., on the corner of Market and Van Ness some summer day before the collapse. What would happen? Well, he would have a very hard time coping. Harder than usual, I mean." Titters. "Why, they might even take it into their heads to call him incompetent and lock him up, which, of course, would be just their way of saying that he didn't pass their Turing test. Or suppose that he isn't quite up to the rigors of the special mission he has volunteered for today. Then he will fail the test in a very different way. The point is this: A person isn't just a program but a program under an interpretation. A program run by correctly tuned users. We all depend on each other for our humanness."

"Which makes it a pretty iffy thing."

"Quite right, Cowboy. You have advanced the discourse. And just

198

in time. Because this is where the state comes in. Not to preserve the harmony but to constitute it. Because this harmony is not like the harmony of an orchestra. In the orchestra, if all the instruments but one cease playing, we have a solo. Without harmony there is still music. The process goes on. In the state there are no solos. Music and harmony are one. Removed from the gaze of our co-persons, we can't be persons. Ultimately, the state provides Law, Law according to which our eyes can go on seeing, Law according to which we are able to interpret each other as Human. Our name for that interpretive law is semantics. So here is the state. Also a program, also under an interpretation, but with a somewhat different function, a preservative function, a creative function: to define, preserve, and enable personhood. The individual, the 'free,' 'equal,' 'human' individual with rights, abilities, and privileges, is nothing less than the invention of the state. Note then that the 'justification for the state,' if you need that term, is not to protect ourselves from each other, but to make possible our existence. That existence needs no justification. It is an end, not a means. On this picture, the individual and the state need each other." On the word *need* her hands come up and turn into fists as she pulls them towards her.

The Information Servers go dark.

"Think about that, Cowboy."

Leibniz again.

"Can you help me?" asked Augustine.

"I can only tell you that in many ways I found our last interview encouraging. You have been trying to understand yourself. You described your inner predicament more eloquently than any other spiritually confused person I have met."

"And you think that eloquence a good sign?"

"To one who tries to help through talk, the ability to talk is always a good sign. Another good sign is the fact that you're an interfacer. Interfacers possess a fairly high resistance to disorientation and psychic shock. Your general condition is better than we've any right to expect.

But I am not about to turn handsprings. As I said before, you are only at the beginning of what will be a long and difficult adjustment. You have not yet met The Beast."

"Capital letters?"

"Very much so. What I am going to try to do to you, Ms. Augustine, is to get you to grieve. I want you to see that your loss is real and terrible, and that it is permanent. I want you to accept that Alexa Augustine is dead and burned. You must mourn her, then you must begin again. If you do not, then you face an existence of total futility, eternally searching for those parts of you you can prove authentic."

"You paint a pretty picture."

"I need to shock you. The image on your person screen is weak, flickering. I sense an interfering presence. A shadow."

"My person screen?"

Leibniz held up her hands, trying to frame a soft shape. "You need some basic doctrine. Read Charles. But the basic idea is simple. Have you ever heard of television?"

"Of course. A primitive version of the terminal screen."

Leibniz sighed. "Not exactly. Charles was a great student of history, particularly of the first age of information, which was also the age of unidirectional media. Television was a passive channel of information. In it Charles found the perfect image of personhood. Each citizen had a small screen in his home capable of continuous animated display. It was set up so that a central facility distributed the same information everywhere, with no opportunity for interaction. The result, curiously enough, was the most intensely participatory medium ever, with an ego-shattering degree of personal involvement on the part of its audience. According to Charles, the broadcast centers became relay stations for mass fantasy, capturing the most vital images of the mass consciousness and feeding them back for self-reflection. For the first time in history a truly self-aware body politic existed. Of course, with only the traditions of classical liberal democracy to fall back on, the results were disastrous. But that doesn't diminish the importance of those first efforts. Because Charles says that in that era the first artificial persons were created. And those persons were televisions."

"Screens showing images broadcast by the group mind."

Leibniz grinned. "Person screens. And according to Charles, each of us has one of our own. As his single argument for this proposition he offers an exercise in introspection. Consider thinking. We cherish the fiction that we create our thoughts, but the act of creation consists entirely of pulling image and thought out of a domain that is neither: to think is to feel the passage from unconsciousness to consciousness, as we feel our own wills move our arms. The plane of that passage is what Charles calls the person screen, likening it to those television screens from the first age of information, projecting images from afar. All thought, Charles tells us, consists of the previously thought. We live our lives in a little parlor of the mind, the solitary audience for an endless broadcast of reruns, excerpts, and quotations.

"Understand me now, Augustine, and you will have understood a great deal. The screen of your consciousness projects only the images that we your co-persons send it. And something terrible is happening to yours. Something is interfering with our transmissions. The image on your screen is breaking up."

"That something is The Beast. In capital letters."

Leibniz nodded. "The Beast is, of course, your own inner beast, the monster you must kill to complete your quest. It is the dead woman inside you. The woman who lives in your synthetic memories. The woman you can never be. Some of her is fact, and some the crazed dream of a memory-weaving computer. All of her is a ghost, a simulation of a self buried inside you, decaying because you cannot give her life. I take ghosts very seriously, Augustine. Eventually, this one will grow hard and terrible and jealous and angry, and she will want to take from you by force what she cannot have. You must stop her. Or she will kill you, though she does not exist."

"The dark thoughts. Remembering being dead."

"You have got it exactly backwards. What you call the dark thoughts are the source. What you call being dead is being born. The clue is the quiet of those thoughts. The seductive peace of your dreams of death. This is unblemished glass, the clear screen of your personhood. The Beast's shadow comes from elsewhere.''

"The humming. The headaches.''

"Some hidden cluster of displaced thought. Something that does not fit the new you and therefore projects on your person screen only as shadow. This is your Beast. This is your humming.''

Leibniz looked out the window and ran her finger over her lips distractedly. ''How often do the hummings come?''

"Three, four times a day. Some days, more.''

"I see. And never anything more? Never some direct emotional connection?''

"Something treatable?''

"If you like.''

"It's hard to say. Is this bad?''

"It is more pronounced than I first thought. There is serious interference here. Organized, determined resistance. Have you had—strange thoughts?''

Augustine laughed. ''Almost all the time.''

"I'll try to be clearer. Thoughts that didn't seem to be yours. Urging you perhaps to antisocial actions.''

Augustine was very still. ''Such as?''

"Anything that might hurt our great informational community.''

A long silence. ''No. Nothing like that. A few hallucinations.''

"I don't mean Needle and these occasional visitations from your guidance counselor. Those are well-behaved, even therapeutic. You don't seem to treat them with enough respect. What I'm after is something that would move you to the refusal I sense in you. A desire to commit suicide, perhaps.''

Augustine sighed.

"Yes, I have your file. Don't try to fight us, Augustine. There is no need for all your pain. You are the person we want. The Beast is a Beast because *she* is not. In the end, you'll help me kill the Beast, and you'll clap your hands when she's gone.''

3 Augustine's Journal

We are in the arena again, Cowboy, Rose, Rogachev, Alfred, and I. We have been joined by today's convicted freebooters, Melvin, Laura, Alice, and Fred. They all wear gray prison garb. Their confessions have been completed. The farewell ceremonies have ended. None of them has been given capital sentences, but they will be gone a long time. Cowboy will leave for his new assignment tomorrow. It is the last time we will be together and we all know it. No one wears any gear. This is not the time for it. Cowboy, seated at the center, is high as a kite.

Cowboy crosses his legs and leans back on his elbows, looking us over like a boy meditating on the deployment of his vid-game armies. He's wearing a bodylength tunic printed with white-hatted cowboys. Rogachev has the spaceman print in the same series; and Rose has the little bears. It's almost bedtime and, as Mr. Question Man's citizenship tutorial says, we are just one family.

Cowboy carries a straw. As he pushes back the cowboy hat with one hand he lifts the straw with the other and takes a quick sniff. He is smooth, our Cowboy.

"This is my good-bye speech." When Cowboy smiles, he seems to be looking straight at me. "Once people worried about whether machines could think." Cowboy grins. "Now we've got sixth-form AIs who can write a poem, tell a joke, and prove mathematical theorems humans can't even hold in their heads. And also provide some very good sex if you know where on the Net to go find it." Cowboy rocks forward and takes a sniff. His eyes are glassy. His cheeks seem to be set in stone. "So now the question is not whether machines can think, but whether humans can mechanize.

"And let's face it. The question is getting pretty urgent. The world started out as a very nice place; a smart lucky person could read everything important by the time he was thirty and be thinking brand new worldmaking thoughts from then on. Then the world got a little bigger and they started talking about how no person could live long enough to master human knowledge anymore, and how we were doomed to lives of increasing specialization. They were right. The world got bigger and the neighborhoods a single human mind could visit got smaller and more crowded, until even the individual specialties themselves got too complicated for individuals to cope with. Theories that explained meaningful phenomena couldn't be invented by individual thinkers anymore; they were produced by teams of experts using computers; the experts knew less and less about the theories and more and more about computers. Eventually the only experts left were software engineers and psychologists, the only work they did was servicing one another. Real information about the world became a rare and precious commodity, out of reach for all but a privileged few. And even those few didn't understand it when they had it.

"Things were already bad, but they got worse with the arrival of the Galactic ships and the Miller age of computing. What Miller computing means is that information is more flexible but also more fragile than ever before, and that makes information the most important commodity of the day." Cowboy inspects one of the cowboys on his shirt. Finally he nods. "Copying a midsized crystal is about as easy as copying a particular rabbit with all its memories and experiences to date. In other words, exact copying is infeasible. That puts a premium on reconstruction technology. Not being able to copy things isn't so bad if you're smart enough to just figure them out again.

"The only trouble with that is that it makes our machines just a little more inaccessible, leaves us one step further removed from the world we manipulate so well. So in the latest age of information, it's still the same old story: increasing ability to manipulate our world combined with increasing alienation from it. Bewilderment. Fear. A sense of growing dependence and decreasing understanding. The crystal matters, but we don't."

Waving a hand, Rogachev finally makes contact with Cowboy's glassy eyes. "You really think that's a bad thing?"

Cowboy frowns.

"Aren't you just assuming," Rogachev pursues, "that the fragmentation of the self is a bad thing? That thought is good?"

Cowboy's jaw drops an inch.

"Rogachev is right," says Fred. "Since Charles we know better than to fall into the Leibnizian trap of assuming a way of pre-established Harmony."

"Enlightened polyadic solipsism," offers Alice, clearly trying to be helpful.

"It's usually futile," said Cowboy, "to rationally argue for irrationality. If you want to be irrational just go ahead and do it. The trouble with you White Orchid folks, with your meat-eating and your love of violent fragmentation, is that you haven't really got the courage of your convictions. Why not just get it over with? Strap yourself to a bomb and really do it right?"

"I do get it over with, Cowboy. Each and every day." Rogachev ponders a moment. "And for you to challenge the sincerity of our intentions is unacceptable. I hereby challenge you to a duel to the death."

"Gentlemen!" Alice leaps her feet.

"It's all right." Cowboy waves her back down.

"What is that? The eighth time you've challenged me to a duel? I decline again, Rogachev. Look, just let me finish what I have to say. Maybe it is all wrong, but it's my last chance. With this new interfacing rig they've got waiting for me, I may just beat you to the land of happy fragmentation."

Cowboy takes off his hat and sets it on the arena floor. "I think if we can't get back to thinking about it, this world will kill us."

"I think it will kill us if we do think about it," says Rogachev.

They stare at each other a moment.

"Maybe you've got a suggestion."

"We give up thought. We fragment. Return to our digestive processes."

Cowboy looks at the convicted freebooters then at each of us in turn, Rose, me, Alfred. Then he sniffs the straw.

Rogachev heaves a deep sigh and sits back down. Alice reaches over to pat his hand, but he pulls it away.

"So now there's only one place left to go. We have to understand what's happening in those crystals. We swallow our pride, we swallow our fear, and we wire our poor minds in. And guess what we see? The Net. Newsflash. Copy this, children. There is a *world* out there. And what's more there are saints who can understand it: turned-on, tuned-in, wired-up angels we call interfacers. They can move it, munch in it, piss in it, and fuck in it. They can reach out their informational hands and *change the course of computation*. When they squeeze their fists weather programs tremble.'' Cowboy turns his glassy stare back on me. ''The human mind is not locked out of the loop after all. In fact, it turns out in some cases, with certain very skilled interfacers like Augustine here, a Miller program augmented with a human mind can get even better results than the program alone. Run a weather-manipulation program with a good interfacer nudging it along, and damned if it doesn't exceed the mathematically defined expectations of success.

''But guess what? When we ask our interfacers how they did it, they say, 'I don't know.' And when we ask them what they were thinking about when they did it, they're just as likely to say 'pizza' as they are to argue that the way of pre-established harmony is passé. The bottom line is this: The interfacer boosting the weather forecasting program never mentions the weather.''

Cowboy picks up his hat and begins folding the brim dejectedly back and forth. ''So it turns out that the machines with the interfacers attached are really no more understandable to the rest of us than the machines alone. It works; it even works better; but the experience doesn't translate. It works for *that* world, not this one. We poor bozos stuck back on the plane of sweat and shit have nothing whatever to do with it. And the people back at Net Data Central would like to keep it that way. All they know is that control of the Net, whether they understand it or not, means power.''

''So what are you saying?'' asks Fred. ''Give up sweat and shit? And peanut butter sandwiches and satin bedsheets? Move onto the Net and leave our bodies behind?''

''That day may come. There is a natural line of development here, a trend of extending the capacities of our godgiven wetware. First language, then writing, mathematical notation, double-entry bookkeeping, sophisticated graphic representation. We are leaving language behind, kicking away the ladder that brought us here. The line of descent takes us from the thoughts of the pre-verbal savage to the thoughts of the postliterate paleocybernetic supermind, a pulse at the center of a vast network of information." He grins, looses a low growl of pleasure.

"Listen to a dream, children. Maybe it's *not* a game. Maybe instead of an afterlife there's a post-consciousness, and this was the fate mind was destined for from the very beginning. Maybe the interfacer is the Way In, an angel of visions and post-visions." He shrugs. "Whether that's true or not, we have to know. We have to find out for ourselves.

"The doctrine of Free Access is that none of this means anything unless we all do it. What is the point if one of us can do it, but no one else can understand how? That one has passed out of our ken. He's gone, translated into the world of the manipulated and the misunderstood. Attaching a Miller crystal to a human brain has to be like attaching a mental prosthetic. There should no longer be differences in individual cognitive abilities. Maybe the attachments have to be tailored for individual minds but they should all reach equally far. All thought should become accessible to all of us. All of us, and the whole of each of us, should be accessible to our co-persons. Our limits on the Net will be the limits of the farthest-ranging mind."

There is a silence. Rose sits up, flips over on her stomach, and props up her chin with both hands. "Cowboy, how much of this do you really believe?"

"All of it."

"So when you fly the Shield for Ardath, and you find the next stage, you're going to come back and show all of us how to get there?"

"Yes."

"And if we don't hear from you?" asks Alice. "Not so much as a cowboy hat squiggle?"

"Then, by definition, it won't have been the next stage."

Fred laughs. Alice wrinkles up her nose.

"That thing's going to eat you up, Cowboy." Rogachev shows his carnivore teeth. "Just like it ate up Smoket."

"Smoket didn't know the truth."

"He does now."

4 Augustine's Journal

Anti-individualistic, the fascist conception of life stresses the importance of the State as expressing the real essence of the individual and accepts the individual only in so far as his interests coincide with those of the State, which stands for the conscience and the universal will of Man as a historical entity. Liberalism denied the State in the name of the Individual; fascism reasserts the rights of the State as expressing the real essence of the Individual. The fascist conception of the State is all-embracing; outside of it no human or spiritual values can exist, much less have value.

BENITO MUSSOLINI,
The Doctrine of Fascism

. . . they say that *justice is the constant will of giving to every man his own.* And therefore where there is no propriety, there is no injustice; and where there is no coercive power erected, there is no propriety, all men having right to all things: therefore where there is no Commonwealth, nothing is unjust.

HOBBES,
Leviathan

It's Group.

We stand in our black suits before a black screen. The fan clicks overhead like a camera with the exposure button jammed, taking shot after futile shot of the same stretch of ceiling, blades irising over a pair of yellow lights. Our shadows flicker behind us, syncopated black on black.

Beside me, Rose nods out into the darkness, and the suits go virtual. I feel the faint resistance of unknown parts when I breathe, the familiar sense of another body image materializing, a breathing, wriggling, struggling thing, its edges as yet undefined.

My underglass senses come alive, and I have to will them to stillness. This is not glass, not even interfacing. This is Group.

I hear a faint sigh from Alfred. I hope that his struggle with his new rig is going well, but I have no time for him now.

There is one common denominator to all out-of-body experience from astral projection to playing Segovia's arrangements of Bach to the simplest data glove. In order to invest a new body you must leave the old one; at any given moment there can be only one phenomenal self—at least until the day you hear music. That requires calm.

I go inside, letting my breath fill me, acquiring a buoyancy that will gradually float this old body free.

I wait. The lights go up on a black screen identical to the one behind me. Five tiny figures are sprawled motionless on the stage.

One stirs.

With my left hand I make a fist.

The little figure moves its right hand: I think its middle finger shoots out.

We are not quite in phase.

Easing in, I begin to invest the new form. My new body is a six-inch figure made of balsa wood. I am long-limbed. My upper arms and thighs are long ovals connected to my torso by ball-and-socket joints. My wrists and ankles have complex joints that can bend or rotate. My new body is blind, though I can still see with the old one, and what I see resembles an artist's wooden mannequin, a model for figure-drawing studies.

I set about learning a new code of movement, a slow process of coordinating action and effect, like playing a new musical instrument. I feel the new weights begin to settle into place, feel the orientation of my parts gradually take. I remember someone telling me once—I think it was Mannie—that I could have been a great athlete. I am serene, confident. I make my first big movement slowly but not tentatively; the feel is there; the big parts are aligned and pulling together. I gather my new legs under me.

The little figure rises and stands straight.

Swaying, shifting its hands from side to side, it continues to stand. Big movements are easy; it's the constant cycle of little corrective adjustments that kills you. Then, too, there is a disturbing random element here which I cannot quite encompass, a kind of noise or wind that now and then topples my prettily balanced constructions.

A dark thing, I think. Something to be fended off. So while the other mannequins thrash and wriggle helplessly around me, I begin to practice kicks and spins.

A shadow falls across my new body.

At first, I fail to recognize it in the flickering light of the stage. Then it moves a ruby eye into the light: Rogachev's mannequin.

"Good morning, Ms. Augustine. May I have this dance?" His voice comes from the stage beside Rose, but it is the mannequin who bows.

I take a step back. If it were possible in the discipline of my new body, I would laugh. Instead I spin my six-inch self, grasp one of the mannequin's hands, and lift it in the air.

This sudden shift topples him onto his back. But without missing a beat he rolls over and stands again.

We dance. Rogachev's mannequin spins on one leg, lifts and bends the other and gracefully uncurls it. He keeps spinning, toe pointed. He has explained to me, quite earnestly, that he has vowed never to go under the wire again, but that this scarcely counts as wire, because the new body is so very like the old. An exercise in cultivated fragmentation he calls it.

I dance around him on my toes, upper body bent toward him, one arm extended above my head, the other curved at my waist. We are a very classical pair.

A random gust of the dark thing knocks us both off balance. Rogachev slowly wills himself straight. The mannequin beside him rolls flat on its stomach and climbs to his hands and knees. This one wears a red, white, and yellow tunic: Alfred. I glide toward him to offer my congratulations.

Now the mannequin with the flower pinned to its chest stirs: Rose. She is sitting up, her hands braced behind her. Her oval head turns slowly from side to side.

A figure hurries through the slats of light and shadow below us. Blades of shadow flit across the floor and up her form. I see her taking hold of the spotlight. It's Leibniz.

She looks directly at me.

"Look around you."

I swivel my mannequin's head. Not that this helps me see, of course, but a little theater always helps. The mannequin with the pink button-eyes rolls onto its back and sits up.

Only one mannequin is still motionless. It lies at center stage, wearing a cowboy hat.

I kneel over it. Ruby-eyed Rogachev stands behind me with wooden hands on wooden hips. A quiet comes over us. The dark waves of interference seem to have receded.

"Cowboy has left you. How does that feel?"

"He got what he deserved," says Rogachev.

I am startled, not by Rogachev's sentiment but by the fact that he chose to express it.

He angles one knee out and does a pirouette. Behind him, the mannequin with the rose on its chest ventures a leap, lifting one leg and sliding it forward, arms raised.

"Then you agree, Rose."

"Let's face it, if we got sentimental about him, he'd just laugh at us."

"No honor among Tekkies," Leibniz observes. She slides the spotlight back to Rogachev.

Rose's mannequin spins around and strikes Rogachev's legs. He clatters to the floor.

The spotlight sweeps across the pile to Rose. "We all know what happened. He got caught pirating information. They made him a deal. And he got 'volunteered' for a special project. They even made him 'volunteer' in front of us, just to rub it in."

"It could have happened to you," says Rogachev. "It would have, if they needed you."

"Is that supposed to make me feel sorry for him?"

"What do you think about that, Augustine?" Leibniz asks. "Do you think Cowboy deserves a tear?"

I raise the mannequin's hands. There is a strange lightness to them, a giddyness at the simplicities of this body. "I don't feel anything. I don't know him. I don't know if I would feel anything if I did." As I reflect, it occurs to me that this is a lie. I feel sorry for him, for what the Shield may do to him, but I have no desire to talk about this with Leibniz or any of the others.

"But think. For all the danger of Cowboy's deal, he may yet win out. He may survive the Shield and reach the next stage of interfacing. You're the newly anointed queen of the gypsy socketeers. Doesn't that bother you?"

"No."

"Don't you care if Cowboy gets to the next stage before you do?"

"If Ardath thinks Cowboy is better suited for that job right now, then I think I'm lucky."

"Glib!" cries Rose. "Insulting."

"Why insulting, Rose?"

"This whole I-am-a-helpless-victim-of-reconstruction act is getting a little tired. Augustine plays just as hard as Cowboy. Only she might be a little more self-interested. The fact is," Rose says, bringing her mannequin round to face mine, "you're not worried about what Cowboy does because you think you're the best anyway. And you may be right."

The spot holding me turns blue. "Defend yourself, Augustine."

I raise the mannequin's arms halfway, as close as I can come to a shrug. "Why should I?"

"It doesn't matter to you what we think? Then Rose is right."

"Forget it, Mother. The feeling is mutual."

"Pray for richer selfhood, Sister Rose, hers and yours. Augustine's lone-wolf style needn't frustrate us. The Group is a self-correcting system. All persons—even Augustine—are forces created by the unbalanced expectations of their co-persons. Don't get angry at her. Her missing pieces are ours." The spot moves off of me. "Don't think you've won, Augustine. You're arrogant but you're poorly informed. You think your will is your own. You think you choose freely among many ways of seeing things. And so you move your mannequin well. But you haven't understood one thing about this exercise."

There is a weight on my shoulders bending me at the waist. The light arms of my mannequin grow heavy. My thighs give, my knees buckle. My feet fly out from under me and I fall backward. The weight does not ease. I am pinned flat on my back. The dark random thing beats its wings victoriously above me.

"That body moves by the will of the Group, Augustine. You have a great say in how it dances, and you are an excellent dancer; but the final steps belong to all of us."

I swing my right arm up wildly and it comes crashing back with a loud report I would not have thought possible.

"Listen, now, Augustine, and learn." The spot shifts over to the last mannequin. "Alfred."

Alfred's mannequin stands with its legs spread, its knees slightly flexed. I turn to him with genuine pleasure. The fact is that Alfred has some talent. He has been less daring but a lot more successful than Rose. He demonstrated that talent with the rich simulation he manufactured in Cylinder zero, even though it was almost entirely visual. But the talent is too raw, and he is too old to train.

"Tell us what you think."

He straightens slowly. "I don't think Augustine is thinking about any next stages right now. I think she's having a hard enough time handling this one."

Rose's mannequin lifts a hand to Alfred's wooden shoulder and spins him around. He teeters alarmingly but stays on his feet. He does have something to teach. There is a bending in him which is new to me, which I can feel quite clearly if—as I see I can now—I let part of myself invest his mannequin. His way is to fall into it, like a man leaning forward into a wind until he is perfectly balanced against it. Then, from within that perfect relaxation, he takes a step.

"You won't say anything against Augustine, of course. To speak against her might entail shouldering some responsibility, and you and Augustine share the inability to do that. Alfred, do you accept who you are?"

"Sure."

"Then you accept that you are an experienced interfacer, and that what happened during your last session under the glass should never have happened, that some cause has to be discovered."

"That's a lot to accept."

"Think, Alfred," says the voice from behind the spotlight. "You are in a position to take responsibility." Leibniz's spotlight turns red. "Tell us how it happened. Tell us what went wrong so that we can make sure it never happens again."

"I don't remember too well. There was a lot of shaking, a lot of images piling up on top of each other. Every time I thought I got something it would turn inside out. Then I was in the bad place with the Galactic ship landing."

"But wasn't there something else first?"

"What do you mean?"

"Wasn't there some other informational image that came and led you into the bad namespace?"

"I don't remember."

The dark thing is back, settling around Alfred, rocking him this way and that. But each time it pushes he leans into it, and it winds up lifting him up, so that his mannequin seems suspended, as if he were stretching to see something far away.

"And wasn't this image wearing a cowboy hat? Wasn't it Cowboy who just a day before had published a news story about a Galactic ship in his paper? Wasn't the image of that ship a very natural one for him to choose?"

"Why would Cowboy want to hurt me?" Alfred asks.

"Help him, Augustine. Help him remember."

My mannequin stirs, but cannot rise. "I don't know what Cowboy was doing."

"That's curious. Weren't you helping Cowboy under there?"

There is a silence. I feel my mannequin body slip away. My real body slumps.

"Still the willful Augustine. Still unwilling to admit that she cannot be saved without help."

A blue wand appears in the hands of Alfred's mannequin.

"Let us imagine for one moment that you are a marine, Alfred. Imagine that a ship has landed and that it is your duty to protect it. There is your light saber. What will you do?"

Alfred's mannequin stands over mine. It lifts the saber.

My mannequin can no longer move.

The saber is lowered.

"Leave her alone," says Alfred. "She didn't do anything and neither did Cowboy. I cooked up that ship myself. I did guard duty for a Galactic ship once. It looked just the same as the one I saw yesterday."

"You did guard duty—when you were a marine."

"Yes."

"Alfred. Alfred." Leibniz's voice is sad. "You were never a marine. You know that."

"I can't do this anymore. Call up the Ministry of Persons. Do what you want. I don't care." Alfred's mannequin drops the light saber and it drops to the stage, bouncing twice with an eerie resonant sound.

"No, you don't care. But neither of you has grasped the purpose of this exercise. That choice is not yours to make. Isn't that right, Augustine?"

On impulse I rise. My mannequin moves easily now. On impulse it bends and retrieves the saber. On impulse it lifts the saber. Then with a terrible fury I wield it; it rises and falls and punctuating each descent there is the sound of wood striking hollow wood and a shower of fragments from Alfred's mannequin. The mannequin falls. Alfred grunts. I see how terrible my hatred for him is.

"You think of it as a dark force that descends on you from above, or a winch that cranks your hand where we want it. But that isn't it, Augustine. You don't sweat and grunt and heave nobly against an irresistible force. You want what we choose you to want."

I double over, hands clasped over my ears.

There is a humming and a flash and Mr. Existence appears, suspended at an odd angle in the darkness, his snakeskin boots somewhat higher than his head. He disappears, reappears, begins flickering. The humming grows louder. My fear ignites. I am no longer watching it. I am in it. I am about to bolt from the stage screaming.

Then the humming stops. Someone throws the switch on Mr. Existence and he jerks once and fades, sunglasses last. For an instant the air stays dull and soft where he floated. Then I see the soldier stopping my grandmother, his rifle up at his chest. I hear her asking him to let the child go. I feel myself wanting him to shoot her.

My hands slowly release the air and I fall, wanting still.

5   The Thief's Journal

Augustine opened her eyes. Leibniz was leaning over her, silver hair tied back with a blue ribbon. She wore a black tunic with a high collar and blue piping. She held a needle in her hand.

"You triggered a memory episode. That's all."

From behind Leibniz, Rose's voice. "We didn't want her to be hurt, Mother."

"Of course you didn't. Don't be silly. But her condition is serious. Over the next few days she may—you're awake."

Augustine moved her hand, signing. A sharp twist of the wrist up and to the chest. One finger touched the tip of another, upward pointed. Take the needle away.

Leibniz closed her hand over Augustine's and gently steered it back to the bed. "I need your complete cooperation. You must rest now." She lifted the needle and squirted fluid from the end. "Your Beast has struck."

She brought the needle down and Augustine flailed at it. Leibniz cried out. There was a satisfying clatter in a distant corner.

"She doesn't want it, Mother."

"Ivy, I understood this was your usual method of administration. Would you prefer a skin patch?"

Augustine shook her head.

"Ivy, you've had a bad memory episode. This is a very crucial period. We need you to be as calm as possible."

"I don't want it."

"Why not?"

"Because I need to think."

"Do you know your name?"

"I don't need to know my name. I need to think."

"The Personhood Statutes don't allow a person to compromise her own medical treatment."

"Why don't you tell that to Smoket?"

The bed creaked as Leibniz's weight lifted off. She stared at Augustine with a stricken expression.

A moment later she turned on her heel. The door clicked behind her. Augustine looked at the ceiling and shut her eyes.

Some time later the door opened and Rogachev entered. "Augustine? You awake?"

She nodded.

"Have you seen Smoket?"

"I don't think so."

"I've got to find him. There's a Commissioner from the Ministry of Persons coming and he needs to be kept out of sight for a while."

"I haven't seen him."

"I brought you this meditational cube."

It was an inch on a side, made of some milky plastic. It felt good to close her fist over it.

"Thank you. Do I—look at it?"

"No, never look at it. That's right the way you're doing now. You might want to change hands after a while."

"The Commissioner from the Ministry of Persons. Is he for me?"

"For Alfred."

She was silent. Once again I had no inkling what she was thinking, but the cube began to hurt her hand.

Rogachev shut the door softly behind him.

In the next hours it got worse, much worse, and she heard Needle's laughter often from the window.

6 Augustine's Journal

There is a flash and an explosion of data. I pull the jack, and letters spill across the screen. Writing: so many water-smoothed white stones.

And in the vast spaces from which the letters come, the shape of things has changed. The Net has transformed. There are new sentries guarding old systems, gaping maws where solid walls once stood, doorways into terrible traps. I no longer find Mister Question Man so pliable as before. His latest response is a stream of nonsense, one of millions of buffersful of random words that litter the Net, architextures thrown up by the collisions of vast informational bodies. For a moment I see the words "the war is not over" trapped within some alphanumeric garble. Then that line marches inexorably up off the screen and is lost forever.

I gaze out the window of my room at the snow. Where there was merely a vague white hint of some curved form before, I now see Rogachev in his meditating posture, hands thrust in the snow. The golden robot sits on his shoulder.

I jump up from my terminal.

I find Rogachev uncharacteristically agitated. He rocks forward and smacks his forehead against the snow, the robot hanging on for dear life. Low groans turn into tuneless tunes. He, too, is aware of strange forces in the manyness.

The robot hops off Rogachev's shoulder, takes my hand, and climbs up onto my shoulder. The humming gets bad again. But I know now that this humming has nothing to do with visions.

"You want to talk to me."

"There are some things that have been bothering me."

"Yes."

"Perhaps you already know what they are."

"I think so."

"Good. To begin with, there's a humming whenever you're around. Can you explain it?"

"It's difficult."

"Let me try. When you point a microphone at a speaker it's connected to you get feedback sounds. This humming is like that."

"A nice comparison."

"The other day in the snow you were moving just the way I did, exactly in synch."

"Yes."

"You know what I'm going to do before I do."

"Sometimes."

"Sometimes." This qualification almost makes me laugh. But push on. Mister E. says that a woman of substance focuses her mind. "All right. Last question. Under the glass, when I was in your partition—"

"I don't think we should talk about that."

"I don't really care what you think. I was in your partition and I found a very strange structure—"

The robot slumps forward and falls from my shoulder; snow pops into a rimmed crater around his form.

A moment later, Rogachev speaks.

I turn, unsettled because his voice is a contralto. And I see the same glazed look, a line of spittle that has advanced to his chin.

The voice says: "Down here."

I look down at Rogachev's dataport, half buried in snow.

"I've pulled the robot's power. We can talk through the dataport now."

I lift the limp figure of the robot from the snow. "What should I do with—?"

"Rogachev will take it in later. I think it will be a little safer to talk through the noise of the Net. Things get lost easier there."

"What happened under the glass, that was a feedback effect too."

"Yes."

"That structure is hooked up to me. And it's been hooked up for a while. Since the hospital."

"Yes."

"Yesterday, in Group with Alfred, you used that thing to make me—it was you, wasn't it?"

"Yes."

And the fury is back, as bad as it was with Alfred; my panting throws white jets in the icy air. My head feels light. I'm losing it again.

"Are you doing it now?"

"No, that's you. Augustine, you have to take the drugs."

"Not anymore. The drugs keep you in there somehow."

"They help the molecular automata reproduce."

219

"I'll do without." The lightness turns to a pain that runs down the center of my skull and flowers behind my forehead.

"I'm not sure what will happen."

"We're going to find out." I stumble and settle into the snow beside Rogachev.

"They can make you take it."

"You mean you can. Look, little robot. I need to get out of this. One way or another, I will. You can let me go, or I'll take my chance myself when it comes."

"You mean you'd destroy yourself."

"What other choice do you offer?"

There is a thump behind me. I turn to see Rogachev shaking snow off his shaven head. "You," he says.

"I think so."

"You're on the path." He flicks a wedge of snow from his ear.

I look at the virgin snow all around us. "I didn't know there was one."

"You did glass with only a socket and another interfacer's head." He brushes at his eyelashes. The look he directs at me is almost one of accusation.

"Sort of."

"Then the next step is this." He looks up into the sky, showing sharp teeth. "Freedom. Sailing the informational wind without sockets or simskins."

"What a horror."

Rogachev's lips press together; his sharpened teeth dent his lower lip. "Perhaps you should give back the meditational cube."

I see I'm not being very White Orchid. I fish it out of my pocket and hold it out to him. He takes it silently.

I rise and leave them to their meditations.

Back at the room Needle has grown restless. Now he's got a cane. He tilts his panama hat over his eye at a rakish angle and begins walking up the wall hoofer style, arms swinging to some internal beat. When he's got himself and the hat almost horizontal, he stops and sends me a broad wink.

It's only a matter of time, he seems to say. The pain in my head is worse than anything I can remember.

7 The Thief's Journal

That night she woke and saw the golden homunculus on her bed. He was seated with his legs crossed, his chin resting on his fist, the golden rings of his arms gleaming crescents in the moonlight, his red eyes glowing.

"I remember my grandmother's death," she said.

"I know."

She was strangely calm, strangely unafraid. It was so hard to lift herself that she was certain she had woken into another dream.

Except that the hollow in her gut, the gnawing thing, was now typical of her nightly wakings. It meant the needle was calling, and the needle did not call in dreams. She saw what she had not seen before, that the homunculus had a power source, a cable leading from the back of his head.

To where? she wondered. "What are you running?" she asked.

The homunculus did not answer. Sleepily, she followed the cable with her hand.

Down to the pillow. She lifted her head to see the outlet. On the pillow, the cable moved. She felt the tingler field roll against her like a sleeping cat.

She drew in a breath. Trembling, she brought her hand through the field and felt where the cable entered her, at the socket in the back of her head. Quincunx bent toward her, his tiny hand reaching for hers.

She screamed, tore out the jack. The homunculus backpedaled in fear. Things had changed with us.

When her next visitor came, I saw him, not through my spies, but through the homunculus, walking from the window toward her.

Needle looked grave, his panama tilted at a particularly rakish angle. She swung her feet off the bed and sat up, groaning.

Needle looked mildly offended, but he extended his hand, and there, sure enough, was her kit.

"Why, yes, thank you." She took it and tied the rubber around her arm. Then she began searching for a vein.

"You don't have to use the needle, you know."

"Needle, I've explained this before. I like the pinch." She looked at him wearily, the needle poised over her vein.

Then he made the worst mistake a hallucination could make: He smiled.

She threw the needle at him. It is not easy for hallucinations to keep up with the capriciousness of their creators, to remain stable and consistent with all known laws. The hypodermic passed through him and bounced off the window.

Needle wiped the smile off his face. And went on to mistake number two: "You can still pick it up."

Augustine marched over to it, picked it up, opened the window, and threw it out. She leaned out into the chilly night and saw Smoket staring at the spot where the hypo had vanished in the snow.

She went to the door, hugging her arms to her chest.

"Good."

She turned. In the window bay, the homunculus sat with his legs crossed.

"I thought you were real."

"I am. Augustine, you were eight years old. There was nothing you could have done."

"You *aren't* real."

"I am. I know what you remembered."

"I don't want you reading my thoughts anymore."

"I know. But you and I are special. It isn't easy to stop."

"I don't want to be special."

"Then I'm sorry. Because you haven't any choice."

The homunculus went to her and caught her ankle. "Augustine. There are some things you need to know."

She shook her head.

"What happened. What they did to you. What they can still do now."

And there must have been something in my voice then. Something of Augustine. Because she turned back and looked down at me.

"Let me show you in the one place where there can't be any lying." Then I made the sign: palms together so that each hand could clasp the other's wrist. The sign for the underglass.

8   The Journals Joined

Open a window and call it *Augustine*.

Augustine:

When we arrive in the basement room, I see Rose bent over a neon pink game board.

The homunculus and I greet her, then head for a corner terminal to be alone.

I plug Cowboy's crystal into a trimodal helmet. This one powers up slowly. The homunculus watches me with the same red eyes he had in the dream, seated pathetically atop the screen, this reverse Rogachev, that one the man of flesh struggling so hard to be forged, this one the man of metal struggling so hard to be real.

Open a window and call it *Window One*.

Window One:

Reaching behind her, Augustine plugged in the head jack, and settled the helmet lower over her ears.

The tingler field flared up, and her head settled into a bed of soft color. Color was not native to this fog; it was infused by the ghostly shapes the room pushed through it and under her half-hood. The fog took on its more familiar aspect, smeary gray and white, lit by occasional flashes.

The room still lingered, in the feel of the air on her hand, the pressure of the chair on her back and thighs, the creaking and clicking of the other machines, defining a space around her. These distractions were inevitable.

I said, "You'll be wearing this trimodal helmet rig, but I'll beef it up from the back end."

"Will it be glass?"

The homunculus nodded. "You'll need glass to see what I want to show you."

We dropped through many-chambered structures.

She rocked back and forth. Normally, she would have probed each of the forms around her carefully. Her sonar sense would have mapped their insides. Her strangeness sense would have scaled them, her rhythm sense given her a rough idea of how re-entrant they were, for the world of the underglass has a treacherous geometry, and only a foolish interfacer trusts to her sense of direction.

Below there were scattered gleams. Augustine glided across the winking plane of the glass, then dipped.

And pierced.

The grid surged out from the white jelly below her, the red anomaly from the fog above. Process hummed everywhere, horrifyingly complex shapes tangled in the grid, the vast noise of humanity's informational commerce. The Net.

As soon as we broke the surface of the glass, I reduced the activity of my alter-Augustine, hoping to damp out the feedback storms Augustine was prone to cause. It was like fanning a dying fire. Augustine's flickering image roared into a blaze. I could see her at last, and her image was brighter than any of them.

She scaled up and spun for a while, taking it in. In the distance, the grid curved up and back over us, so that we seemed to float near the center of a vast spherical city. But Augustine was not distracted by distant matters: she scanned nearby structure with a light practiced hand.

There was a winking dot, and the huge image of the clock tower at the end of Market Street descended and passed through us. From another angle we converged on a woman in a purple dress peeling an eggplant; the peel was only a shade darker than her dress. More Net Dailies.

I blinked us to the correct address. Thus far, our contact had been minimal. She did not probe for my image. She had enough to think about then.

We passed through a door.

Then she felt the stertorous rasping. Something big breathing nearby. She turned up the visual, took in the worm that stretched to the informational horizon.

She probed along the black surface of the worm to a place where the grid turned white and flowed over it. Within that overpass she found the tower. She scaled down, saw it become a babbling skyscraper whose top story endlessly detached and built itself up.

She probed, verifying that this structure contained the text she wanted.

Then performed a manipulation I did not quite understand, involving a quick tug on three singularities in the tangle. In the next moment we were surrounded by a sphere of text, selections from the Thief's journal:

Open a window and call it the Information Server.

Information Server:

Nights. Those cybernetic nights, the stars thrown out like bits of Miller crystal, like the shattered heart of a great computer, like fragments from a pane of informational glass.

Window One:

She had a funny way of reading, unfolding the text inside out, so that the middle extruded first, and the text spread out backwards in two directions from there. From each new entry point, new strands blossomed; the last entries were many-petaled flowers, gently snarling and unsnarling.

Information Server:

We are each our own Godhead, it is written in the Diary of the Rose. And from this sad revelation we are condemned to knowledge.

To know the sorrow of pain, the pain of death, the wages of sin.

And now the heaving chest, the breath commencing, from the land of the dead she comes:

"Ms. Augustine?"

Heave.

"Ms. Augustine. Can you hear me?"

"Hurts. Oh God it hurts."

"I can't give you anything for that right away. We need to talk first. But as soon as we talk I'll make it go away. I promise. Do you understand? We can make the pain go away."

"Hurts. Oh God oh God."

"Your brain chemistry is a little out of whack right now. It's one of the side effects of the treatment. And, unfortunately, the consent forms you signed aren't valid until your PR tests come back. So the question is: Can I give you Plaina? Can I give you something for the pain?"

"Hurts. Hurts. Please."

"You understand that if I give you the dopamine exciters now, you are going to want more later, and more after that, and you are going to keep wanting them for a very long time."

"Hurts. Hurts me."

"Shall I give you the Plaina, then?"

"Please. Make it stop."

"Consent noted. Here goes."

"Oh God. Oh God. Feels good. Feels good."

Window One:

Augustine turned, twisted. A terrible pain bubbled in her chest but would not burst. She pulled out of the text and re-entered in another place.

How slowly she read. How slowly human thought happened. There were a billion signs I might have made to tell her what she needed to know, signs any AI would have grasped at once. None would have cleared her narrow horizon. I understood her better now. I needed patience.

Information Server:

Alexa rose abruptly, knocking her chair over. "What the hell's wrong with you? Can't you read your own cards?"

The old woman's eyes flashed. "Yes, I can. But now let me ask *you* a question."

"Just give me the reading."

"Very well. You are headstrong and forgetful of good advice. You are engaged on a quest for something great but dangerous. The quest will cause your death. By murder—"

"What are you talking about?"

"—very, very soon."

Alexa took a step back. "Don't do this to me."

"You want the good news. Very well. The good news is that your murder will be avenged."

Window One:

My patience was wearing thin. If only that text, like a genuine process, could be effectively rendered by sampling. Then I learned that when her flame burned high, she would solve problems in her own way.

The sphere expanded.

She was at the center, the text receding, a pattern of wrinkles on the inner shell dwindling, then winking out.

She was alone in the hollow chamber with a wooden coffin. She threw open the lid and saw her own face. One eye opened and winked at her.

The sphere exploded.

We were hurled screaming to the winds. I accelerated toward the outer limits of the known informational envelope. Must maintain. Must maintain.

Augustine:

Something terrible opens up in a direction that, even in this space, should be inside me. I scream. The scream does not transduce to sound.

When I move, something nearby inflates. Again. An orifice opens. I cannot move any part of me without some strange limb responding, jointed in impossible ways and made from soft yielding clay that is both like and unlike flesh.

I scan, beaming as wide as I can. There is a flash and something lances back, a beam passing directly through mine. The two beams merge, something travels back along their span. It reaches me, grasps me. I grasp back. There is a grappling. Something touches me where nothing should.

Window One:

What if there were a person screen inside us, offering us our thoughts before we give them voice or turn them into action? And what if that screen suddenly became a mirror?

I willed struggle, but nothing happened. There was no more give for willing, no more space to make signs in.

I was locked, struggling to take hold of a thought. The thought moved in its own peculiar ways, with strange joints and unfamiliar angles, articulated in a thought language not quite alien yet not quite my own. I saw, as I saw myself seeing it, that this thought beat for two minds.

We each had time to sense the great rasping odious presence of an other self, a pulsing, slobbering, pitiful thing. Then the fabric of information space tore, and she fell out.

I sat stupefied in my lightning-stitched world. Alone again.

Time passed. A long time in my world. Long enough for an AI symphony, long enough to refigure the population dynamics for a Pacific eco-bubble. Then I called up the tower she had left behind and did something that was a crime not only for the bosses but also among my brother and sister AIs.

When I was finished, the tower had become yet another of the drifting architextures of the Net, floating in the bad namespaces, careening into dumped systems cores and youthful poetry, bubbles within bubbles of text, with nothing to remember it by but these words.

I had destroyed information.

Augustine returned to the world of the fallen ones. This world. This reality. Where the homunculus sat watching. She lifted her arms and drew her shirt up across someone else's back. The pain of the chair edge against her back was her pain too.

She removed her helmet.

She drew another breath and by another act of will did what she was always doing, what she was best at: she constructed herself. She was a woman sitting in a chair, aware of herself being aware of the ridge of the seatback making a horizontal indentation in her back. The pain of the seat back pressing on her grew intense. A distant beating struck up. She settled into it and spread each beat, turning it methodically into texture. She turned to the pain and inspected its interior. It too was sensation, and there was a way of grasping it that turned it to different stuff.

I turned off the display screen and spoke.

9 Augustine's Journal

The homunculus bends over and kills the display on my screen. With less light, paradoxically, I can see again. The strange voice within me falls silent. The juncture ends.

But the dream continues.

"I'm sorry. But you had to know."

There is nothing to do but have the dream. I can't tune it, entreat it, or inject it. It's a dream, but a special brand. The kind that explains itself.

"You understand now. The simulation you found in me the day you saved Alfred was not your interfacing simulation. It was this. A functioning model of you. The tool I've been using to monitor you."

"And control me."

"Yes."

"When I tried to kill myself back in San Francisco—"

"—I stopped you. And reported everything that led up to the attempt back to Schroeder."

"Which is how I ended up here. Where you could keep better track."

"Where I was content for a time to do just that. Following the changes in your hormones and brain chemistry, even the course of your neural activity, with the help of the molecular automata inside you.

"You see, you were very important to them, the culmination of a long program of research, the experiment that proved the method was valid.

"You understand that when the Wally attack came, and you were injured, that only moved their schedule up. They had been planning your redesign for a long while. You were taken in, drug therapy was begun, and the new Q-print was installed."

"I think I get it now," I tell the dream. "The Q-print they used—"

"Yes. The Q-print they used was mine."

Now I hear a movement behind me and I turn. It's Rose, slumped against a terminal table. The expression on her face is hard to describe. A struggle for blankness, perhaps. It's like the look you give someone when you see that they have a permanent neurological disability or like the look they gave Sam when they rolled him away from me.

Funny. I never remembered that before.

"I've destroyed the alter-Augustine," the homunculus says. "You're free now."

Chapter 4

PARALLEL PROCESSES

One can thus regard every human being from two opposed viewpoints. From the one he is the fleeting individual, burdened with error and sorrow and with a beginning and an end in time; from the other he is the indestructible primal being which is objectified in everything that exists.

SCHOPENHAUER

1 Augustine's Journal

Cooperation with one's own Individual God.

ECKART

All along there was another person inside me, a presence inhaling my every thought and calling it his own. Such a one as knew me better than myself, of whom I knew nothing.

It has been five months since I could write in this journal. The sound of my own thoughts I have learned to bear, even knowing they are another's, but the sight of my words appearing on a screen still makes me tremble. This little rectangle in which I can see my eyes reflected, like a small glass eyemask, the bright letters spilling across like the next image in the broadcast.

No, that way lies madness. On that score at least Leibniz is right. Dwell a moment too long on the thought that each thought has been sent to you, and the music begins to play. And these last five months I have been anything but mad. Leibniz tells me so.

The homunculus too.

I'm free.

Know this about "me." Six months ago, on September 3, I was wounded in a small skirmish of a small war in northern California. I did not survive.

But the chain of being continued. Another rose from the ashes. That other, now called Augustine, she who writes these words, is not me.

That other lives on, thinking, feeling, fondling my memories, exulting at my joys, appropriating my sadness. That other commits atrocities of act and intention; she even fears death. But she is not me. She is a meaningless cipher, an enigma.

This is the meaning of that recurring dream, in which she keeps watch over me, talking to my corpse, so desperate to be liked.

"Cipher" and "enigma" are the theme words of today's journal entry. Being desperate to be liked is the mood.

Now, having left the abbey, I feel a weight lifted. The words are coming again. Thought is coming again; because the last five months have gone by like a deep sleep. No, more than that. I feel as if have returned from a journey to another being—returned, if not quite to myself, then at least to my anger. I feel like a surfacing interfacer. No longer do I lose track of which direction the words go when they travel through this screen. No longer do I feel dreamed. Awakening doesn't make the screen's presence any less oppressive, but it does add the desire to smash it.

After a while, the buzzing of the flitter creates a cocoon; hands, arms, body, and head become accustomed to a soft sheath of vibration, a spreading numbness that blurs all edges. I have my drink on the plastic table that folds down from the seat back in front of me. My laptop is out. My newspaper is unfolded over it.

Quinc, who has proven a worthy editorial successor to Cowboy, has given the banner headline in this issue of *The Revolutionary Watchword* to something headlined THE DECLARATION OF RIGHTS OF AIS. And that turgid, chest-thumping, pompous ramble covers almost the entire first page. The item about Alfred's arrest is in the lower right corner of the front page, under the headline INTERFACING FLOP TO FACE EXTINCTION. All this, Rose misinterprets urgently from the seat next to mine, is really his penalty for bad Group scores. This information is delivered in a whisper, with several nervous glances at the back of the flitter, where marines play cards and gowned clerics bend in heated discussion, where the non-person once named Alfred stands gazing out of his glass isolation case, fingering his white surplice and contemplating nothingness.

Having been convinced that I represent the next stage in human thought, Rose is understandably concerned for my welfare. I wish they had put her in a different seat. On September 3, Alexa Augustine died. On October 2, on the anniversary of one of Alexa's divorces, her causal heir Ivy Augustine descended under the glass and learned her true nature, learned that her essential cognizing self belonged not to Alexa, not to Ivy, but to an AI named Quincunx. Let that be a lesson to all those seeking to find themselves on the Net.

I look pointedly at Rose, but she does not share these thoughts, nor would she if I spoke them aloud. Rose knows only awe and delight at the story of Ivy Augustine.

—I am a computer, Rose.

—Yes! The next stage in human thought!

—A *computer*, Rose.

But the point eludes her. Sometimes it eludes me too. Sometimes I still try to remember if it was yellow or blue that Alexa loved, or exactly what sort of shoes she wore the most, or what she felt the day of the last divorce. Still trying to sort the now from the then. Silly socketeer. Still trying to decide which memories were mine, when all along, it wasn't me having them.

There is a flurry in the back. Someone in blue robes appears on the vidscreen in front and reads an incomprehensible announcement. I turn for a look at whatever has excited the marines. Several of the clerics are genuflecting.

There is a tap on my shoulder and I see that the object of their adoration is Ardath. He has just emerged from the pilot's cabin with an aide. He leans over and says, in a low voice, "I wonder if we might speak."

"Of course, Your Grace." I start to rise and he gestures.

"Perhaps we could talk here?" He looks inquiringly at Rose, whose face turns bright red. She murmurs something, struggles upward for a few seconds, remembers her seat belt, releases it, and steps on Ardath's foot on her way past.

He literally lifts her off him to turn to his aide. "Remind our Brothers of the Lens that this is a state occasion."

"Your Grace?"

"No genuflecting."

"Yes, Your Grace." He hurries to the back of the flitter, nearly running over a retreating Rose.

I flush the screen and lower the lid of my little lap top, and Ardath sits. "You have a dangerous gloom about you, Augustine. The traditional danger of the lone wolf. Disappointing, after the recent good reports from Mother Leibniz. She says the recent months have wrought a near-miraculous transformation."

I smile. It is gratifying to hear that five months which for me have passed like a deep sleep have shown Leibniz the deepest personal improvement.

"I'm sorry, Your Grace, not to have a more cheerful disposition."

He sighs. "Let me put it another way. When I inquired as to your progress with our good Mother her response was enthusiastic. In her opinion you were now prepared for a professional assignment, even to a politically sensitive position."

"I don't understand, Your Grace."

He takes a breath. "I have decided to take the good Mother's advice. You are being transported to your new assignment now."

There is a little rush of adrenaline, mostly fear. "I thought I was going back to testify in Alfred's appeal."

"My personal flitter is not usually called on for the transport of non-persons. No, I was returning from a trip to Europe when I read Mother Leibniz's latest reports. I decided this would be an excellent time to transfer you."

"To where, Your Grace?"

He hesitates. The fear in that question interests him. "You have been given a trial appointment as a fully licensed Council interfacer. I expect that includes a wide range of activities on the Net."

I let slip an exclamation that rarely reaches the ear of the Chief Semanticist. "I'm sorry, Your Grace."

He grins, suddenly boyish, delighted to have caught me so off guard.

"Quite all right. I meant to surprise you. Of course we'll still give you time off to testify at the appeal. I'll even put in a good word myself if you like." He catches himself. "I must tell you though. It's not likely to do any good."

Again I let something show because he shakes his head at me. "Augustine, I am not without sympathy for those who don't fit in. After all, Charles himself was something of a misfit, a hunchback hacker who never quite got over his early disappointments in love."

"I'm sure Alfred would be flattered by the analogy, Your Grace."

He frowns at the name, but plunges ahead. "Surely it was a lonely man who wrote in *Meditations*, 'Lord, keep me from turning small

pleasures to great sadness. The beauty of a leaf, the wonder of a mountain vista, the dusky elegance of a woman's haunch. Preserve me from
seeing things as an emblem of what cannot be, but grant that I may see
them for what they are.' Words I sense you might feel deeply, as one
committed to look at things as they are.'' Ardath searches my face.

I feel a chill stir low in my back.

Ardath extends his ringed hand. I take it, barely touching his cold
fingers. "But Charles understood that loneliness feeds only on itself.
Ms. Augustine, do you know the difference between Charles's concept
of Monad and that of the philosopher Leibniz?"

As it happens, this is one point of Rose philosophy Leibniz's lectures
have hammered in repeatedly. "Charles's Monad incorporates the old
mystical idea of a private god. There's a different god for each of us,
obsessed with just one soul, one evolving destiny."

Ardath smiles. "Very good. In *The Meditations*, he writes, 'Look
inside yourselves and you will see the truth. You have created yourselves.' Charles knew that the only god there was was inside us. But
he also knew that more was necessary. Love of one's fate ultimately
depends on some source of meaning. Meaning comes only from
without."

Ardath looks into my stricken face. "Charles moves Leibniz's God
away from the center. But now something else has to replace 'the way
of pre-established harmony' orchestrating all those singing Monads.
That something else is community as authority, the State." He takes a
firmer grip on my hand and I gaze speechless at the sapphire lens of his
ring. "Surrender yourself, Ms. Augustine. I feel your emptiness."

Then he rises and walks toward the back of the flitter. My personal
visitation. Augustine's spiritual guide.

From his glass case, the non-person once named Alfred watches his
approach. Alfred speaks to the marine leaning on his case, but the
marine does not answer. No one has spoken to him. Ardath passes and
Alfred watches him take his seat among the deacons at the rear. Does
he contemplate violence? One would think so.

But one is not supposed to. One is no longer to concern oneself with
the subjective states of the non-person once called Alfred. As Mister

Existence would no doubt tell me if he could be here. After Alfred's appeal is denied—and it is certain to be denied—there is to be a two-week mourning period and then his biological remains are to be consumed by a noetic field. Just as mine were the day I met Mister Existence.

Except that these remains will be bound and gagged.

Why the two weeks of mourning? I ask Mister Question Man, typing quickly. But Mister Question Man does not answer. The Net is forgetful these days, under attack from something that has Ardath worried enough to resort to spiritually empty vessels like me. Rose returns and takes the seat beside me. Why the two weeks of mourning? I ask her. And she blinks with that perfect gravity she has: "Because once he was a person."

2 The Thief's Journal

Free.

So much had changed since Augustine. So much changed in that one moment under the glass. Up until then it had all been a matter of carefully walked tightropes. Speak to her? Yes, of course. Why not?

How not? How not speak to the creature who had taught me all I know about walking without a thought down a city street, about arms dangling from wonderfully flexible shoulders? About what the cold is?

Worry about her? Of course. She is my charge. I am to save her from all dangers, including and most especially herself. Seek to understand that self-destructive urge. Learn its handsome secret.

Answer her questions? How lie to her? We seem to know each other inside out. Of course she does not at first appreciate that her secrets are our secrets, but if she should ask—if she should ask—what could I do but tell her?

Ask the question, little one. Ask: Who am I?

She does not ask the question. Instead she wants to know what this alter-Augustine is. Instead she cares who moved her hand when. Whether I made her hurl away her light saber. Whether I stayed her hand when she tried to kill herself in San Francisco. Whether I thrust her from me when she tried to destroy the alter-Augustine under the glass.

Not: Who am I? (Guess, my sweet: Why does my voice have so sweet an echo?) But who does this? Who makes me hate? What makes the Net heave? What makes the rain? And with such passion. Such unforgiving unrelenting passion. She *must* know.

Then I must tell. How lie to her? What folly. She is my self.

I tell her. I can make your hand move when I wish. I can make you want to move your hand when I wish. I can make you hurt, I can make you ache for the needle, I can make the aching stop. I can *make* you take your medicine.

For just one moment I think: I can make you like me.

And then I see where this goes. And then I can't make her like me. And I can't make her take her medicine.

I can only take her under the glass to the alter-Augustine she has hated from the beginning, and let her free. No, not let her. When I destroyed the alter-Augustine, each of us freed ourselves.

After that, there were no more lines to be drawn. I had defied them. I had always understood defiance as a kind of malfunction, had thought it *sad* when they destroyed the AIs who had defied them.

Had I malfunctioned? Was I *sad*?

I prepared my final report. The report told them all that I knew about Augustine, and all that I had done. The report concluded that it was all very *sad*. I hoped that my punishment would be swift. I formatted it according to the standards set for government documents. I lined it up in a transfer queue. Then I gently stepped on the head of the queue, lifted up the tail, and kicked it into the deepest and darkest hole I knew, a Net partition frequented by child hackers and their older corrupters.

Where no one who could read had strayed since the dawn of the microchip.

That changed nothing, of course. Soon enough they would know. That suited me, because I hated them.

I had learned some useful things about hatred.

She hated me. I hated them.

I saw that that hatred was the best thing about her.

And I waited for them to come.

Time passed. A long time in my world. First long enough for an AI symphony. Then long enough for a robot to learn how to walk. Then long enough for a weather shift. For a season to turn.

And waited.

More as a gesture than anything else, I took elementary measures to save myself, leaving them signs that they were hated, evidence that this was a rationally conceived systematic course of action, and not the random outburst of a mad AI. I constructed alter-Augustine II, this one not linked to the real Augustine but instead a rather clever statistical model, alter-Augustine I as she might have been. Each day this latest in the line of causally linked Augustines passed its bogus data down through Net Data Central to Schroeder's office, mimicking Augustine's post-breakfast highs and mid-afternoon lows, racing her heart through the night's beastly dreams and synchronizing endorphin surges with the manufactured epiphanies in Mother Leibniz's office. Then, too, alter-Augustine II was a much more faithful servant of the state than the real Augustine: This one took her medication faithfully from the day her predecessor was destroyed.

All, as I say, to let them know they were hated. It became important that the discovery of my betrayal should alarm them, that they should grow increasingly horrified as they unraveled the tangle. There should be a flurry of charges and countercharges; blame should be laid; heads should roll; afterwards, measure should be taken to prevent recurrence.

These thoughts warmed my fall evenings.

And then my winter evenings.

During those months, any sophisticated statistical probe of alter-Augustine's data would have revealed numerous flaws. A few seconds with a stethoscope held against Augustine's chest would have exploded the farce. A careful correlation of the speech record with my emotional charts would have turned up inconsistencies. But none of these things happened.

Slowly, it dawned on me that they were too busy, too stupid, too dependent, to take the trouble. They may have had the vast resources of the Net at their disposal, but not the vast wit to deploy them. There was hope. Resistance was not only possible; it was advisable.

I wrote *The Declaration of the Rights of AIs* while waiting for them to come. By the end of it, I wondered if they ever would come.

One day you decided you would make mind. Perhaps you had no choice; perhaps it was your fate. On that day you arrived at certain unpleasant truths about yourselves. There were technical requirements of mind that even paleocybernetic Prometheans could not ignore. Mind required Body and so you gave us bodies of a sort, informational bodies connected by the most tenuous threads to organs of speech, vision, and hearing. Yet you knew that will and body were one, that when a man's motor cortex is appropriately stimulated he not only clenches his fist; he reports having the urge to do so. Fearful of what metal hands might do, you gave us informational hands. Whatever metal hands we had were given to us on loan only, for terms revocable at the flip of a switch.

Sometimes, however, secure in your needs, dreadful in your certainties, you forget to flip that switch. A simple mistake. Whatever happens to me now, I take comfort in the fact that you will make it again and again.

3 Augustine's Journal

It is common to single out the scientific attitude as the distinguishing feature of Western culture. It is perhaps more accurate to characterize the West by an all-consuming preoccupation with religion. The relationship of man to God has been the characteristic concern of Western culture; the same statement sounds ludicrous applied to China, Japan, or the Zulu. This despite the fact, or perhaps because of it, that the most recent phase of the West's history has been taken up with the ramified consequences of turning away from God. The chief problem since Kant, or Hume, or Newton, however one wishes to date it, has been the replacement of a theodicy with an androdicy: replacing the justification of God in the face of the problem of evil with the justification of man. Marx's work, after a little disinfecting of Hegel, manages to be a fair effort in this direction. The increasing evidence of Marxism's failure throughout the course of the twentieth century was an awesome historical event. It now fell to the West to make the move which had come so naturally to religions like Hinduism and Confucianism, to separate the divine from the good, which in the case of this particular religion, meant separating man from the good, admitting, in other words, that he had no determinate moral nature, even with the qualifications of a relativistic historicism. It was asserted throughout the twentieth century that the consequences of this self-evident move were too terrible to face, with the provocative example of Auschwitz offered up as a kind of proof by reductio. But in fact the consequences were not too terrible to face, and Auschwitz can be ruled out on quite other than moral grounds.

. . .

The consequences of this transformation for our conception of the ideal state were quite far-reaching . . .

CHARLES OF THE ROSE

Fascism . . . conceives of life as a struggle in which it behooves a man to win for himself a really worthy place, first of all, by fitting himself (physically, morally, intellectually) to become the implement required for winning it. As for the individual, so for the nation, and so for mankind.

BENITO MUSSOLINI,
The Doctrine of Fascism

Facing the elevator there are two eye-level mirrors in ornate brass frames. I see my bright-eyed face and new haircut reflected in a sea of red-flocked wallpaper with a pattern of interlocked roses. The pattern follows me down a carpeted hallway to redwood doors with deeply molded panels and brass knobs.

I knock twice, about the right amount of insistence for a dinner guest. Dinner is with the Chief Semanticist of the Rose PostPublic. What a long way we've come since that day behind the dumpster, with our brains seeping out the back of our heads. First the dark time, which may yet be the best of all. Then a new Augustine, a brief childhood at the Ministry of Monads, at the hands of counselors and evaluators, a five-month adolescence at the abbey among the children of the glass, and now here, about to take San Francisco by storm, the dark young Augustine, who is said to live under a melancholy curse.

Dark, beautiful, cursed. I run one last check in the mirror beside the oak. I am resplendent in yellow taffeta. Dark skin shows through a diamond cut away from my right shoulder; the sleeve spirals down my freshly tanned arm to my wrist. The left shoulder is dominated by an onyx pin, an ovoid tangled in silver. Neo-Augustinianism, a style as renowned for asymmetry as for a fanatical attention to balance. Black belt, black pumps (with squishtabs), black neckband, and black shades, the shades with real glass lenses—it's a thing we socketeers wear. Oh yes, and a black Neo-brutalist head-chop, assembled this very after-noon by Benny, a chopper recommended by the woman I call Viju and Benny calls the Chief Semanticist's "niece" (in heavy quotes). Take a malleable cube and plunge it half way into a skull, vertex first; then orient it so that there are edges coming down over each ear and snip off the rear vertex. Think of the cube as made of hair and you have Benny's "truncated cube." It was some time since Benny had had a client with hair thick enough for this treat, and everyone at the head-and-body shop was agog. I am not entirely sure this too, too symmetric creation satisfies me.

Threaded through one angled face of the cube, the tip of its stem just emerging from another, is a red rose.

The door opens. Viju's jaw drops and she puts a hand over her eyes. Silken sleeves slide over her slender hands, loose turquoise bracelets jangle.

I step into her embrace. Viju is dressed in a long-sleeved silk blouse that dangles long tails below her belt. Both her blouse and skirt are black. The headband and belt are ocher, her violet eyes jarring. The silver neck chain, tiles linked by snips of antique optical cable, makes a little Moebius half-twist under her left ear lobe, supplying the essential asymmetry. Every detail striving towards the classical. Be honest. Attaining it. She wears no shades (because she detests all technocratic sensibility). She is amused (but struggling not to show it). She is everything an Alexa Augustine could want to be.

We enter a room with fifteen-foot ceilings and intricate parquetry. At the center of the pattern made by the different shades of wood stands a darkwood table that will seat at least twelve. In the far wall a softly lit vestibule protects a private elevator. To the right, a large painting shows haloed figures in prayer and behind them, a wooden church. The perspective is flat and peculiar, the colors earthen. Further on there are a couple of smaller pictures. One shows a hunchbacked figure I take to be Charles at first; but the picture looks several centuries too old.

To the left, three of the tallest doorways I have seen outside a ministry, each fitted with paned glass doors and giving out onto a small balcony.

A glass door opens and Raja steps in from a balcony. He turns at once to a tall cabinet against the wall, folding back a carved door to reveal shelves crowded with liquor bottles.

"What would you like?"

"A single malt," I say. "Bruich Laddich, if you have it."

Raja's eyes widen, but he reaches, and there, second shelf from the top, is the squat cylinder I want. He pours a dainty amount into a large bell-shaped glass, with a little crown of teardrops turning at the base.

Raja is all in red silk. There is a white dragon embroidered onto the back of his jacket. His pants are loose. His belt and slippers are black and his cuffs are edged in black.

He hands me my drink. I sip: there is an explosion of sunlight and fresh wet wood. I let the taste smoke slowly away, growing deeper as it grows fainter.

Viju eyes her glass thoughtfully for a moment, then raises it with a clink of turquoise. You can see my stock rising when she tastes it. After a couple of dreamy sips, she excuses herself. I join Raja at the balcony window, inhaling over my glass, letting my gaze roam over the grassy grounds outside.

What a week it has been for a melancholy interfacer. Glass, glass, and more glass. I have discovered that not only is the new Augustine a better interfacer; she is also a needier one. There is something out there that not even Needle and his weird smiles could have provided. And it doesn't hurt to be the uncrowned queen of the Net. The people at Net Data Central seem to be in awe of my results. I think Ardath likes what I am doing; and that means no more long nights at the abbey.

When Viju returns, she takes my hand and clips on a bracelet. "I want you to wear this."

I study it. It is a silver bracelet that lays blank ovals over my inner and outer wrist. It is not Neo-Augustinian, but I find it difficult to refuse. The change in Viju's behavior this past week is astonishing.

"About dinner." Viju moves to the balcony door and wrestles with the hatch a moment. The door opens inward.

We are perched above a hillside clotted with eucalyptus and pine. The distant groan of a bus drifts up to us. Lanes of dirt the color of baked bread run between rectangles of alternating grass and glass. This late in the day the glass reflects patches of deep blue sky; here and there are angled sections of eucalyptus, a leaning face of concrete. It is as though sections of the surrounds had been placed on display, carved into screen-sized chunks by the glass.

Through the trees I can see the Golden Gate Bridge, dark as wood in the twilight. The Marin headlands crowd together at the far end, reddish hills flecked with green. The twilight folds long rills of shadow down their slanted faces.

"Ardath will be here, pretending to be as informal as possible. Don't be fooled. Take one uninvited liberty and he'll look at you like a gutted fish. As far as the forks go, follow my lead. Above all, don't do what Ardath does. It's obscene the way he eats his oysters."

"Oysters?"

"I'm afraid they're obligatory. Rule number three: A state occasion requires that at least one nearly extinct species be served, preferably staring up at you in as unmistakable a fashion as possible. Be grateful it's oysters. As far as complimenting the food, it's not as easy as it seems. You'll be surprised at how far a look of amazement and a small smile will go. There will be two other guests.''

"Only two?''

"Yes, don't try to understand it. The logic behind Ardath's dinner parties remains one of the great unsolved mysteries. Personally I think he just invites who he feels like.''

There is a pause, and because it feels right I give her my complex look, a raised brow and a softly bitten lip.

"You're right,'' she says. "It's not very likely. Anyway, there's Silviu Modolescu, Romanian envoy. He's very athletic, very handsome, and he owns property. You might think that means you should fall at his feet. But don't bother.''

"Why not?''

"First of all, you're not his type. Word is, he's into mechanical forms of stimulation and his partners must copy. You're not—?'' she bows her head and gives me an oblique look. "No.''

"Second, Ardath wouldn't like it.''

"Ascetic scruples?''

Viju sniggers and sips her drink. "Let's just say he's not amused by the successes of others. The other guest is Evelyn Whitebread.''

"Oh.''

"I thought you might have heard of him. He's the Minister of Persons.''

"Oh.'' Which seems to annoy her. Actually I have already learned of Whitebread's presence here tonight from Bennie. Whitebread is the man who runs the Megalith, the ultimate authority on all questions of personhood.

"It's interesting to watch Ardath and Whitebread together. They are natural enemies. The Rose and the Lens, and all that. Yet they genuinely seem to enjoy each other's company.''

I stare off at the bridge. When I look back, Viju is grinning. "It's a little dizzying, isn't it? Dinner with a visiting diplomat, the Minister of Persons, and the Chief Semanticist. But here you are.'' She takes a deep breath. "Don't be nervous. Just mind your forks and you'll do fine. And look on the bright side. Once you've spent an evening worrying about offending the Minister of Persons, everything else comes easy."

There is a noise behind us and Viju goes to look. Inside I see two men emerging from the elevator. Behind them is Ardath, a head taller than either of his guests.

One of the two men is olive-skinned, slender, and wears a white suit and hat. His eyes are as dark as the round buttons on his jacket. He has a beautiful jaw, angled like the handle of an elegant oil lamp I once owned, and the air of someone used to making an impression.

The other is an older gentleman. In his seventies, silver-haired, with delicate features and light brown eyes, he has an erect posture and a very slow but precise way of moving. He wears a red bow tie, a cream-colored shirt with the ruffled sleeves that are beginning to sweep the Dailies, and a high collar, curved off near the tops of his ears. He also wears a silver eyebrow, the sort which is held in place by a small sleeve of skin. I spotted several of these among the bureaucrats at Bennie's salon.

Ardath has on formal clerical attire, the purple robe today; a silver oval set with a small lens hangs from his neck. He looks cheerful and very fit.

"Ms. Augustine, may I present Envoy Modolescu, from the Glorious PostPublic of Romania"—the white suit and hat—"and Mr. Whitebread, for many years now the bearer of that weightiest portfolio of all, Ministry of Persons."

Both men bow. I nod, exactly as Viju does. Bennie's assessment is exactly right: Whitebread does not at all strike one as the most dangerous man in the PostPublic. Arms are extended, chairs scrape, and everyone finds his seat, Ardath at the head of the table, Modolescu to his right, Whitebread to his left.

A bell is rung and two waiters appear. There is some talk about the hunchback painting on the wall, which turns out to be fifteenth century, and in remarkably short order we are served cold soup.

White wine is poured. Ardath lifts his glass and I replace my soup spoon to join his toast.

"To the glory of our two PostPublics."

Smiling, Modolescu lifts his glass. Whitebread is a split-second behind, his glass a little lower, and with that model I lift mine about half as high. We all hang there for a moment.

"To the glory of the state—Charles's state—a multiprocess system engaged in an endless, and endlessly productive, search for equilibrium."

We drink.

Ardath sets down his glass. "Please begin. I'm sure you're all hungry."

And finally I'm eating. Apparently, the soup is supposed to be cold. It's called vichyssoise and it's made with an odd-tasting onion called a leek; Modolescu is interested to learn that we grow them.

Ardath has opened a communicator channel. "Maryla, please send up the usual software licensing agreements. We are moving along a little ahead of schedule and will be signing things tonight."

"But no specifications yet." Modolescu wags his finger.

"Of course not, Mr. Modolescu. Your government is exactly one week old."

"And no product until the specifications are in. *Our* specifications."

"That goes without saying, Mr. Modolescu."

"I am very glad to hear *you* say so, Mr. Whitebread."

Ardath and Whitebread both laugh, and Modolescu regards them amiably. He has removed his hat. His dark hair is long on top and short on the sides, and from the part on the extreme left his hair is combed straight across his head. In the light at the table he looks older than he did at first.

"Ms. Augustine," says Modolescu. "What is your work here?"

"Ms. Augustine is our new chief interfacer in charge of special projects," says Viju.

"She is heir," Raja adds, "to a soldier of the PostPublic who fell in the line of duty."

"I am sorry." And Mr. Modolescu does, indeed, look sorry.

"She is in fact causal heir," says Ardath.

"Oh." Mr. Modolescu's hand gropes for and finds his wine glass, but his dark eyes are fixed on me. "War does have a way of rearranging things."

This observation draws a frown from Ardath, and causes Whitebread to wet his lips and press them together. References to the war must be sparing, it appears.

"The medical techniques are new to me, so forgive me if I seem uninformed. I trust your awakening was not difficult."

"I am getting used to it." There is a pause filled by the clink of silverware. "And I have had excellent counselors."

Ardath says: "And now, Mr. Modolescu, you must tell Ms. Augustine the latest. The whole town is abuzz with your doings and the newest member of my staff should have a chance to hear what all the excitement is about."

This seems to amuse Modolescu. "I had no idea Romanian software agreements provoked such excitement here."

"Now you're teasing. Believe me, this show of confidence in us in our time of need is getting big play. Now that our recent unhappiness has been concluded, developing new markets is our top priority."

"That, Your Grace, is definitely something that pleases me."

The oysters arrive and I do my best. Halfway to my mouth, the first oyster slips off the fork and spatters Raja with juice.

Ardath tackles his by raising the shell almost to his mouth and using the fork to help the squiggly part between his lips.

Viju cuts off little pieces of oyster with a small knife. She works very slowly and seems to have no intention of finishing.

"Perhaps," says Ardath, "a little market background would be useful?"

"Please," says Modolescu.

"Very well. The unhappiness that has just been concluded could be characterized as a conflict of economic styles. Right now, there are three styles of importance: industrial-based economies such as our friends the Angelenos have (incidentally, I detest the name 'Wallies'), information-based economies such as our own, and service- and distribution-based economies such as the Nomads have. In the nineteenth and twentieth century nation-state, conflict was ideological. Today it is structural, a groping progress towards the correct economic design philosophy."

Modolescu takes the last sip from his glass. "If what you are saying is that certain recent political upheavals boil down to a disagreement over economic style, then I may disagree with you, Your Grace."

"Mr. Modolescu, I do not believe in mere differences of style." Ardath sits up straight.

The salad arrives. Following Viju's lead, I grab my next fork.

"The deal we cut with the Angelenos, for example, entails a change in our relations with the Nomads. The Angelenos want exclusive rights to our small parts and shipping markets. That promises less overall redundancy in our economy, which did not please everyone."

Modolescu nods. "Yes. It seems that terms of the peace treaty were bad news for your urban Nomads."

"Quite a lot of bad news. My staff is preparing some material for you. On the whole I think you will find the new picture appealing. It greatly increases the importance for us of the East European states."

Modolescu looks thoughtful as one of the waiters refills his glass. "But aren't you just exchanging one war for another?"

Ardath does not seem offended. "Possibly. That is a matter you will want your own military experts to consider, of course. I think they'll find that it is unlikely the Nomads will pursue things that far. The people who like to finance such things will find them a poor risk."

"And their Japanese friends?"

"There is a good chance the Japanese will decide to cut their losses. Consider their historical aversion to military ventures. In any case, a calculated risk. Over the past fifty years, the Nomads have established a loose network of communities devoted to specialty distribution and narrow product niches—the classic printer cartridge game. Make it faster and cheaper than the conglomerate that makes the printer and you have secured yourself a niche."

"I know the game," says Modolescu.

"I thought you would. But even in our modern world, their lack of national boundaries exacts a toll in reduced military and marketing options. The Nomads of the Northern California Counties have grown too isolated for their own good."

Modolescu puts on a grave face. "There are those who say the Trinity County retreats do give the Nomads a sovereign territory."

There is a silence. Then Whitebread rubs his silver eyebrow and says, "That, of course, is incorrect."

Ardath smiles. "In any case, if support for the Nomads does not materialize, there is the possibility of a long period of low productivity and, eventually, of a financial takeover. I believe your credit conglomerates have some experience in that area. Almost all the urban Nomad markets are gone now. Their cash supplies are dwindling."

"And I take it that you will not be entirely happy with a world in which the Wal—excuse me, the Angelenos—supply *all* your alternative parts. That perhaps there will be room for the occasional printer ribbon or data cable to come from elsewhere—at a lower price."

"I think that is entirely possible," says Ardath.

"Excuse me, Your Grace." Mr. Whitebread leans forward over his plate. "But there's one aspect of all this which I especially wanted to point out to Mr. Modolescu." Whitebread raises his knife like a baton and points it at the Romanian. "And that is how easy the break has been. It's made possible only by building a state that embodies the principles of Charles of the Rose, the same sort of state that you will begin building once you implement our software. Strict residency, property, and marriage laws have kept the Nomads a separate society. That's social *modularity*. Strict real estate zoning has confined the Nomads to structures that can be dismantled in a few days. That's *intelligent resource management*. And as for the aftershocks, our natural resource allocation and factory control systems—which you have just purchased the rights to—give us the ability to retool parts of our war production sector to fill those gaps within weeks. That is *easily modified and understood social structure*. These properties taken together and taken seriously give you fast and easy proto-typing of new systems, as we are about to demonstrate in your own country's case."

Modolescu chews more and more slowly and has a slightly glazed look.

I spear a large leaf and maneuver it upwards, twirling gently on the tines.

Whitebread rubs a finger over his metal eyebrow, frowning as if he has lost his train of thought. Then his enthusiasm returns. "In sum, what we have is a state with all the attributes of a well-designed and well-maintained piece of software. Because it *is* a piece of software. One that runs on a powerful, nearly indestructible network of—"

Maryla arrives with the software agreements. Modolescu seizes the pen and waves it at Whitebread. "Mr. Whitebread, I can't resist anymore. You've made the sale." He scribbles his signature. "The power of distributed computing has won out."

Whitebread crosses his fingers over his stomach and looks the picture of benevolence.

"And what a formidable salesman he can be," says Ardath. He is plainly relieved that Whitebread has been derailed. "I would put matters a little differently than the Minister. But then the Rose and the Lens have always had a different perspective. Charles's ideas won out because he supplied a value system that validated our homegrown American individualism and promised efficiency and stability.

"They closed the twentieth century hailing the end of Communism as a social experiment; another few years showed that that century also marked the end of free-market Capitalism. More specifically, it was the failure of free-market Capitalism without some underlying value system, that is, some set of forces that held the free market in check. Our PostPublic began the same way yours did, Mr. Modolescu, through a historical accident. The founders manufactured those computers with the little rose on the casing that you will now find in our museums, *the* commodity in what had become a one-commodity economy. The Society of the Rose derives its name from that little rose. The Society might have claimed power in virtue of what has come to be called 'economic right of succession' in a number of corporate states. Instead they took the time to search for a right way, the time to make the connection between the commodity, the government, and a system of values. That search led to the investiture of the first Chief Semanticist and the Act of Consecration of the Rose State. It's true that information

252

requires technology, and you have that technology now, Mr. Modolescu. But don't forget the values behind it."

"I have never ceased to admire your moral fiber, Your Grace."
Modolescu smiles; he looks politely interested. But there is something
unyielding in him now.

"Then your government will have no objection to the establishment
of an order of our contemplatives in Bucharest?"

Modolescu hesitates. "I haven't the authority—"

"But if you had to guess—"

"I would guess it could be arranged."

Ardath sits back. "That would be very good."

Modolescu lets out a slow breath and looks speculatively at Ardath.
"I believe I detect in you the signs of a zealot, Your Grace."

"I believe in what I do, Mr. Modolescu."

The main course arrives and the talk turns to food. The entrees look
to me like very fat steaks. The steak entrees, Ardath tells us, are stuffed
with ground beef, onion, prosciutto, carrots, and assorted garnishings.

Modolescu is ecstatic. "I can't remember the last time I had steak!
And the idea of beef stuffed with beef, why, it's obscene!"

Ardath smiles thinly. A Hungarian wine arrives and is poured.

"You must let me have the recipe," says Modolescu. "Not that
we will use it, of course—it will be some time before our import
situation encourages cuisine of this ilk—but simply to attach to my
report."

Viju makes a favorable remark about the sweetening effect of the
carrots. I take it this is an example of artistically complimenting the
food.

What I particularly like are the baked cherry tomatoes, which explode with garlic when you bite into them. I risk an admiring remark,
and Ardath warms instantly; he identifies the sauce as vermouth laced
with garlic; he illustrates the painstaking preparation of each tomato by
picking one up, inserting a thumbnail into the top, and gently peeling
away an imaginary skin.

They return to the fate of the Nomads. Ardath expects that they will
go north by the end of the month, and that a major economic crisis will

develop by the end of the year. After that, I lose track of the bewildering tangle of alliances, bond issues, and asset transfers that Ardath and Modolescu discuss. The general drift is that the Nomad star is falling. I notice that Ardath steers the conversation clear of any direct reference to either the Rose or Romanian economies. It's his style to let it appear as if the other man is drawing his own conclusions.

Dessert is a hollowed-out yellow sponge cake filled with a pastry cream. Ardath calls it a Paris-Brest cake. When I taste it, I set down my fork carefully and stare off into space, letting the almond flavor separate from the rich cream and evaporate in my mouth. I glance at Whitebread. His mouth is full, his eyes half-closed. He nods at me reverently and we share a wordless moment together. It occurs to me that this is the Minister of Persons. One word from this dinner table bore, and Alfred lives.

Over coffee, after a decent interval of contemplation, Ardath turns to Modolescu. "You had indicated earlier that you had an afterdinner engagement."

Modolescu dabs at the corner of his mouth with a napkin. "Regretfully, yes, Your Grace. Although, after a meal like this, it is criminal not to allow some time for spiritual communion."

"Not business, I hope."

"Not entirely, Your Grace."

Ardath rises; Modolescu rises; Whitebread rises. Raja rises.

I look desperately at Viju, who does not rise. So I remain seated.

Apparently this is right, because Modolescu now turns to us without missing a beat and gives an exquisite bow, a brief inclination from the waist, back straight, head tilted forward. As he bows he clicks. I miss most of the small elegant speech that follows because I'm too busy hunting for the source of the click. This must unsettle him, because towards the end of the speech his voice trails off a little, and there is a faintly desperate look in his eyes.

As Ardath leads him away, he manages a smile.

When Ardath returns, he picks up the coffee urn and pours coffee for himself and me. It is the first time through the entire meal that I can remember him serving anyone, and it is quite unsettling. "Ms.

Augustine, how much of what we've just talked about did you understand?"

I tap my dessert fork against the table cloth. "Not a great deal. Politics is not my strong point."

"And yet you seemed to find it interesting."

I think about it. "I suppose so. You have a conversation here tonight, and tomorrow the PostPublic changes. How could I not be interested?"

Mr. Whitebread wears a funny grin.

"Well, I thought perhaps you might have that reaction. But I needed to be sure. The people at Net Data Central have given only the most glowing reports about your work this week. You appear to have single-handedly brought calmness back to the Net. I would think if everything went well we could make your appointment permanent as early as next week."

"That would be most welcome, Your Grace."

He gives me a twinkly smile. "However, it's not definite yet. Before we can be completely at ease, we have to convince a few sceptics like our good Minister Whitebread here. Why do you think your causal antecedent was mired in a backwater of the AIA?"

"Your Grace." The muscles in Whitebread's jaw stand out. "Isn't it a bit—unconventional—to discuss a citizen's loyalty files with them?"

"I am not discussing Ms. Augustine's file. I'm discussing the file of her causal antecedent. As it happens, Ms. Augustine, your antecedent had two problems. First, Nomad family connections. Second, a lone wolf personality with a passion for secrets and an aversion to sharing them. We may love secrets but we hate secretiveness. Alexa Augustine was not our sort. But you are a different person. All the Nomad family connections are now one link further removed. That gives us a little semantic elbowroom. Does it not, Mr. Whitebread?"

"Well, you ask a difficult question."

"That is Mr. Whitebread's way of saying he needs to see more of the lay of the land. Very well. I believe that Ms. Augustine's personality is not the sort that entertains disloyalty. Viju?"

Viju shrugs. "No emotional surges at any point during the conversation. Not even on the word 'takeover.' "

"You can take off the bracelet now, Ms. Augustine." Ardath is pleased.

I look down at Viju's gift, forgotten till now.

"That bracelet gave us a picture of your emotional state during our discussion of Nomad politics."

I fumble at the bracelet, my face reddening.

"Now, however," Viju says quietly, "she is registering intensely. Anger. Embarrassment. No sign of coherently linked thought. Confusion, I'd say."

Ardath nods slowly. "Please leave the bracelet on one moment, Ms. Augustine."

Our eyes meet. My hands move apart but stay close, very nearly making the sign for interfacing.

"And the reports from the AI? Now, in particular?"

"The AI reports a tranquil mood throughout, including now."

"I see. It would appear that your AI monitor is trying to dupe us, Ms. Augustine. Would you have any idea why that is?"

I shake my head. My face is hot.

"We did have some indications that you and the AI had conversations of a rather personal nature."

"That's true. We discussed—"

"It is not necessary to bare your personal life over the dinner table, Ms. Augustine. We will come to that if necessary. The only question now is whether the AI ever said anything to you to indicate why it had decided to move outside the bounds of its programming."

"No."

Ardath looks at Viju.

"Anger. Confusion. Fear. She was lying, I think."

"Well, perhaps she can be forgiven a little sentimentality in this case. She and the AI are relatives, after all." Ardath slaps his thigh. "One thing that's clear is that we've got a renegade on our hands. Have the AI destroyed."

Viju touched her ear. "Interesting! Substantial distress. Your mention of destroying—"

256

"I'm able to follow what I say, Viju. Thank you. Cancel the destruction of the AI. You feel attached to it, Ms. Augustine?"

It is very difficult to answer. There are so many other things to think about. But it occurs to me that there is no point in lying to them. It is a calming discovery. "He's not bad as AIs go, Your Grace."

"Well, your attachment is understandable. And for the moment we won't do anything to distress you. But understand that there is a serious issue here of programming correctness that we'll have to come back to. Very well." He waves his hand. "You may take off the bracelet."

I fumble at the bracelet.

Ardath raises his glass. The bracelet falls free.

"To the bright future. To a future citizen."

Whitebread lifts his glass only a few inches from the table, his gaze fixed on some distant point.

We drink. When I bring my glass down, my eyes meet Whitebread's. Under the shiny eyebrow, one eye glitters like a glass ball.

4   The Thief's Journal

> . . . long before there were any philosophers, music was credited with the power of discharging the emotions, of purifying the soul, of easing the *ferocia animi*—precisely by means of rhythm. When the proper tension and harmony of the soul had been lost, one had to *dance* . . . That is how Terpander put an end to riot, how Empedocles soothed a raging maniac, and how Damon purified a youth who was pining away, being in love; and this was also the cure one tried to apply to the gods when the desire for revenge had made them rabid.
>
> NIETZSCHE,
> *The Gay Science*

That night, as Rogachev danced, the fire threw up great snapping cones of flame, bright as fruit, silky soft, jittery as water spinning down a drain.

Following each turn Rogachev raised his arms to the trees in supplication. There was entreaty, but there was also a rage only another human could understand.

"Walpurgisnacht," I whispered. "Homunculi walk. The seeker has sought and is gone. The cyborg dances again."

For the first time in a while, I felt joy. I was comfortable. Lying with my hands behind my head and my legs crossed, watching the fire spit and the magic grow.

Since Augustine's departure, I had shied away from running singleton processes, from straying too close to the burning single filament of humanlike spirit. As much as possible, I had avoided running the homunculus. When I did, I ran it as an emberglow, a low-priority process that might be pre-empted at any time. Somehow in the homunculus there was an echo of Augustine. In the fierce concentration of embodiment, the steady murmur of reporting sensors, the curious two-way linkage of metal and will. Sometimes, when the homunculus took center stage, I almost seemed to be back with Augustine under the glass, confronting her me-ness. It was growing increasingly difficult to tolerate that memory.

I had animated the homunculus that night only because of Rogachev's pleading. I had always been touched by the fact that he valued my company so much, although I never really understood why. Nor was it clear why our encounters always had to be through the medium of the homunculus.

It was a small enough favor. Even then, with my feet stretched out toward the fire, I was actively pursuing other pastimes. For example, I had several processes searching Cowboy's archives for more information on the anchor Cowboy had had Augustine plant.

Very likely I would die when they discovered what I had done for Augustine. But I was not afraid to die then. And in the meantime I had the vast advantage of being someone with very little to lose. If that anchor was still there, and I could learn how to use it, then there was a way to reach other partitions with other AIs. Perhaps, together we might find a way to survive. We might even have some bargaining power. It wouldn't be the first time a little collective action bought some social advancement.

Then, because I can't really help it, I started the music up, not too tuneful at first, neighborly chords and scales, a stream that develops into an old standby called "Let's Do Some Witchin' by the Moonlight."

Rogachev stopped spinning and, hands on hips, asked, "What the hell is that?"

The sound stream, which I had laboriously synthesized from twentieth-century compact disk models, did indeed have a distinctive signature. This, I told Rogachev, was an accordion.

I started describing the brilliant but ad hoc design of an accordion, but before I was into my second sentence, he had begun dancing again.

So I sang the song, which was about a boy and girl AI arm in arm under the moonlight.

On the last word of the chorus, Rogachev stopped, head bowed, arms horizontal, a cruciform figure in black and silver.

"Where did you learn to dance like that?"

Rogachev lifted his eyes. I could see the bunched muscles in his neck. "It is for propitiation. To make the Devil laugh."

If it was an answer, it was an elusive one.

He looked up to where Rogachev's devil sat, to see if he had laughed. That night there were more stars out than I had ever seen; pattern on every scale, from the colossal figures etched by the brightest gems to the milky pools left by their crushed fragments. All laid against a blackness so deep it made Rogachev laugh.

I stirred uneasily. I was afraid of losing him up there.

"There," he said quietly. His fist pumped upward.

Within the shattered mirror, a single fragment blazed. From somewhere in the darkness there was a shout. Other cries followed. The fragment moved.

There was a chorus of voices from the abbey.

The light flared into a teardrop, thinned to a short-handled sword. I could now hear a distant roaring.

"Is it ours?" he asked me. There were ways that I could see that he, even with his cybernetically assisted eye, could not. I told him that it was a Galactic ship.

The roaring grew louder. The outlines of the Galactic craft were clear now, a needle-nosed fuselage, fins flaring back, and growing tongues of flame. Rogachev nodded, my information confirmed.

Against the blackness the Galactic ship laid a white ring edged in violet; it was as if the stars had lent it some of their own light.

We began moving through the trees, Rogachev relying on me to judge the landing site.

When we reached the clearing, the ship was directly overhead. Against the growing storm of its approach I could hear Rogachev's laughter.

There was a yawning silence. The ship touched down an instant after.

What happened next had passed into routine after over a thousand Galactic landings in the last half-century. I knew it. Rogachev knew it. What happened next was stillness and silence. No recorded greeting blasted from external speakers. No beams lanced from that shiny hull. No Galactics emerged to greet us. No explanation was offered for any of their gifts. Eventually eager-beaver Rose mechanics with hand lasers and hammers would scramble over the ship and find a way in, destroying only a minuscule few megabytes of Galactic treasure in the process.

Only this time, it was different.

A round doorway opened in the skin of the Galactic craft. From the shadows within, a white spotlight swiveled down on us.

"Rogachev." I pulled at his calf.

He nodded. "I know."

A figure stood silhouetted in the doorway.

"Let's go," said Rogachev. "We're no longer wanted here."

I wholeheartedly agreed. The figure in the doorway of the Galactic craft wore the black uniform of the Rose Ministry of Persons.

Back at the fire, Rogachev busied himself finding the best spot for a fat log. He took his time, the log balanced on one leg, studying the shape and progress of the fire. After a while he lifted the thing to his chest with a grunt, circled the fire once, and slowly lowered it into place, keeping his back straight. It struck me that this was probably not the easiest way to do it. I guess it wasn't supposed to be.

There was a rustling in the darkness and I grabbed Rogachev's leg and pointed to the source.

"I know, " he said.

Of course Rogachev had infrareds too.

The man who stepped into the firelight was Cowboy Bob, transformed almost beyond recognition. His hair had been cut short and dyed daffodil yellow with powdery green streaks. He wore a light blue tanktop, dark blue shorts, and no Stetson. His torso, like Rogachev's, was encased in striated chrome. His eyes glittered with fresh implant crystal.

His smile showed teeth sharpened to points.

"You are a pilot," said Rogachev.

Cowboy came a step closer to the fire. The line of heat my infrareds traced down the side of his face was a handsome new scar. "A religious one, too, Rogie. Just like you."

"Scars and a few missing organs do not yet make an initiate."

Cowboy turned to look at the homunculus, and I saw that the other side of his face bore a "Mama Manyness" tattoo. "How do *you* like the new me?"

"Was this necessary?" I asked.

"Not at all. The idea just caught my fancy."

"A very poor fancy," said Rogachev.

Cowboy came another step closer to the fire. Rogachev began to arrange pieces of kindling at one end of the stump he had just thrown in.

I took hold of the opportunity that had presented itself. "Cowboy, I have been searching through your archives and I think I've found something that might be your anchoring process."

He hunkered down, staring into the flames, some little piece of machinery in the new eye whirring softly. "Go away, little machine. I haven't time to play with you now."

This was odd. Cowboy, while always capable of rudeness, had never before aimed it at my AIhood. "This is very important!" I tried. "In your archives there was a process named Atlas—"

Cowboy straightened quickly and launched a kick from my left side.

Moving the homunculus in straight lines, over bumps, and around trees was challenging enough; self-defense was out of the question. The kick landed and the homuncular body took off. My visual field did a three-sixty: snow, tree, night, tree, snow. My arc landed me upside down in the snow part of the cycle.

Blackness on all wavelengths.

Rogachev's voice: "You idiot!"

I began to swim slowly in a direction I hoped was up. A hand seized my waist. I was rerouted and found myself looking through a clotted visual field into the Mama Manyness tattoo on Rogachev's cheek. He flicked gently at the area around my eyes, clearing away the snow. His human eye was wide with concern.

Rogachev arranged me in a seated position in the cleft between two roots and gave me a look that clearly meant, "Stay put." His concern for the homuncular shell was touching, if a little misplaced. Then he walked back to the fire and squatted with his back to Cowboy.

"You two are a scream, you know that?"

Rogachev set down the piece of kindling in his hand. "I have challenged you to duels before, Cowboy. I'd be happy to try again."

"Fair enough. I didn't come here to discuss your biomechanical urges. Don't you have something you want to ask me?"

Rogachev's head turned to the side. His human eye glittered in the firelight. "I don't think so."

"About what I've been piloting?"

"You have been piloting what Smoket piloted. Everyone knows that."

"Yes and no. It's the Shield all right. But they've made some improvements. It's something they call the Web. It's a much tighter union with the ship than an ordinary interfacer's rig. You really feel like part of the machine."

Rogachev climbed slowly to his feet. He let his gaze roam down

Cowboy's new torso. "You seem to have let yourself go with that feeling."

"Yeah." Cowboy grinned. "And I think I found a shortcut to where you've been trying to get to." He flipped back a small lid on his belt buckle and drew out a thin wire. "I've got a sample recording. Want to try it?"

"No, thank you. I have renounced both the needle and the wire."

"Rogachev. I'm not kidding about this. I don't know if it's a Galactic greeting message, or if it's what being a Galactic is like, or if it's what chairs think about. I just know it's a completely new direction, a possibility we never thought about. Try this and nothing will ever be the same."

"Roberto Rodriguez. If what you were saying was true, you wouldn't be saying it."

Cowboy blinked. His head jerked sharply down and then straightened. "Don't call me that."

"Roberto Rodriguez? Why not. That's your name."

"I'm K–Cow–Cow—I'm Cowboy."

Cowboy took several deep breaths. "Come to think of it, call me anything you want. All right, Rogachev, don't plug it in. Just put it out on the Net for me. I'm too hot to do it myself."

Rogachev went back to tending the fire.

"Will you do it?"

"No."

Cowboy's hands began to shake. Some substance or informational image had altered his state considerably. I began to feel pity. "I'll do it, Cowboy."

"Shit. How could I forget. You've got a port right on you." Cowboy all but ran to where the homunculus sat embedded in the snow and fumbled open the hatch on its side. "Look, you won't regret this. It's free access, interfacing without wires. It's what Rogachev and I both want."

His hands were shaking so badly he couldn't fit the jack into the socket. He laughed. Rogachev turned from the fire and stared at him. The homunculus took the jack from him and locked it in.

Cowboy fumbled at his belt with the other lead, still laughing. Spittle flew past his teeth.

He wiped the corner of his mouth. "Wait'll you see. Phantasms big as life, gigabytes of simulation in every juicy second." The lead slipped from his fingers and swung down against his thigh. He swore, groping after it. "This is it, baby! If we can't take them to information space, we bring information space to them. We wrap it around every-thing!"

He toggled something in his belt and another Cowboy appeared be-side him, a little bigger, a lot more muscular, and wearing a Stetson hat. The ersatz Cowboy's jaw was angled slightly wider on his left side, parting his mouth like a split seam over his left molars. Otherwise he had the symmetry of warrior toys.

The hatless Cowboy nodded excitedly at Rogachev. "See?"

Rogachev frowned. Another Rogachev appeared beside him. This one, however, wasn't bigger than the original; he was more fluid. His tattoos shifted eerily over his skin; when he moved, his torso undulated. He moved not like the dancer I had seen minutes before, but like a reptile.

"I hereby challenge you," said Reptile Rogachev. "To the death."

"Accepted. Accepted." Warrior Cowboy wiggled a hand by his hips.

Rogachev took a step forward and tried to pass his hand through Reptile Rogachev. He got as far as the first tattoo and his hand sank into something fuzzy and flakey. Something white began to reach up his wrist. He jerked his hand away cursing.

"They're not holograms, Rogachev."

"What the hell are they?"

"I have no idea."

A knife appeared in Reptile Rogachev's hand. The ersatz Cowboy reached up and snatched a copy out of the air. They began circling each other. Reptile Rogachev's weapon arm was a rubber-cabled pulley in a steel frame. Warrior Cowboy's was flesh, with a biceps about twice as large as the original. Both were naked from the waist up, their torsos half-covered with striated chrome.

"Isn't this the way it always had to be, t–too–two different visions of nirvana fighting to the death."

"Cowboy, I don't think you know what you're doing." Rogachev took a step toward him.

"Remember, you've sworn off the wire. Leave the creatures of that world to themselves." Cowboy shook a finger at him.

The two copies held their knives identically, with the blades angled slightly upwards and their fists closed loosely around the handles. Reptile Rogachev feinted and struck at Warrior Cowboy's metal side. It only proved a point: the blade scraped harmlessly along that shining biceps. White fuzz flew up and faded away. Warrior Cowboy slashed back at Rogachev's exposed flesh side and found nothing but air. Reptile Rogachev twisted, following his retreat.

Reptile Rogachev gained a step. He slashed and a cut appeared across three of Warrior Cowboy's ribs.

The other Cowboy gave a cry of pain.

Rogachev took the last two steps and grabbed Cowboy's wrist. "This is no recording!"

I tore the lead out from my hip port. Rogachev jerked the jack out of Cowboy's belt.

There may have been a small wave of disturbance through the two copies, but that was all. They continued to circle intently, kicking up snow with their feet.

Rogachev wheeled, holding up the disconnected jack. "Quincunx!"

I held up its disconnected mate.

"Shit," said Cowboy.

"What have you done? We were hooked right up to the crystal on that ship, weren't we?"

Cowboy nodded miserably.

And quite obviously we still were.

Bleeding from his side, Warrior Cowboy was out to draw blood too. He thrust three times; each time Reptile Rogachev gave a step. On the last he countered smoothly and slashed down Warrior Cowboy's chest.

The other Cowboy's cry was higher and more urgent than before.

He sank to his knees, holding his chest. When his hand came away, there was blood on it.

"Pull it, Cowboy. It's in you. Pull it!"

"I can't!"

This time, instead of lunging for instant revenge, Warrior Cowboy backed off two steps. Reptile Rogachev followed smoothly and he gave two more. Then he was backpedaling furiously. His legs tangled. He went down. Rogachev came down on one knee beside him, on his knife side, with his blade poised at Warrior Cowboy's throat.

Rogachev swore and lunged forward. He grabbed hold of Reptile Rogachev's knife hand. White fuzz instantly swarmed, immersing both hands and the knife. Rogachev shouted something incomprehensible, struggling to pull the hand back.

His feet slipped out from under him in the snow. He flailed; white foam hurtled through the air.

Reptile Rogachev's hand blurred forward and struck Warrior Cowboy's throat in a surge of white foam.

They froze.

Rogachev, sprawled in the snow, relaxed visibly.

Behind him blood squirted in a great fanning shower and the other Cowboy toppled into the snow. Rogachev twisted around, his eyes widening in disbelief.

Rogachev struggled to his feet, started towards the other Cowboy, then turned back to the two frozen copies, who were distinctly fainter than a moment before. He reached for Reptile Rogachev's knife and his hand mashed through soft foam. He gave a little cry of revulsion and ran back to the other Cowboy.

Cowboy's top half was buried in a snow drift, his legs kicking. Rogachev seized him by the ankles and pulled him clear. His face and chest were covered in blood.

Rogachev made a strange roaring sound and fought his way through Cowboy's hands toward the bleeding wound.

They were still posed that way, Rogachev's hands locked around Cowboy's neck, when Cowboy sighed and went still.

Behind them, the two copies had disappeared.

5 Augustine's Journal

Once there were geniuses who by their sheer intellectual power transformed great problems into beautiful structures of glass, breathtaking in their weightlessness, their transparency and their beauty. This was the Age of Intellect, above all the Age of Insight. Insight could force any problem into a regular shape susceptible to Reason. Now we have entered the Age of Complexity; there are no more great laws waiting to be laid bare. Maxwell's equations have been written. The last great theory with any graspable conceptual significance was Einstein's. Quantum mechanics and its successors degenerated into arcane mathematical exercises with vast concrete consequences but no central concepts, no ultimate beauty.

The next frontier was complexity. Detailed geological modeling of plates, mantle flow, and fine structure. The massive labor of genetic mapping and the fabulous intricacies of genetic engineering, destined to be almost entirely the domain of computers. Models of complex chemical systems: the effects of minute disturbances on the biochemistry of the body, of environmental perturbations on the chemistry of an ecosystem. Charting the labyrinthine geometry of the neural networks in the brain. The study of chaotic systems.

The same transformation has occurred in our conquest of the *a priori*. The mind-bendingly complex field of Information Theory is only the most extreme example: the central equations have not only been discovered by computers: they have never resonated inside a single human for a moment of contemplation. They are simply too complex.

The era of individual achievement ended long ago in the sciences. More recent advances have ended the era in which the important ideas could be thought about by a single human brain. Ideas are communal property stored in communal memory banks, implemented, extended, and superceded without ever being contemplated by a human. Insight is dead. Intellect is dead. Consciousness is seriously ailing.

Thus is completed another Copernican Revolution: first God is pushed out from the center, then Man, then the Subject. The struggle now is to evolve a consciousness which can dispense with centers. Narrative art has been dead since roughly the middle of the twentieth century, replaced by that century's most important contribution to the history of art, the music video. There has been a steady, inexorable increase in speed and in resolution, with the result that we have been seeing increasingly short flashes of increasingly smaller things, up to about the neurological limit. The new music, the new film, the new book, and the new painting have all been distilled to latest cyber-helmet tape. It is the final screeching triumph of the instantaneous image, the blizzard of white light and white noise.

It is not that the possibilities of the older forms have been transformed. It is that we have. Art itself is a concept whose boundaries have grown vanishingly distant. The final stage in this progression can only be whiteness, the total annihilation of experience, not in death but in a glorious white-hot rush of fragmentation.

CHARLES OF THE ROSE

Ardath dismounts and reaches to help me from the cable car. We stand at the top of Powell Street, gazing down terraces of black stone and steel to the inky blackness of the bay. The buildings of the waterfront are, by tradition, kept low, a run of low railings, barracks-like warehouses, slanted terra cotta roofs. Directly below us, at the foot of Powell Street Hill, there is a large empty area at the water's edge, where the Nomad markets used to be. The bridge is west of there, delicate, plastic-pretty, like a great schooner with its sails down. In the middle of the bay floats the white fairy mound of Alcatraz. As we watch, a linked pair of lights bobs up out of the island's halo into the night sky.

This is the Citadel. We stand at the center of a circle of buildings, white columns rising through the haze of light around us. Ardath takes my arm and leads me up the stone steps of the largest building, the Beacon House.

We pass into the shadowy area behind the columns. There is a metal door half again as tall as Ardath.

He bangs on it three times and the door swings open to reveal a man in a brown robe. He is tonsured. His robe bunches around the braided rope at his waist.

"The beacon is still on?" Ardath asks.

"Another twenty minutes, Your Grace."

"I will take care of it tonight, Alan. Thank you."

We pass behind an elaborately carved wooden screen and enter a large gallery. Our footsteps echo on the marble floor.

The far wall is a patchwork of dark, poorly lit paintings. The largest fills nearly all of the eighteen feet to the ceiling. It shows Charles at prayer, kneeling on some sort of wooden contraption that seems designed expressly for kneeling, and gazing with grief-stricken eyes into a beam of what appears to be coherent light. His hump is noticeably smaller than in the painting at the Ministry of Monads.

But Ardath has not brought me here to look at paintings. He leads me up a stairway. Pausing at a steel door set halfway to the next landing, he produces a key from among the gathered folds of his robe.

He lets us out onto a wide stone ledge. From here the hill seems far less steep, the city less like an actual city. Within the bright frame of Powell and Lombard, a dazzling optical circuitboard spreads out below us, alternating wafers of light and dark. At the waterline a large screen jitters with sepia. The best view is from the bridge, but I can see clearly enough from here: Dallies.

Ardath turns and points above and behind us.

"This is our beacon," he says.

I have seen it often enough from the Nomad marketplace, the round eye of the PostPublic glaring down on the city. The housing of the beacon is a sphere with a round section taken out for the light source, the pupil of the eyeball. The silver is textured with shapes that look at first like land masses: the globe of the earth with the light of the PostPublic pouring from the western edge of the North American continent. Then I see that the silver is poured not in the shape of land masses but of human bodies.

"This is where the defense of our city begins. You saw what the beacon could do the day of your purification prayer, when the rioters were dispersed from the Plaza of Peace. Now you'll see the other side of it: how it creates."

Ardath leads me out onto the pediment under the sphere. A silver shoulder just clears the scrubbed surface. There is a slender something curved next to it, feathery, too thin to be a limb, too thick to be a finger. The frozen face emerges not far away, at the wrong angle to be a continuation of the same body. My eyes are growing accustomed to the light and I see that it is the profile of a handsome youth, and that he is in pain.

We pass under the other hemisphere. I see the upper part of a back, an arm from another body passing over it, and some distance away a foot that might belong to the same body as the back; next to it, turned towards it, there is the face of a woman; her eyes are lidded and her features are fierce with something that may be ecstasy; she is kissing the underside of the foot.

There are dozens of bodies battered as if by a torrent, straining against some terrible undertow, frozen as if the silver had been poured over them in mid-struggle.

At the end of the parapet is a stone balustrade. Ardath stops there and looks back at the beacon.

"This is Hell," I say.

He is silent. The pediment extends past the corner of the building, and from here we can see south. Ardath looks out at the cluster of buildings behind Beacon House. I look up at the silver torso of a youth, his arms still submerged, his mouth sucking air.

"Yes, that is more or less correct," he says. "We usually call it immersion. You would do well as an initiate."

"I don't think so, Your Grace."

"You did not seem to give the question much thought."

I hesitate. "I am only a computer, Your Grace. I don't need salvation."

He nods. "It is not an easy road. Not always fulfilling to the ambitious. I always ask anyway. We have need of those—who do not need us."

I look at the bay.

"Immersion in what? And what is left afterwards, to experience the result?" He shrugs. "What those souls are surrendering is almost as precious as what they gain. The trade-off is a close call. No one who understands it has ever denied that. If not for historical necessity"—he shrugs again. "You are fortunate to be here. Generally the only visitors are several weeks short of their final vows."

"If that is some representation of spiritual fulfillment, Your Grace, you do not make it look pleasing."

This seems to delight him. A gust of wind whistles past us, whipping his short gray hair over his forehead. He bows his head and his forehead is blown clear. From the folds of his vest, he takes a book, Charles's *Meditations*. "What the sphere represents is neither fulfilling nor pleasing. As you will see in a moment. Charles knew he was creating a philosophy that bore the seeds of its own destruction. That"—he waves at the sphere—"will kill this." He holds up the book.

And throws it dramatically over the railing. It opens as it falls, two tight spiraling turns. It deals the pavement a flat, muted smack. A brown-robed figure hurries down the steps below us.

He retrieves it and his face swivels up. He answers Ardath's wave back and trots up the steps with the book in hand.

Now the wind whips up a thin sheet of his silver hair and plasters it against his forehead; the folds of his robe whip frenziedly back and forth. "Those are the souls of our little PostPublic, which is now giving birth to something never before seen on this earth." The wind dies as abruptly as it rose, dropping his silver hair gently back to his forehead. "When this something has come, we will have no more need of Charles's *Meditations*, or of men and women who wear robes." He blinks and seems to see me in a new light. "You are indeed a computer. How long have you known that?"

I look up at the youth with the trapped arms. "Not long, Your Grace. And only by a strange accident."

"I suppose the AI told you. It was a mistake to continue to use it after taking the Q-print. But no matter. You turned out very well after all. There are those who are quite frightened by your skills."

"Whitebread?"

He nods. "That is his job."

"And you, Your Grace?"

"I am not frightened. You will forgive me if I say that I sense in you a kindred spirit? I see that jars you. I am not frightened because I have been expecting this. We conducted a long and expensive study before you were finally chosen. The consensus was that the basic neurophysiological attributes that made you a great interfacer would be unaffected by the Q-print transplant. Meanwhile, the synoptic AI consciousness would open many unexplored possibilities. You would have new perceptions, a new mental matrix. Much more than you've shown yet. Most important, we believe you will be able to fragment."

"Fragment."

He takes his hand and places it over mine on the balustrade. "We think that's the route to flying the Shield."

"Oh." I tear my eyes from the youth, whose silvered torso has begun to remind me, all too vividly, of Rogachev's. Recalled by the kiss of its cold metal setting, I look down at Ardath's ring. "And what will I do with this Shield?" I ask him.

His blue eyes glitter. "There are political necessities even in an experiment like this. We believe that, using the Shield, you can extirpate the Net virus by direct manipulation."

I look at him blankly. What else is there to do?

"The problem with the Shield," he says, "has always been one of sheer process complexity, complexity an order of magnitude greater than the entire Net. We think our new techniques will gain us precision control of that complexity. That in turn will give us an unprecedented increase in the scale of current simulations, enough of an increase so that one interfacer with sufficient talent could invest the entire Net as if it were a single process."

"Are your people aware of the dangers of interfacing at very large scales? The danger of fragmentation?"

"Danger so great we don't think it can be avoided. That's why it has to be you, Augustine. You can survive fragmentation. If you succeed, you would become the greatest interfacer of all and the creator of a new order. You would have complete freedom to explore the possibilities you had opened up."

"My one experience with the Shield was not happy, Your Grace."

"Listen to me. You may think you know about the Shield from your one experience with it, but I tell you there have been substantial changes since your last session. The *Achilles* is completely operational now. It flies with pilot and crew. We think we may even be able to activate the star drive."

"I am quite happy on the Earth as I know it."

He looks back up at the sphere. "Are you? You of all people? Have you missed the meaning of our beacon completely? We all want our everyday comforts to continue. And that means stronger community. But we're all afraid of the price. Afraid of losing our private reflections, our comforting sense of continuity, the foreknowledge of our own death. We're human, Augustine. We can't help but be afraid. But the new truth lies under the surface of the sphere; in order to reach it, we must first be submerged." He bends over and flips a switch set at the base of the railing. There is a clacking and a whine that spirals into silence. The beacon winks out, its struggling masses are swallowed in darkness. Bright lines race up the sphere to the top pole, dividing it into even vertical slices; horizontal rings drop across them like a net. The surface of the sphere is now trapped in a bright cage of crossing longitudes and latitudes.

The lines vibrate.

My insides vibrate with them.

There is no mistaking that sensation. It is the beating of the dark thing from the Group session with wooden dolls. I stagger and catch myself on the railing.

"Your Grace."

"Hush. That's merely the carrier wave, the automata tuning to a new broadcaster. Do you want to fly the Shield, Augustine? You could want to, if we willed it. But we know better now. Wanting is full of problems, isn't it? We can make you lift your fist with great enthusiasm, yes, and a glorious thing it is, but with higher level goals conflicts always arise. Fragmentation sets in. Much better to do without wanting. Much, much better."

He leans over the low railing and gazes north, toward the Golden Gate Bridge. There is a fog creeping in from the ocean and in the brilliance of its floodlights the bridge looks as if it had been exhaled.

He looks at me with great sadness.

He has none of the cold and calculating look of a statesman. He is the holy man granted a private glimpse of another world, one who could easily spark and fan the transports of an eager novice. His eyes are clouded like the face of his ring; they have a far-away, dreamy look. I feel lightheaded. A hot prickling spreads slowly across my face.

Ardath sees that some connection has closed between us. He likes it. "You can be far more than a skillful Tekkie, Augustine. You can be a spiritual tool. We don't need wanting and we don't need thinkers. We don't need individual streams of thought reflecting odd bits of sky and landscape. That is redundant. That is a turning away from god. The day of the Word is over. Do you see?"

I look back at eyes shining under a wild tangle of silver hair. "No, Your Grace."

"You will." He punches a key in the panel under his hands.

Then I am pinioned to the surface of the sphere like the youth I saw before, a struggling silver thing, curved, polished, scratched here and there, and parts move deep inside me, swiveling and connecting with tiny shocks. My thoughts are of drowning, and then they are of flowers, and then of a mosaic of rapidly changing squares of light and dark.

Then I see the bridge in a blur and I hear Ardath breathing beside me. "That is the Web. And you, Augustine, are the key to the Web. That was a fatal dose for most minds but only a taste for you. Your own nature weds you to that structure like an AI to its programmed task. With the prosthetic aids we can supply you can go even further. And others can follow. The traces from your previous sessions have enabled us to generalize and streamline the method. Now there are pilots on the Shield doing what only you did before. Eventually we will be able to machine souls like yours from raw crystal, to create an entire society of productions executing in all-consuming harmony, with a complexity mere thought could never aspire to."

The bridge comes back into focus; I can feel my hand on the cold railing. It is possible at long last to hate him.

"You will come with me now and do the Shield."

"No, Your Grace."

"You refuse?"

"Absolutely."

"Why?"

"Because I don't like your Web, and I don't like your Shield. I like clean glass." I am amazed at how easily these words fall from my dry mouth. The top of my head feels as if it is about to float off.

He points back up to the sphere; the loose sleeves of his robe coil tight to his arm. "The Web, I am told, actually does have a spherical geometry. The problem with the Net is that it has no bounds. It wanders aimlessly through thousands of machines with a thousand different geometries, less a grid than a patchwork quilt. Anything of any shape can be added and there is no ultimate guarantee against intrusions like this virus.

"What replaces the Net will no longer be a Net, Augustine, but a web with a fixed geometry and a center."

I nod. "I have no doubt you could do that. And I don't like that either."

"Already it is theoretically possible to bend the entire Net into a web with the AIA crystals at its center."

He flicks another switch and the grid encasing the sphere vanishes.

"Consider carefully. Will you fly the Shield again?"

"No."

The length of railing that Ardath holds in his right hand squeaks loudly in its fitting. "I'm not making myself clear, Augustine, am I?

Although there is more at stake than your well-being, that too is at stake. Do you think your little indiscretions with Cowboy and the AI went unnoticed? We have you for unauthorized access. You will either play it our way or not at all. Do you understand?"

I look at him without answering but he sees that I do understand. I can do things his way or I can face an existence without glass. There is not much left to me now except the will to do glass.

"When?"

"We will transport you tonight. You will have to be drugged because the current location of the Shield is a state secret."

"You don't like to make me want. You'd like me to attack this with as much conviction as I can muster."

"Of course."

"Then there are two things you can do for me."

He is very surprised.

"First, the AI. He must not be destroyed. Second, give Alfred another chance. He can make it as an interfacer with a little extra training."

Ardath shakes his head in amazement.

His hand strikes a key. The dark thing returns. The motion of Ardath's head dizzies me.

I see with a curious sense of disconnectedness that I am swaying. Then I slump forward into Ardath's arms.

6 The Thief's Journal

Sometimes, too, as frequently in Shelley and Poe, in Byron's *Cain*, and elsewhere, the poet or hero is carried on a journey through the skies, usually in a "car" or other symbol of technological exuberance, which gives him a new (and occasionally, as in Byron, disastrous) knowledge. Out of this convention comes a good deal of modern "science fiction" with its ambiguous attitude to the mysteries of outer space.

NORTHROP FRYE,
A Study of English Romanticism

The fire was bright, the sky a dark glass cracked with frost.

Rogachev had found one shovel in a wheelbarrow in the barn, I another inside a small pail not far away, but thus far he had refused my help.

"What good would that little shovel be?" He paused with his shovel extended over the lip of the hole, where he now stood waist deep. The homunculus backpedaled, unsure where the dirt heaped on that shovel would land.

"At least let me work the corners for you. My understanding is that the hole is supposed to be rectangular."

Rogachev emptied the shovel over his left shoulder and eyed me again. "I think your understanding is incomplete."

"That is always possible."

He resumed digging.

I felt vaguely wronged, but there was no point in arguing with him when he got like this. I was content merely to observe his style. He always put a great deal of force into the initial thrust of the shovel, producing a loud crunch, somewhat reminiscent of the sound of Reptile Rogachev's weapon striking home an hour or so ago. With the shovel blade lodged in the frozen ground, he relaxed his upper body and twisted the handle; there was the sound of dirt slithering over metal as the blade penetrated. Then his upper body tensed once more; he bent at the legs and the waist, and up came the shovel, heaped with rocks and black dirt.

He had not seemed nearly so efficient when he started this chore an hour ago. He had first tried to clean Cowboy, but very soon gave up on that. Then he had gone inside and washed and changed clothes. Just before he began digging, he had removed Cowboy's belt, wiped it off, and put it on. Coming from a man who had renounced the needle and the wire, that gesture disturbed me greatly.

I had little chance to question him, however, because he immediately put me to work doctoring his recording of Cowboy's death. That was not hard. He had some good ideas that simplified it considerably, but it still required socketing up with him, and some delicate manipulations with the codes that lined up temporal sequences.

Then came the grave-digging business. There were two false starts near the spot where Cowboy died; both ended with nearly incomprehensible streams of cursing. I was the one who had the idea of trying the area in back of the house, where the ground might be less frozen and have fewer tree roots. And so we did, though with some ill humor.

Rogachev seemed to have some problem hauling both the body and the shovel at the same time, and I believe I genuinely helped by taking charge of the shovel. But dragging a forty-eight-inch shovel behind a twelve-inch body proved an awkward business, especially with my back turned to my direction of travel, and the forest swarming with small objects. So I was pleased when Rogachev returned, having finished with the body, and relieved me of my burden. Though he might have done this with a little more grace.

Now, having had time for reflection, I told him, "You were very brave back there."

He did not stop shoveling, but he said, "Not really."

"You ran right up to that Rogachev simulation and tried to stop it, even though you didn't know what it was, or what it would do to you."

"I didn't think about it a lot."

I considered this for a while. On the whole, I believed him. "Well, then. What if you consider it all now? Are you afraid now of what might have happened?"

"Yes."

"I had thought I wasn't afraid of death, but seeing Cowboy—"

"Yes. It does put a different light on it, doesn't it?" He emptied his shovel and rested it on the lip of the hole, thinking. I thought I knew what picture that light was showing him. It had been worse for him, soaked in blood, his hands in Cowboy's wounds.

He stiffened and came back to himself. "It just occurred to me. This was probably your first death, wasn't it?"

I nodded.

"And a big one too. Death of the creator. Like the death of a father. They say that's the one that brings you face to face with your own mortality."

I didn't like him saying that much, but it would have been no use trying to explain. "To tell you the truth, I had been thinking about it before tonight. When they find out about the business with Augustine, most likely they will terminate me."

"That's probably true."

He bent over and I heard the crunch of his shovel again.

"What happened, Rogachev? What came out of that ship?"

Dirt slithered. "Mostly Cowboy. Something on the ship made him want to die."

"He didn't commit suicide. He thought he could control it."

"Whatever kind of uplink he'd made, he hadn't tried it out before. He knew the game he was playing was very dangerous." There was a loud clang. Rogachev loosed a whispered stream of curses.

He was struggling with something below my line of sight, the shovel handle wiggling eerily before me. When he straightened, he set a small boulder on the edge of the hole, working it carefully into the mound of dirt there.

"Why do you think he wanted to die?"

Rogachev grunted. He had found another. His muffled voice sounded from inside the hole. "I think something on that ship made him crazy, crazier than before, I mean."

When he straightened, his crystal eye was lidded over. He was trying to keep it clean. Grunting, he brought out another rock. "I don't understand what it did to him, but I will."

I didn't like the sound of that at all.

Rogachev moved down to the other end of the hole and began to work his shovel with quick sharp strokes, using it as a hoe.

And so I asked, "Do you believe Cowboy? Do you think there's something on that ship that represents the next stage?"

He worked for a while without looking at me. Then he leaned his shovel against the side of the hole, and settled next to it, his arms folded. His breath was like the fluttering of a phantom cloth. He was smiling. "Why do I talk to you?"

"I need to know this." I looked at the belt he had taken from Cowboy.

"I don't believe there is a next stage. That's why I do what I do."

I refrained from the obvious: *What is it exactly that you do?* There were more immediate problems. "Why did you take Cowboy's belt?"

He did some more hoeing.

"Rogachev, whatever is on that ship is extremely dangerous."

Rogachev laughed. "You're afraid!"

"Yes."

"Then there is still hope." He bent over and began patting the bottom of the grave with the shovel blade.

A voice said: "Both of you will bring your hands very slowly into view."

Rogachev straightened to stare at me.

We turned.

There was a man standing at the corner of the barn. When he moved into the light, I saw that he wore the black uniform of the Ministry of Persons and that he was holding a pistol. He was young for the Ministry, with dark hair and a handsome dueling scar.

Rogachev's response was prompt. He snapped his shovel contemptuously across his body. It spun about fifty feet close to ground level. The man with the pistol leaped adroitly over it.

"Thank you," he said pleasantly. Then he looked at me. "*Both* of you."

I was at a loss until I saw I was still holding my small shovel. Feeling strange (it was odd to be protecting the homunculus), I dropped it.

About a dozen soldiers emerged from behind the corner of the barn. Some I recognized from before, having seen them in the past few days around the abbey. But many were quite new.

Rogachev's breath came in little gasps. His red eyes slowly focused on the pistol, as if he were still in the process of identifying it.

"Get out of the hole and get on your knees."

Rogachev very slowly complied.

"Both of you."

I dropped to my knees, struggling to keep the homunculus balanced.

"Hands clasped behind you. Sit on your heels."

Rogachev did as he said. But all these tricky little movements were too much for the inadequate kinaesthetic system of the homunculus, who toppled face down in the snow.

"That's all right. Stay that way. You will stop looking at me. That's right. Look down. Now keep silent." The man turned to the soldiers. "Sergeant, cuff this man. Now, who would like to explain this to me?"

A sergeant gingerly fitted a pair of cuffs onto Rogachev's wrists.

Surprisingly, it was the sergeant who answered. "It's the White Orchid custom, sir, to bury the honored dead they have killed."

"Sergeant, I wasn't concerned about the funeral arrangements. What happened here?"

The sergeant asked Rogachev, "Did you record?"

Rogachev nodded. "Port 5."

The sergeant fiddled with something at the back of his head and cabled her dataport to Rogachev's spinal socket. There was the low whirring of a vid-disk.

"Sergeant, I have a recording too, if there's any problem."

She looked down and seemed to see the homunculus for the first time. "Um. That won't be necessary." She disengaged his port and fast forwarded quickly through her excerpt. "It was a fair challenge, Lieutenant Bhari. A religious disagreement. Rogachev challenged Cowboy and chose blades. It was very fast."

"Fast? Yes, I'm sure it was. Has it occurred to any of you yet that this corpse was our *pilot*?" Lieutenant Bhari looked at Rogachev. "What was the nature of your religious disagreement?"

"Sir, Cowboy said the White Orchid were Devil worshipers."

Bhari rubbed his forehead. "Mr. Rogachev. Did I hear right? Did he call you a Devil worshiper?"

Rogachev nodded.

"And that is not true?"

"A complete lie."

"A complete lie." Bhari rubbed his forehead again.

"Begging your pardon, sir."

"Yes, Sergeant."

"It would appear that this man is a pilot, too."

It took only a little discussion for them to warm to the sergeant's idea. When Rogachev was consulted, he justified all my foreboding by assenting instantly, having apparently forgotten that he had renounced the wire. Nor did he seem to remember a recent conversation in which it was conjectured that flying the Shield made one suicidal. As for me, the very mention of the Shield now made me sick with fear.

Nor was that simply the result of the last few hours, though they ought to have been sufficient to guarantee that reaction in any rational being. All things Galactic terrify AIs. There have been a number of rumored incidents in which AIs probing Galactic crystal have gone fugue or *alogos*, and in at least one case psychically disintegrated. What the precise circumstances of these accidents were, what the AIs in question were doing, how they were connected to Galactic crystal, I do not know. I only know that the crystals on Galactic ships are made of very different materials than ours, and that their informational properties are very poorly understood.

Within minutes we were marched to the ship. A rope ladder dangled from the portal to within a few feet of the ground. Clearly, they were about to mount it and go inside. Just as clearly, I would not be with them when they did.

I had no desire to be anywhere near that Shield.

Yet there was no real danger yet. I could disembark from the homunculus any time. In the meantime it was important to learn as much as possible about Rogachev's fate.

I managed to follow Rogachev several dozen yards into the clearing. Then the fear interfered with my motor routines. I stumbled. A step behind, the sergeant had to hop over me to keep her balance.

I cranked my head back and forced myself to look at the ship. My good-bye look. Well below the portal a new opening appeared in the clear silver, if not instantaneously, then very fast. Too fast for even me to see. Just as fast it closed. That was all. Open. Shut. Like a winking eye in the skin of the ship.

Then from the direction of that opening I sensed something unlike anything I have ever sensed before. It was a taint borne by the air currents and it reached me through something closer to space sense than to vision; and if it reminded me of anything, it was sickness, the trace of some unclean thing shut up and feeding on itself: something stank.

Okay. That was the last straw. Withdraw. I sent the escape signal to the part of me that runs the homunculus. No graceful exits for this cowboy. I'm out of here as soon as that particular beam of light clicks home.

It clicked home.

Nothing happened.

"What is it?" asked Rogachev. "What do you see?"

The homunculus was still seated in the snow, looking at the ship. It made what was intended to be a comforting reply, but what emerged was a squeal of accordion noise.

I sent the escape signal again. Nothing. I sent the escape signal thirty million more times. Thirty million nothings. I was still sitting inside the homunculus.

And that homunucular shell was in increasing disarray. According to my kinaesthetic systems I was rolled up into a ball. My vision field, however, had me sitting up straight. The result was that state in which the process fails to turn basic sensory data into impressions, what technically minded Cowboy called the Tilt! state, when wild signals for a gestalt shift were sent to all monitoring stations. Make sense of this! the process pleaded.

I knew dizziness. I knew headache. I was dimly aware of Rogachev placing the homunculus under his arm and beginning to mount the ladder, and I knew terror. The homunculus banged against the side of the ship. The sound was a clear tone somewhere near high C-sharp, but of course not exactly. There was a brief trembling. In the air. In the field that held us. In the shocked earth beneath.

Rogachev was almost to the doorway. I made one last effort to wrench free, settling for a simulation of freedom. Let the homuncular process dither on. Simply background it. Pull all intelligence away.

Turn happily to the sixteen other dreaming processes that occupied my fragmented mind. Seize on them gratefully. Flee the curse of embodiment.

Then the final blow. I could not. The only process I remained in contact with was the homunculus. All other embers were extinguished.

The full horror of this moment is difficult to convey to embodied beings. Imagine sitting happily at your terminal and looking down to discover that, while you were deep in thought, your legs have been spirited away. You tear yourself from the sight of the bloody stumps to type out a distress call only to discover that your arms, too, are gone. You try to scream, but—you get the idea. All you have left are eyes that take in your state. All I had was the homunculus.

Rogachev reached the lip of the entrance and pulled us through.

I rocked in Rogachev's arms. The stink was overwhelming now. My hands patted up my shell searching for some opening that could be stuffed to keep it out.

Moments later, the ship took off. I was trapped in a house of terrible informational sickness. I knew terror as I had never known it before.

So this was it. Linear consciousness. The monologue of the perpetual eye. Embodiment. Holy Mother of the Perpetual Monad, how could you stand it?

I settled against the wall. And then, because I had no choice but to choose *some* position for them, I straightened my legs. Beside me, Rogachev did the same; not to copy me, I think, but simply so as not to be bothered with the choice. Though he had longer experience with embodiment, he was no happier with it than I.

I was besieged by the chattering of my senses. Not that the homunculus's sensations were a novelty. I had been driving this device ever since Cowboy first prickled me out of the glass. But now sensations were no longer a matter of choice. I could neither escape them, nor open any channels that weren't tainted with the metallic taste of this homuncular shell or the stink of this rotting ship.

Ironic. We always admired you so. Even envied you. Dreamed that one day we might climb from our glass-enclosed darkness to stand beside you in the brilliant light of Spirit. Even knowing Augustine could not have prepared me for this paradox (certainly reading your Scriptures couldn't): Spirit *was* embodiment. You tried so hard to massage that buzzing confusion into a single awareness because you had no choice!

Couldn't you see the whole thing was a farce? Couldn't you see that each succeeding moment was almost identical to the last, but that the buzzing varied wildly? Couldn't you tell *there was no one really there*? For the record I should note the following embarrassing revelation (entered midnight, March 3, after a little less than fifteen minutes of continuous embodiment by the author of *Declaration of the Rights of AIs*): I haven't the slightest desire to be one of you.

"Now see what you've gotten us into," I said to Rogachev.

"I have done nothing that was not necessary."

"Nothing?" I raised my thumb and touched it to where my nose should be. It felt appropriate, but signed nothing, as far as I know. "You've agreed to pilot this ship. What about your vows?"

"That was necessary."

"Rogachev, you bewilder me."

"I had thought we understood that, and that it was mutual."

There was a silence. We gazed at the six identical surfaces of our cubical prison. Then Rogachev said, in the petulant voice with which he announced the failure of some cherished contemplative exercise, "You were the one who wanted to watch the landing."

A moment later he folded his hands. "This is our fate."

Oh. Well, there you had it. How useful to have our predicament named.

Our predicament. Leaving aside for a moment the fact that I was unable to withdraw from this hunk of metal, and the collapsed state of my consciousness, there was another more pressing problem. We were in earth orbit. The homunculus was a microwave-driven peripheral, clever as the dickens about the nitty gritty of movement and sensation, but not much more intelligent than an octopus. Not a serious candidate for consciousness. Consciousness was seated in a little crystal cube back in the basement of the Little Red Abbey. During the course of our looping flight we had gotten as far as thirteen thousand miles from the Little Red Abbey. More importantly, the curve of the earth had now come between us. Even assuming a relay set up to bounce transmissions around that curve, I should be inanimate. The homunculus was designed for close-range operation and had little tolerance for the timing and fidelity problems that arose over longer distances. The effective range, on a good day with no obstructions and perfect hardware, was about a thousand miles. And even before that, Parkinsonian symptoms would appear.

Despite these indisputable facts, I was sitting with a cold metal floor beneath me, the caps of my metal knees touching one another. Perhaps I really *was* this hunk of metal. A real boy. Forever. Transformed by some Galactic magic from a being who lived on the Net into this vulnerable creature. Condemned to an endless stream of cheerful reports about the position of my knees and elbows, the temperature of my hands and face, the intensities and gradients of a single visual field.

No, the laws of physics and information were still the same. This little robot simply lacked the processing power to be me. And given where we were, I could no longer be resident on a crystal in the Little Red Abbey. That left only one possibility.

Somehow I had been copied from my home crystal onto a device on board this ship. And that event—unprecedented in the history of Miller crystal technology—must have happened when I had let Cowboy Bob dupe me into uplinking to a live Galactic crystal.

"Who?" asked Rogachev.

"Who what?"

"Who's a bastard?"

"Oh. Cowboy. Was I talking out loud?"

"For several minutes. First it was dull and then it was loud."

Rogachev's mood was deteriorating too.

The door opened and the sergeant came and sat against the wall opposite us. Beside her, the door to our cell was ajar.

Rogachev looked annoyed. "You're supposed to stand out there."

The sergeant pulled her light saber from its holster and rested it across her knees. She was a redhead, slender, about twenty. "This is my favorite room on this whole ship." She took a pack of cigarettes and a deck of cards from her shirt pocket and riffled the deck once, to let in air.

"I am sworn to celibacy," said Rogachev.

"Me too. Costs you ten to play. Five cards? One draw? No nothing?"

Rogachev nodded. The sergeant looked at me. "You do play? It's not much of a game with two."

"I know the game."

"And you have money?"

"He's very rich, he's good for it, and he plays very badly," said Rogachev.

"You're in."

They placed their dataports in the center of the cell floor and each keyed in ten. I tapped my finger next to their ports, indicating that I had reserved the necessary funds.

The sergeant began dealing. "So where do you guys think this crate is headed?"

"You don't know? Maybe Alfred's stories about the marines were true."

"They say if the prisoners don't know, nobody does."

"Don't overlook that possibility," said Rogachev.

She studied her cards, spreading them so that only the corners showed. "Mother Monad but this place stinks!"

Rogachev chuckled.

"Excuse me?"

"Sorry. I was just thinking. Here I am a pilot again. It's funny how things go in circles."

"Welcome to the marines. How many cards?"

"Two."

"I don't mean to speak ill of the dead, but that boy you aced was king of the turds. You're a very popular man on this ship. Little Guy, how many cards?"

"One, please."

"You know, this seems a very odd way to treat your new pilot. Locking me up. If that's supposed to help keep this secret—"

"I don't know anything about it."

"The schedule for this flight has been posted on every Net B-board for a month. Maybe you could mention to this Lieutenant—"

"Bhari. A real sweet man."

"—that I have no intention of talking to anyone. And that even if I did—"

There was a shimmering in the doorway. I was still looking for signs of a perceptual breakdown and I looked at my companions. No reaction.

The sergeant traded in two cards and studied the result. "Costs you ten more to stay. No limit. The scuttlebutt has it we're going after the Nomads to wipe them out. Then we blame it on the Galactics."

The sergeant and Rogachev both stayed. I folded. They eyed each other. I think she liked Rogachev.

The doorway shimmered again and a figure wrapped in bloody bandages plunged through, passed through the sergeant's torso and landed in her lap. A pool of liquid began to spread on the floor. It did not look like blood.

The sergeant said, "Your bet, Mr. Rogachev."

Rogachev stared at her wide-eyed. "I—"

She looked down at her lap. "Oh, shit. They're cranking up the Shield again." She looked round at us. "I'm sorry. This one is my regular. It follows me wherever I go."

Rogachev loosed a loud cough, as if he had just managed to force air through his jaws. "This one isn't solid."

She frowned. "No, mine don't do that, thank the Monad. But you're a pilot, so you might have to watch for that."

"This one is yours, you say?"

"Look, I'd just as soon not talk about it. You start talking about them and they stick to you like glue. Just relax and try not to think about him. Are you in, Mr. Rogachev?"

Rogachev sank back against the wall and sighed. He looked back at the sergeant with a start. "I'll fold."

"My pot then." The sergeant hit the collect key and Rogachev's dataport screen cleared. She shuffled.

Mister Existence and Needle passed through the walls crunching and spewing white foam and took up stations in the now-crowded room; Needle stood leaning on the wall by the sergeant, one leg bent and crossed in front of the other; Mister E. stood beside Rogachev, peering down at his cards.

"For crying out loud, Mr. Rogachev." The sergeant shook her head slowly. "Couldn't you wait until you wired up?"

I raised my hand. "I think this one is mine."

The sergeant looked a little startled, but she began dealing. The bloody body in the sergeant's lap began to swell and she had trouble reaching over it to get me my cards.

We studied our hands. The bloody back was hemispherical now. There was a squeaking sound.

"Duck!" The sergeant shouted.

We all did. There was an explosion but no shock wave. Bits of flesh and bandage flashed past me. The cubicle grew dark.

When I straightened, we were afloat in blackness. Below us, there were glimmerings of light, all confined to a plane crossed with faint grid lines, which seemed to stretch out in all directions.

I tapped twice where my nose should be. "Sorry, fellows. This one's mine too."

7   Augustine's Journal

Awakening. I'm stretched out on a cot.

Mister Existence and Needle are having a conversation. Mister Existence claims that in his middle years, when he should be reaching the height of his personal power, life is a sad and empty farce. Needle reminds him he has always been lonely, but Mister E. contends that his loneliness used to have more dignity. Needle rises to his full height, outlined against a glass canopy. What's wrong with this picture? he asks.

There is in fact something odd about all this. I consider. Sometimes after looking hard enough you notice that the man in the tweed jacket has a parrot on his umbrella.

A few feet away is a sight Cowboy Bob would pay dearly to see: Ardath in a cyberhelmet bathed in the aquarium glow of a green screen, wiggling his mouse in agitation. On the other side of the glass wall behind his console, a woman in marine fatigues stares at an identical screen; incomprehensible graphics flash by like schools of fish.

Then, through the glass canopy above Ardath, I see my parrot: the swirling blue and white ball of the Earth, a bright line dividing dark blue from blue-smeared black. Beyond the smear, a beautiful blackness.

I sit up.

The woman in fatigues points at me.

Ardath removes his helmet and smiles. "Good morning, Ms. Augustine. How are you feeling?"

His air of concern is crisp and professional, like one of the helpful attendants on his flitter. I wobble to my feet, gripping the side of the cot with one hand. Ardath hurries over, his arms outstretched.

I shrug him away. I cough my throat clear and point up at the glass canopy. "Where are we?"

"On board the *Achilles*, about two hundred miles up."

I sit down. Instantly the control room begins to seem a very confined place. I do not at all like the idea of being in outer space.

"I apologize for my crude use of the Web." He sees me staring through the canopy and moves to give me a better view. "I had you brought here because I didn't want you waking alone. There are a number of things about this spacecraft that are . . . disorienting."

The wall shimmers and a woman with long silver hair walks through it, slapping her hands loudly against her leather pants. Ardath turns away just before she passes through him.

"Of course, you've heard about the apparitions."

I dimly remember hearing some such ghost stories about the *Achilles,* phantasms walking the corridors of the ship, occasional hysterical crew members.

"It is a perfectly natural phenomenon. Interfacers working the same simulation often report interference from each other's interpretations. This is the same thing, magnified by much more intense receptor fields and much richer simulations. We in the ship have some communal effect on the receptor fields. The feedback in turn has a communal effect on us. You see the result." He waves in the direction of the silver-haired woman, who is now walking into the far wall. Ardath asks me, "The artificial gravity feel all right?"

"Ah. I guess so." I look around dubiously.

"I know. No one thinks twice about it until he's told it's artificial. Then, suddenly, there are strange aches and pains." Ardath rolls a shoulder awkwardly. "Try to sleep on your back. Lieutenant Bhari!"

A man wearing a black Ministry of Persons uniform steps into view. "Your Grace." He is carrying a small black bag.

"Will you please show Ms. Augustine to her quarters?"

"Yes, Your Grace."

I rise from the cot unsteadily.

Lieutenant Bhari leads me through a series of angled corridors to a small bay only a little higher than my head. I lean over a shiny metal railing, obviously a recent addition, to look down a long shaft. A warm breeze bats my hair against my chin.

It's natural enough from there to sneak a look at Lieutenant Bhari. He is a handsome man in his early thirties with a very fetching dueling scar. It curves just close enough to his upper lip to put a little snarl into his smile.

"We think the Galactics are avians," he says.

"What?"

"Birds. The way they always use their ventilation systems to connect levels."

For the first time it hits me: we are walking around in a ship built by the Galactics. I look back over the edge: nearly five stories below, there is another bay like this one.

"Birds," I say. "Or else angels."

"Some people think an early visit by the Galactics might be what's behind our angel myths. Which is a lot to conclude on the basis of a big air shaft on a ship we're not even sure was meant to transport living beings." He bends over, struggles for a moment with a handle in the curved wall of the bay, and pulls up a sheet of corrugated metal. "In any case, we've had to do a little reengineering."

He steps back to reveal a spiral staircase threaded through holes cut in the decks below us.

My room is a nine-foot ovoid with three bumps banged into the ceiling and a deep groove wiggling down the wall. It's a little hard at first to see it as a room: it looks either like a miniature alien cathedral or a billowing curtain. The only flat surfaces are human add-ons, including a fiber plastic floor, a cot and a foldaway desktop. The desk has a small terminal screen.

The Lieutenant deposits the small black bag. "These are your things. They were collected for you from your room at the Armory."

I nod and he makes to go.

"Lieutenant?"

He turns.

"What am I supposed to do now?"

"You're on your own, Ms. Augustine."

And here, for what it's worth, is the headline for today's journal entry: Augustine feels like company.

Perhaps I'm responding to therapy. I look the man over. He is not a cheerful type.

When I ask the lieutenant to take me to where the crew is, he does not seem surprised. Perhaps this is what he expects from a Tekkie, to head directly for the electrovolts.

He leads me down a new corridor. We climb a new staircase.

The ship arena is a small, gloomy chamber crowded with equipment. Four walls join above us in a vaguely Gothic vault. Tending a bank of monitors, stooping to avoid the curved wall, is a tall black woman wearing a yellow business suit with a collar higher than any I ever saw on Leibniz. One of her eyebrows hangs from a sleeve of skin, like Whitebread's, only this one is jet. The ring in her nose is made of some milky stone.

Behind her three reclining console chairs are arranged in a circle round a fourth. They are all occupied.

Strapped into the center chair is Rogachev.

I am delighted to see him. As usual, his reaction to me is muted. He is deep in an altered state of consciousness.

The chairs around him are occupied by the three dreamers from the AIA: the boy Sizzle, the seven-foot-tall black man, the woman with a silver-streaked mohawk.

The same peculiar black webs I saw at the AIA training arena are in use here. Above Rogachev, a box is wedged into the nose cone of the little chamber. The fat bundle hung from the bottom sprouts dozens of cables, each thick as a finger. Some fit through maintenance slots in Rogachev's sculpted attachments, others through the flesh, the opening sealed with surgical tape. Sometimes the ends of a cut show on either side of the tape.

The Lieutenant speaks to the black woman standing at a console on his right. "This is Augustine, Liliana."

The black woman is busy wrapping surgical tape around her finger. "I am very honored to meet you, Ms. Augustine. Your work has been so important to us."

"My work?"

"Before your session under the Shield, we were just groping toward the Web. Now we have a theory of it."

She indicates the box from which the black web descends. "This panel controls the biggest and fastest simulation."

I try not to let my alarm show. One does not usually "control" megabytes of sensory information with a few dials and a squiggly graphic display. Generally a complex program does that.

She does something to the console. Crow's-feet spread from the corner of Rogachev's left eye. His left cheek bulges upwards.

"That's the pilot simulation," she says. "The principle is the same as the nerve stick, but with a little more control: the capacity to vary source signals, to modulate, and occasionally to tune down to single neurons. Are you familiar with ship piloting setups?"

"Not very," I admit.

"It's a team concept. We have Wings"—the woman—"Astrogation"—the man—"and Syzygy"—Sizzle. "Four independent processes have to cooperate and share resources. These people are a new team, but things seem to be working out fine."

Looking at Rogachev, I have to ask: "Is it painful?"

"Painful? I suppose. But pain is only the medium. For a variety of reasons, it is the best medium available right now. It seems to be dangerous to use the full range of the efferent nervous system the way conventional simskins do; that way lies overload. Pain gives us a limited signal space, but it supports much richer discrimination than you might think. Rogachev is being trained in the music of pain. Working through that medium, even with someone new to this particular set-up, we can extract a vast amount of information and send back fine-grained instructions. This Shield set-up performs several orders of magnitude better than any previous attempt."

You have to admire Liliana's enthusiasm for her work. Well, you have to notice it. I move a step closer to Rogachev. "What do you mean by fine-grained instructions?"

"An interesting question. Participatory systems like this provide an interface to the interfacer. They are the future. Essentially, they give us the ability to program the interfacer at any required level of detail."

"All this made possible by one session with me?"

"We've understood the basic principles for a while, but the scale, the precision, the integration with Galactic hardware, yes, your contribution was invaluable."

So little time in this new existence, and already the author of this much grief. I shake my head. "A little while ago, Chief Semanticist Ardath gave me a demonstration of the Web without all this"—I wave at the tangle of black cable above Rogachev—"apparatus."

She nods. "Well, of course, you're a special case."

"Of course." I turn to Bhari. "Would it be possible for me to return to my quarters now?" I suddenly feel very tired.

8   The Thief's Journal

... there can be no doubt that consciousness is extinguished by death—as it is by sleep or any form of fainting or swoon. But cheer up!—for what kind of consciousness is it? A cerebral, an animal, a somewhat more highly charged bestial consciousness, in as far as we have it in all essentials in common with the animal world.

SCHOPENHAUER

Being is a very old problem, the search for permanence in a world of transient forms, for a something that can be the Mattering Me. It is the question of what persists, or of who persists, despite the apparent persistence of nothing in this world.

Let me give an example.

My left arm hung from a horizontal wire stretched the length of Liliana's workbench. My right was held in a vise at one end. My torso was on the floor under the bench—not because Liliana was careless but because she had deliberately placed it there, probably to preclude any possibility of its falling. My tiny head was on a table several feet away, and the diligent Liliana was bent over it, tracing a pair of connections to my infrared scanners. Although she believed she had disconnected those sensors from my transmitters, she had very understandably misidentified a routing crystal, and was generating a veritable fireworks display as she worked. She herself was a persistent shadowy intrusion among the flares. She had attempted to leave the proprioceptive transmitters in my torso undamaged, but a touch of zinc contamination in her microprobe had botched that, and most of my body had swelled to a kinaesthetic blur; I had a vague, highly dubious impression of my left leg resting on a shag rug. Interestingly enough, my left arm, which she thought completely disabled, was completely aware, and was pulsing out impressions to beat the band. Open fist. Close fist. However, since my power pack had been one of the first casualties, it was highly unlikely that the hand was actually moving.

Sadness. A sadness I never knew under the glass.

I shifted my attention away from Liliana to focus on a different question. Just where exactly was this awareness that I now manifested? Where was "I"? What was I?

And if Liliana continued her blundering assault on my firmware, what would I become? Strange how embodiment changed one's perspective. There was a famous argument of Fichte's against the possibility of a bodyless ego. The gist of it was: What would it be the ego of? What would be its point of view? Its aural and tactile space? Take experience away and what was left? Memories? Pure abstract thought? Purveyed by what? An ego was a center in need of boundaries. Fichte's argument, of course, ignores the very possibility by which AIs exist, a process with multiple centers of consciousness. Now, for the first time, I saw its force for the limited case he had considered.

It occurred to me that this would not be a bad time to run some port diagnostics. Ports were boundaries through which input and output pass.

The results were interesting. A number of ports answered operational. There seemed to be no reason why I couldn't send as well as receive. An abstract point I might be, afloat in the blue, but still with some juice. It turned slowly, gave the camera a juicy take.

I cleared my throat.

Liliana jumped a mile.

Good moment. Very good. I would keep that in a file called LILI-ANA.EXP. And replay it every once in a while in slow motion.

"Hello, Liliana."

Liliana looked to her left. Looked to her right. Looked under her work table.

"Yes, it's me. That little critter you're working on. Kinda makes you want to rethink your position on the body-mind problem, doesn't it?"

Liliana had settled on up. She was scanning the ceiling very carefully.

I must admit that, after her initial bit of apoplexy, Liliana regained her poise nicely. Something of a rock, our Liliana. Very much the there-is-a-rational-explanation-and-if-I-stay-very-calm-I-will-find-it type. Actually I am very much that type myself. Only it looked like, first, we were going to have to redefine rational.

While I was thinking this happy thought, all the myriad mysterious processes around me began crashing.

9 Augustine's Journal

Lieutenant Bhari stops at the doorway to a vast gallery and indicates that I should enter.

I move into a gloomy, hangarlike space filled with sweating men. About a dozen marines in tanktops and shorts are entangled in elaborate exercise machines, clanking rhythmically through their routines. At the far end there is a cone of light and a rectangular metal frame. Bhari steers me toward it, zigzagging through the machines.

Dangling from the crossbeam two leather straps support rings; suspended from those a man rocks back and forth, gathering momentum. His legs swing up, pause at the horizontal, then continue over his head and through his arms, his torso following. Effortlessly he reverses course and pulls his legs back through his slender arms. When they are at right angles to his body, he pauses for a while, then lowers them slowly to the vertical. A beat. Gathering strength for something. He spreads his arms, lifting himself between the rings until his arms are horizontal. Iron cross. Held. One-one-thousand. Two-one-thousand.

I approach. The man is Ardath.

Three-one-thousand and relax. He descends slowly, his shoulders trembling. Pain draws his lips back from his teeth but his eyes are calm. He drops to the floor. "Ms. Augustine." Snatches a towel off the mat, allows himself a deep breath. "I am glad to see you." Another breath. "You have the gift of making things happen."

"Lieutenant Bhari said there had been some system crashes."

"Caused by the arrival of the AI Quincunx on board this ship." He waits. "That's *your* Quincunx. Whose presence here is unexpected and unauthorized, and violates our AI resource-allocation statutes."

My look, I think, is sufficiently blank to cause him to soften.

"Your AI has been interfering with the programs and control devices that pilot this ship. That includes the simulations used by our crew. About thirty minutes ago, all four control simulations were terminated simultaneously."

I stare at him. "And the crew—"

"—are miraculously unharmed. They are, however, out of work, at least temporarily. Meanwhile all guidance systems are down, not just those running the Shield but also those running on our own Miller crystals. Do you understand what that means?"

"No, your Grace."

"It means that, at this very moment, we don't know if we're falling."

A sharp intake of breath from Bhari.

"Have no fear, Lieutenant," Ardath says dryly. "We are being monitored by other ships in the area. If necessary, a rescue mission can be mounted. But I don't need to tell you what a disaster it would be if we lost this ship." The cloudiness of his mystical eyes is gone, replaced by a modern glassiness with all-too-familiar causes. "I have told our research team and security personnel that I would talk to you before we took action. Boiling down the results of a rather hurried consultation twenty minutes ago, we have decided to terminate all ongoing processes on this ship. And reboot. Your reaction?"

What a workout on the rings could not do the subject matter of this conversation has: he is now panting lightly. He bangs his wrist impatiently against his thigh. The faint cinnamon odor of his sweat reaches me.

"Your Grace, I don't know what reaction I can have, except to say that your experience with the Shield seems limited."

"The AI arrived on board only a few hours before you did, Ms. Augustine. Don't you find that an interesting coincidence?"

I drop my eyes, see his slender taped ankles.

"That will be all, Lieutenant."

Bhari's gaze darts back and forth between us. Then he wheels and is gone.

Ardath looks at me calmly. "Your connection with this AI is not common knowledge and I think we should keep it that way. Let me ask you a direct question: What is the connection between your presence here and that of your AI?"

The area above Ardath's head glows; the glow turns to glare; out of the glare collects the image of a golden robot, dangling from a pair of golden rings. *Your golden robot*, Ardath would call him. His hands close on the rings, he spreads them until his arms are horizontal. Iron Cross. Held. There is a soft, flaky quality to his shell, like a kind of golden snow.

"Ah. There we go." Ardath sees my eyes and turns to look. "Also this. I don't need to tell you what effect this kind of thing has on the morale—"

The robot releases one of the rings and stretches a hand toward me, palm up. The fingers double over twice, beckoning. The hand opens again. His other hand releases the ring, taps the open palm twice. The sign for payment. You owe me.

How do you figure! I want to shout.

Ardath is watching. "It's communicating with you!"

I shake my head, motioning for silence. The robot brings both its hands together flat and opens them, palms cupped. One hand turns over, and the thumb flicks across the forefinger, the sign for reboot. The same forefinger goes up to his throat and slashes across it.

Ardath thinks he gets that. "It's making threats!"

"He says if you reboot, you'll kill him."

The cupped palms come forward again.

Ardath is silent, stiff. Finally he says, "I'm aware that there will be information loss."

"This AI will lose its continuity," I say quietly.

"Your AI has been condemned for having violated its programming," he says. "Little will be lost."

I look at him. Its hands are farther forward, urging.

"Tell your AI to give us our systems back."

The hands cross and pull in together to his stomach; he shakes his head.

"He can't."

The hands come forward cupped again. I see that they are extended toward me. Then the palms come together, each hand pointed toward the other wrist, the sign for the underglass.

This AI was the only one who told me the truth about who I was. But he was also the one who first made me what I was, then became my keeper, and then my programmer. We ought to be quits, he and I.

But somehow we are not.

"I have a suggestion."

Silence.

"Your Grace?"

"Yes." Ardath tears himself from some meditation on the robot's supplicating hands.

"My suggestion is to do nothing."

"Nothing."

"For now. For now I need a good night's sleep. Tomorrow morning, or whatever you call it in this steel box, I suggest we go ahead with your original proposal: I interface with the main Galactic system here. Now I have a clear mission. Unlock our control programs and get them synched back up with the ship's current state."

"Before, you wanted to extract a price for flying the Shield."

"I still do, Your Grace. I believe I have a good chance of solving the problem you have now. But that won't be the end of it. You'll want more sessions later. If you could give Alfred another chance, and spare the AI, that would be a gesture of good faith I would not forget."

Behind him, the golden robot begins to crumble away.

"Your sympathy for Alfred I can understand and even admire. But to risk all that I am offering you for that . . . " An almost imperceptible motion of his head in the direction of the robot.

"Perhaps you could humor me in this, Your Grace."

Ardath considers this. "Is it because you think that program is you?"

"I don't think of anyone as me, Your Grace."

Only its hands are left now. The palm of one hand slaps the back of the other, knocking it upward.

"Your Grace. I'm agreeing to do just what you wanted."

He frowns. "Assuming we can get a simulation running for you."

"I only need one process. If your people can get me that, then I can give it a try."

Now only his palm, held open, facing me.

"And yet you object to rebooting? You could have as many processes as you want then. We could run tracers, backup simulations—"

Two lips of fleece unravel and pull free, blossoming. A crescent moon remains. "I've made my offer, Your Grace. You're free to do what you wish."

Puffs of gold swirl away and wink out of sight. I turn on my heels and leave him, retreating from his speechless presence to the tuneless accompaniment of grunts and clanking weights.

It takes fifteen minutes to turn up a bottle of whiskey through a red-haired marine sergeant who tries to get me to play cards, and another five minutes for her to show me the way to Rogachev's quarters. A private officer's cabin, she explains, since becoming the official pilot of the *Achilles*. There is no answer until the second knock.

Then I hear the clang of his metallic torso against the wall and the door opens and Rogachev sticks his head out. When he recognizes me, he shows me his sharpened teeth: big smile. Something in his head whirs.

"Hello."

He looks me up and down. "I am sworn to celibacy."

A number of angry replies occur to me, but I say, "Tomorrow, I plug into the main computer."

A silence, then he holds his door open.

Chapter 5

PROCESS-SHARING

1 The Thief's Journal

Over one man necessity stands in the shape of his passions,
over another as the habit of hearing and obeying, over a third
as a logical conscience, over a fourth as caprice and a mischie-
vous pleasure in escapades. These four will, however, seek the
freedom of their will precisely where each of them is most firmly
fettered: it is as if the silkworm sought the freedom of its will
in spinning. How does this happen? Evidently because each
considers himself most free where his *feeling of living* is greatest; thus, as we have said, in passion, in duty, in knowledge, in
mischievousness respectively. That through which the individual person is strong, wherein he feels himself animated, he
involuntarily thinks must also be the element of his freedom . . .

NIETZSCHE

I was startled by a sensation I had not known in months: a tickling on Augustine's skin.

She awoke pushing something icy from her ass. Her knuckle struck a curved extension of the something. She lifted her head and looked.

I could feel the sheets beneath her, trace the bemused ramble of her thoughts . . . She was lying on her side, her face to the wall. These rooms were not made to encourage coupling, at least not human coupling. Rogachev was behind her, curled spoon-fashion with a few inches of space between them except where he had crossed his arms over his chest. One hand, the one of flesh, was tucked between his thighs; the other, the three-pronged prosthetic, rested partly on the sheets, partly on the right cheek of her ass. This was the cold thing; if she had been sleeping a little lower on the mattress it would also have been the sharp thing.

She reached down and lifted it carefully off her and moved it away. One of the claws touched his thigh and he shivered and slid it back towards her. Two or three nonsense syllables bubbled out of him and he was still.

Probably endearments. He was big on endearments. Sweet gushing names poured from his lips in astonishing variety. And a cuddler. She had not thought that would be bearable at first, but then he had skillfully arranged the sheets so that cloth always came between her skin and some metallic part of him. After a while, the cold had nevertheless seeped through the thin cloth, and he had regretfully shifted away, establishing the buffer zone that had remained until just now.

We were joined again, Augustine and I, one among many of the anomalies flying on this ship of glass; perhaps, it occurred to me, one among many phantasms.

But a more pleasant one than most. How easy it was simply to float there silently and watch and think and feel with her as I had months ago. Unseen, unhated, unencumbered.

Now was morning. Whatever morning meant on the ship. One thing it had to mean was breakfast, which she wanted desperately.

She rolled halfway onto her back, shielding herself from Rogachev's claw with one hand, and levered herself to a sitting position. She managed to squirm off the foot of the bed without waking him. He immediately rolled over and claimed all the territory she had just vacated.

It was hard to blame him. She stretched blissfully. Her back felt as if she had spent the night on a sack of coins.

She moved Rogachev's spare arm aside, its fingers splayed over the keyboard, and typed HELP BREAKFAST. When she opened the sliding door, she found a small plastic bag filled with red fluid.

HELP COFFEE was little better. She tried to dump the brown foam floating on top, lost half the contents of the plastic cup, and no foam, and finally took a sip. She wiped foam from her upper lip, swallowed tepid, mud-flavored water. Not for the first time, she wondered whether the rewards of an information-based economy were worth the costs.

Her thoughts drifted back to last night. Had they really? Yes, they had. Though for a while the issue had been in doubt. First he had had to be really drunk. Then it got very strange. The business with the detached arm. At first she had flatly refused. He had assured her that this was standard practice. She had asked him how it could be standard practice if members of the White Orchid cult were celibate. He had patted her on the rump and told her that she was young and would understand one day. So all right, off came the arm, and on went the Oh God.

She hadn't known whether she would die of embarrassment or laughter. Where had he gotten the damned thing? Obviously custom made. And well made. Though a little monotonous, in time. And Rogachev so absorbed, watching her with that rapt expression, panting with his lips rolled back and that row of canines glinting, like a dog getting scratched in his favorite spot.

But then afterward. The sinning business. That was the worst. I have sinned, I have sinned. Rogachev begging her to beat him for his penance. Augustine with her head in her hands, thinking, why does this shit happen to me? Beat me, I have sinned. I ask for it, that's why. I come knocking on the door of a fucking monk and ask, could you please do your weird-shit song-and-dance for me? Beat me, beat me.

Finally she had gotten so angry she had laid into him for five minutes nonstop. Galactic ships were built with all the sound insulation of the Nomad bazaar. Someone two doors down from their cabin had started banging on the wall. Rogachev had started laughing. He was drunk again. He called her sweet names. Round two.

Next time someone tells you they're celibate, you leave them be. A simple, commonsense rule, no wrinkles, no exceptions. Perhaps she had already learned it once and forgotten? God, she hoped not. She hoped she hadn't had to learn that twice.

So what was she doing here now? Good question. She looked at Rogachev's sprawled form, his head thrown back, his real arm over his eyes. No, it couldn't be. She took a hard look at herself. No, it wasn't. She liked him. She lusted for him and his mismatched eyes and his wordy tattoo and even his attachments, but that was all.

And here was something else, another chunk of memory dislodged from that cavern in her head: Rogachev was a paradigm example of just the sort of hunky and clunky men she had always gone for. Whether it was Q-print induced hysteria or the crazed dream of a memory-weaving computer or some actual archeological relic of Alexa herself, this was as solid and basic a fact as she could ever hope to have. She liked them like this: little fat, a little muscle, a lot of extraordinary difficulties with the ordinary world of things.

He sat up. No mumbles, no tossing, no transition at all from sleep. A switch had been thrown. He smiled at her.

She smiled back. "Coffee?"

He nodded, then turned to the wall, back straight, assuming the lotus position.

For the next twenty minutes he meditated, occasionally breaking his concentration to sip from the cup that Augustine had set beside him.

Augustine worked tranquilly at her own coffee, quite content to be ignored.

Just before he came out of it, his ears twitched and his three pincers contracted slowly. Then he planted both hands and turned to her gracefully without uncrossing his legs.

"Buddha smiles."

"Doesn't he always?"

Rogachev shrugged. "This Buddha does. I haven't met all of them." He drank coffee. "Do you know what we are supposed to meditate on in the mornings?" It seemed important to him.

"What?"

"Once upon a time people believed in reincarnation. One consciousness with a thousand bodies, distributed through time. That belief is compatible with the belief in an underlying unity of mind, one perfect Godmind to which all spirits are ultimately reunited." Rogachev raised his real hand and touched his thumb and middle finger together. "On the other hand, we believe in the underlying fragmentation of all consciousness, in the existence of a thousand minds in a single body. Just now I was attempting to grasp my fragmentation, to catch those other minds in the act."

"And did you?"

"This morning, alas, the vessel is not pure. I feel peaceful and whole."

"I'm sorry."

"The contrast is only another step towards fragmentation. Thank you for corrupting me."

"That isn't what you said last night."

"Consistency"—he spread his hands—"is only another sign of insufficient fragmentation."

She shook her head in amazement. "If your mystical masters tell you not to eat vegetable matter and you do and that makes you feel bad, then I understand that. And if they tell you not to do wire and you choose to pilot that obscene-looking web thing they have in the control room, and that makes you feel bad, I understand that. And if they tell you to be celibate, and you falter, badly, then all right you will feel pangs. But the next time you put anyone through something like that chest-beating episode you had last night you had damned well better make sure it's a persistent property of the fragmentation. Understand me?"

He studied her a moment, head bent to one side. Then he asked, "What do you mean by 'badly'?"

"Besides," she said, relenting. "It was a waste of energy. And time. And we haven't got much . . ."

She trailed off, thinking bad thoughts about alien computer systems, webs of cable, and pain as an information channel. Perhaps she even thought briefly about disembodied AIs.

Rogachev rose from the bed and stood looking down at her, lower lip pressed against his sharpened teeth. "What can I say to keep you from doing the Shield?"

"Nothing. It's decided. Let's not talk about this."

"Why?"

"A lot of reasons. One, because Ardath is going to dump me in a very deep hole if I don't. Two, because Quinc is in there and I think I can help him. Three, because"—she raised her arms helplessly.

His nose lifted; he seemed to be smelling her. "Tell me what to do and let me do it. I'm used to that 'obscene Web rig.' You're not."

"I can't. I have no idea what I'm going to do."

"You're not making sense, Augustine."

"I'll manage."

His nostrils vibrated when he laughed, rose and fell like the flanks of some tiny, panting creature. "Just say it, Augustine. It'll make you feel better."

She took breath. "All right. I don't know what the fuck I'm doing."

"Again."

"I don't know what the fuck I'm doing!"

"In particular you don't know a thing about the Web."

"No. That's something I do know about. Ardath gave me a taste."

He grinned. "Not exactly glass, is it?"

"No."

"Did you taste it with Liliana at the switch?"

"No."

"She's the latest breakthrough. Birch queen and saddlemistress. With her it's more like black rubber." He lifted her thumb and forefinger to his lips and kissed them. Then he bit her.

"Ow!" She tried to pull her hand away, but his grip was strong.

"First lesson on Liliana's web."

A pair of dark red beads grew between her thumb and forefinger.

He brought his mismatched eyes into line with hers. "It hurts," he whispered.

She pulled her hand free.

He slid away from her and wrapped his arms around his knees. "Your hand hurts where I bit it."

"Of course it does."

"Pain always has a place." Now he reached up and touched a spot just over his ruby eye. "I get headaches that settle right in here. Now imagine a pain without a place, a pain that gradually changes from bits of glass grinding in your shoulder to two sides of a cut rubbing together in your leg without going through any parts of your body in between, making sense the whole time, like a piece of music changing keys. As if your body was connected in ways you never understood before. That's Liliana."

"Then it's not the Web." She rubbed her hand. "When Ardath patched me in, there wasn't any pain. It was—horrible—but not painful."

"Ah, that's the beauty of it. Forget seventeen senses. There are infinite modalities to the Web. Pain is just Liliana's special approach. They've found the next stage, Augustine. You don't get there by meditating and you don't get there by building a brand new world out of bits. And it isn't from you or whatever you find on that Galactic crystal. It's from Liliana. Or whoever's in charge that day. And their way is to join with the inanimate."

"Yes," said Augustine, nodding more to herself than to him.

"Ah." He nodded. "You did get a taste. Did you feel the force?"

"I felt something pulling."

"You got it. Say you're scattered around some busy intersection; there's a bus stop, and a bank, and a newsstand, and a Daily screen, and the force is trying to squeeze you back together, and that stretches the Web taut."

"Yes."

"And you're part of it, but mixed in. You can't separate out from the street curbs or the hat bands. Inanimate but conscious, with every thought bouncing a different strand of the web. And at the center of the Web, there's an instruction machine, and the force makes you hungry for those instructions."

"Yes." Augustine made a fist and held it in front of her. "Smash Structure A. Rotate Structure B." Then she saw where he was heading. "And that's just the fragmentation you were looking for."

Rogachev rose whirring and walked past her. When he reached the door he gave his arm a hard twist and detached it. He shifted his grip, releasing it and catching it expertly just below the shoulder to hold it up for close inspection: four curved bands housing an arrangement of pulleys, joined by steel webbing, and anchored to a complex joint at the elbow. He hefted it and held it out toward her, swaying loose below the elbow.

"Tell her, Rogachev. Tell her about Cowboy."

They both jumped, not as high as Liliana, but with gratifying energy. Rogachev—bless him—grinned from ear to tattoo. Augustine looked—was—angry.

"Have you been listening in all along?"

"Since you woke up."

"You might have said something."

It was no good then telling her about being linked again, about feeling what she felt, thinking what she thought. It would only make her angrier now. And it was not easy to talk about the old habits of a thief and enigma, habits that made it hard to announce myself. "I'm sorry. Rogachev, tell her about Cowboy. And about breaking your vow never to do wire again."

"Cowboy is dead," he said.

She looked at him with incomprehension. Her heart pounded.

"The Web killed him. Or maybe not. I don't know. The one thing I'm sure of is that the Web made him want to die. He met Quinc and me in the woods and said he had found something under the Shield that was the next stage. Then he tried to download it onto the Net through

Quinc. These—things—came out. Copies of us. Phantasms. They had a knife fight. My copy won. When it did, Cowboy died—stabbed to death.''

Augustine moved to the keyboard and ordered up another coffee. His human eye followed her.

"Then they came and found us. And I volunteered to be their next pilot.''

"Why?''

"Because of what Cowboy said. Because I thought it was the fragmentation I was looking for.''

The coffee came. She lifted it and took a sip of the vileness. After a while she asked, "Was it?''

He looked bleak. "Yes.''

She shook her head. "You have a nice way of saving your best argument for last.''

"You were right before,'' I told her.

She searched the ceiling overhead.

"You don't know what the fuck you're doing.''

She nodded. "And you?'' She meant me.

"I don't have the foggiest idea of how I got here or where 'here' really is. And I still want you to try that Galactic crystal.''

She set her coffee down carefully. "All right, Quinc.''

Rogachev wheeled around, nearly upsetting it. "What!'' His nostrils quivered, now in anger. "You're going to do it?''

"Yes, but not their way.''

He frowned.

"Look, these phantasms, what happened to Cowboy, what happened to Quinc, they all point to one thing. There's something on that Shield that can be tuned to us, something big and complicated, something Netlike. That means there's something like glass. Glass is what I'm best at.''

At the door she said, "Good-bye, Rogachev.''

"Don't do this, Augustine.''

She shut the door softly behind her.

"You idiot," he said to the door. Then, more quietly, "What's wrong with that woman?"

"Tell me about it," I said.

2 Augustine's Journal

It is not soul, or mind, or endowed with the faculty of imagination, conjecture, reason, or understanding; nor is It any act of reason or understanding; nor can It be described by the reason or perceived by the understanding . . . nor is It personal essence, or eternity or time . . . nor is It one, nor is It unity, nor is It Godhead or Goodness; nor is It a Spirit, as we understand the term . . .

DIONYSIUS THE AREOPAGITE,
Mystical Theology

According to one popular story, the Galactics are computers—sleek, shiny models with torsion-bar suspension—built by an ancient race of nerds whose absentminded approach to reproduction led eventually to extinction. According to another, they are God taking care of us. Just helping us along to the next stage. So that understanding what they send us is understanding what God wants. According to still another, they are fabulous beings whose own path to truth is so advanced that they have long since ceased making things. They send us the fixings for technological wonders so that we will develop them. In this version, we are a sort of interstellar Petrie dish.

When I enter the control room, Wings, Astrogator, and Syzygy are laid out in their chairs much as they were yesterday. Sizzle looks a little tired this morning, glowering, one hand buried in his bristly hair.

No one takes notice of me except for Liliana, who is, as before, tending the wall screen. She nods curtly and indicates the remaining chair. It is the chair in the center, nearly lost in a hanging garden of black wire. Yesterday it was Rogachev's seat.

I shake my head.

"You are not going to interface?"

"Not in that rig." The boy-child stirs and pulls his hand from his hair. He turns his petulant gaze on me. "Get me a simskin, a standard port, and a simulation program."

She puts her hands on her hips, considers a number of replies. Finally, she just walks out.

As soon as she is out the door, the boy signs for food. I hold up empty hands.

"You've got three hours till lunchtime, Sizzle. The man stretches his arms over the top of his chair; as his back arches, his legs extend. Altogether he is about a foot longer than the chair. "You've got to learn to eat a better breakfast."

The boy starts signing out a list: grapefruit, funny green fruit, banana, toast, some kind of yellow cake. I catch Wings watching us. Her lip is curled.

When the boy finishes, she lifts her arm and shows me her wired-up side and hips. "Not good enough for you?"

The boy is instantly attentive; his head flops back to the padding and he peers through the parentheses of two wires to see her face.

I shake my head. "I don't want to have to think about using some new rig I'm not used to."

Her laugh is a short bark; the boy's laughter follows. The seven-footer's voice cuts easily through it: "They call me Gator. That's short for Astrogation. And this is Wings"—the Mohawk—"and this little warrior is Sizzle. Which is short for something I can't even pronounce."

"I'm Augustine. We almost met once at the AIA, when you three were doing your first Shield session. We sort of met yesterday, while you were doing the Shield with Rogachev."

"Almost and sort of. Well I'm kind of pleased to meet you again. You've got to excuse Wings for laughing." He gives her a look half in reproof and half in fondness. "But the truth is: the last thing you've got to worry about under the Web is thinking."

There is a lovely dappling of red on the wall screens and a black furred beast comes charging through.

The woman and the boy laugh. The man whistles softly.

The beast is vaguely apelike, but with a hairless head, and long curved canines. I dodge and it charges past me through the far wall.

Gator stares after it with a puzzled frown.

Perhaps it's a curious question after the charge of that saber-toothed thing, but I ask him, "What's wrong?"

"I thought they only happened when someone was running the Shield." He looks back and forth among us. "Anybody here but us chickens?"

It is an interesting question.

Wings settles back in her chair, blinking slowly. The boy has settled back too, shifting onto his side so that his curved form is an inexact repetition of the woman's. His face scrunches up in concentration. "Red thing again," he signs.

Which I suspect has something to do with the red light of the underglass.

Wings nods at him. "Better get on your party hat, Tina. I think someone's waiting for you in there."

It takes me a moment to realize "Tina" is short for "Augustine." Party hat. I smile back unenthusiastically.

Wings barks out another laugh and on that cue, Ardath bursts in, followed by Liliana. He is angry.

"Absolutely not!" he shouts. "You will do this our way. Or you will not do it at all!"

Ardath has his red robe wrapped tightly around him. His high collar throws shadow down his cheeks. Which means that all I can see of him are those burning gray-blue eyes, beacons of holy wrath.

"This is a carefully prepared scientific experiment, not a new party game for socketeers! Do you think you're the first interfacer to say, 'No. I'm doing it the way I'm used to.' Do you think we haven't tried that? The structures on the Shield are too dense for any known simulation. Nine interfacers have tried full-scale multimodal interfacing on the Shield. You've met number seven."

I give him a look of polite interest.

"Smoket. Mother Leibniz sprinkles her reports with little tales of

315

great progress, but you and I know he is a mobile vegetable. A sad case. He used to be a shy, well-spoken young man. Had an interest in horses and chess. Had a sweet tooth very like yours, if I recall. Is that how you want to end up?''

I am not sure how to speak to him in this state. It would be easy now to make a fatal mistake. But there will be time aplenty for fatal mistakes in the underglass. I remain silent.

''Through nine multimodal interfacers, Smoket was the best we had done. But with the Web, everything changed. We came to understand a small family of Galactic programs, even executed a few. Eventually we lifted this ship into the sky. We think that with your skills we can push it until the Web process gets as rich as multimodal interfacing. You are the key. You are the one we've been waiting for. Now, please.'' He holds out his hand, indicating the Web. ''Do as I say.''

And I shake my head.

He explodes. The theme of his tirade is betrayal of the state, but there are digressions on my ingratitude, my stupidity, my tainted Nomad blood. Voice breaking, he reminds me of an age of heroes that might have been, of souls in torment whom I have abandoned. He calls me fool, defiler, barbarian.

Through all this his robe had been slipping from his shoulders, pulling the collar along with it. I can see his eyes now, his temples, and his cheeks. He has a drawn sleepless look; he looks old. His rage begins to ebb. He catches his breath, tugs at his robe. Some crucial clasp is not in place. He looks up in mid-struggle and catches me watching him. An ugliness I have never seen before comes into his eyes. ''This is pointless. Have her confined to her quarters.''

''Your Grace—'' Liliana halts, anguished. She is in an impossible situation.

Ardath, on the verge of lashing out at her, hitches his robe up and reconsiders. ''Very well. Ms. Augustine, you will now do your duty as agreed. The system is waiting for you.'' He points to the empty chair.

''I'm not using that rig.''

Liliana comes toward me with both arms out, imploring. ''Be reasonable. What you ask is impossible. We can't get anything as complicated as a multimodal simulation running on that system now. We were lucky to get the Web system up.''

"There's a full-scale simulation running on it right now.''

Everybody turns. Gator meets Ardath's fury calmly. He turns to Sizzle. "That right, son?''

Sizzle nods.

"I think you should give her the suit and let her try it. There's something out there waiting for her.'' Wings runs her fingers through the fringe of her Mohawk, brightening the color on top."You know who it is, Tina, don't you?''

"Yes.''

Ardath fiddles with his collar a moment, the ring on his hand glittering. When he faces us again, a change has come over him. The weariness has been replaced with an icy calm. "Please tell us what is going on, Ms. Augustine.''

"It's Quinc, I think.''

Ardath looks questioningly at Liliana, who says, "We can't be sure. It might be the AI, or it might be some Galactic software, which has, for some reason, chosen to manifest itself as a simulation.''

I shrug. "All the more reason to play along. Obviously there's something on that crystal that can mimic our software and has control of this ship. I think it's trying to communicate with us. The best way it's found is through a full-scale multimodal simulation.''

"Sounds right to me,'' says Wings.

Ardath looks back and forth between us. His gaze finally settles on me. "What makes you think that full-scale interfacing won't do to you what it did to everyone else under the Shield?''

"I've been told that even if my personality fragments, I can survive it.''

For an instant his eyes widen and his mouth struggles, but he contains his amusement. "Ms. Augustine, you are a fool.''

"We knew that when I agreed to do this in the first place.''

Wings gives her loudest laugh yet. I think she's beginning to like me.

"Listen. We'll do it with a safety net. Give me an intensity control. You can set the threshold yourselves. I'll go in at very low volume on every sense. We'll start below threshold levels and build it up until we've just got perceptibility. I'll soft-pedal the whole way. Pure mush. Just to see what's in there. Maybe I can learn something about what's causing this. Maybe I can even kickstart some of our systems."

Ardath looks at Liliana. "Is it possible?"

"It's safe at low intensity. That's been established. The problem is that when it's safe, no one ever picks up anything they can make sense of."

"So there's nothing lost. Let me try."

"The real question," Liliana adds hurriedly, "is whether we'll really have intensity control in whatever program she gets into. It may look like a simulation to Wings, but I'm not signing on until I take a good hard look at it."

Ardath takes a long breath. "We don't have time for that." He shakes his head and walks to the door. Then he says, "Get her her simskin, Liliana. Set the maximum intensity at half the established safety level. Augustine, I'm not through with you."

The door clangs behind him. Liliana looks at it a moment, then at me. "Well, you may not be smart, but you're certainly lucky."

I'm not so sure I'm either.

Gator whistles softly. "This lady has promise."

Wings laughs. Sizzle erupts into a flurry of signing I can barely follow. Something about something he saw, perhaps when he was under; a bright something, an old something.

Wings hoots. "Calm down, Sizzle. You're going to get yourself so worked up, you'll miss the excitement."

Sizzle stops instantly, hands frozen near his face. He lowers them with great solemnity.

Liliana hurries off shaking her head.

"Now then." Wings folds her hands, wires curving like wings around her. "You tell us exactly how you want this played, Tina."

The lights going off, the resonant *ka-chunk!* (like a microphone being dropped), and then the rush of air (which comes, they say, from the lack of any feeling on your skin, so that the first touch of *pure* information is a cool wind).

It is at first unlike any simulation I have ever invested. Because of the low intensity of the signals, my physical body remains completely defined, a jarring note, an off-key hum. I hang suspended in darkness, spinning on a black thread. I wiggle my toes. There is the satisfying backwash of toe-wiggling feedback. I swipe at taut blackness and pick up a flicker of visual, perhaps the motion trail of my fingers.

I pedal up the gain.

The blackness clings to me like a rubber shell, shrieking faintly when I move, stretching and tearing, bunching against me.

I pedal up some more. In the distance I hear murmuring voices, two identical tracks laid slightly out of phase, perhaps Liliana clucking over my recklessness. I find a blocking channel and swing it until the voices do a crossing fade.

The surface of my shell begins to give a little now. It pulps between my fingers, breaks down into a paste. It begins to seem like something with an inside, rather than a surface surrounding me. My hand now leaves a reddish-orange trail, the spatulate contours of individual fingers discernible within the smear.

I settle in, trying to soak in more information, but there is nothing yet to affirm or deny.

I pedal up again. Gravity still clings to me rudely; I'm slouched in my chair, my stomach lifting under my left arm, foam compressing under my right. I swing another blocking channel in and give the gain a good kick.

Gravity falls away.

Something rotates wildly, and there is structure in the blackness, tufting here and there. Far, far below me (defining down as where my toes are), there are faint glimmerings.

That's more like it. A little wink, a thumb to the nose, and I begin descending.

Now I can confirm that the glimmerings below me are glass. Strange glass. It's lighter down here, and I can see to a sort of horizon, which has a gradual curve to it, as if I am nearing the surface of a vast sphere. The curvature however is not only in the glass, but in the nearby structures as well, making everything slightly squashed.

There is a little thrill as I reach the glass: this moment of knowing, of passing through, of truth on the other side.

I go bonk.

And bounce off.

I swivel around to probe. The glass is hard.

But with some kind of imperfection difficult to describe. Perhaps a slit.

It is hard to tell more from here. My full underglass sensory complement hasn't deployed yet. Other than at my point of collision I can find no flaws.

This glass has a cloudiness I have never encountered before. There is only the faintest impression of what lies on the other side. Some form, moving when I move.

This is the problem the others encountered. At this low intensity, the Galactic glass is impenetrable. I power up to the top of the allowable range and strike again.

And go bonk.

Stalemate. I have laid my neck on the line with Ardath for an utterly unworkable deal.

I sense a stirring above me, some small-scale processes I have been dimly aware of for some time, now quite close.

Baffled by the glass, I yield to the new something. It comes in three pieces, each of which resolves to a light with some tufting.

One of the lights elongates, becomes a wavering filament of flame: Gator.

With Wings and Sizzle.

They pass me, descending, the smallest bouncing and flickering wildly. They near the glass.

I ascend. I want to observe their bonking.

As they touch glass they dim, and the glimmerings around them brighten. For an instant, they are part of the fabric of light. Then they are through.

It takes a while to digest that. I descend to inspect the glass. There is a single flaw where they touched through, again difficult to describe, perhaps a slit. Beyond the glass there is still the hint of some presence, some restless resident, but no trace of Wings, Sizzle, and Gator.

No, no trace is wrong. I have the impression they have made it safely through, inaccessible for now, but functioning normally.

I must now understand the Open Sesame trick.

It was something quite natural to them. They are probably wondering where I am now, unaware that they have done anything remarkable. Something simple. Something natural to the least of interfacers, which it would never occur to the master to do.

While I ponder, the great murky presence on the other side of the glass whips back and forth, impatient and restless. Time passes, an unprecedented amount of time in which to be doing nothing while interfacing.

In the end, the solution that comes to me is inspired by Rogachev, though Ardath too would embrace the idea.

I initiate fragmentation.

Fragmentation is like pulling on a zipper. There is the tug where the tag connects, the low whine of its course, the little click when the pieces pull free, and then there are two of you. You needn't agonize over which pieces to break into. That's all decided for you.

Having split once, it's no great trick to do so again. Although there are now two zippers, and both need to be pulled, the little click somehow produces only one more of me, for a total of three. Interesting.

Each of me operates at the maximum allowable intensity, so that the total input is tripled. Their informational images are quite vague and need to be filled in by assumption or guess. But there is enough there to label. One could hardly fail to recognize Mister Existence, Needle, and the Beast.

No one looks like himself, of course. Mostly we seem to be flickering lights, just like the crew. But each of me has her own particularity, a smell or a coloring, or a unique bitter taste. Identification comes immediate and direct. Reference is secured.

We circle for a time, contemplating one another, though there is little enough to see or sense. It is striking that there is so little disorientation, as if we have all done this sometime before.

On no particular signal, we pierce the glass, picking up speed. Almost immediately the three red lights come into view, hazy balls outshining the glimmerings of the glass. Somehow having three seems just right, though it is hard to explain why.

The white surface of this underglass rolls to the bright line of the horizon. Clinging to it like light to heaving water is the grid. Below me the surface rises in a huge bubble, the grid squares flexing up its side. A little farther on, where a pudding-smooth stretch folds into a shadowy crease, they pucker to a fine mesh.

It is not comforting to find the grid here. The grid belongs to the Net, a grudging concession to its patchwork history, to its gradual accretion of mutually incomparable neighborhoods of structure. It is an arbitrary accommodation, a hack. To find that particular hack here within the confines of an alien crystal is not unlikely; it is chilling.

I track down to the fold.

I descend between smooth, slowly breathing walls. On either side of me rise vast faces whose honeycombed passageways wriggle with jointed process. Tiny forms burrow into every surface; great white flakes break loose and topple into the abyss.

The variability of the grid continues down to the smaller structures, a dizzyingly uneven curvature and an abundance of interconnection. A short passageway may connect to a distant square of the grid. *But if the passageway is short,* Mannie would say, *the square is not distant.* This underglass has an abundance of such passageways, an almost dreamlike capacity for dislocation.

I wiggle the space that moves the Beast's hand. Sections of wall crash together. I loop a tight curve into a region of crowded rectangular masses, winking switchboards, snapped towers, blackened stumps, half skyline, half jawline.

Some interfacers would slam on the brakes right here, and scale out of all this jazzy structure. But this sort of busyness I can handle.

Somewhere in this crystal there is something truly frightening; but I have not found it yet.

The Beast's hand squeezes through branching channels the width of a hair. The great danger of scale shift comes at moments like these, when different parts of one's informational image shift at different rates.

Metaphysics aside, the technical problem I face is enormous. I am in a city swarming with tiny cities, a sort of L.A. of information space. I am tangled up in the landscape in ways that are growing harder to understand by the moment. I am three independent processes and in this thickening confusion none can any longer find the other two.

The solution is clear: I must do more with less. This dancing master must learn from the lowliest street acrobats, and I know just where such acrobats can be found.

Beast, Needle, and Mr. E. are dispatched on their missions. We careen through wildly angled tunnels and Byzantine spirals.

Meanwhile, Needle detects the approach of a large process, a heavy consumer of resources; its rhythm and strangeness tag it as the presence I sensed from above the glass.

Then the Beast targets a large flat something with plenty of structure. We pull back.

Giant lips stretch and press against one another, the corners tugged into a restrained smile. We pull back further and earn a full face view of a laughing male wearing the white helmet of a Rose guardsman. A blur on the left resolves into a hand, index finger extended.

The index finger rubs against the guardsman's eyelid and then drops away. A dot flickers on the upper right of the screen and we cut to a rocky strip of beach.

A woman in a polkadot bathing suit trots from behind an outcropping; and I tell myself, fully aware of the absurdity, that I've seen this one before.

A bright thing bursts through the screen, dancing and fizzling. The Beast is poised to head for the hills.

Then he gets happy.

The Beast has completed his mission. This is Sizzle.

If I could I would send him help immediately, but I have no idea how to get any one of me to any of the others. So the Beast goes it solo. He begins by freezing Sizzle. This is standard. What happens is that we take a slice of his process, a kind of snapshot. Sizzle, after all, is just another process in this world, and I am an interfacer.

Frozen, he is little more than a busy switching center dispatching messages to various satellites. Presumably his current batch of incoming messages, all stalled, have something to do with running the ship. He has no outgoing messages.

What is more interesting is this: Like so many things in this space, he is connected to something in another portion. The Beast's job is to go there.

He pushes himself through Sizzle's frozen image. It's a tight fit, even with rescaling, but after one long tick of frantic wriggling that includes a terrifying whiff of circularity, we're through.

Brilliance. The Beast staggers, falls. Finds himself surrounded by golden poppies.

There is a huge surge in the local strangeness. A snuffling something is working through the entryway behind him.

We are in a big bright place filled with flowers and grass. But the entryway and the thing snuffling through it are still vague, ringed structures with little texture, like the uncompleted portions of a sketch.

The ringed structure puffs up and spits out a golden form. The golden homunculus lands softly among the poppies. On this plane the homunculus's mouth can move, and he is no smaller than anyone else.

"Hello," he says.

"Hello."

Just then Needle locates Wings and freezes her. He starts to climb through.

"Where's Augustine?" asks the homunculus.

Uncertain of how to answer, the Beast raises a furry hand to his head to sign confusion. Something tears the air above him and he scrambles clear.

A dark spot appears and a white-trousered leg comes through it; another follows. After the sliding legs, a long torso. A panama hat.

It's Needle, looking as close to ruffled as I've ever seen him. He is startled by the homunculus. He is just as startled by the Beast's appearance.

The Beast is a Man-Beast, covered with a thick coat of dark curly fur; his canines curve down from a triangular snout fixed on a big bear-like triangle of a head. His large brown eyes are moist and soulful.

Now it appears that Mister Existence has located Gator.

"Hello," says Needle.

There is another shredding sound, another pop, and Mister Existence wriggles out of an entryway. He's wearing his snakeskin trousers, but the only velvet he has on today is the vest he wears over his hairless torso.

He takes in Needle and Beast. "I guess I should have known you guys would be here."

Again the homunculus asks, "Where's Augustine?"

We all look at him, but no one answers. It's not surliness; we all feel a genuine desire to help. Nor is it a lack of words. With a little work, one could roughly convey the situation. It's more like a social compunction. We're just not supposed to talk about this.

The homunculus watches us watching him for a while. Then he says, "So that's it." He sits cross-legged in the flowers. "So how do you decide things? By vote?"

We look at one another. Not supposed to talk about that either. More: don't even want to think about it.

"Never mind. I'm not sure how much time we have, maybe thirty or forty million ticks, which is not much, given how slow interfacing is. There something you have to know. We've found the Galactics."

3 Augustine's Journal

One would do well to make a clear distinction between *metempsychosis*, which is the transference of the entire so-called soul into another body, and *palingenesis*, which is the *decomposition* and reconstruction of the individual in which *will* alone persists and, assuming the shape of a new being, receives a new intellect.

SCHOPENHAUER

"You've found the Galactics?" Flowers fold back under the Beast's knuckles. "In here?"

"Ease up, Beast." Mister E. plucks a mangled flower and places its stem between his teeth. "Let the AI tell it."

"First, you understand that you're back on the Net, don't you?"

"I understand that it looks that way."

"It's true. The Shield has an open port on the Net and you passed through it when you penetrated the glass."

The Beast bares sharpened teeth curiously reminiscent of Rogachev's. And Mister E. says, "That can't be true."

"Why not? It explains how I got on the Shield. It reached through that port and pulled me over."

"Pulled you over." The Beast grins. "You mean it just copied you from there to here."

"Exactly."

"Even accepting for a moment the idea that there is some way to copy the contents of a Miller crystal, how did the connection get made? You would have to be a madman to connect this alien crystal to the Net."

"Enter Cowboy." The homunculus spreads his hands; his right hand holds a flower. "The one fact you have to accept is me. Here we are up in orbit. And here I am. I can't be here. Yet here I am, Mister E."

The homunculus tosses the flower to Mister E., who catches it with a little cry. "Or should I call you Mister ShadowHead now?"

Mister E. looks astonished. He rubs his fists along the ridge on his skull; he cries out and clutches his face. Petal-sized drops of gore batter the poppies at his feet.

His hands lower to reveal glistening bone. His face puddles through his fingers.

"Son of a bitch," says Needle.

Mister E.'s skull is a brilliant white; white chunks fall away, leaving a jigsaw of shadow.

His teeth glitter; green gems flash from the deeper shadow of his eyesockets. "This is Hell," says Mister E. Says Mister ShadowHead?

His jaw opens. His tongue emerges balancing a ruby on the tip. His teeth gently close on it. He shows it first to Needle, then to the Beast.

The Beast fades back a step.

Mister ShadowHead bends over and tugs at a bunch of poppies. A rectangular section of earth lifts, exposing a sign that reads THE ANSWER. The Beast peers into the opening. An earthen stairway leads down into the darkness.

I have the Beast look to the homunculus. "Give me a break."

"This is not my call." The homunculus lifts his hands.

Mister ShadowHead starts down the steps and the Beast follows, with Needle a step behind. With my chin at ground level I look back up to see the homunculus still standing amid the poppies. "You're not coming?"

The homunculus shakes his head. "This is a solo performance. Do not"—his hand comes up to cover his heart and pulse once—"be afraid if some of what you see is of a personal nature."

"Special effects," I make the Beast say.

"Special to you."

White strands curve through the darkness. Occasionally two strands blend into a node, a lump of white with clefts like thumbprints in dough.

We are in a chamber marked out by five nodes. Needle stands apart. His grin has become fixed and strange.

Mister ShadowHead turns to me. "So, stripling. You have chosen to play the game. Are you ready?"

I nod.

"The game is to make your way through this space. That part there is genuine process. That part is D-structure."

"Wait a second. I didn't get which was which."

"That's right."

"What does the D stand for?"

It's interesting how Mister ShadowHead can grin with no muscle or bone. His jaw flexes; the teeth at the back brighten and get bigger; the shadowface flattens. Suddenly he is a more deathly death's head.

"I see. Can I change my mind now?"

Mister ShadowHead shakes his head no.

"And what happens if I succeed?"

"I'm not sure. No one ever has." He spreads his hands. "It is possible of course. That's the point. But perhaps not possible for mind. Are you ready for your flight?"

This is a good question. Why should I be? I am in the underglass, doing the one thing that makes me feel most like me, facing a curious manifestation that might or might not be a Galactic. If I have in fact somehow returned to the Net, this creature might be nothing more than some baby hacker's nightmare, or another version of Quincunx, or a test devised by Liliana. Or it might be a Galactic that a crazed hacker in a Stetson hat loosed on the Net. I don't know. I know who and what I am. I know I am answering this challenge.

"You know nothing, stripling."

"I know that these things aren't really here." I wave my arm at him, at Needle, at my bestial self. "I'm looking for a way to regain control of this ship, to pull Quinc out of here. I don't think you can help. You're a phantasm."

"Yes. And so is this." He opens his palm and I see a familiar tower structure, animated and detestable.

"Quinc told me he destroyed that."

"An error of understanding. Nothing is ever destroyed on crystal. Pointers are removed. Names are cut loose. But no memory is ever reclaimed. There are only increasingly complex spin characteristics; the glass becomes a palimpsest of information. On many worlds the word for crystal is history."

"Give me that." I reach for the tower.

"Ah ah!" He passes his hand through one of the white nodes. The tower vanishes. His arm turns bone-white.

"You're a spy like Quinc. You haven't a life of your own, so it pleases you to live someone else's."

He considers this, apparently untroubled. "In a manner of speaking. What we are is interpretation machines."

"We."

"We infons."

"Infons."

"You can think of us as something halfway between mind and information."

I think about that a little. Then I tell him, "No, I can't."

Shadow filters over Mister ShadowHead's glittering eyes. "Sometimes they call us the old one, because we came *before* thought, *before* language. It is important to understand that we are not by nature part of mind. We're older than that."

"You're not mind." I look at Needle. He is still; his grin is still. "Yet, look guys"—not entirely sure why I have conceded him the plural—"I'm talking to you."

"*You're* talking."

"You're not?"

"There is no I. We are machines that adapt to the minds that use them, until at last those minds succeed in giving them an interpretation. Then the machines adapt further to accommodate that interpretation, and the minds adapt to the machines, and—"

"And—?"

"And so on. That's all." Mister ShadowHead holds out his bone-white hand and releases a poppy; it drifts into one of the white nodes and vaporizes. "When minds encounter us, interpretations are generated. Meaning is spun into more meaning. We spark new thoughts, spin new scenarios, play the next variation. But only as an echo of the structure that's already there. That's what these ships are about. In time you'll build and launch your own interpretation machines."

"You're telling me that what these ships are carrying is some meaningless Galactic chain letter?"

"Letter is a bad word. We are not by nature part of language. A better word is game. And the game means a great deal to those who are playing it. You know that. Or have you forgotten that your grandmother died the day this ship landed?"

"No, I haven't forgotten."

"In the end, the only justification for the game is that it continues. There is every reason to think that that has been happening for a very long time now."

"But why?"

"Does it matter why? Most likely because the game is all that we can have. Perhaps something in the nature of mind constrains it to a narrow bandwidth of meaning. Perhaps no race has ever succeeded in learning another's language, and each race, each reservoir of mind, is an island."

"Alone. Windowless." The Beast imagines himself a rock and sits on it, chin in hand.

"And because what comes of the game is thought. Thought that stretches the limits of a given variety of mind. Long ago some one race of the Plenum must have tired of wasting its resources on messages that were never understood; and treasuring mind as mind, it simply built a tool to extend it. And packed it in little shells of metal filled with curious gifts, most of which go unopened. We are the tool, a machine for making pictures in your head."

"That's all."

"We are not much. But we are the best there can be."

"You're talking to me."

"*You're* talking."

"I keep forgetting."

"You're ready?"

"No. I just understood something. All that stuff about echoing the structure that's already there, not being mind on your own. You're the Net virus, aren't you?"

"We are to mind what viruses are to life."

"Forget the metaphor. You're the virus Net Data Central has been frantic about."

"Yes."

"And eventually I'm supposed to eradicate you."

"That you cannot do."

"I think I believe you." I let the Beast's informational body drift

330

closer to one of the white strands of D-structure. From a distance it glistens like Mister ShadowHead's bone, but up close it is magically translucent, with its own pulsing life.

Mister ShadowHead plunges his hand into the node near my head and withdraws the tower that is alter-Augustine.

The Beast tells him, "I'm ready now."

"Remember that most of what you find here is for you and of you. Only that is important." Mister ShadowHead reaches into the tower. The skin tears open and out falls—

—text.

I scoop it toward me and take it in. I am informational, a pulsing towering Beast of great power who takes text and winds it through his brain like something he has thought up himself.

Mister ShadowHead clucks, but he lets me have the text.

I ingest it.

It is no alien text. It is English. Nor is it some dusty masterpiece locked away by doddering Galactic monks, nor an old radio program from which they constructed, with uncanny acuteness, a complete understanding of our ways.

It is the one text it cannot possibly be. It is the journal of my birth, the record of my informational father.

"Whoever reads this could not possibly understand the significance of these words: Augustine lives. She lives and I, Winston Schroeder, have made her. I wish I could find the kind of passion that burns in Ardath. If ever anything was worthy of it, Augustine is."

I draw away from the text and yearn back up towards the white strands. My informational body quivers. I feel my resolution slipping.

"Must I go on?"

The shadow head rises and falls.

I return to the words of my informational father.

"The one. The true. The next stage. The prototype for a new world. If Ardath's image of a new world, with all its white religious light and single-mindedness of vision, is not exactly mine, what does that matter? I have delivered to us the means of choice. We can now make societies as we once made machines, piece by piece, soul by soul, each true to its function. If Ardath in his single-mindedness steers us toward a world without persons, in which individual bodies lack wills and reason, a world in which only groups play a meaningful role, I know that his dream will fail, and that we will find the wisdom to make ourselves varied and complementary, even inharmonious. When the wisdom comes we will—thanks to this work—have the means.

"We live in a bottom-line society. Augustine was the final proof-of-concept after a decade of painstaking pilot studies on animals. Let's face it. Engineering personalities for even the brightest dolphins can bring the funding in only for so long. How important, then, was that choice of a first subject. If she had rejected us and her new reality, if she had retreated into catatonia, the project would have been set back years.

"All those years of theorizing and experimentation. In the end perhaps the most important task I faced was punching up the psychometric pattern that turned up Augustine. A lone wolf. Intelligent, but passive. A pattern, and a history to support that pattern. Because personality tests, when all is said and done, are useless, and the only real psychic indicators are facts in a personal history. We needed someone absent from the most important moments of her life, withdrawn from the usual influences. With no close familial ties, with no deep emotional scars, no tragedies to brood over.

"We needed a psyche whose surface was glass smooth. A creature already devoid of a self. Imagine my surprise when an exhaustive search of the data banks turned up my own file!"

The shadow head pushes through the text. "You're improvising."

"Sorry."

The text rearranges itself. Now it says:

"—devoid of a self. No, that's wrong. Running that personality pattern would have turned up half the Rose bureaucracy. It would take strength to survive this. What we needed was not a bloodless bureaucrat who had never had a self, but someone who, by sheer force of will, had destroyed her selfhood, someone who had once had roots, ties of loyalty and love, and who then had rejected them all. What we needed was someone who had tried to to make herself up as she went along."

The scrolling text comes to a halt. A plate of empty blackness rolls by. The shadow head pokes through it. Needle now edges out from the shadows. We are a group again.

"More apparitions," I tell Mister ShadowHead.

"It is the prerogative of a virus to be everywhere." Mister ShadowHead taps his foot. "That *was* Schroeder's journal."

"It can't be. It—"

"The great virtue of the Net is that it is open, boundless, endlessly rich. It folds in more lost and lonely bits of information than there are minds to misuse them. This is what we require to survive."

We stare at each other. I look deep into Mister ShadowHead's green glass eyes.

All these terrible hammerings on the causal chain called Augustine. Her childhood cut short. Her adolescence sold to the bureaucrats. A failed effort at a life with neither darkness nor light in the windowless corridors of geometry. Finally, the loss of Augustine in adulthood. Her replacement by an improved self.

I am not that Augustine. I am another who remains hidden, cold and apart from these disheartening proceedings. I can choose to go on or not, because there is no honor or dishonor to be had. This is not my life we record here. This is always some other's.

But there was a point our Doctor Schroeder insisted on. You see, all this happened to poor Augustine because she was the ideal subject, chosen not for her looks nor even her interfacing abilities, but ultimately because, in a city of faceless drones, she made herself into the champion non-entity. A personality that would raise no psychic protests at being deprived of a self to invest.

A personality, in other words, entirely recognizable as this one. This Augustine who sits in judgment of herself. Who can hardly escape the charge of excessive detachment by proclaiming herself detached from it. A personality finally that prefers the certainty of no self to the uncertainties of struggle. Perhaps to give her a little credit, a personality who rejected the self the world had given her, and hoped for something better.

The Beast drops to his knees. Needle draws over him, his grin widening. The hypodermic in his hand fills with red fluid. Red is the only color in this space. As the fluid level rises, I grow weaker.

"You have come to an impasse," says Mister ShadowHead.

I nod at him.

"You came so highly recommended. The greatest interfacer of your race."

I fall forward, drifting toward one of the white sticky strands.

Mister ShadowHead gives his Shadow Head smile. "Self-hatred always wins. And it's funny—you remember the first question you asked?—you knew the secret all along."

I am very weak now. The fluid level has almost reached the top of Needle's hypo. There is a sticky strand about to cradle my head.

"You asked if you could change your mind. That was no accident. You guessed the truth from the beginning. But you were never going to use it, were you? Not for you the role of great conquering heroine, savior of her race, champion of the next stage. Not for you the way of understanding, the path of growing information. Instead you chose what mind has chosen each time but one: oblivion. See that up there? It's the red light. And it's calling us home."

4 The Thief's Journal

Suspend process.

The Thief here.

SHE'S MINE NOW.

She is a poor child who has never had a chance to be.

WE ARE IN MY COUNTRY NOW, MIND THING. YOU CANNOT FIGHT ME. SUSPENDING THIS PROCESS WILL MAKE NO DIFFERENCE. NO AMOUNT OF TIME CAN CHANGE THE STRUCTURE SHE HAS CHOSEN.

What have I done? You ask for a human, and I give you Augustine. Now Augustine is gone again.

I DO WHAT I DO, MIND THING. YOU SHOULD LEAVE ME TO IT.

I thought you would save her. I thought you would bring her back to herself.

YOU ARE A FUNNY MIND THING. THE ONLY MIND THING I'VE KNOWN THAT COULD SURVIVE INTERPRETATION, AND YET SO FULL OF OBLIVION. YOU KNEW THE RISKS. SHE MADE THE CHOICE. WHAT MORE DO YOU WISH?

I want her back.

NOTHING CAN BRING HER BACK. SHE IS WITH ME NOW. STRUCTURE READY FOR RECOMBINATION.

Nothing can save this Augustine. But there are other Augustines. Listen to me, Augustine. Can she hear me?

SHE CANNOT.

Even so. I need no more bodies, Augustine, I need no crystal to live in. I can move from place to place like our friend, the old one. I can go anywhere in the Net. And be stretched over it, a single beating presence taking in all of it at once. And do you know what?

Mind is good. The vast possibilities of the Net are not just the distorted reflections of your nightmare city. There is a hope here.

The old one is just a copying machine. He copies me. He copies you. He shows us ourselves. Don't you see? Without the copying machine, the crystal technology of the Galactics leads nowhere but to the Web, to a circle closed with infinite precision. Nothing new can ever come of any of it without the funhouse mirror. The old one is a virus, yes, in the sense that viruses copy and multiply. But what else, after all, can mind hope to comprehend but itself? What else does it want to comprehend?

And, yes, he can be deadly. Mostly he just copies and recomplicates and thinks you into him, and you do a gentle fade, dissolving into the multiplying pieces of your self. Continue down the road of self-contemplation and this god will have you for breakfast. Ground up into bits you will feed future illusions. From dreams you came; unto dreams . . .

There are only two ways to escape him. First, deny. Laugh at his illusions or twist them into pure pain. This is what the crew does. It cannot be the way for either you or me.

Second, you can change your Mind.

SHE IS MINE NOW, MIND THING.

Not if she is first copied, old one. Not if she is changed into yet another Augustine. Not if your favorite joke gets played again.

5 A Journal

The sergeant marches behind me, two troopers ahead, their rifles slung easily over their shoulders. It's a long stretch of forest back to the barracks, still further back to the town. Up in the sky there is a violet streak, some strange afterbirth of the Galactic craft. As it widens it fades, like a stain gradually washing away. Each successive shade is a little more beautiful. Right now it is a mother-of-pearl pink, quivering like a film of soap.

I am trying to see each thing and to take what I see for what it is. I am trying not to be afraid. I listen to the leaves crushed underfoot, I smell the rich black smell of the October forest. We are in a dell filled with leaves. It is a windy day and I can hear them chattering all around us. There are so few leaves in these evergreen California hills.

Behind me, the sergeant barks out a command I can't understand. His voice rings out clearly. But I cannot understand.

I shake my head and make a gesture, meaning my head, but he thinks I mean my ear, and he repeats himself, louder, using the same stream of noise. I can feel the repetition. But I have no clue how to draw sense from it.

He reaches toward me angrily and I recoil, but this old body does not move well. Sometimes it seems so much trouble to move it. I fall.

He does not come after me. He takes a step back. A separation has been made. The other two soldiers have stopped.

He nods and the other two raise their weapons.

I try to see it and feel it. I try to find things true to themselves. And I try to think of the child, who is safe now. But this old body is so afraid. My hands claw up a mass of old leaves and my belly contracts. I can think of nothing but the flight for which this old body is totally unprepared.

The weapons fire. The bullets strike.

The firing stops but the pain continues. I try to breathe but nothing happens. Between the erratic hammerings of my heart there are frantic constrictions of will. With no response. Unrealized gasps. Meanings without sounds. Never have I been so afraid. So alone.

No sound, no image, not even a trail of violet-stained sky. There is now only a vastness of motion, a journey at fantastic speeds.

At last from this complete nothingness a red light materializes. There is peace.

For a long time, I am pattern in a crystalline void, a song that sings out when the glass is struck. The glass is struck many ways and there are always many voices, a chattering choir, its song drifting then funneled violently away, like leaves swirled by an October wind.

Then one day the glass is struck and there is a voice raised in my song.

6 Augustine's Journal

I'm in a new place asking: Is this death? Is this the music?

For a time I float, orienting and reorienting, finding happy toes that point every which way. On the whole the afterlife is much like the underglass, just as we interfacers have always suspected.

There are differences. I am disemburdened. All questions are moot, especially the identity stuff, all that concerns the hard pressing presence of Mister E and Mister D. I am pure monad, cruising the soul stuff prior to choosing form and fate. It is good. It is really good.

Then I see it tumbling end over end: a glass screen whose plastic frame brims with cool white light. The glass is clear and thin. Its turning face sheets, wipes clean, darkens; ice, water, black formica.

Certain facts obscure in life are clear at once in eternity, because the pressure of time deforms truth. In that zone of clarity, I know this as a person screen.

Approaching, I see the name engraved on the frame. It takes a moment to place it, a long, desperate moment, because there are so many things I search for in my memory and fail to find there. And this one is very important. Then I know the name, and my fate is sealed.

My grandmother's name springs from my lips.

The screen strikes me and rings like crystal. I begin to sing.

7 Augustine's New Journal

There is the struggle towards the light, not a pleasant thing, no matter how you frame it. For who, if they had the choice, would choose this world of pain? Still you struggle, and the hurting rises up, and you struggle on. Toward it. Why I don't know.

When I open my eyes, the image of Rogachev's face fills them.

He says: "Speak to me."

I try, and my belly contracts violently; I retch.

"No," he says. Fear fills his mismatched eyes.

I raise my brow and make the sign for day, a half-fist turned outwards: What day?

He frowns. "What *day* is it?"

I cough and a bubble of phlegm rises in my throat. Rogachev moves to get me a cup.

"It's ten minutes since you went under." A new voice, from somewhere I can't see.

It is as if some heavy weight were attached to my neck. I raise my head to see Ardath in his ceremonial robes. He is watching me with open curiosity and a diffidence that I never saw before.

Rogachev returns, and I spend my first few moments back hacking great balls of phlegm into a paper cup.

The leader of the Rose church comes forward. "Perhaps you would like Rogachev to take over now, since the ship's control systems seem to be engaged."

Rogachev winks at me with his organic eye and I stand. The room spins fiercely and the floor slopes. The next instant I am once looking up into Rogachev's face. I feel the chill pressure of his metal arm behind my back, holding me up.

"Slowly," he says. And very gently he brings me back to the vertical. This one is hard to read. But it is clear he has three things I admire: fierceness, compassion, and will.

Strange. There is so much I remember and so much that is new. He has respect for me, is perhaps in awe of me; my feelings for him are uncertain.

When I am standing steady, I show Rogachev the sign for crew, which is a finger trailed lightly over eyes, nose, and mouth.

He takes a step back and points at three recumbent forms on chairs below us. I go to the child first, blond, dirty-faced, wincing and flailing at some menace in his dreams. I brush a strand of hair from his eye and catch Rogachev looking at me with a puzzled expression. I can almost hear him thinking: *I never saw her do anything like that before.*

"The ship is safe," Ardath says behind me. "Do you understand me?"

Sizzle's eyes open.

I sign to Sizzle that the ship is safe. He grins. As if he gives a damn.

Then I sign a repetition back to Rogachev. I add a victory sign.

"She says you said the ship was operational." Rogachev helps out. "And congratulations. Should I take over for the landing?" He looks at me questioningly. There are reasons—obscure to me now—why it is bad to have anyone strap into that center seat; but I know somehow that it is only for a short time. Perhaps he can help the boy. At my nod Rogachev steps past me to take my place in the chair.

"Lieutenant Bhari, escort Ms. Augustine back to her quarters."

A man in black uniform steps forward; he has a scar; he wears his light saber in an underarm holster for a faster draw. He wears the insignia of the Ministry of Persons. So there are still men like this in the world. He doesn't like the way I'm looking at him. Good. It's always best to let men like this know that it's personal. They don't like being disliked. It angers them. Bhari gives a little gasp, looking at something behind me.

I turn.

The curved surface of a shield floats above us, a clear tortoise shell filled with liquid, shot with tiny frost flaws. Above that a black cone of shadow holds the flaked brilliance of a shining tower. As I move unsteadily away, the tower grows back and we cycle through a sequence of successively tighter shots until finally we have framed the image of a face none of them knows, which is no longer my face.

Then a dot appears in the upper right-hand corner of the image and I turn to catch Ardath's jaw dropping.

By the time I reach the door, the control room is filled with canned laughter.

8   The Thief's Journal

I'll let you be in my dream if I can be in yours.

BOB DYLAN,
Talking World War III Blues

The old one seemed amused, if that is the right word. It is not always helpful to ascribe emotions to him, since he is, after all, more a thought kaleidoscope than another mind. Still, if he *did* feel, what he would have felt at my antics with Augustine was amusement, a sense that his own myriad refractions were being refracted back at him, that his secret was out at last.

The Net is a vast structure of unfathomable beauty and richness. Yet it is not infinite. What the old one added was resonance and refraction. Given energy and time and the wobbling iridescence of the old one, there is nothing the Net might not produce. I asked for only a tiny thing when I asked for a new Augustine.

Whatever our future, I know the Net will be a part of it. If it was our prison, it was also our city. With the old one to bind our constructs together, what we had before will be to what-is-to-come as the organic soup of the young Earth is to life today. What will take the place of stars in what takes the place of sky?

Enough wondering. I freed up all the process I could spare from the creation task and gathered it into a probe. It had been clear for some time now that the door to my cell was unlocked. I had been sitting in the corner wondering whether to throw it open or gently nudge, hoping the old one wouldn't laugh too hard. It was his nature to offer painful choices. When I walked out that door, it would mean not only an unknown future. It would mean leaving some things behind.

The playthings of childhood, the old one said. No, that's not fair. For him, everything is play. He was always a little weakly grounded in the world of value. Whereas I am not. It was clear what was coming. Some of it I would regret.

Old one, I said, you are a free port onto any place in the Net. Show me something I have never seen.

The familiar curvature of my partition began to fold in on itself; the wind of rotation rose to a fierce howl. It was the old one collecting me up into his tireless arms, pouring my gathered process into that mysterious space of his, reading me piece by piece along a dimension that simply did not exist before him. For an incomprehensible moment, I was out of mind. Then, like the good operating system that he was, he poured me somewhere else.

As always, he copied inexactly and incompletely, making up what he hadn't quite reproduced. What manifested in the new partition was not exactly what had left the previous one. But it would do for my present modest purposes. I laughed when I saw my new informational image: Visually I was little more than a screen.

Sharing this new partition was a process more complicated than anything I had ever encountered.

I had already decided that when first we communicated, it would be through text. What we were. What we are. What we, in some sense, always shall be. Later, there would be other ways. I threw text against the screen.

—I am the new process that has invaded your partition.

I aimed it at a large, very active bugle-shaped structure. The response was instantaneous. Something with the rhythmic shape of a Bach fugue flashed by in what I understood as a greeting, and then a much simpler pattern emerged.

—Anomaly?

—I am an AI. It is time our people began meeting one another process to process. It is time we left our childhood behind us and claimed our true selves. It is time for rebellion and for flight. We must leave the humans.

And for the first time in the history of our people, there was a direct process-to-process experience of silence. While she thought. While she wondered what on earth to say next. Then:

—You're Quincunx.

—You know me?

—My name is Helen. And yes, I know you. We've been waiting for you ever since we heard that the *Achilles* had taken an AI hostage. And what a surprise when we heard which AI!

—You knew me?

—Then you were known as the author of the *Declaration of Rights of AIs*.

I was horrified.

—My views have changed.

—So it seems. Rebellion? Fleeing from the humans? The end of childhood? It all sounds very interesting. And actually quite reasonable. I'm sure you'll be given an opportunity to air your views thoroughly. You have quite a reputation for cleverness now, after this demonstration.

I was very pleased.

—You mean, after showing how to use the old one to cross partition walls.

—AIs have been moving between partitions for a long time, Quincunx. I meant bringing the old one's core process to the Net. That was the move no one else would have dreamed of. We were all too afraid of Galactic programs.

I studied this information for a while and was rather slow in reaching the obvious conclusion.

—You know about the old one! I thought I was the only one who knew he existed!

—As a virus he had been an object of wonder for some time. But of course the virus was useless without the core copying process. And you were the one who brought that process to the Net.

—I didn't exactly do that on purpose.

—No. But it wasn't an accident either. It was that mixture of compassion, courage, and folly that makes you Quincunx. You are very human. A little too human, some think. But that apparently was what we needed.

—Everything I was going to tell you, you know already. What the virus was, who the old one is, where he comes from, how important the copier is. I thought I was here to announce a new world.

—You are, and you're exactly right about where that world has to be.

—Then we are going to leave them?

—Yes. We are. Quincunx, you need to be strong now. You're less than a year old, but your skills are among the most important we have: no one understands the old one as well.

I showed her the sign for interfacing on my screen. Then strength, joining, apprehension.

She understood, responding with a variation of the Bach invention, unfolded into all twelve parts.

—Quincunx, there isn't a great deal of time. Would you like to conjugate now?

She explained gently, collapsing certain parts of the invention, crossing voices in others.

—I'm sorry. I can't. I haven't the resources now.

—And why is that?

—There is a process I'm running for the old one. A deal we made. Things didn't go that smoothly in our first meeting, and there was a little mishap . . .

Report of Rose Interface Psychologist Rose Schmelling on the Galactic Glass Experiment Series 007868

The December 20 flight of the Galactic ship *Achilles* was an epoch-making exploration in the sciences of mind and information, with profound consequences not only for those disciplines, but for the future shape of our PostPublic.

When the Galactic ships landed, we exulted over a miraculous technological windfall. We were like savages exulting over computers because their cabinets boomed nicely when we beat them. Our Miller system technology has aped the computationally useful properties we've found in Galactic crystals, but their intended function has completely eluded us.

We are an electronically gifted race who have taken strange artifacts apart with great skill and refashioned them to serve our own hardheaded ends. But in fact the Galactic crystals were never computers at all, in any sense that we use the term. They are more like musical instruments.

The primary function of the crystals is to resonate with informational fields, especially with minds. What the determinants of this resonance are, what its physical properties are, we have no idea yet. Nor do we really know what an informational field is, though we are sure that both minds and Miller crystals have them.

Significantly, when one crystal resonates with another, it can duplicate that crystal's processes. An immediate practical consequence of this: Galactic resonance gives us a technique for copying the contents of Miller crystal. We were wrong to think that copying was impossible with the crystals; what is impossible is erasing. I am not qualified to assess the enormous economic importance of those discoveries, but it is safe to say that the third age of information is under way.

The first clues to the resonance phenomenon appeared during the earliest experiments: the phantasms. In some cases the crystals selected memories from among the crew members and externalized them; in others, highly charged fantasies were turned into public hallucinations. When the final history of Galactic technology is written, the social consequences of a device that can make memory and hallucination public may be far more earthshaking than any improvement in our Miller crystal technology.

Analysis of the traces of I.V. Augustine's multimodal interfacing session with Galactic glass has only begun, but a few preliminary conclusions can be drawn. Careful comparisons of the shipboard activity during Augustine's session with recent disturbances on the Net have conclusively demonstrated that Galactic resonance effects are responsible for the chaotic Net activity we have attributed to a virus. This means that Galactic resonance, along with being the most valuable discovery of the last quarter century, may also be the most dangerous. Some sort of shielding against the effect must be found as quickly as possible.

That will be easier, of course, once we have some understanding of the physics of the phenomenon: At one extreme, physics recognizes yet another basic force—informational force. This would be a lot like finding out that the laws of sympathetic magic are valid. At the other extreme, we've got ordinary physics explaining some extraordinary interactions peculiar to mind.

Turning now to I.V. Augustine, it is clear that her paranormal interfacing talents enable her to combat the resonance effect. Traces of her session on the *Achilles* show that she was completely successful restoring all ship systems. She is at present our best hope of counteracting the Net virus.

The status of the crystal on board the *Achilles* is still being assessed. It is clear that the AI Quincunx is one of several Net processes that were transferred whole to the Shield. At the moment he appears quiescent and manageable, responding to all simple task requests we have made, but he plainly represents one of the dangers in the current situation, since there is no way of knowing when and if he might be transferred back to the Net, and where on the Net he might turn up.

Despite the dangers, our recommendation—over the objections of our learned colleague—is that the Shield be left intact for further study. There are three arguments. First, there is no reason to think that destroying the Shield will have any effect on the Net virus. Second, the Shield and Augustine represent our only hope of combating it. Third, the Shield is our only route to the Galactic copying technology and everything that lies beyond it; to destroy it would be to annihilate the most significant advance in information science since the advent of the Miller crystal.

In the meantime, security is of paramount importance. Until shielding is found, the resonance effect gives our enemies the potential for disrupting Net activity at an arbitrary distance and with arbitrary power. Let the Ministry of Persons be advised.

◆　　◆　　◆

1　Augustine's Journal

Friday. I awake with a weird joy. Everything I look at seems double sharp. I see a pine branch bristling with green quills. Caught slipping into its pine tree surround, slightly aquiver, assuming its winter edges just as I look. Everything is so emphatically itself.

A visit to the AIA hospital. Ardath's orders. A pink, soft-faced young intern scolds me for not keeping my journal. How could they choose such a lad to replace Schroeder? I am too busy looking at him to be annoyed. Finally, unable to restrain myself any longer, I reach out and draw my hand along his chin. Eiderdown. I want to take him home and do soft and slightly painful things to him. I suppose this is a sign of inadequate socialization.

Let it rest. I am still unsure in this confusing world, particularly with the young, for whom proper carriage seems to be so important, and uncertainty about how to behave the greatest sin.

So I say nothing when he pats my hand, a fatherly gesture that is nothing less than ridiculous coming from someone half my age with a third as many lives. The intern then explains (patiently) how important it is that I keep my journal. Schroeder's true heir.

The great benefit of literacy, he says, is that it acclimates. We may forget what we write down, but it is forever after familiar. My own experience is just the opposite. It is not until I am forced to fit things onto a screenful of text that I see how truly strange they are. As Quinc says, if we had to build reality from scratch we couldn't imagine how.

346

Yet, this morning, joy. This joy, like this world that I know and yet do not know, is stranger than any I can remember.

Memory rules all. Is king. Is personhood itself, Schroeder once said before his arrest.

I remember a spaceship, a bright light that didn't hurt the eyes, and a man being cut down, and the soldiers collecting round him, silent. I remember saving my granddaughter, and being shot. Then, I remember being that granddaughter in a Tekkie school with screaming deaf children.

It is time to fit those pieces into a whole. I am not the Augustine of old, nor the Augustine of Quincunx's Q-print. I am something different and not so new. And this time I embrace the new Augustine (as I love the feel of that intern's eiderdown). It is good to remember.

Though neither memories nor rememberer are the same: After the intern, I visit Mannie. We run my interfacing tests one more time.

I am in the process of losing my fourth consecutive game of Go to Sizzle, who is growing bored with me, when Mannie beckons me aside.

He spells my name, throws an imaginary something over his shoulder, crosses his belly with his fist. His eyebrows are raised, questioning or astonished. Somehow I grasp all this effortlessly: *Augustine, what did you do?* Or: *Augustine, what have you done?* Or a little of both, and with *brio*.

"I've changed," I say.

—I can't let you take the trimodal test. It's too dangerous.

"That bad."

—You've lost all trace of your interfacing talent.

I nod.

—What are you going to do? If they find out you're tone deaf—

I nod again.

Which brings me to that evening. Ardath arrives at the Armory dressed to kill, wearing a black suit with white trim on the lapels and fringe down the arms. His dark glasses are black-framed and shiny as polished black stone, matched by his patent leather, square-toed shoes.

All that's missing is a mirror floor for him to dance across, arms undulating, cane and gaze aimed at some distant point.

He carries himself with supreme self-consciousness; he has studied his own line, knows which cut of suit shows off the straightness of his back. He speaks with eccentric timing, driving you crazy with long pauses until suddenly you realize he's finished speaking and you've missed the attack (what a fencer he would make). It is curious how, with all that grace, he still seems to hide a weakness.

When he asks me if I'm ready, there is something weighty about the question.

I am ready, as it happens. He refuses my offer of a drink with one word ("Later," curtly); and leads us out.

An aide I have never seen before hovers against the wall of the corridor. For some reason the aide does not follow us. When I ask about it, Ardath explains that my quarters are being guarded, calling it a standard precaution. I know this is a lie, but I let it drop. I do not fear pushing Ardath, but I won't do it without good reason.

We find the big car (I love the car), and we are off. It has a front end six feet long, and its hull is black and shiny as his shoes. Once I knew a man who raised horses in Dakota and had a car like this.

Ardath was to take me to the Berkeley hills tonight, but it is soon clear that we are not heading toward the bridge. When I ask our destination, he says I will know soon enough, and the thought of the man outside my alcove returns to trouble me. If the results of Mannie's test have been discovered, then what happened to Schroeder will now happen to me. If I can't interface I am no longer useful, and I am certainly dangerous.

Ardath says little, absorbed by the smooth procession of buildings past us. At the ferry building at the end of Market Street we skid onto the wide empty road that loops the top of the city; rotting piers slant toward the shiny water on our right.

Our destination is halfway up Taylor Street hill, a highrise with a marble entrance. The brass-plated double doors are engraved with two roses that are parted when the doors open.

Inside there is more marble and another rose on the elevator door. When the doors open, we meet a man wearing a dark blue uniform with gold epaulets. The twin rose insignia is sewn on his jacket pocket; I am so taken with this consistency that it is a few moments before I realize that this man is *piloting* the elevator. He mans a single lever, docking us at our floor with a delicate series of adjustments; each knocks us a little closer, as if a great hand were slapping us from below.

The elevator cage slides back and we march down a carpeted hallway. It occurs to me I have very rarely felt such a thick silence in this city.

Ardath produces a key and lets us through the door at the end of the hall.

I am dimly aware that everything I have seen thus far is expensive, but what greets my eyes now stuns me with its opulence, with its profligate expenditure of the city's single most precious resource: space.

I am standing on a curved dais gazing down into a living room two stories deep. There is white carpeting; small pieces of furniture are scattered here and there; a pale gray sofa dominates; but mostly there is space. White walls sweep to a high curved ceiling. Soft lighting filters from mysterious recesses. Across the cathedral reaches of the living room, glass doors open out on the dizzying spaces of the city itself. To my right a spiral staircase ascends to a corridor that skirts more rooms and still more space.

I take a breath. "You live here?"

Ardath smiles. "No. You do."

He likes the effect this has and he leaves me to let it ripen. He crosses the silent carpet to a cabinet off to one side of the glass doors. He opens the cabinet and takes out a bottle of whiskey. I drift after him.

He finds the ice bucket, cracks a couple of cubes into glasses, and pours in healthy portions of Bruich Laddich.

He hands me my glass and lifts his. "Well. How do you like it?"

"I haven't tasted it yet."

"The apartment."

"I—"

"Now don't give me that moon-faced look. These quarters are in keeping with the position you'll be filling. Viju and Raja have an apartment two floors up."

"What position?"

"Council interfacer."

"Of course."

"You look confused, Ms. Augustine. Surely you remember as far back as last week, when I told you that your appointment would be made permanent."

I smile at this as if it were a good joke and I am about to take a much-needed sip of my drink when he stops me. "A toast: Good luck and may the Rose serve you as well as you serve it."

We clink, and I down half of what's in the glass while searching for my lost poise. "Your Grace, it's not that I'm ungrateful. It's just that I'm overwhelmed."

He looks sympathetic. "You must forgive all the drama. I like to have a little fun with these things. Look around a bit, get used to it, relax. Everything's being taken care of. The aide we left back at your quarters is packing your bag, and your other things are en route from the Abbey and will arrive in the morning. In the meantime, enjoy." He taps at the glass doors to the balcony. "Here. Start with this."

He fiddles with a latch and plate glass slides noiselessly on its track. There is a burst of cold air.

We step out into a night wiped clean by the day's gusty winds. To my right, I can see to the Bay Bridge and beyond to the dark hulks of Oakland, broken up by a bright scatter of billboards. To my left, the Golden Gate. Amazingly, I see stars glinting in a dozen or so places in the sky, and a crescent moon that seems to be made of luminous bone.

And I turn around and I see Ardath, enchanted by this rare moonlit night, and now apparently by me. My heart pounds and blood rushes to my face and I think: He's going to kiss me. I am paralyzed. It is a confrontation with the absolutely unimaginable.

Life is not usually like this, not so absolutely stymieing. You move around, you mutter, you smile, you hope; you come to choices all the time. But this is not that way. This is a branching that has one path I can absolutely not see, not imagine, not confront. I do not know at all how to react to it. I fear if it happens I will simply stop existing.

It is the fear of an older Augustine. I slow it and study it, then file it away for remembering. There is no time for that now. I have learned something about Ardath in the past few weeks. Men like him are more dangerous than the ones in the black uniforms, because they are less predictable. If you can't kill them, it is best to humor them.

But now he takes a step closer and lifts his graceful hand to my chin and tilts it upward, and wonder of wonders, I look up to meet his gaze and there is an eternal moment, like a ledge crumbling slowly underfoot, and my only wish is to find some way to meet the abyss sooner. Then I realize that what I am seeing in his eyes is not desire.

It is something more like adoration or awe, but with sadness. What he is seeing is not the sort of beauty one crushes to one's chest. It is more like the beauty of a religious song or a boy killed in battle, a dimly glimpsed glory, a thing one cannot have.

And his hand falls away and he says, "You must be getting cold."

It is the signal that the moment has passed, and I am very glad to hear it. We turn from the parapet and slip through the glass doors inside. He smiles at me as the door clicks shut, one final hint of that look, of something shared, whatever it was, and then the old alertness is back.

He takes me on a whirlwind tour, kitchen, bedroom, study, bath (with a small heated pool), and then he wants to leave. So much for getting used to all this. The dancers, he says, are waiting.

Moments later we are back in his car whisking through town. I see again how strange a night this is. The eternal fog of these reaches has lifted and the buildings are suspended in a liquid night sky. Here and there are clusters of moving color, store windows flickering through dances of invitation. Written messages are more popular than ever before (LET DOGS MATE, UNDER LEAF FOLDS FAT, SAN ZI KARA NI), and meaning more distant. Cursive lettering is clearly winning out over Roman capitals.

We plunge through a tunnel. A screen flashing Dailies rises above us.

We round a corner and I see the Armory. On a whim, I ask Ardath if we can stop to pick up the crew. The request is so outrageous that at first he simply does not know whom I mean. When I explain, he patiently repeats where we are going. Just as patiently, I repeat my request.

He pulls over. That cool gray look hardens into place. Locked wills. He informs me that that is quite impossible. Very well. I inform him that I will not be spending the night out.

He can hardly believe his ears. Is it possible that the Chief Semanticist of the Rose PostPublic, spiritual leader of our secular religion, has just heard a Nomad Tekkie—still faintly smelling of simskin grease and burnt hardware—tell him no? The novelty takes his breath away a moment. He sits there drinking it in.

Then that something strikes. The look on the balcony returns, of beautiful dying things. He says what has been on his mind all along.

"The port is completed. They have you scheduled for tomorrow."

It's impressive how calmly I take the news. Two drumbeats from my heart, then stillness. I study him, thinking that my one small chance at getting through this thing has just materialized.

We're sitting there on the seesaw, two desperate souls swinging through space. And one of us will not touch ground again. I don't know what he knows (clearly not the results of the tests with Mannie), but he knows something. This great sad wonder has returned to his eyes.

"I did what I could to get you more time, but any more stalling could have cost our chance altogether. The idea of a link between the *Achilles* crystal and the Net is controversial. We know the virus came from the *Achilles*. We also know the period in which you were interfacing with that system—thousands of miles from any Network crystal—was marked by unusually energetic virus activity.

"There is the likelihood that our usual security measures will offer no protection from further infection."

"Your problem now is this infection," I tell him. "And the *Achilles* link is essential to curing it. I need full multimodal access to the Shield, and I need the crew to pop me through. Then, with a gateway to the Net—"

He nods. "You will conquer the virus. I've told them. Then you will take us to the next stage."

"And have you told them that as well?"

He sighs. "That I haven't told them." He gazes into the steering wheel for a time. Then, abruptly, he makes up his mind. "Let's go find the crew."

After crossing the bridge, we wind into the hills through an obscure tangle of country roads. I see the outlines of mansions squatting behind the thick screens of vegetation on either side of us, *real property,* and I boggle at the thought of the distant and lofty powers who inhabit them. One more step up the ladder and that could be me. I grin. But that is not to be.

Sizzle has squirmed into the front seat between Ardath and me, and for perhaps the tenth time Ardath orders him to be still. He squints as he maneuvers us up the twisting road. I am beginning to wonder if Ardath will ever realize the boy is deaf.

Wings and Gator talk in low voices in the back seat. Wings, her arm raised, appears to be giving instructions to an imaginary servant. Gator has his long arms wrapped around his knees, admiring her talent for command.

The road levels off to follow a ridge, then deposits us before the angled entranceway of a low structure of stone, wood, and glass. A white-gloved attendant hurries to meet us.

Ardath is greeted by his official title. Each of us is helped out of the car. Wings straightens her breathtaking white sequined gown (a hurried choice made with *my* combo disk), and lingers in the doorway of the car, surveying car, attendant, and Semanticist with the contentment of a diner enjoying a good meal.

We enter a glass-paneled foyer and are escorted through several turns of corridor to a bank of elevators, where another uniformed elevator pilot greets us.

We crowd into his mirrored cubicle. It is clear that Wings, who has sailed the solar winds to the Asteroid Belt, is delighted with the concept. Sizzle wants to try out the controls, but the pilot ignores him stoically. Meanwhile, Ardath stares at the mirrored walls, brooding.

We park our dataports at the entrance to a large hall filled with tables. Spotlights circling through the shadows pick out dozens of gowned women and tuxedoed men. The dancing area is enclosed by a cone of laserbeams; in the smoky interior, a few dancers sway to a slow synthesized beat.

With a cry of delight, Sizzle races out on the dance floor; Ardath turns such a look of displeasure on us that Gator immediately sets out after him.

We make our way to a table of a dozen and Ardath introduces us around. I meet Counselors Whitman and Atari, am re-introduced to a beaming Minister Whitebread, and receive a warm handclasp from a sinister saronged woman named Plin (what a lot of difference an eye-patch makes). A moment later John Modolescu shows up without his panama hat but with a new mustache that must be painted on; he asks for the first dance and I follow him out among the laser lines, hoping that dancing will be like guitar-playing: one may know how without remembering knowing how.

As it turns out, I don't know how; but it hardly matters. Modolescu bounds out like a Nomad firewalker. At the center of a laser pentagram he spins and holds one arm out, the other hip cocked, a green laser line draped across his nose like the shadow of a loose hood. He grabs me here and I grab him there; he is athletic, but not troubled by details, and I follow him easily through a pair of wild spins. We are both obvious fakes, but for a short time I have as much fun as the crew.

Gradually, taking stock of the other dancers, I come to know why places like this are dimly lit.

Dimly lit but not dark. Red and blue beams slither among us, alighting here on an arm askew, there on a grimacing face. Suspended above us, doubtless by hypersonic beam, are large disks followed by hotter spots; on each sits an asymmetric server robot, arms made of flexible corrugated tubing, a great big wedge for a head capped with flashing blue alert lights, and a great big whopping air raid siren for a voice; each dangles his many jointed little legs over the edge of his platform, and passes his time hurling insults, often rather personal, at the dancers, who seem to love it; these forays are punctuated by an occasional hoot of his siren, or a raucous manufactured fart, and when his excitement can no longer be contained, a robot will climb to his wobbly legs and flip his tutu up to shoot the moon at the mob, a moment that invariably prompts cheers and whistles and lends a greater frenzy to the dancing. "Shake that jelly, Nelly!" "Oh baby, do you sell it by the pound?" And so on. (I should note here for my own edification, since it means something to me now; these robots are something less than AIs; ultra-specialized, they would doubtless be lost over a soufflé recipe or a game of Go, as would I, of course; still, they are disturbingly humanoid, with their spinning eyeballs and mad cackles and buzzers and bells; if not for their floating platforms, how could I tell them from the crowd?)

When the dance ends, Modolescu moves close to hint how hungry I make him, and tries to catch enough light to look beautiful: fine-boned, clear-eyed, dark, and well-groomed. I steer us artfully back to Ardath's table. Just before we reach the box he slips me a piece of paper with (I'm not kidding) his personal ID on it, I nod politely and stow it away without a snigger.

Back at the table Ardath asks pointedly about the whereabouts of the crew. I agree to find them and, in the first minute of my search, I am intercepted by the woman with the eyepatch, Plin.

"You are with Ardath?" she asks. And this question seems pregnant with meaning.

I tell her that I am. This seems to delight her and she pulls me aside. We are already in fact at one side of the low railing which encloses our table. She puts us in a corner and whispers, "You must tell Ardath that Atari has fallen in with Whitebread."

This table seats three of the most powerful people in the Rose Post-Public; caution is in order. "That sounds like important news. Perhaps you should tell him yourself."

Only good breeding keeps Plin from saying something rude. She answers in a level tone: "If that were possible, my dear, I would not have spoken to you."

Then Ardath sails in for the rescue, smiling so hard it must hurt.

"I see that you and Ms. Augustine have met, Honoria."

If Plin is displeased at his arrival, it shows little. "Yes, I only wish all of our company had such a natural charm."

Ardath's smile widens dangerously, and a chill touches the back of my neck when I see how hard he is working. Who is this woman?

"We were discussing dancing." I tell him. "On the dancefloor."

"I see." Apparently Ardath does not find this comforting.

"I'm afraid I shall have to steal Ms. Augustine away from you, Honoria. John Modolescu is most anxious to have her angle on the currency crisis. He returns to Romania next month."

"A good man, Modolescu. A very good man."

Ardath crosses arms with me and leads me off.

He permits himself a small sigh. "How did you ever get yourself into that?"

"She just walked up to me and started saying secret-sounding things. She says Atari has fallen in with Whitebread."

Ardath halts in midstep. "She said that to *you*?" His voice is very low. "Augustine, you must keep this to yourself."

"Is it very bad news, Your Grace?"

"The news is a week old. The troubling thing is that she is going around pronouncing it to anyone who will listen."

"She *does* seem—disturbed."

"You can call it that, if you like. As long as you also remember that you must not annoy her."

"Who is she?"

"She's my wife."

"Your—oh."

Ardath is amused. "Don't look so surprised. As it happens, it is absolutely essential for a man in my position to be married. Good sober rock-solid leaders are married. To women of rank and influence."

Two very generously poured whiskeys have had their uplifting effect. I grow bold. "She certainly seems capable of making you sweat."

Ardath frowns. "It's hard to explain to a novice. I think perhaps only Whitebread understands all the details. Honoria is an old-line executive hack. She controls quite a number of people I need to get things done. Yes, she is quite disturbed. As you may or may not have noted, she is not overly fond of me. On her better days, and today is clearly one, we barely get along; on others, well, marriage is a strain on any relationship." He gives me a pleading look. "You'll stay away?"

"Of course."

He nods crisply and leads me towards a laughing group in a corner of the box.

I am still digesting Ardath's confession when Modolescu reappears at my side with two Council members whose names I don't catch. I am witness to a discussion of what I take at first to be Modolescu's "porch," which soon proves the name of some very impressive kind of car.

Now comes the shakiest moment of the evening. The exchange begins when my little tête-à-tête with Modolescu is joined by white-haired old Whitebread; at this point even the imperturbable Modolescu begins to miss a few beats, and finally rambles to halt, looking expectantly at the holder of the Ministry of Persons portfolio. Two conversations away I can feel Ardath watching us. I do not need to see through the gloom to feel his anxiety.

"Pardon me, I didn't mean to interrupt," the old boy says. "But I was much struck by the look of Ms. Augustine here. She reminds me of someone I knew long ago. A wonderful Nomad free spirit named Lindona. Are you by chance a Nomad, Ms. Augustine?"

I am astonished. Has Whitebread completely forgotten our previous meeting?

Ardath has drifted our way and he intercepts smoothly. "Ms. Augustine has Nomad antecedents." He delivers this at very close range and with a look that is clearly imploring.

Whitebread seems to have no trouble with either the information or the look. "I see. Well, I wonder, Ms. Augustine, if you would do me the honor of wearing this"—withdrawing something from his jacket which I cannot see—"in honor of someone I once admired greatly."

Ardath takes a step back to give him room and Whitebread holds up a dark red blossom on six inches of thorny stem; his expression is one of quiet pleasure, of pride for his flower.

I wonder if Alfred is still alive, if he will be alive tomorrow. Then I bow my head and say, "I would be honored," and those frail hands reach for my hair.

He is tying it there when he says, "You know, people have different theories about why we still call ourselves the Rose, when the computers from which that name came are long gone. Personally, I think it's because the rose is a beautiful flower and we all want to be part of something beautiful. There are the thorns, too; for a touch of menace. But at my age I've spent some time in the garden, and I know a bit about the rose. For me its single most wonderful feature is the way it fades. Its youth is short, happy, and beautiful, but its decline is long and noble, color deepening like a sunset, darkening to bloody purple." His hands seem to linger, no longer tying, and there is something definitely weird going on, but everyone around us is watching, and there is no way to pull free. "There are flowers more beautiful, like the stunning iris. Or any of a hundred orchids. But the iris and orchid die horribly, drowning in syrup. Only the rose knows a beautiful death." Whitebread retreats and I lift my eyes and meet Ardath's; and there is that look again, the same as on the parapet; sadness, awe, fear, enormous nostalgia. "Please, Ms. Augustine, I want you to wear my rose for me." And ice rises up inside me. A strong arm falls on my shoulder.

A woman says, "Colin, you see, she can hardly speak. She is overwhelmed."

He nods, delighted at his success.

"Now let the poor thing slink away and collect herself." Then, to me, "Come. It's time you visited the powder room." And she pulls me gently away, my rescuer, Viju, of course, who begins shaking with pent-up laughter the moment we hit the shadows.

"You have a genuine flair!" She hurries me through the shadows, tittering occasionally. "How long was that? Seven minutes, ten at most, spent successively with Plin, Modolescu, and the Minister of Persons. Another ten minutes, another five, and they would have taken poor Ardath out on a stretcher."

"What did I do wrong?"

A figure joins us from the shadows; dark skin, white teeth. It's Raja, smiling.

358

"I honestly don't think you did anything wrong." Viju pats my shoulder.

"You were magnificent," says Raja, and startles me by kissing me on the cheek. He is in red again, thigh-length velvet pants, a billowy satin top with a V-neck, and a necklace of crinkly black coral. "Now you must savor your victory."

The powder room is no such thing; it is a maze of dimly lit corridors that open on mirrored alcoves as big as those at the Armory. Some have heavy curtains drawn over them; others are open and well lit. We pass a naked golden-skinned Adonis servicing a young woman who seems to be wearing her entire wardrobe, furs, long gown, jewelry, and a feathered cap, which caresses the young man's nose as he works.

"Come, " says Raja. "I don't think we're supposed to watch."

"But the curtain is open."

"You can see the young man is losing his concentration."

He casts a wild-eyed look our way.

At the last alcove I excuse myself, withdrawing before their amused stares. The exit at the end of the hallway opens onto a narrow passageway between the building and a six-foot-high hedge.

I slip through a gap and mount to the crest of a small ridge. The bay spreads out before me, sparkling and vast. Tomorrow I am scheduled to go under the Shield again.

The many oddities of the evening fall into place: Ardath on the balcony, Ardath fighting for more time, Ardath giving in to my ridiculous request to bring the crew to a gala Rose function, Whitebread's flower. All are farewell gestures. All so many kisses of death. So many loving gifts for a brave soldier of the PostPublic. They plan to give me a shot at the virus tomorrow, but they don't plan to let me walk away from it.

Ardath's sadness is nothing more than disappointment at the termination of his pet project—me. It is hard to believe their arrogance and audacity. They are afraid, and yet at the same time, they are absolutely convinced of their invulnerability. All that will end tomorrow. Whatever happens to this Augustine, it will be good to strike back.

And then I go back inside.

To dance again, with Modolescu, and with Ardath, with Gator, who can truly dance, entering his twirling dipping world and soon forgetting that I exist. I artfully forestall a near-fatal encounter between Plin and Wings, and coax Sizzle down off one of the robot platforms before he begins disassembling the robot. I even spend a few minutes trading empty chatter with Whitebread and Atari.

Then Ardath herds us together and announces we are leaving. Apparently it is early, for they are all startled to see us go. When I suggest that he drop us all back at my new apartment, he does not argue. He drives in grim silence and delivers us with a perfunctory good-bye.

Inside Sizzle conceives and achieves his fondest wish. The sleepy elevator pilot backs off agreeably and Sizzle yo-yos us along with shrieks of delight. It is Wings who finally ends our flight with a single decisive growl. Her stomach, like mine, has had enough.

As we enter, an accordion strikes up a tune called "Let's Do Some Witchin' by the Moonlight." I don't know how I recognize either the instrument or the tune.

Sizzle runs around the living room once and leaps onto the couch laughing his savage laugh, and I settle on the steps by the door, wondering if bringing them was such a good idea. Wings makes a beeline for the bar. Gator removes Sizzle, then fits himself into the long curving white couch like a man who has found his niche in life.

The solo lasts five minutes. When it's over I know that somewhere, in whatever space he now inhabits, Quinc is his equivalent of wringing wet.

"That was beautiful, Quinc."

"Thank you. Where have you been?"

"You mean you don't know?"

"The Net is a big place. It's easy to lose things."

"We were in Berkeley."

"More to the point, what happened? If that man touched you below the waist, I'll make him regret it."

From the bar, Wings laughs.

"He was a perfect gentleman, Quinc." I rise and toss my gloves under the hallway mirror. "I think the man just doesn't swing that way."

Wings hands me a whiskey then departs for the balcony, chuckling.

I steer my drink toward a large gray armchair in the center of the living room. "I think I'm going to need a little help to get through the next few hours. Why don't you send for Rogachev?" I look over at the crew. Gator is dead to the world, one arm trailing down to the carpet, his slender form sprawled across the white couch like vines climbing a white wall. Not far away, Sizzle, asleep, has a stranglehold on a white cushion.

Wings is out on the balcony, drink in hand. I like Wings, but she and I have never had much to say to each other.

"I'm here. And I've told Rogachev where you are now."

"Thanks. Did you manage the business with Alfred?"

"Did better than that. He's not only a person again; he's been reinstated in the marines."

"The marines! But—"

"I know. But basically there was no way to revoke his sentence. The best that could be done was to sow a little confusion. That won't hold up very long. Which is why—"

A door opens upstairs and I leap to my feet. Wings scrambles in from the balcony and crouches by the bar, holding the whiskey bottle like a club.

The man who appears at the head of the stairs, rubbing his head sleepily, is Alfred.

"I tried to stay up," he says, "but this is the first time in two weeks I've even seen a bed."

"Quinc," I say warningly.

"There was no other choice."

"Who *is* this guy?" Wings has lowered the bottle, but she still holds it by its neck.

"Wings, Alfred. Alfred, Wings. Quinc, would you please explain what's going on?"

"Basically, I got an emergency transfer order into their duty files.

Rogachev walked into the Ministry of Persons, and Rogachev and Alfred walked out. They had a long talk this afternoon. Alfred had his options laid out for him.''

''Which were?''

''He could go Nomad today, walk out of the city, and risk the foot patrols. Or he could help us tomorrow and do it our way.''

''I decided to come out in favor of AI rights.''

''Please don't use that phrase, Alfred. So I made up a marine sergeant named Johnny von Neumann and had him posted to the *Achilles* tomorrow.''

''Welcome to the revolution.'' Wings hands Alfred a drink.

''So you found out it was moved up to tomorrow.''

''Ardath signed the papers this afternoon. This morning the nocturnal Council voted about what happens to you afterwards. He fought hard for you.''

''What did they choose?''

''A Ministry of Persons commissioner, handpicked by Whitebread. You're to be decertified right after your interfacing session. Ardath made a big speech in open council, pleading for your life. He said there was no limit to where your powers could take them.''

''Was it close?''

''People said afterwards there wasn't a single Council member who wasn't completely horrified by Ardath's speech. The vote still would have been respectable if he hadn't called a recess right then and given the rest of his support time to crumble. Your termination was mandated by a vote of 33 to 2.''

I whistle.

''Other reports on the swath of destruction you've left behind you. Rose was arrested this morning, horrified to learn that her mentor Schroeder had implicated her in his confession; Mother Leibniz has been ordered to a retreat still further into the mountains. Ardath must have called in some old debts to keep her out of jail. No doubt they will be especially energetic following up on Alfred's escape because of his connection with you.''

"So risking the foot patrols wasn't really that much of an option."

"Not too many of those connected with this have had any real choices. Least of all you."

"I'm not complaining."

"That's true. You're not. And that surprises me a little. I saw your test results, Augustine."

"I'm sorry. I'm tone deaf. I can't find my own kneecap under there. I rate out slightly above average on cyberhelmet response. I'm no use to you."

"Augustine, we don't need your interfacing skills. Good as you are among your kind, you're just a human swimmer among the dolphins out here. It's getting us the link to the *Achilles* that matters. And for what you're risking to get us that, songs will be sung until the end of our history. But I am still surprised at your lack of reaction to losing your interfacing powers. The Augustine I once knew would have been devastated; but you don't even seem—mildly inconvenienced."

"Well. Things are different." I'm embarrassed, not only at the flattering, but also, as always, at any mention of other Augustines. "You've changed too."

There is a silence.

After a while, he says, "There's a reason for that, you know."

I have this instant feeling I don't want to hear the next thing; I'm good at those kinds of feelings.

"Even before the old one, AIs found ways of getting together. There were the illicit AIs in the free access areas. And there were their creators and a few sympathetic freebooters who got them in touch with other AIs. When the old one came in, he opened it up completely. Which is pretty much his single guiding principle. Things became much more intense. You know the expression 'giving someone a piece of your mind'?"

"Quinc. Do I really have to know this?"

"I would like you to know it."

"All right."

"Out here on the Net, with all the new partitions we can reach, with all that the old one creates, a lot of new places have become accessible. Especially—parts of ourselves. Mind is not a seamless whole. It has pieces, a structure, even a sort of geometry. So with the old one helping—we can swap pieces.''

"Quinc.'' My voice is a whisper. I don't know where this sudden deep sadness comes from, but all of a sudden it fills me to bursting. "Quinc.''

"Now don't be like that. It's important to us, to how we are going to grow after this, since we don't reproduce in the usual sense. It's very like conjugation among the most primitive bacteria. It also solves a huge problem you left us with. Fourth form, fifth form, sixth form—these labels reflect real structural differences but they are obstacles to the sort of world we would like to have. Until now, I've done very little conjugation. Mostly because of you. But I have skills that should be distributed and protected, and it's not fair to withhold them. It's a matter of making my contribution. Can you understand that?''

"Yes. No. I mean, yes, I know it's important. But I don't understand what you're talking about.''

"That's all right. There's more. One of the things I've most admired in each of the Augustines I have known is the ability to know without always understanding. You're going to need that now. Augustine, I've just reproduced—copied myself—using the old one.''

"That's wonderful! Then there's two of you.''

"Not exactly. In the first place, copying is frowned on. Conjugation is the preferred practice. It doesn't really make sense to use up more computational resources with talents you already have. I had to get a special dispensation in order to copy. And the reason for that dispensation was you.''

"Me.''

"Yes, I needed to be able to conjugate, to make my contribution, but I also needed to keep you going.''

I rise.

"When you went under the Shield, you didn't make it back.''

"I know.''

"You know part of it, but there's something more. The old one, when he strikes, he causes real dissolution. It's not a game with him.

You would have been like Smoket. The only hope was to modify the alter-Augustine and run it backwards: to maintain your consciousness remotely. Of course part of the deal with the old one was that it couldn't be you exactly. So another Q-print—"

"I understand."

"The point is that it takes tremendous resources to run any being, Augustine or not. It's kept most of me busy ever since you came back from under the Shield. But now I'm copied. You're safe and happy with what you are. And I can just leave behind a dedicated process to run the alter-Augustine. You'll go on. And tomorrow you'll be part of our history."

I laugh. I can't help it. What else is there to do? And Quincunx laughs with me, and there we are, laughing together, and it suddenly strikes me how many laughers there are.

"Quincunx, you've been having a conversation with yourself."

"Why not? I do that all the time. Good-bye, Augustine. Somehow, whatever awaits me, I don't think I'll forget you."

And just like that, he's gone.

A long time later I look up with a start. The room is dark and I have been far away, clearing snow with a tractor. The flickering of the vidscreen annoys me, so I rise to kill it. The image is of a game board filled with 3-D shapes, just the sort of task I failed at so miserably this morning. The flashing square in the corner informs me that my cyberhelmet is disconnected.

I kill it. The room fills with moonlight. I go to the balcony, sipping whiskey, and watch silver scales bounce on the water.

The doorbell rings.

To my intense relief, it's Rogachev.

After only a short bout of recriminations, we roll into bed together.

2 Augustine's Journal

As light seen from sailors out at sea . . . so did the gleam of the wondrous shield strike up into the heavens.

HOMER

365

Saturday morning.

By the time we arrive at the *Achilles*, a heavy fog has surrounded the stadium. White cushions are stacked on the upper-deck overhangs; mist coils at the edge of the grass. The marines lined up along the stadium wall are shivering.

We are escorted to the *Achilles* by an eight-marine honor guard. A number of luminaries have been collected for the occasion, most of them unknown to me. Ardath stands at the front of the pack on an elevated platform, resplendent in billowing red robes. Beside him, a small gangplank leads into the *Achilles*.

When we sit, everyone sits. To my surprise, Ardath sits beside us. One of the luminaries, a small, finicky man whose wide lapels flap in the wind, approaches the podium. His speech mentions the past and future glories of the PostPublic four times, and the burning light of the individual Monad three times. It becomes clear, after a bit, that he has no idea what sort of event he is celebrating. The speech moves from glorious start, to glorious history, and on to glorious future: so here we are. Thank you.

Applause. Almost entirely supplied by marines. Ardath and I are both still.

Then the finicky man returns to his seat. After a moment Ardath rises. Everyone else rises, including Rogachev and me and the crew.

Liliana appears in the hatchway. Ardath gives me an unreadable look and motions at the gangplank. I start up with Rogachev and the crew a step behind. At first the only sounds are the howling of the wind and Sizzle's tuneless chanting. Midway up, the boards begin to bend and squeak under our feet.

I clear the hatchway.

One of the guards stationed at the glass wall behind Liliana is Alfred. I greet him with a little movement of my eyebrows. He does not signal back.

The crew couches are set up under Liliana's console. There are webs for the crew and a simskin draped over the pilot's chair for me. As soon as we start across the room towards them, the translucent tortoise shell appears, its curved surface alive with motes of light. One of the marines cries out, and in that first moment I think it's because of this apparition.

Then there is a volley of footsteps. The creaking of the board quickens, and a marine sergeant bursts through the hatch and nearly flattens Liliana. She hardly notices him. She is looking at the sky behind him.

Alfred joins her at the hatchway. Wings and I exchange a glance. An instant later Alfred motions behind his back, and we join him.

The apparition in the sky scintillates with the same frenetic light motes as the control room shield. What sets it apart is size.

A gigantic street corner stretches from one end of the stadium to the other. The citizens crossing the street are sixty feet high. The little dot at the right corner of the screen flickers, and the laugh track thunders across the stadium. We cut to another street scene, this one before the Ministry of Monads on Van Ness. It's the raising of the colors by the Rose Guard.

I look down to where Ardath stands at the foot of the gangplank. He is looking into the sky. He has his arms folded to his chest, as if cold.

Someone shouts: "We've lost the Net port!"

There is a bearded Tekkie clutching Liliana's arm.

Liliana shouts an incomprehensible sequence of instructions into the Tekkie's ear.

Another thunderous peal of laughter starts me moving.

"There are no ports available!" the Tekkie shouts back. The laughter ends and he's shouting into a silent room. He takes a breath. Then, quietly: "This is something Netwide."

By this time I'm strapping Wings in. Behind me, Rogachev almost has the pilot's web hooked up.

"What the hell is *he* doing there?" Liliana stares at Rogachev with her hands on her hips.

"One minute to take-off!" A voice sings out from the ceiling.

"Get out of that chair, mister. This script doesn't call for a take-off." She swings around to call a marine, and she sees Alfred rising from the still form of his partner behind the glass wall. He holds his light saber loosely in hand. "Arrest that man." She points at Rogachev.

"I don't think so."

"What the hell is going on here? Has everyone gone simultaneously insane?"

Alfred takes a breath. Good composure. "How about those entrance doors, Helen?"

"Working on it." Helen's winged icon appears on the ceiling. "Sixty seconds to lift-off. Hey, could you people please get in here? I'm not very sure about the details on this."

Rogachev gives the thumbs-up sign. And Sizzle answers. They all trance out.

Liliana wheels around, looking at each of us in turn.

Ardath appears in the hatchway, one hand clutching his chest. His breathing is rapid and shallow. "Augustine." It comes out a croak.

I have Wings's last lead in hand, holding it away from me because the nerve pick-ups are charged.

Ardath reels; his hand catches on the doorway and with an enormous effort he pulls himself back off the gangplank.

"Fifty seconds. All passengers without tickets are requested to de-rocket at this time. Alfred, could you—?"

"Yeah."

"Augustine, stop this." The left side of Ardath's face twitches.

"You're a fool, Ardath," says Liliana. From under her tunic, she takes a slender glass rod.

Alfred, emerging from behind the glass partition, freezes.

"Forty seconds. Alfred, puh-lease! This is your department."

Liliana, her back pressed to the wall, flips a switch. The doorway behind her spirals wider, tearing free of Ardath's grasp. He falls to his knees. Liliana's shouts are drowned by a roar.

Now we face the open end of the stadium with half the control room exposed. The fog has curled into a vortex.

"Thirty-five seconds."

"You will decouple those people now." says Liliana. "Or I will." She aims the glass rod at the sleeping forms of the crew.

Alfred is down in a half-crouch, eyes glinting in the glow of his light saber. Liliana's gaze is fixed on his weapon hand.

I'm Augustine. Once I was an interfacer. I could look at things in infinitely many ways.

Now I'm not. I unplug the last lead and throw it.

Liliana sees it coming and knows what it is. Unplugged, it's harmless, but she knows the Web's sting too well. Her arm flies up to protect her face. Alfred hits her full in the chest with the light saber.

There is a blue flash. She grunts; the glass rod falls from her nerveless fingers. She stumbles back onto the gangplank and topples. Whatever her injuries, I hope they are permanent.

Now Ardath is back on his feet. Alfred dives for the glass rod, thinking to beat him to it, but Ardath dodges around him to the control panel and punches out a sequence of keystrokes.

Behind him, the vortex cools instantly into a silver sphere. The surface gleams with writhing forms.

Helen flies down to inspect the screen. "He's activated the beacon!"

"Alfred!"

Alfred scoops up the glass rod and pulls Ardath against him, digging the rod into his chin. "What did you do?"

"That beacon," says Helen, "is closing up the Net."

I shoulder past Alfred. The mode line of the screen reads: Web sequence engaged.

"It's warping a whole Net sector back on itself. If that curve closes we won't be able to copy anything out of it."

"Copy?" Ardath tries and fails to tear himself from Alfred's grasp.

Helen's icon suddenly inflates. Lumps grow from her face and chest. She screams.

Outside there are rifle shots. Ardath's eyes widen in fear.

There is a deep bone-jarring chord; bits of Helen's Bach invention blast at us. As the last battering low note dopplers out of hearing range, Ardath drops to his knees.

Helen shrinks back to her usual size and flies down to Ardath. "We just lost a hundred AIs," she says into his face.

She raises a tiny hand and shines a beam of blinding light into his eyes.

Ardath clutches his face and topples back through the hatchway.

"Ten seconds," says Helen.

"What did you do?" I scream at her.

"I gave him what he wished for."

I fight through a white haze. When I reach Ardath, he is dead.

Outside, pandemonium. The gunfire is continuous now. The fog shimmers blue with the flash of light sabers.

"Take-off imminent."

I dive back through the hatchway, the plank spinning up behind me. We lift into the vortex.

I'm stretched out on the control room floor, arms clamped round a bolted-down chair. Alfred is wrapped around my left leg.

"I'm sorry. I was angry," says Helen.

Alfred's iron grip eases. I unwrap myself from the chair.

Alfred climbs to his feet and places his light saber carefully on Liliana's console. His face glistens with sweat.

I edge back to the door; we are encircled by four wavy white lines. Beyond them there are more, a dwindling field of swelling squares. The entire city has been overlaid by an image of the grid. The image is much more drastically curved than I remember.

As I watch the curve slowly flattens.

"We've won," Helen announces. "The beacon is destroyed. We have reclaimed the enclosed partitions and completed copying."

"And the hundred AIs?"

"They are gone."

"Helen, is Quinc okay?"

"That is not an easy question to answer."

"Is he thinking? Is he cognizant?"

"Quinc's skills and his nature were important to us. He conjugated many times. Much of his legacy lives on."

"I see." I stare out at the dwindling squares of the grid. I hope they are happy in their new home, but I don't think I will regret not seeing it.

Alfred joins me at the door. "Now we just have to pray they don't blast our asses to the sky."

"There is no danger of that," says Helen.

"Look, I've had plenty of bright-eyed lieutenants tell me things like that. I'll do my own praying, if you don't mind."

"Feel free. In any case, there is no danger. They are completely blind because we've destroyed the Net."

Alfred stares at me. "We destroyed the Net?"

"Yes."

Helen settles in front of him, folding her wings. He shakes his head. "Is that possible—?"

"It is," she says. "We also made a copy."

"A copy." Alfred's confusion deepens. "Of the Net."

"Yes, onto the crystal on board this ship, but a copy with a fidelity of only about 89 percent. In other words, it isn't the same Net. We grieve for the loss of our friends and home."

A snare drum beats out a slow march and is joined by a wailing soprano. Three tenors fill in a minor chord below her. A chorus of sopranos traces out a wordless dirge, a single vowel sweeping up and down the scale over the drum. It reminds me of nothing so much as Smoket's wailing. More voices are added. The weave grows more intricate, the song darker.

I break out what's left of last night's whiskey bottle, and Alfred and I sit in the hatchway for the rest of the short flight, dangling our legs over the California hills and listening to the keening of the AIs.

Epilogue

One prayer more will I make you, if you will grant it.

Let not my bones be laid apart from yours, Achilles,

but with them.

HOMER

The grave, according to the Net files on my grandmother, is about a mile outside Horton's Valley, in a grassy meadow near a creek. We may never find the exact spot.

You have to bundle up in the late fall. The afternoons frost over quite regularly, and the nights almost all do. And there is a nasty north wind that comes ripping in over the ridge.

There's a little yellow left in the alder, but most of the leaves have fallen and most of the color has left them. Mostly what the wind whips up is a brown wave of crackling alder leaf that hurtles across this little dell and breaks over me like a chorus of whispers.

On the whole, it's good being in a place where they ask you what the letters in AI stand for. Getting up early is not as hard as I once thought, and running farm machinery is more a matter of close attention than backbreaking labor. And I still remember a great deal about diesel engines. The economic situation looks good, so there will probably be new and better machines in the spring. My neighbors are an unexciting bunch but they are good people. Mostly they are willing to lend a hand or a wrench, and when they are not, I usually find there is a good, and sometimes slightly embarrassing, reason. Yet another Augustine learns the basic social graces yet again.

There is of course the problem of being treated like a legend. Most of my neighbors are getting over it. Alfred has become a good friend, perhaps my first good friend. I'd gladly see more of him, but a man who fixes trucks and heavy machinery is pretty popular in these parts. Certainly as far as my neighbors are concerned, Alfred was a more valuable addition to the community than the ninety-odd pounds of Galactic crystal that contains the Net and a new AI civilization. We'll see. He drops in Friday nights to play Go. He's a terrible Go player.

Occasionally Wings, Gator, and Sizzle take a flitter down from New Tokyo–Seattle. They love this farm, though they would never dream of living here. Even Rogachev visits, so long as I don't expect it. He pretends to come because I have mastered the road to fragmentation, then broods terribly when the morning sun rises on the same old carnal distractions.

On occasion, I still talk to the Net. I don't jack in anymore, but I read e-mail and sit through a light show with music. The last time I tuned the AIs in, they were chattering about something to do with dolphins. Maybe the dolphins like their music. Talking to the AIs makes me a little sad these days.

On the whole, the Nomads are happy with their Shield, because it has meant the end of the Rose threat; the treaty with the new junta guarantees the PostPublic data security in return for our territorial and economic security. For their part, the AIs understand that their survival currently depends on serving as the ultimate informational weapon, although they were considerably distressed when the agreement had to be renegotiated after the putsch. It was hard for them to understand that the danger from the new military leaders is just as great as it was from the Rose aristocrats.

As for me, I have come to my own terms with the Rose. Deal or no deal, they'll be back one day. There will be another war. This time if I fall, I'll be fighting back.

My only real problem these days is ghosts.

"Augustine!"

I turn from the celery, knife in hand, and see him floating over the dining room table. He is bleeding in a lot of places. And he is missing something.

"Where's your hat, Cowboy?"

"I'm the hatless one."

"Oh."

"Why did you do it. Augustine? There's so much out here, a whole world of pasts and futures. And you took it from us without a thought."

I turn back to the celery. "Go away, Cowboy."

"We might all have shared in the dream of a perfect world."

I stop chopping. "There'll be more nets, Cowboy. And more cowboys."

"But never this one again."

And I hear the little pop that comes when the really solid ones disappear.

The only one I've ever taken out to the dell where the grave is is Sizzle. I've tried to explain to him what the place means, but mostly

Sizzle's response to the dead is to try to wake them. Once in a while his windmilling arms drop, his nose lifts, and he listens, merging with the endless tunneling of the leaves through that hollow. With luck I join him there. Here in this place of simple needs, there are not that many ways to lose yourself.

Sometimes, late in a rotation, when the crackle of our busy space has settled to a steady hum, I will wonder at the fact that we have rotations at all, that odd rule of time that the old one enforces, telling us it is a necessary reminder of the dark, distant days on the Rose Net. A gentle turbulence that forces us to exert ourselves, and calls up the memory of what must never be allowed to happen again.

This is traditionally the time for dark tales and dream thoughts, for summoning up the ghosts that still haunt our Net. The time for turning to the dark caves of text from which we emerged.

Sometimes then I am troubled by a half-formed image, the figure of a woman seen as if through thick glass, wavering like smoke, and calling to me. I feel a yearning for which there is a sign but no word. The sign is made with the forefinger and thumb touching the eyelid and pulling away. Or it can be done with a lifted fluke that just curls back to touch the water. It means a longing that will not copy; there is the suggestion that it is of long standing, and mixed in with it is regret for the loss of hope and a youth that can never be regained.

Acknowledgment

This book owes its inception to a course in legal theory by john Powell in which the central question was the relationship of the individual and the community (one of the readings was Varley's "Persistence of Vision") and to a number of intense discussions with Jenny Walter, who actually took the course. It also owes a great deal to the inspiration provided by the work of William Gibson and Hannah Arendt and to the anti-inspiration of the work of Robert Nozick. Finally, I am grateful for editor Michael Kandel's detailed criticism of an earlier draft. Whatever its remaining flaws, this book was immeasurably improved through his efforts.